⸺⁜ House of Secrets ⁜⸺
BATTLE OF THE BEASTS

ALSO BY
Chris Columbus & Ned Vizzini

House of Secrets

HOUSE OF SECRETS

BATTLE OF THE BEASTS

CHRIS COLUMBUS
& NED VIZZINI

Illustrations by GREG CALL

BALZER + BRAY
An Imprint of HarperCollinsPublishers

Balzer + Bray is an imprint of HarperCollins Publishers.

House of Secrets: Battle of the Beasts
Text copyright © 2014 by Novel Approach LLC
Illustrations copyright © 2014 by Greg Call

Library of Congress Control Number: 2013956357
ISBN 978-0-06-219249-3 (trade bdg.)
ISBN 978-0-06-229594-1 (international ed.)
ISBN 978-0-06-219250-9 (pbk.)

Typography by Amy Ryan
15 16 17 18 19 PC/RRDH 10 9 8 7 6 5 4 3
❖
First Edition

For Eleanor, Brendan, Violet, and Bella
—C.C.

To my grandmother
—N.V.

House of Secrets

BATTLE OF THE BEASTS

Brendan Walker knew the package would be there by eight a.m. It had to be. He had selected "FedEx First Overnight" on the website; he had confirmed that in his zip code (in Sea Cliff, in San Francisco), "First Overnight" meant eight a.m.; he had even woken up continually during the night to hit Refresh on the FedEx tracking page. If the package didn't arrive at his house by eight, how could he go to school?

"Brendan! Get down here!"

He turned away from his laptop and went to the trapdoor that was the only exit out of his room. Sometimes he thought it was strange that his room was actually the attic of a three-story, Victorian-style house, but mostly he thought it was cool. Besides, it was one of the *least* weird things about his life.

He hit the latch. The trapdoor swung away, unfolding into steps that led from the attic to the hallway below. He hopped down and folded the steps back behind him, tucking the rope that hung from the trapdoor inside, so it dangled down several inches less than normal. This way, if anybody entered his room while he was at school, he would know.

"Brendan! Your breakfast is getting cold!"

He ran toward his mom's voice.

In the hallway, Brendan passed three photos of the home's former owners: the Kristoffs. They had built the place in 1907. Their pictures were faded, overlaid with pastel colors that appeared to have been added years later. Denver Kristoff, the father, had a grim face and a square beard. His wife, Eliza May, was pretty and demure. Their daughter, Dahlia, was a cute, innocent-looking baby in the photos—but Brendan knew her by a different name, with a different set of skills.

She was the Wind Witch. And she had almost killed him half a dozen times.

Fortunately, she hadn't been a problem for six weeks. She was . . . *How would the cops put it? "Missing and presumed dead,"* Brendan thought. Brendan's little sister, Eleanor, had used a magical book to banish her to "the worst place ever" and they hadn't heard from her since. Which meant it was probably time to take down her picture. But whenever Brendan's parents brought up that idea, Brendan protested, along with Eleanor and his older sister, Cordelia.

"Mom, the house is *called* Kristoff House. You can't take down the pictures of the *Kristoffs*," Eleanor had said the other week, when Mrs. Walker showed up in the hallway with pliers and putty. Eleanor was nine; she had strong opinions.

"But we own the house now, Eleanor. Wasn't it you who suggested that we start calling it Walker House?"

"Yeah, but now I think we should respect the original owners," replied Eleanor.

"It gives the place historical integrity," Cordelia agreed. She was three years older than Brendan, about to turn sixteen, although she sounded like she was in her thirties. "It's like when they change the name of a baseball stadium to Billionaire Corporation Field. It's fake."

"Fine." Mrs. Walker sighed. "It's your house. I just live here."

Mrs. Walker left, allowing the Walker siblings to speak more freely. Just looking at the pictures brought them back to the fantastic adventures they had been on in Kristoff House—the certifiably crazy, never-talk-about-them-because-you'll-be-put-away adventures. The adventures about which Brendan thought: *If any of us ever* gets married, and we tell people, "The best day of my life was when I got married," we'll be lying. Because the best day of our lives was when we got home safe, six weeks ago.

"It really does make sense to keep the Kristoffs up," Cordelia said. "They're the ones responsible for this whole . . . situation."

"What situation? The situation where we're rich?" Eleanor asked.

It felt weird to say. But it was true. At the end of the Walkers' certifiable adventures, when Eleanor had made the wish in the magical book (or cursed book, really) to banish the Wind Witch, she'd also wished for her family to be rich. The Walker parents had ended up with *ten million dollars* in their savings account as a "settlement" for Dr. Walker. Now the family was living very comfortably because of it.

"There's that," Cordelia said, "and there's the situation where we live in mortal fear because the Wind Witch could come back." She looked at Denver Kristoff's picture. "Or the Storm King."

Brendan shuddered. He didn't like to think about the Storm King, the persona Denver Kristoff took for himself after he became a wizard warped by *The Book of Doom and Desire*. The book—the same book that had given the Walkers their newfound wealth—was blank, but if you wrote a wish on a piece of paper and slipped it inside, the wish came true. As one might imagine, prolonged use of such a magical artifact had terrible effects on the body and mind, and, in Denver Kristoff's case, had turned him into the monstrous Storm King. All of that was scary enough, but the real problem was that the Storm King was AWOL—the kids had no idea where he was.

He might be living in Berkeley.

"Here's what I think," Brendan said. "For the month or however long it's been since we got home, those pictures have stayed up, and we haven't had to deal with the Kristoffs in real life. Is that a coincidence? Probably. But in this house, you never know. So it's safer to keep them up."

Eleanor grabbed his hand. He grabbed Cordelia's. For a brief moment, they all made a silent wish that it was really over.

Now Brendan rushed past the pictures down the spiral stairs to the kitchen. The room had been nice when the Walkers bought Kristoff House, but after the ten-million-dollar cash infusion, Mrs. Walker had gone a little nuts, picking up a fancy French stove that cost more than a Lexus.

"Here," Mrs. Walker said as Brendan took a seat between his sisters at the marble countertop. His mother handed him a plate of warmish blueberry pancakes. He looked left and right: Cordelia was leafing through a copy of *Teen Vogue;* Eleanor was playing a game on her mom's iPhone.

"Look who decided to wake up," Cordelia said.

"Yeah, what were you doing up there?" Eleanor asked.

Brendan tucked into his pancakes. They were good. But they had been just as good back in their old apartment.

"Wuhting fuh uh uhmportunt puhckuge," Brendan said with his mouth full.

"Ew! Could you chew and talk *separately?*" Eleanor said.

"Why? Who's watching me?" Brendan washed down the pancakes with almond milk. "We're not in the dining hall, are we? Is one of your new friends who owns every single American Girl doll going to see me?"

"It's not like that," Eleanor said. "You're just supposed to have manners and you *don't*."

"You never cared before," Brendan said.

"Families that are rich are supposed to be *nice!*"

"Okay, hold on," Mrs. Walker said. She looked at all three of her children. In many ways they appeared the same as they had before the family moved into Kristoff House: spiky-haired Brendan; Cordelia with her bangs over her eyes like a shield; Eleanor with her nose scrunched, ready to take on a challenge . . . but they all felt different.

"I don't want to hear you use the *r* word, Eleanor. I know things have changed since your father's settlement—"

"Where *is* Dad, anyway?" Cordelia asked.

"He's out for a run," Mrs. Walker said, "and—"

"All morning? Is he training for the marathon?"

"Don't change the subject! Now, even though we are financially in a better place, *we are still the family we always were.*"

The Walkers looked at one another, then at their mom. It was tough to believe her when she was standing in front of so much high-end kitchen equipment.

"That means that we respect each other, so we don't do things like chew and talk at the same time. But it also means we're *kind* to each other. If we're offended by something, we *nicely* ask the other person to change what they're doing. Is that clear?"

Cordelia and Eleanor nodded, although Cordelia was already back in her music—she had found a band from Iceland that she liked; they sounded . . . *"Cold" is the best way to put it*, Cordelia thought. *They make the coldest music I've ever heard.*

And Cordelia liked feeling cold these days. Numb. It was one of the only ways she had to deal with the craziness that had happened to her. She could never tell anyone what she'd been through—never write about it or speak about it. It would be better to forget it ever happened. But that wasn't easy, so she tried to distract herself; for instance, she'd had a TV installed in her bedroom. At first it was to keep up with Brendan, who'd had both a TV *and* a beef jerky–dispensing machine installed in his attic (or as Cordelia liked to call it, his "not-quite-a-man cave"). But it had grown to be a source of comfort for her, along with music, because it allowed her to numb the swirling emotions she had about where she'd been and what she'd done. Reading used to provide that escape for Cordelia, but books were harder for her to enjoy now—books, after all, were what had gotten her into trouble in the first place! *I'm changing*, she thought. *And I'm not so sure it's a good thing.* But she couldn't dwell on this now, because Brendan had spotted the FedEx truck outside.

"Brendan! Where are you going?"

He was tearing out of the kitchen, rushing past the suit of armor in the hallway, under the chandelier, out the big front doors, into the chilly San Francisco air, down the path that slalomed the gigantic oak trees on the pristine lawn, past the new driveway with his dad's new Ferrari parked in it . . . all the way to Sea Cliff Avenue, where the truck was parked by a man in a blue-and-orange uniform.

"Brendan Walker?"

"That's me!" Brendan said, signing for the package and opening it on the sidewalk. He pulled out what was inside . . . and gasped.

Cordelia and Eleanor were down the path and practically on top of their brother before he could appreciate his delivery. He held up—

"A backpack?" Cordelia asked.

"Not just *a* backpack," Brendan said. "A *Mastermind* backpack, from Japan. You see this skull logo on the back? Real diamonds."

"Like the crystal skull from Indiana Jones?" Eleanor asked.

"No! Cooler than that! This is one of the most exclusive backpacks in the *world*! There were only fifty of them ever made!"

"Where did you get it?" Cordelia asked.

"From a website . . . ," Brendan said.

His mother was coming down the path. He gulped. He'd been rehearsing for this moment.

"Brendan! What is *that*?"

"Well, Mom, it's a—"

"Diamond skull backpack from Japan that he probably spent a thousand dollars on," Eleanor interrupted.

"Nell!"

Brendan started putting the backpack on. Maybe if his mother saw how great he looked in it, she'd let him keep it. "Mom, look . . . Bay Academy is a great place. . . . I mean, it's the best school in San Francisco. Everybody knows that."

His mother's eyes narrowed suspiciously, but she was listening. Cordelia and Eleanor shared a look of annoyance. Brendan went on.

"It's also a really competitive place. And I don't mean like in studying. I mean, we're going to school with high-powered kids. Kids whose parents are bankers and CEOs and baseball players. And my wardrobe, it just . . . needs a status piece."

"A status piece," his mother repeated.

"Have you ever heard me complain about all the clothes you order from L.L.Bean? No. But they're just normal clothes that every kid wears. I need something that I can wear when I'm walking down the halls and have people go, 'Wow, who's that guy?' Because otherwise, I'm invisible. Or visible in a bad way. Like a stain."

"Mom!" Cordelia said. "You're not buying this, are you? He's giving you a sob story for a thousand-dollar backpack!"

"Will you stop with the thousand dollars? It didn't cost that much," Brendan said.

"Well, how much *did* it cost?" his mother asked.

"Seven hundred."

His mother's forehead turned into upside-down arrows of wrinkles. "You spent seven hundred dollars on a backpack?"

"Including shipping."

"How did you pay for it?"

"Your credit card."

"Have you lost your mind?"

"It's all good," Brendan said. "I wrote you a check to pay you back."

Brendan pulled the check out of his pocket. It was one of Mrs. Walker's, made out for the exact cost of the backpack, but Brendan had crossed out Mrs. Walker's name on the upper left-hand corner and replaced it with his.

"You wrote a check to me from *my* account," said Mrs. Walker. Her face was crimson now.

"Yeah. I mean . . . I figured some of your money is technically *my* money, too," said Brendan. "I know you and Dad put away money for us to go to college. So I figured I'd use my college money to buy the backpack."

"You have no idea how much money we put away for college!" Mrs. Walker snapped. "You're sending that bag back immediately!"

"But it'll help me become popular, and by becoming popular, I'll be invited to more extracurriculars, and by doing more extracurriculars, I'll get into a better college. Think of it as an investment!"

"You know what would help you get into a better college? Getting rid of the S's from your report card," Mrs. Walker countered. (Bay Academy Prep didn't do letter grades; it had E for excellent, S for satisfactory, N for needs improvement, and U for unsatisfactory—or as the students called it, *uh-oh*.)

"I'll get all E's this semester," Brendan said. "I'll be like Cordelia. I promise."

"Don't believe him," Cordelia said. "The last thing he wants is to be like me."

Brendan looked at her. *That's not true*, he thought. *Deal's still the smartest person I know. She's just been acting a little weird lately.*

"I'm *very* angry with you, Brendan," said Mrs. Walker.

"How are you gonna punish him?" asked Eleanor.

"Shush, Nell," said Brendan.

"Make him do chores!" said Cordelia.

"Chores?" said Brendan. "What are our three cleaning ladies gonna do then? Do you really want to put people out of work in this economy? Just to punish me?"

"No," said Mrs. Walker, "what you're going to do is make this backpack count as your birthday present."

"That's not fair," said Brendan. "My birthday isn't for six months."

"Or," said Mrs. Walker, "you can get a job at In-N-Out Burger."

"Are you kidding?" asked Brendan. "One kid at Bay Academy sees me making animal fries, my entire life is over!"

"Your decision," said Mrs. Walker. "And if you ever use my credit card again, I *will* take that backpack right down to Glide Memorial and give it to the first homeless person I see. Don't think I won't."

Brendan shrugged and sighed; he knew this fight was over—and he'd gotten to keep the backpack. It just meant he couldn't get a moped for his birthday like he was planning. "Yeah, fine, okay, Mom," he mumbled. "Thanks."

"I can't believe you're letting him off so easy," Cordelia said.

"Look, I took you and Eleanor on a shopping spree when we got the settlement."

"Yeah, but . . . but . . ."

"But you're girls?" Brendan said. "Sorry, equal rights."

"Brendan! Stop antagonizing your sister and get ready for school!"

A few minutes later the Walkers rushed out to Sea Cliff Avenue with bags full of homework and books to meet the black Lincoln town car waiting for them. The driver, Angel, a portly, cheerful fifty-seven-year-old, was always early. He turned down the music of the great accordion player Flaco Jiménez as the kids came toward the car.

"Good morning, ladies and gentlemen Walkers!" he said. He always said that. "We ready for school? Mr. Brendan! Looking sharp! What is that? A Mastermind diamond backpack? Aren't there only a hundred of those out there?"

"Fifty."

"Fifty?!" shouted Angel. "The girls are gonna be swarmin' all over you, dude!"

Brendan raised an *I told you so* eyebrow to his sisters as they piled into the car, where magazines were laid out next to that morning's *San Francisco Chronicle* and fresh bottles of water. Brendan and Eleanor cracked two bottles; Cordelia ignored them, listening to her music, and turned up the heat in the backseat.

"What are you doing?" Eleanor asked. "It's gonna be like eighty today!"

Cordelia pulled her earbuds out. "I'm freezing," she said.

"It's not cold!"

"Yeah," Brendan said. "Maybe you need to eat more, Deal."

"Both of you leave me alone," Cordelia said.

Brendan and Eleanor gave each other a look, but then Eleanor said, "It's fine. Put it at whatever temperature you want. I'm going to read my new book."

Eleanor pulled out an Encyclopedia Brown book her mother had given her. She was very proud of how she could read Encyclopedia Brown now. She could usually solve the cases, too—*Probably because of all the mysteries I had to solve on our adventures,* she thought. To try and get her in a better mood, she showed the book to Cordelia.

"Look how close I am to being done. Today I'm gonna finish!"

Cordelia stared at the book, shrugged, and looked out the window, ignoring her sister. Eleanor's face fell.

Brendan noticed. "Hey, Deal, what's your problem?" he asked. "Angel? Could we please have some privacy?"

Angel raised the dark glass panel between the front and

back seats. Now it was like the Walkers were in a private, rolling chamber.

"Deal," Brendan said. "What's up with you? You haven't been acting like yourself. You're not reading, not even about Will in Kristoff's books. Is that what this is about? Will? I know you miss him."

That got Cordelia's attention. Will Draper was a World War I fighter pilot, a character from Denver Kristoff's novel *The Fighting Ace*. He had collided with the Walkers when their house got banished during the first Wind Witch attack . . . and, to be completely honest, he'd had a bit of a crush on Cordelia. And vice versa.

"Why should I read about Will?" Cordelia said. "He clearly isn't thinking about us, or he would have been in touch. Maybe we imagined him. Maybe we imagined all of it."

Brendan sighed. Losing Will was the hardest thing the Walkers had faced after their adventures. When they went back to San Francisco, they brought him with them, and he had promised to meet Cordelia at her school the next day—but he never showed up.

That was six weeks ago.

The Walkers did everything they could to find Will—searched the internet for reports of a confused man who thought he was a British pilot, put up posters depicting a sketch of him—but nothing had come of it. Cordelia had gotten sadder and sadder as days passed and she never heard from him, and then her sadness had turned to anger. She didn't like the idea that someone had the power to make her feel so bad.

"Maybe he drifted magically back into *The Fighting Ace*," Brendan said, "and he's there now. We know Kristoff's books are weird, cursed things. Maybe they can absorb a character if he gets out."

"I just hope he's okay, wherever he is," Eleanor said.

"Yeah," Brendan agreed. "He was kinda like the older brother I'll never have."

"I miss his corny jokes," Eleanor continued.

"And the way he held my hand when we—" started Cordelia, who quickly stopped herself, realizing that Brendan and Eleanor were staring at her.

"I thought you said he wasn't real," Brendan said.

"I shouldn't have," said Cordelia. "I know he's real."

They all thought about Will for a moment, about how great it would be if they had one more person they could talk to about the things in their lives that they couldn't talk about with anyone else, when the car *screeeeeek*ed to a halt.

"Hey!" Angel yelled from the driver's seat, so loud that they could hear him through the panel. "Are you crazy? Crossing in the middle of the street?"

Brendan powered down the window. Cordelia was the first to speak: "Dad?"

3

"Mr. Walker?" Angel asked, suddenly worried about his job. "I'm sorry. I didn't recognize you!"

Their father would have been hard for anyone to recognize. He was wearing a ski jacket, torn jeans, loafers without socks, a tattered San Francisco Giants cap, and aviator sunglasses, with a plaid scarf wrapped around his neck. He was crossing the street in a hurry, headed for a deli, while a double-parked cab waited across the way. Mr. Walker saw Angel and put on a smile.

"Kids! Hey! Angel, don't worry about it." He walked to the rear passenger window. Cars honked at him. He looked like he'd been up all night.

"Mom said you were out for a run," Brendan said.

"I was working. Your mother tries to shield you from the amount of work I do. But I'm really trying to get my old position back, and that means doing time-consuming research."

"We understand," Eleanor said. "We love you, Dad."

"What kind of research?" Brendan asked, concerned about his dad—and wanting to believe him.

"Medical research. Blood flow and reward centers in the brain. Look, I'm grabbing a sandwich and going home. You kids have a great day at school. I love you." He kissed his hand, reached through the window, and patted each of their heads.

Then he was off, into the deli. The Walkers looked at one another.

"Maybe he's going insane. Maybe the book cursed him," Cordelia said.

"Or maybe he's just got too much money," said Brendan.

"Maybe I should have wished for like half as much," Eleanor said guiltily.

They rode in silence the rest of the way to school.

4

Bay Academy Prep was situated on a sprawling campus with a duck pond. You had to drive through a gate and up over a hill past the pond—which was home to a few cute ducks and more than a few big, dirty seagulls—until you arrived at the main building, which resembled a red sandstone cathedral. It was listed as a San Francisco landmark. It had been very impressive to the Walkers at first, but now it was just school.

The Walkers gave one another fist bumps and went their separate ways.

Eleanor headed left, down a path where she was joined by other kids her age. The third graders had two forces acting on their bodies as they walked to class—the weight of

their backpacks, which pulled them back, and their desire to play with their phones, which hunched them forward. Eleanor texted her mom on her starter phone as she walked in. There wasn't much else she could do on the phone, since it couldn't go on the internet. Eleanor didn't mind; she was just happy to be able to text her mom when she needed her.

I miss you mom

Is everything okay?

Before Eleanor could answer, she realized that two girls were walking beside her, one on either side: Zoe and Ruby. Not the nicest girls. Both taller than Eleanor, and (she had to admit) prettier. *But they've each got models as moms—what are they supposed to be, short and ugly?*

"Hey, Ruby, did you see what I posted last night?" Zoe asked, speaking right across Eleanor as if she weren't there.

"Oh yeah!" Ruby said. "It's awesome! And did you see? I just Instagrammed the funniest picture of my French bull-dog."

Ruby held out her phone directly across Eleanor's face, so Zoe could see the photo. Eleanor realized they were showing off their phones.

"I know what you're doing," Eleanor said, rolling her eyes. "You don't have to be so obvious. I know my phone's not as good as yours."

Ruby looked at Eleanor like she was surprised to see her there. "We're not doing anything. We were just talking."

"You think you can make me feel bad, but you can't. I've done a lot of amazing stuff that you would never ever understand. I've taken down a real witch."

"A *real witch*?" asked Zoe.

"What are you talking about?" said Ruby. "You got in a fight with Ms. Carter?" There was a rumor going around school that Ms. Carter, who had dreadlocks and a skull tat-too, was actually a witch.

"No, I—" Eleanor started to explain, but then realized that if she told them any more of the story, she would sound completely bananas. So she just muttered under her breath: "Forget it."

Ruby put a hand on her shoulder. "You need to calm down. You're not, like, so important that we just gang up on you to make fun of you."

"Really?"

"Yeah," Zoe said. "But you should probably get something better than a grandpa phone."

Ruby laughed, just a little, and the two girls breezed past Eleanor into school. Eleanor's head was spinning. She looked back at her phone, at the question *"Is everything okay?"*

She wanted to get into how Cordelia was mean on the ride over, and how they'd run into Dad and he looked terrible, and how these two girls were making fun of her and she almost spilled the beans about the Wind Witch, and how she just wanted things to go back to normal, the way they were before . . . but instead she wrote to her mom:

Everything's fine

She had a feeling that was the way grown-ups handled it.

Brendan, meanwhile, was in the building that had classes for sixth, seventh, and eighth graders, and he was *rocking* his backpack. It wasn't just an accessory; it was like a force field that let him walk in a different way, with his chest jutting out, looking at everybody. *Because what if they look back? What'll they see? One of the best backpacks in the world, that's what.*

The bell rang; Brendan was late for class. *But so what? I can't walk fast wearing this. This is a backpack for strutting in.* He went to his locker and fiddled with the combination without even noticing the guys behind him: Scott Calurio and his posse.

"What do you think you're wearing?" Scott said.

Scott was Brendan's own personal bully, a junior-varsity wrestler, beady eyed and muscular, with meaty hands and a neck wider than his head. He had curly blond hair, which Brendan thought was a big reason he got away with so much. Nobody suspected a bully with cute, poofy hair. Scott targeted people he felt were different, stupid, and poor, and he had a bunch of wrestler friends who helped him in this mission.

"It's a skull backpack from Japan. With real diamonds on it."

"Where'd you get it? Off eBay?"

"None of your business . . . why are you even bothering me? What did I do to you?"

"You're walking around like you just scored a winning touchdown, which we all know could never happen in this universe," Scott said, sharing a laugh with his group. "And hey . . . I've been wondering . . . what happened to your ear?"

"I got shot," Brendan said, touching his left earlobe. Scott and his cronies laughed, but it was true. Brendan's missing earlobe was a small souvenir from his adventures in Kristoff's books—the pirate Gilliam had blasted it off. Brendan didn't miss it too much, but it was pretty sad that for the past six weeks, his parents hadn't even noticed it, because they were caught up in their own problems, and now here was Scott Calurio pointing it out.

"Yeah, right," Scott scoffed. "Your cat probably licked it off!" His goons all laughed—and then they grabbed Brendan and pushed him to the ground. He fought, kicking and clawing, but he couldn't get any leverage—there were too many of them.

"Hey! Stop! Help—"

"*Shh*," Scott said. "We're not gonna hurt you. We're just gonna take a closer look at this."

Scott pulled off Brendan's backpack and squinted at it. The diamonds gleamed under the fluorescent lights. Brendan struggled but it was no use; he tried to scream but a hand covered his mouth. *I could bite*, he thought, *but then I'd get made fun of as the kid who bites people.*

Scott palmed the inside lining of the backpack until he found a tag. He tore it out and held it up for Brendan.

"What's that say, huh? I'll read it for you, in case you're dyslexic like your little sister. 'Old Navy.' *Old. Navy.* Now why would a backpack from Japan have an Old Navy tag on it? I'll bet these aren't diamonds either. I bet they're made of glass!"

And with that, Scott ripped six or seven "diamonds" off the backpack, put them in his mouth, and . . . *chewed them up!* When they were ground to a fine powder, Scott spit them in Brendan's face.

"Told you!" growled Scott. "You can't chew real diamonds. This backpack's fake. Like you. Like your stupid family that came out of nowhere."

Scott threw the backpack down onto Brendan. People were passing him in the halls while all this was happening, pointing and taking pictures on their phones. The teachers were no use; they were in their rooms drinking coffee, which was probably better because if a teacher saved you from a kid like Scott, that was even more mortifying than being targeted in the first place. But the worst part? *Scott's right*, Brendan thought. *I am fake.*

"Hope you didn't spend more than ten bucks on that," Scott said, before walking away down the hall with his minions. The ambient noise of the building took over. Brendan got up and stuck his head far inside the shadows of his open locker. He didn't want anyone to see him crying.

6

Cordelia was feeling a lot better than Brendan. In fact, since she'd started going to Bay Academy Prep, she found that she was happier at school than she was at home, which was a little sad but which she didn't mind. She looked at the place as an opportunity to reinvent herself; at her old school, everyone knew her as the girl who was reading all the time or the quiet girl or "Brendan's older sister," because Brendan had such a personality—but not here. Here Cordelia was the person who had started the Student Tutoring Program.

It hadn't been so hard, and it had come together quickly. In her first two weeks at Bay Academy, Cordelia noticed that a lot of freshmen and sophomores were getting tutors outside the school, which seemed silly, because there were very smart juniors and seniors who could tutor them just fine. And those juniors and seniors wanted extracurricular activities for their college applications, so Cordelia thought: *Why not start a program that turns older students into tutors for younger students?*

She went to the Student Union Office to talk about the idea. There she met Priya, student body treasurer, who liked it and liked her. That was how Cordelia found herself participating in student government—or "school politics," as people called it, but for her it really wasn't about politics; it was about helping. She set up the Student Tutoring Program in two weeks and it was a big success, with twenty pairs of tutors and students already signed up.

Maybe helping people is what I'm supposed to do, she thought now as she passed the Student Tutoring sign-up board in Douglas-Kroft, the building that held high-school classes. *Help people. It feels good, and it makes me stop thinking about myself, or Will, or what I've been through.* Priya had suggested to Cordelia that maybe she should run for class president next year. It was an idea that scared Cordelia and excited her—or maybe it excited her because it scared her.

Cordelia went into her first class, history, with Mrs. Mortimer, and sat in the middle of the room. She tuned out her thoughts and got into the work of school, which was something she always had the ability to do . . . until she felt someone looking at her.

It was a nasty, prickly feeling. Cordelia had felt it a few times in the last few weeks, at school and at home, and she always stopped what she was doing to try and catch the watcher. This time was no different. She sat stock-still and moved only her eyes. Was one of her classmates looking at her? She dropped her pen to give herself an excuse to look behind her. No, it wasn't any of the students—but it was someone!

Suddenly she saw somebody—out the window, moving away. She couldn't see the person's face, just a long black body that quickly disappeared.

She stood up, aghast, but stopped and sat back down.

Something was happening to her hands.

It started with the veins. Below her skin, which was fair, her veins were not things she paid much attention to. But she knew she didn't have veins on her fingers. Who had veins on their fingers? Old people.

And yet: She had them now. They were dark, and thick, and rising to the surface of her skin.

It was like she was seeing it from outside her body; the veins were stretching, *fattening*, and the skin around them was shrinking, becoming paler and paler, drying up as if it were going to flake off, like she had a disease, or . . .

Like I'm getting old, Cordelia thought.

This is a nightmare. It has to be. I'm not really even at school.

My mind is sabotaging me. I'm not here at all. She flipped her hands around—her palms had deep lines. Her nails were growing, turning orange, becoming dirty underneath. As she looked at them, a piercing cold hit her side, like a frozen bullet biting into her. Cordelia wrenched over in pain, biting her lip to keep from crying out.

Her hands were curling now, becoming like tangled, dead-gray roots. She remembered something she had learned about foot binding in social studies, how when Chinese people used to foot bind women, the goal was to make their toes turn inward, to make a "golden lotus," the most beautiful kind of foot there was, a foot you couldn't even walk on, and that's what her hands were turning into—a dead lotus, cold inside—

She screamed.

Everyone in class turned to her. Cordelia quickly hid her hands beneath her desk.

"Cordelia? Are you all right?" Mrs. Mortimer asked.

"May I please be excused," she said. It wasn't a question. She shoved her old-woman hands inside her bag, got up, and rushed from the room, using her elbow to open the door. Mrs. Mortimer protested as kids behind her gave one another looks and started laughing.

But Cordelia felt a different look. She felt the look of the person who had been watching her—back again, seeing what she was going through, and feeling pleased about it. She whirled around at the window, but no one was there. *I'm losing it!*

She could only think of one place to go.

7

Cordelia dashed down the hallway with her hands in her bag. Why had she not worn something with pockets today? *Because*, she thought, *I wanted to wear leggings with this vintage sweater.*

Tim Bradley, from her chemistry class, suddenly appeared at the end of the hall. He was tall, on the basketball team, with shaggy red hair, blue eyes, and a sweet smile. He sneaked glances at Cordelia in chemistry when he thought she wasn't looking—but Cordelia always knew when someone was staring at her. Especially a cute guy.

Still, Tim never talked to her. Maybe he didn't have the courage. Except now he was waving at her, holding a hall pass.

"Hi, Cordelia . . . are you okay?"

"Can't talk!" Cordelia said, moving past him. She couldn't believe it. *Boys never knew how to time anything.*

"But . . . wait! You're going into the—"

I know, thought Cordelia as she dipped inside the women's faculty restroom.

She closed the door. The faculty restrooms were like hidden temples at her school; no one had ever been inside them, and they could contain anything. Luckily this one was empty. Cordelia pulled out her hands to examine them.

They were worse. Like gnarled old sticks with gray hide pulled over them. Like fossilized snakeskins. With great difficulty, she managed to lock the door, noticing as she did that her hands were *still getting older,* shriveling and cracking in real time, like they were going to fall off and leave her with stumps—

Like the Wind Witch, she realized. *Who had a hand like this? Dahlia Kristoff, that's who.*

Cordelia's hands were cold. Ice-cold. Suddenly she had an idea. She used her elbows to turn on the sink's hot water.

When we were on the pirate ship, what did the Wind Witch do to me? She turned me to ice. And what's the opposite of ice?

Cordelia shoved her hands into the sink. The water burned; she jerked back but held firm. Steam rose into her face. Tears came out of her eyes.

This is good; this will help. Beat the ice. Beat it with heat.

She wiped her eyes on her shoulder. When she looked down, her hands were back to normal. They were swollen, crimson, and throbbing, but they no longer resembled Dahlia Kristoff's hands. Cordelia collapsed on the bathroom floor.

She returned to class. Nobody said a word. She guessed that Mrs. Mortimer had warned them to respect other people's privacy. But now everyone would be talking about her. She needed to find Brendan and Eleanor ASAP, to discuss what the heck was going on. But not until they got home. Talking about the Wind Witch in public was dangerous.

At lunchtime, Cordelia didn't feel like eating, or talking to anyone. Fortunately Bay Academy had a sushi bar, so she grabbed a tiny prepackaged container of salmon sushi and sat by the window.

"Hi, Cordelia."

It was Tim, from the hallway. Cordelia had a momentary burst of excitement before she remembered the crazy situation she had been in that morning—then she felt a quiet numbness as she realized she'd need to lie to Tim.

"Yes?"

"I just . . . seeing you before . . . *are* you okay? I mean, you seemed upset—"

"Oh, I'm fine. I thought I was getting the stomach flu, but I'm okay now." Cordelia forced a smile, took a bite of sushi.

"Look," said Tim, a bit nervous, "I was wondering . . ."

"Yes?" asked Cordelia, taking another small bite.

"If you're not too busy this weekend, would you like to go to a movie with me?"

Cordelia blinked. *Somebody put this day in the calendar! The first time a boy has officially asked me out! Hopefully the freaky thing with my hands won't happen again. Maybe I imagined it all. Maybe everything's just fine.*

But there was one thing that wasn't fine. The last time Cordelia's heart had raced like this, it was because of Will, and she still missed him. . . .

But you know what? Will's gone. He had his chance and he never showed up. And Tim is right here.

Cordelia didn't want to appear too eager. She took one last bite of sushi, for dramatic effect, ready to answer yes, when she heard a *chunk* and felt a tugging in her gums. *Now what?*

She pulled the piece of sushi out of her mouth. The salmon was covered in blood.

Protruding from the top of it, like a gravestone, was one of her teeth.

Tim Bradley stared at the tooth in horror. He looked at Cordelia, back to the tooth, back to Cordelia. . . .

"Uh," muttered Tim, "I just remembered. I have to get a haircut this weekend. Maybe some other time."

Tim backed away, bumped into a table, and made himself scarce. Cordelia cupped the tooth-sushi in her hand and rushed out of the cafeteria. Kids gasped and stared, but there was nothing she could do—she needed help. She barreled down the hall and pushed open the door to the nurse's office, screaming: "You need to put it back in! Can you put it back in?"

"Put what back *where?*" Nurse Pete said.

Bay Academy's school nurse weighed almost three

hundred pounds, with big sweat stains in the underarms of his dress shirt. He was bald, with a small gray goatee, black glasses, and fuzzy blue Uggs. The office was covered in posters about depression and lice.

"My tooth fell out!"

Nurse Pete pointed to a bench. Cordelia sat while he took the sushi, then handed her a towel to stop the bleeding. As it subsided, he placed the tooth and sushi in separate Ziploc bags.

"Can you explain what happened?"

"It just came out like a baby tooth." Cordelia moved her tongue into the spot where her tooth had been. She could feel her exposed, ragged gumline.

"Baby teeth get loose before they come out," Nurse Pete said. "Was this tooth loose?"

"No—"

"But sushi's very soft. It's nearly impossible for food that soft to extract a tooth. This is very disturbing, could be serious."

"Like how serious?"

"Gum disease, mouth ulcer, oral cancer—"

"*Cancer?*"

"Don't jump to conclusions."

"You're the one who said cancer!"

"Here." Nurse Pete handed Cordelia two Advil and a Solo cup full of water. "Take these. And most importantly . . . you need to see a dentist. A *dental specialist*. Have your mother make an appointment."

Yeah right, Cordelia thought as she took the Advil. Nurse Pete meant well, but of course she couldn't discuss this with her parents. Her parents would send her to a bunch of specialists, but they wouldn't find anything, because this was no normal tooth decay. This was a curse. And it had something to do with Kristoff House.

Come to think of it, Cordelia thought, *should I even tell Bren and Nell?* If she told her siblings that her hands were turning geriatric and her teeth were coming out, what would that accomplish? It would be one thing if she were the little sister and everyone was expected to take care of her. But she was the oldest—she was supposed to be the strong one. *How can I expect to be successful at anything if I can't even handle my own problems?*

Once she was out of the nurse's office, Cordelia scratched at her arm as she walked down the hall. Nurse Pete had told her to go home but she didn't want people to start talking about her, so she was just going to sit in class, keep her mouth closed, and eat broth and triple-whipped smoothies to protect her remaining teeth. But now her *arm* was itching something fierce. *What's going on?*

Cordelia began to pull back her sleeve. When she reached the itchy spot, several peach-colored flakes fell onto the floor. Cordelia picked one up and examined it. *Skin!*

There was a torn patch on her arm, as if the flesh had been peeled away like cheap black ink on a Lotto card. Like she'd been scratching for hours, getting *through* her skin—

And under it was ice.

No veins. No muscle or blood. Just clear blue ice.

Terrified, Cordelia tapped the ice with her fingernail. It made a small clacking sound. She pulled her sleeve back down. Her flesh was cold beneath it. She wasn't going to look. She wasn't going to say anything. She wasn't sure how, but she was going to deal with this herself.

9

On the way home from school, as soon as Angel had rolled up the partition in his town car (he was shouting at sports radio, "No way should that bum get into the Hall of Fame! He ate steroids like M&Ms!"), Brendan asked Cordelia, "A frozen Snickers?"

"Yeah."

"I don't know what's worse: you lying to me, or you expecting me to believe such a ridiculous lie."

"It's *not* a lie."

"Do you know how many lawsuits Snickers would have if people bit into their candy and lost their teeth?"

"Sorry for not following the Snickers lawsuit blog. But I do know it happened to me. Anyway, what happened to your backpack?"

Cordelia pointed to the plastic bag below Brendan's seat, where he was carrying his books, having ditched his knockoff Mastermind bag in the locker room trash. Eleanor looked at it too. Brendan had a lot of explaining to do.

"I, mmm . . ." He fumbled. "I met a collector."

"A collector?"

"Yeah, a guy whose hobby is collecting Mastermind stuff," said Brendan.

"This 'collector' just happened to be hanging out at school?" asked a skeptical Cordelia.

"Mom said you're not s'posed to talk to strangers who hang out around school," said Eleanor.

"It wasn't a stranger," said Brendan. "It was someone I know."

"Who?"

"Norm the janitor."

"Norm the janitor's kinda weird," said Cordelia.

"Yeah," added Eleanor. "He's always asking me if I wear Louboutin shoes."

"Anyway, he offered to pay me one hundred dollars more for the bag than I originally bought it for," said Brendan.

"The school janitor is going to pay you eight hundred bucks for a backpack?" asked Cordelia.

"Yep," said Brendan. "Then I'll be able to pay Mom back and—"

Eleanor interrupted. "That's even stupider than Cordelia's story. You *both* need to stop lying."

Brendan and Cordelia looked at the floor. It hurt to be called out.

"All right, it's my turn to tell you guys what happened today," said Eleanor. "But *I'm* telling the truth. These two girls told me I need a new phone." Eleanor pulled out her starter phone. "Is this really so bad?"

"Yeah, Nell," said Brendan. "You should ask Mom for a new one."

"But I like it! It's good enough for me! I don't need all this fancy new stuff we have. I don't even like being driven around in this car! It's weird."

"You're the one who made all this happen," said Cordelia. "You wished for the money. Think how broke we would be if we didn't have it!"

"I don't care," said Eleanor. "And think if you're Mom. Would you want to hear me asking for a new phone the same night you hear that *you* lost your backpack and *you* lost your *tooth?*"

Eleanor was getting upset.

Cordelia gave her a hug, and then Brendan did.

"Don't worry," said Brendan. "After she finds out how messed up Deal and me are, she'll be happy all you're asking for is a new phone. And if those girls at school make fun of you again, just get your big brother on it."

"Yeah?" asked Eleanor, still held tight by her siblings.

"Sure," said Brendan. "You shoulda seen what happened when Scott Calurio started hassling me today. Let's just say he won't be doing it again."

"Thanks, Bren," said Eleanor.

Brendan gave her a big fake smile. Cordelia noticed this and realized her brother was lying. But she didn't say a word. She just felt cold. *We're all lying about something. Maybe even Eleanor.*

The car went over a big bump and their hug separated.

Back at home, Eleanor waited for the right moment to approach her mom. She decided that after dinner, when the dishes were cleared and the dishwasher was on, she'd send a text with a riddle she heard at school: *What do you call a snoring bull? But she wouldn't add the answer: A bulldozer.* Then she would make up a story about how her phone was broken and some of her texts didn't always get sent.

When the time came, though, Eleanor decided, *I'm not lying to my mom. We've got enough secrets in this house.*

"Hey, Mom!"

Mrs. Walker was on the couch. Brendan and Cordelia were off upstairs. Dr. Walker had never showed up for dinner.

"I think it's time for an upgrade." Eleanor presented her phone. "I know you don't want me on the internet a lot, but you can get me a data thingy with tiny internet, or I could just take Dad's other phone if he doesn't want it—"

Mrs. Walker sat up straight. "What do you mean, 'Dad's *other* phone'?"

Eleanor backpedaled. "I meant, Dad's *old* phone."

"No," said Mrs. Walker. "You definitely said *other*."

"Right, well . . . you know, being dyslexic, I sometimes screw up words," Eleanor said.

"You and I both know that isn't part of being dyslexic," said Mrs. Walker. "Does your father have a secret phone?"

Eleanor gulped. Her mother's eyes were . . . Eleanor looked for the word. Not mad . . . not sad . . . *Anxious. And that's worse than anything.*

"I don't know. I don't want to talk about it."

"Look." Mrs. Walker took Eleanor's hand. "Your father hasn't been acting like himself, and I really need to find out what's going on. I can't promise you that it will be easy, but if he has a secret phone, and you show it to me, it will help us figure out what his problems really are."

"And then we can solve them?"

Mrs. Walker nodded.

"And be a normal family again?"

"Well. I don't know if any family is normal."

"We used to be *more* normal."

"I will grant you that."

"Okay," Eleanor said. "I'll show you, Mom. But you can't tell anyone what I've been doing."

E leanor brought her mother into the kitchen and said, "First, you need to cook up some pizza rolls."

"What? Now you're hungry? I thought you were going to show me the phone—"

"It's in the attic."

"Yeah . . ."

"Brendan's in the attic," said Eleanor.

Mrs. Walker made a face, knowing this was underhanded. Still, within five minutes, the pizza-roll smell was wafting through the house and Eleanor was pulling her mother out of the kitchen as Brendan ran down toward it.

"I've been going to the attic when Bren's not around," Eleanor admitted as they went up the back staircase.

"Nell! It's his room! Why would you do that?"

"To pretend—" started Eleanor, but she was cut off as they heard Brendan chanting: *"Pizza rolls! Pizza rolls! Pizza rolls!"*

"What do you pretend when you're up there?" asked Mrs. Walker.

"That the house is a big ship," Eleanor said, "and the attic's the captain's quarters, and I'm the captain. Or that it's the starship *Enterprise* and I'm Spock. Brendan does this thing where he hangs the rope in a certain way to try and catch if people go in there, but I know how to put it back so I don't get caught."

"Nell," Mrs. Walker said admonishingly, "it's important to use your imagination, but it's equally important to respect other people's space."

Eleanor nodded. She couldn't admit the real reason she played in the attic: to look out the window and remember how it felt when she first saw the forest outside Kristoff House. Back on their adventure. When everything was so exciting. And when the Walkers were working together, facing challenges, being close—not lying to one another.

They reached the attic steps. Eleanor explained to her mom: "Okay, so sometimes, besides playing in the attic, I play in the dumbwaiter." She pointed to the square metal door in the wall.

"That's awful!" said Mrs. Walker. "I mean, if the thing

broke, you would—"

"Fall and break my neck?"

"What on earth are you going to tell me next? That you're joining a gang?"

"Relax, Mom. I'm just *explaining* how I saw Dad go into the attic."

"Oh."

"Friday after school, I was playing in the dumbwaiter, and I saw him go in. Like, *secretly*."

Eleanor led her mom up the stairs.

There were two big piles of magazines in Brendan's attic—*Sports Illustrated* and *Game Informer*—and one continuous snaking pile of dirty clothes that led to a hamper, which curiously held no clothes. Posters on the wall had started to peel off and been reattached with gum. A plate of blue-tinged grilled-cheese crusts rested on top of a goldfish bowl where Brendan's goldfish, Turbo, refused to die.

"Dad was only in here for a minute," Eleanor explained, "but after he left, I came up to see what he was doing. He left that bottom drawer open. Just a crack. When I looked inside . . . I found the phone. It was tucked under Brendan's old dinosaur pajamas, which he would never wear."

Mrs. Walker went to Brendan's bureau and opened the drawer. Nestled under the bright green pajamas was an iPhone.

Mrs. Walker picked it up. The phone was locked. She

tried to unlock it with Dr. Walker's birthday: 0404. That didn't work. She tried her own birthday, 1208, and sighed.

"What?" Eleanor asked.

"No matter what I find on here," said Mrs. Walker, "I know he's still thinking of me."

Mrs. Walker went to Recent Calls, but all the outgoing calls were made to just one number.

"415-555-1438," Mrs. Walker read.

"What's that, Mom?"

"We're about to find out."

"No, wait, what are you doing?"

"What does it look like I'm doing?"

"We should get out of here! What if Brendan comes back? Or Dad?"

"It's already ringing, Nell."

"Then at least let me listen!"

Mrs. Walker knelt and held the phone so her daughter could hear it. A voice answered, "Doc?"

11

It was a man's voice, thick and gruff, like the voice of someone with two raw slabs of bacon wrapped around his vocal cords.

"Doc? You there? Whadda you got? Niners are three over this week, Warriors are—"

"Who is this, a *sports bookie?*" Mrs. Walker asked.

Click. The call was over.

"Who was that?" Eleanor said.

"Some coward," her mom said, calling the same number again.

This time, the man answered on the first ring. "Listen up—"

"No, you listen! I'm Jacob Walker's *wife,* Bellamy

Walker, and I *demand* to know—"

"I'm guessing you ain't got picks for the doc?"

"No! And what you're doing is completely illegal—"

"Hey. Mrs. Walker. Don't judge. I just do business with your husband. You got a problem with that, you take it up with him. And tell the doc if he wants in on this week's games, he better call back. And one final thing—"

The man spat a very nasty curse word at Mrs. Walker. *Click.*

Mrs. Walker looked stunned. Eleanor looked at the floor. "Are we in trouble?"

"Not at all," her mom said. "Mommy's going to handle everything."

"We should go, I think I hear Bren."

Mrs. Walker stuffed the secret phone back in the bureau, and the two of them climbed out of the attic. Eleanor placed the rope back in the same position that Brendan had left it in. On the back stairs, Eleanor stopped and turned to her mom. "See, I was telling the truth!"

"You were."

"And this will help our family, right?"

"Yes. Sure. Of course."

"And do you realize, Mom? We just went on a little *adventure?*"

"Sure, honey. An adventure. Dad is spending all our money on sports bets. Big adventure." Suddenly Mrs.

Walker had tears in her eyes.

"I don't understand when I lost this family," she said. "Do you? Did you see when it happened?"

Eleanor shook her head sadly. All she could do was hug her mother.

The next morning, Dr. Walker was sitting at the breakfast table, dressed in jeans, a bright polo shirt, and an argyle golf sweater, as if everything were all right. It made Eleanor want to scream.

"Yes, that's right," Dr. Walker said, speaking into his legitimate phone. "No, we're perfectly happy with the service. . . . We're just on a tighter budget now. He was really very good at his job. I'll miss him. Thanks."

He hung up. "Who was that?" Eleanor asked.

"Limousine company," Dr. Walker said. "I got rid of Angel."

"What?" Brendan asked.

"Why?" Cordelia said before sipping some water. She

was using it to mush-ify the muffin in her mouth so she could eat without chewing. She had woken up today and run her tongue across her teeth only to realize with horror that they *all* felt loose. Like piano keys, wiggling back and forth, ready to come out!

"Because with our family's unforeseen expenses, we need to cut back," Dr. Walker said. "And before you complain: It affects me too. Angel was supposed to drive me to my conference today. So I'll take a cab."

"Where's your conference, dear?" Mrs. Walker asked innocently.

"Downtown. I'm planning on asking Henry for my old job back—"

"But it's Friday."

"Yes . . ."

"Isn't Henry on call Fridays?"

"People's schedules change," Dr. Walker said. "Why are you always questioning everything I do?"

The room got quiet. Mrs. Walker turned away. Dr. Walker stood up, put a hand on her shoulder. "I'm sorry. I don't know where that came from."

Brendan waited until his parents had an awkward hug before he spoke. "How are we getting to school?"

"You can walk. It's only thirty minutes," Dr. Walker said. "Beautiful San Francisco air, friendly people walking their dogs . . . Cordelia will go with you to make sure you don't get lost, and then she'll go to her dentist appointment."

"I dunno, Dad," Brendan said, "I think it's against the rules for kids to walk to Bay Academy. They like their students to be dropped off by shiny, expensive cars. They might expel us for walking."

"Our family did just fine before we had Angel," Dr. Walker said, "and we can do fine without him. No new income is coming in, you know. This money won't last forever."

Because you're gambling it all away! Eleanor wanted to scream. She saw that her father was still trying to be nice, but that didn't stop her from wanting to call him out. She gave a questioning look to her mom, who shook her head: *Not yet.*

Outside, the Walkers started off on a trek through heavy Golden Gate fog. It was rolling up from the bay onto the street like a clammy quilt. Not only was the air not beautiful, they couldn't see a thing.

"I hate when this city is actually foggy," Brendan said. "So cliché."

"Guys," Eleanor said in a very serious tone.

"What?" asked Cordelia.

"Dad's in trouble."

Brendan and Cordelia both looked at her, but now the fog was so dense that they could only see a small, determined shadow with hands clutching backpack straps.

Cordelia asked, "How?"

"He's gambling."

"Dad?" asked Brendan. "No way. Dad's not cool enough to be a gambler."

"There's nothing cool about what Dad's doing," said Eleanor. "You think it's cool that he lies to us all the time? You think it's cool when he says he's going to 'conferences,' but he's really betting all our money?"

"How do you know?" Brendan asked.

"I can't tell you"—Eleanor didn't want to reveal she'd been in his room—"but I know, and Mom knows, and we're going to have to—*agh!*"

She tripped, landing hard on her elbow. A man was sitting with his back against a stone wall, his legs stretched across the sidewalk, almost impossible to see in the fog.

"What do you think you're doing?" she said, getting up. "You can't just sit in the street like that. I almost just busted open my whole face!"

"Nell," Brendan whispered, "forget it. It's just some homeless dude. Don't get him mad."

"Spare change?" the man asked, and as the fog wisped around him, the Walkers could see his thin beard and cap; his dirty skin; and the old Starbucks cup in his hand, with a smattering of coins inside.

"Yeah, sure, no problem," Cordelia said, digging into her pockets.

The homeless man suddenly tensed, pulling his legs close to his body. He sat up straight, got to his feet, and stared directly at Cordelia. Through the tendrils of moisture that drifted over his head, she could see his bright blue eyes. Cutting eyes.

When the man spoke, she noticed his English accent.

"Cordelia Walker?"

Cordelia couldn't speak for a moment. Then she said in a small voice: "Will?"

13

A bolt of shock silenced the Walker siblings. It was the same dumbfounded disbelief they'd experienced when, after giving up all hope of seeing their parents alive again, they showed up back home and saw Dr. and Mrs. Walker, unharmed and perfectly healthy.

Wing Commander Will Draper stood in front of them.

"Amazing! Incredible! It's *you*!" he said. "What good fortune! I want to hug all of you, but I need a proper shower first!"

"Will, what's wrong with you?" Cordelia asked. "Why are you in the street? You were supposed to meet me at school six weeks ago!"

"I'm terribly sorry," said Will. "I never got the chance.

Things went a bit off the rails. It's all rather embarrassing."

"Have you been here all this time?" asked Eleanor.

"No. I was in jail."

The Walkers exchanged nervous glances.

"It started with that hotel, the Days Inn," said Will, turning to Cordelia. "That's where you advised me to stay the evening we came back from our . . . adventures."

"I remember," Cordelia said. "That's also when you agreed to meet me at school the next day."

"Yes, but you can't imagine how difficult it is, being a visitor to the future. It's quite disorienting. From the moment I left your house, I started seeing things that *boggled* me. You know, where I'm from, Saint Paul's Cathedral is the tallest thing around. I arrive in San Francisco, I'm looking at the Transamerica Pyramid!"

"I'm sorry," Cordelia said. "I never should have sent you away without preparing you—"

"No need to feel guilty," said Will. "We had all just been through an exhausting journey. None of us were thinking clearly. I'm just so happy to finally see you!"

"What happened that first night?"

"I arrived at Days Inn," said Will. "The man at the front desk brought me to my room, where there was a large box that displayed moving pictures. It was loudly playing some panto about a yellow-skinned family that ate pink dough-nuts—"

"*The Simpsons!*" said Brendan. "Classic show."

"Hideous show!" said Will. "I just wanted to get some sleep. But I couldn't find the lever to turn off the box. So I went back and asked the man for help, and he muttered, 'Crazy limey lunatic.'"

"Uh-oh," Brendan said.

"I didn't appreciate being insulted by this person who, to be honest, smelled like my nether regions after a long air battle. I told the man, 'Your Days Inn operation is an embarrassment. Our hotel standards are much higher in London!' He said, 'Then go back to your country, Sally.' Now why would he call me 'Sally'?"

"No clue," said Brendan.

"And then," continued Will, "he said something *very* nasty about the royal family. And *that* . . . put me over the edge."

"So what did you do?" asked Eleanor.

"I punched him."

"Oh jeez," said Cordelia.

"He went down like a sack of bricks and gave me my money back."

"So why didn't you come to us?" said Cordelia. "We would have helped you."

"I had this mad notion," said Will, "that if I could just get into an airplane . . . I could fly back to London."

"Home," Cordelia said sadly.

"Exactly. Where it might be easier to acclimate to this time. And then, after I got my bearings, I would return to San Francisco, reunite with you lot."

"Don't tell me you went to the airport," said a cautious Brendan.

"Yes," said Will, "and when I arrived, I asked a woman if I could please fly a plane."

"Are you insane?" asked Eleanor.

"That's exactly what she said," said Will. "But I told her, 'How can you deny a war hero the right to fly?'"

"Airplanes are kind of different these days," said Brendan.

"I realize that," said Will. "But with my experience, I figured it would take a day, maybe two, to learn."

The Walkers exchanged a roll-eyed glance. Even though he was living on the streets, Will's ego was healthier than ever.

"The woman refused my request," said Will. "So I was left with only one option. Climb over the runway fence—"

"Oh no."

"Find an unoccupied airplane—"

"Bad move."

"Climb into the cockpit, and learn the controls."

"So what happened?" asked Eleanor.

"I didn't even get halfway up the fence before I found myself surrounded by eight bobbies!" said Will. "They took me to the station house, and when I asked the desk sergeant to call the Walker family on Sea Cliff Avenue, I was told there was no one by that name on that street."

"Wait . . . I know," said Cordelia. "We had just moved, so we were probably still listed at our old address."

"The next morning I met with my court-appointed lawyer, and I told him the truth: how I was originally a character in a novel about World War One, how I met you three . . ."

"I'll bet that went over well," said Brendan.

"The lawyer told me I could be let off on account of being mentally unwell, and after a few weeks in city jail, that's what happened. I hit the streets, scavenging garbage containers for food, begging for money, and here I am."

"Why didn't you contact us?" asked Cordelia. "We would have helped."

"I didn't want you to see me like this," said Will. "Down so low. But this morning . . . I realized, after spending three weeks in the Tenderloin, being screamed at by pedestrians, kicked, punched by drug addicts, spit on by gang members . . . I knew I had to come back, that I had to find you. I realized that if I didn't see you all again, I would die a second time."

Will looked down, then up. There was a sad flatness to his voice. "So what are you going to do with me?"

14

The entire time Will spoke, Cordelia had run her tongue along her teeth. It was a nervous response to his tale, which she felt responsible for. She should have known better than to send him downtown. While she had spent the last few weeks worrying about the Student Tutoring Program, he had been worried about *eating*.

"I'm taking you home, getting you cleaned up, and giving you some money," she said, grabbing Will's hand.

"But Cordelia. You said that your parents—"

"They're gone. Dad is off at some conference—"

"Gambling, you mean," Eleanor cut in.

"And Mom is at . . . what day is it, Friday? She's at the gym. C'mon, Will. You've been through enough."

"Um . . . Cordelia, can I talk to you in private?" Brendan asked.

"Why?"

"C'mere." Brendan pulled Cordelia away from Will. Eleanor joined them, and suddenly Will was left standing by himself.

"I'm not sure we should trust him," Brendan whispered.

"How can you say that? He's our friend—"

"Exactly," said Brendan. "The Will we know would have come back to us the next day. This guy could be evil-clone Will; he could be the Wind Witch pretending to be Will—"

"You're wrong," said Cordelia. "I completely trust him. A hundred percent."

"But you've got a big blind spot."

"What's that supposed to mean?"

"You wanna smooch him."

"No!" Cordelia said. "I just want to help him. What do you think, Eleanor?"

Eleanor looked back at Will. "He looks kinda gross, but I think you can trust him."

"So that's two against one," Cordelia said to Brendan. "*And* I took that self-defense class last summer. I think I can handle myself around Will."

"Suit yourself," Brendan said, "but I don't trust him."

Cordelia hugged her brother and said, "I appreciate you

looking out for me, I really do." Then she turned and went to Will. "Have a good day at school, guys!"

Brendan and Eleanor waved good-bye, and in a few moments they were continuing on while Will and Cordelia walked back toward Kristoff House.

"Aren't you upset about missing school?" Will asked.

"This is an emergency." Cordelia squeezed Will's hand.

A strange thing happened as they walked home: Cordelia's arm began to feel cold again, like it had before, when she saw the ice under her skin. She tried to ignore it at first but found it was easier to *let the cold feeling travel through her,* to feel it in her heart and guts and limbs. That way Will felt warmer. He was holding her hand tight, as if it had been a long time since he felt a person's touch. Cordelia liked that.

"Your hand is freezing," Will said.

"I know," said Cordelia. "Hopefully you'll warm it up."

They exchanged a smile.

When they got to the house, the fog was clearing. Cordelia led Will down the pebbled path—then yelped and pulled him behind a tree.

"What?"

"That's my mom's car. She must've skipped the gym."

"I can leave," said Will.

"No, c'mon." She led him around the side of the house, dashing from tree to tree, and pried open the window that led to the back stairs. Then they tiptoed up to the second floor and entered Cordelia's bedroom, which had its own bathroom, all while Mrs. Walker was downstairs, on the phone talking to Gamblers Anonymous. Cordelia told Will, "Take a shower."

He didn't have to hear that twice. In thirty seconds Will was under the hot spray, singing "Keep the Home Fires Burning," his favorite song from back home. With each verse, he got louder and louder, completely losing himself—

The door to Cordelia's room opened.

"Cordelia?" Will asked.

No answer.

Oh no, it's her mum!

Will rushed out of the shower, still dripping. *I have to hide!* He tried to find a place, but he was totally at a loss, desperate, as Cordelia entered with a black garbage bag.

"Whoa!" She snapped her eyes shut. "What are you doing?"

Will jumped back in the shower. "I thought you were your mother!"

"Nope." Cordelia took Will's dirty clothes from the floor and threw them in the garbage bag. "I'll put these in the compost."

She left, placing shaving supplies and some of her dad's clothes on the back of the toilet. Will finished showering and shaved—but when he left the bathroom, he found Cordelia sitting on her bed, her head in her hands.

"What's wrong? Cordelia?"

"I don't know."

She didn't look up. Will sat next to her.

"You saved my life today," he said. "You should feel wonderful."

She took a long pause before saying: "There's something wrong with me, Will. I'm sick. And I don't have anyone to talk to"—she cracked a hopeful smile, keeping her lips closed—"except you."

"Cordelia, what's happening? What's the matter?"

Cordelia opened her hand. A tooth sat in it.

Will gasped. The tooth was on a tissue with a bit of blood.

"That just fell out," said Cordelia.

"*What?*"

"It started yesterday. This is the second one. And all of my other teeth . . . they're loose as well. I think it's linked to my entire body feeling ice-cold sometimes."

"Are you saying it's a *spell?*"

"It's possible," said Cordelia. "I feel like I've brought back something from the world of Kristoff's books. Something inside me."

Will put his arms around Cordelia, trying to comfort her. But instead of warming up, Cordelia found herself getting even colder. She pushed Will away, looked down at her hands, and screamed.

The skin was transparent. And underneath . . .

Nothing but ice.

"We should get you to the hospital," said Will.

"No," said Cordelia. And she looked up at him.

Her eyes were gone, replaced by discs of clear blue ice.

Will was a hardened, fearless war hero—but he still cried out in terror.

"Cordelia, what is happening—"

She jumped to her feet and ran out of the bedroom and down the stairs. Will started to go after her, but then he heard the front door slam, followed by Mrs. Walker yelling, "Cordelia, come back! Where are you going?!"

Will didn't want to be hanging around Cordelia's bedroom in case Mrs. Walker came upstairs. And he didn't like the idea of Cordelia being alone in the world, with some kind of spell spreading through her body. He opened a window and climbed out of Kristoff House, determined to find her, but then he realized he had no idea where she'd gone. Except . . . *Perhaps she went to school, to meet with her brother and sister?*

But what school? Will waited behind a tree until Mrs. Walker pulled away in her car, off to search for Cordelia herself, no doubt, and then sneaked into the kitchen and took Brendan's report card from the bulletin board. (He saw Brendan's grades: lots of S's and one E—in gym.) The report card had the address for Bay Academy Prep, so that's where Will headed. He walked quickly down the sidewalk, appreciating that he looked like a proper young man, in Dr. Walker's clothes, as opposed to a homeless, insane wannabe plane thief. Within twenty minutes he reached the school's imposing black gates.

15

Will reached out to open the gates. Locked. He could climb them, but that would almost certainly lead to arrest on the other side. He wasn't sure what to do. Until . . .

A FedEx vehicle crunched the gravel as it drove toward the gates. Will backed off and gave a friendly wave to the driver. The driver identified himself over the intercom. This was followed by a loud buzzing, and the gates opened. *Like magic*, Will thought. He ducked behind the truck, hopped onto the rear bumper, and rode into Bay Academy Prep.

Looking past the duck pond, Will spotted a big, modern building next to the school's main building. He leaped off the truck, scampered over, dashed inside a service entrance, and found himself in the enormous kitchen of the dining hall. The place was bustling with workers, all dressed in yellow smocks, preparing the day's lunch (and vegan option). Will spotted a laundry basket filled with freshly washed smocks, snatched one, and put it on. Suddenly, a hand grabbed his shoulder.

"Hey, you! What're you doing standin' around?!"

The head cook, a burly woman with chin whiskers and a hair net, was a dangerous type. Will tried to explain to her, "I'm new"—but she was already shoving him out of the kitchen and directing him to the hot-food bar.

"In about thirty seconds there's gonna be a stampede of hungry little silver-spooners! You're on mashed potatoes and green beans, so shut up and get to it!"

The dining-hall doors burst open and students raced inside. Will made himself busy dishing out portions over and over from the steaming pans as the kids made ungrateful faces. Then he heard, "Will?"

He looked up. A confused Brendan faced him.

"What are you— Why are you—?"

Will raised a finger to his lips: *Shhhh*. He placed mashed potatoes and green beans on Brendan's tray, but took extra time, arranging the serving to make a message for Brendan in green-bean letters: *Outside*.

Will stepped away from his post and rushed toward the rear exit. The head cook stopped him.

"Where do you think you're goin'?"

"These working conditions are deplorable!" said Will, whisking off his smock and throwing it on the floor. "I quit!"

Will left with the head cook staring at him open-mouthed and the other workers cheering. No one ever talked to her like that!

Outside, Will met Brendan, who kept his distance.

"Okay, so now you're showing up at my school in my dad's clothes, working the cafeteria line. . . . Can you give me one good reason I shouldn't be totally creeped out?"

"Cordelia's gone," Will said.

"What?" Brendan stepped toward him. "What did you do to her?"

"Nothing. She ran away. Something's wrong with her, a spell—"

"You mean the tooth thing. She told us it was a frozen Snickers. What'd she tell you?"

"Just that it started happening out of nowhere . . . and it terrified her—"

"So my sister lied to me and not you?"

"That's not the point—"

"Yeah it is, Will. My sister's not supposed to trust you more than me!"

"Bren. She needs help. She's scared. She's not herself—"

"And whose fault is that?"

"What? . . . You think it's *my* fault?"

"Duh. She's in love with you. You kinda broke her heart. She's been missing you since you disappeared."

"Well, that's . . . that's . . ." Will struggled for the right words and found them in his past. "There's one thing I've learned from fighting in a war and sleeping on the street. That kind of experience teaches you a very valuable lesson. Do you know what that lesson is, Brendan?"

"I don't really care—"

"It's that problems like love are what you worry about when you're *safe*. And right now, your sister isn't safe. And we need to help her. If you're not up for the task, that's fine. But I'm going to find Cordelia and protect her. I thought you were going to help me. Are you?"

Brendan looked into Will's eyes. He saw the same deep worry he felt in his own gut.

"Fine. Tell me everything you know."

16

Will filled Brendan in as they walked, including the details of Cordelia's icy skin.

"Sort of sounds like how she's been acting lately," mused Brendan.

"What do you mean?"

"Cordelia hasn't been herself. I mean, she could always be annoying, but now it's like she doesn't even care enough to annoy us. All she cares about is this tutoring program she's doing at school. Have you tried calling her cell?"

Will stopped walking. "I've been eating out of garbage cans for the last few weeks. How could I possibly afford a mobile phone?"

"I actually see a lot of homeless people with phones,"

said Brendan, "but I get your point." He called Cordelia and waited through four rings. Her voice mail answered. He tried again. Still nothing. But the third time—

"Bren! Bren, I can't talk right now—"

"Deal, what's going on?"

"I can't—I left Will—left the house—not in control—" Her voice was strangely *gulped*, as if she were speaking while someone tried to drown her.

"Deal, slow down—"

"I can feel it, Bren, it's *inside* me—"

"Where are you, Cordelia?!"

"I'm at"—her voice cracked—"where it all happens, Brendan. *Where weaving spiders do not come*—"

The phone cut off. Brendan tried calling back. It went straight to voice mail. He tried again—same thing. He looked to Will.

"We need to head downtown."

E leanor would have been furious had she known that Will and Brendan were going off on a mission without her, but she was busy with her after-school riding lesson. Her horseback riding, which started after her parents got "the settlement," had become one of the most important things in her life.

Eleanor felt at peace around horses. They liked her; they *respected* her; she could get the most troublesome ones to walk, trot, canter, and gallop. That gave her a sense of confidence that was missing everywhere else in her life—and it made her feel more grown-up, because she was actually good at something. Plus there was one horse she truly loved: a powerful, shiny thoroughbred, Crow, who galloped so fast that when Eleanor was on him, the world blurred and she could imagine she was back in Kristoff's books.

Today they practiced turns and jumps; Eleanor and Crow worked seamlessly, as if they had discussed their plans the night before. The two-hour lesson felt like it ended almost as soon as it began, with Mrs. Leland, the instructor, telling everyone to return to the stables. Eleanor dismounted, still wearing her helmet, and led Crow inside.

"Good job today," Mrs. Leland told her. "You're becoming one of my best riders."

"Thank you," Eleanor said, feeling so proud that she wanted to say something more, to make some grand statement. But her mother taught her to simply say *thank you* when people gave compliments, to keep it simple.

Mrs. Leland looked around. All the other students had gone home. "Eleanor, I have exciting news for you. It's time for you and Crow to enter a competition."

"Really?" Eleanor was thrilled—and frightened. She had always dreamed of being in a competition with Crow. But it would be hard work. All the other riders would be really good. *Wait a minute, though; what about the times you cheated death like five million times with Bren and Deal? A riding competition is nothing!*

"That sounds great," Eleanor said. "I'm ready."

"Good to hear," said Mrs. Leland. "I expect big things from you. Oh—here's your father."

Mrs. Leland pointed to the far end of the stables. Eleanor saw Dr. Walker lazily walking up to different horses and patting their heads. She beamed. It meant a lot to her that her dad would come and pick her up. *Maybe,* Eleanor thought, *Mom was right! Now that we discovered what was going on, Dad will get better.*

Eleanor ran to Dr. Walker.

"Hi, baby," he said. "Did you have a nice lesson?"

"Yeah! Guess what Mrs. Leland told me?" Eleanor lowered her voice: "I'm gonna be in a competition."

"That's wonderful!"

"Yeah, I'm gonna work really hard and come back with a blue ribbon. Well, two. One for me and one for Crow."

"I'm so proud of you." Eleanor's father touched her chin. "You're really growing up."

She turned away, blushing. "You haven't said hi to Crow."

"He'll be happy to see me. I brought him a special treat."

Dr. Walker pulled out a fresh Gala apple and gave it to the black horse. Eleanor grabbed his arm—

"Dad! That's not Crow."

"Oh, I'm sorry—"

"You know that! That's always been our family joke, remember? His name is Crow, but he's a palomino!"

"Right . . . of course I remember."

Dr. Walker turned to the actual Crow, the palomino opposite—but now Eleanor was suspicious. Her father had met Crow before. The joke about him being a palomino was part of their family's repertoire, like the joke about how when Brendan was a baby he would only eat rice and soy sauce. Now, looking at her dad's face . . .

It looked wrong.

The skin was too loose. As if her dad were made of wax and standing too close to a hot stove.

Eleanor started to back away while Crow sniffed the apple—then nosed it aside. It hit the ground and sent up a puff of dust.

"I guess Crow doesn't like apples—"

"Dad? What's wrong with you? Why do you look so . . . so weird—"

"*Weird?*" Dr. Walker turned toward her. "You think I look weird?"

Eleanor glanced behind her. Mrs. Leland had left the stables. The door at that end was locked. When Eleanor turned back, her father was locking the door at the other end, trapping them inside. And then he started coming toward her.

"Eleanor, I want you to listen carefully," Dr. Walker said.

Eleanor backed up, terrified. The stables weren't supposed to be completely closed. Not ever. It was dark inside; the only light shone through cracks in the wood. The horses whined and reared up on their hind legs—*NEIGHHHHE-HEHEHEHEHE!*

"Daddy! What's wrong? Stop—"

"Don't talk, listen. Or on second thought"—he chuckled, a nasty gurgling sound—"watch."

Dr. Walker dug his nails into his chin. Eleanor couldn't turn away. Even in the weak light she could see how the skin puckered around each of his fingernails, and then there was a tearing sound and Dr. Walker *pulled his chin off*, revealing something darker underneath.

"*Dad!*"

Dr. Walker wasn't finished. He tore his hand into his cheek, gripping and pulling—and his cheek came off. He tossed it into some hay and grabbed his nose. That came off quickly. Then his other cheek . . . his ear . . . his scalp—he wrenched his whole face off as if it were a cheap mask of Silly Putty.

And now . . . the man's real face was visible.

The Storm King's face.

Eleanor screamed. The horses screamed with her.

Denver Kristoff was staring right at her with his orange eyes and his purple, pitted, deformed skin. The flaps that served as his nose wheezed up and down.

Eleanor dropped to her knees. Little pieces of hay poked into her. "Please don't kill me."

"Kill you?" Denver Kristoff said. "After all you've been through . . . you still fear death? Trust me. There are worse things."

He curled his mouth into a smile—or a Denver Kristoff smile, with one end of the mouth turned up, the other down. "I won't kill you, as long as you answer one very important question."

"What's that?"

"*Where is your sister?*"

Brendan and Will hustled toward 624 Taylor Street, in downtown San Francisco. The landmark building, known as the Bohemian Club, had a huge guard in front of it, with a shaved head and big rings on each finger.

"Maybe this isn't such a good idea," said Brendan.

"It is if Cordelia's inside," said Will. The building was made of limestone and brick, occupying a whole city block. Carved in the facade above the door were an owl and an inscription: WEAVING SPIDERS COME NOT HERE.

"How did you know that was there?" asked Will.

"I know a lot about old San Francisco buildings," Brendan said. "When Cordelia and I were little, we used to walk by this place and try to spot all the owls on the walls. And when we learned on our last adventure that this is where Denver Kristoff was trained by the Lorekeepers . . . I've been keeping a close eye on it ever since. Let's look for a secret entrance."

"What makes you think there is one?"

"US presidents were members of this club. They'd never go through the front door."

"Could I help you?"

The guard approached. Up close, he was as big as two people stapled together.

"I noticed you lookin' at the building," he said. "You wanna walk away, or you wanna get free handicapped passes for life?"

"Free handicapped passes for life?!" Brendan shouted. "That means I don't have to wait in line for roller coasters! That's awesome . . . so what do I have to do?"

"Let me put you in a coma," said the guard.

He grabbed for Brendan—and Brendan and Will took off running around the corner of the Bohemian Club. The guard came after them, gathering momentum with his trunk-like legs. They dashed into an alley at the side of the building and raced under bluish shadows, skirting smelly Dumpsters. Brendan glanced back—there was the guard, huffing his way forward, closing in fast. Brendan knocked over a garbage can—and then saw steam rising ahead. He noticed a nice smell too, very different from the reeking garbage. . . .

"The laundry room!"

"What?"

"Follow me!"

Brendan ran up to a metal grate in the sidewalk. The steam was rising from it. He dropped to his knees, pulled up the grate, and revealed a ladder leading down.

"This way!"

Brendan started going down. Will followed. The guard came to where Brendan had knocked over the garbage can—and yelped as he slipped on some old kale soaked in vinaigrette and his legs whizzed out from under him. He hit the ground on his back, getting the wind knocked out of him.

"Urf! Huh . . . *Huh!*" (That's about all you can say when the wind is knocked out of you.)

Down below, the ladder ended, and Brendan and Will crawled into an air duct that blew out laundry steam. They moved forward, coughing at the heat—and at the pieces of lint that blew into their faces. Within a few minutes it was getting *very* hot and stuffy, and Will started kicking frantically at a seam in the duct. Brendan realized that it could be a very slow death for both of them: They would collapse in the air duct and suffocate; their bodies wouldn't be discovered for months; then, instead of the pleasant odor of laundry, the smell of their rotting corpses would pour out. . . .

Finally Will's kicks worked and the seam split open. They slid out of the air duct, hitting the concrete floor below.

"We—*kaff koff*—we did it!" Brendan managed.

They were inside the Bohemian Club. But you wouldn't know it from the laundry room. It looked like any other laundry room. Only when Brendan led the way out did they find themselves in the place they had expected.

The walls were deep, rich mahogany with mother-of-pearl inlays. Bookshelves were placed throughout, holding leather-bound volumes with spines embossed in gold and silver. Between the shelves were items on pedestals: Greek warrior statues, daggers encased in glass, and preserved animals in jars.

Brendan pointed to the ceiling: cameras. He and Will hugged the wall and walked sideways next to each other. They were totally silent, until they passed one of the preserved animals and saw that it was a muskrat *with two heads.*

Brendan screamed. Will put a hand over his mouth.

"Quiet now, they probably just took two of those creatures and sewed them together."

"Then why does one of them have a normal head . . . and the other one is all small and shriveled up and weird looking?"

Brendan shook his shoulders to get the chills out. Up next was a staircase, which led to a hallway full of disturbing taxidermy, including an owl with a glass lens in its belly and a mouse skeleton inside it. That hallway led to another staircase. Brendan and Will went up to the second floor, where they heard someone talking.

They were in a corridor that was open on one side, facing a breathtaking main hall with a crystal chandelier. The entire building was arranged around this grand space, which had long hanging tapestries and a table fit for a king's feast. Surrounding the hall were two rows of giant portraits of former Bohemian Club members, including Teddy Roosevelt and Richard Nixon. The pictures looked down at the table. There, dwarfed by the room, were three figures.

First was Denver Kristoff, wearing a hood thrown back to reveal his hideous face, striding up to speak with the second man.

The second man was Angel—the Walkers' ex-driver! *What is he doing here?* Brendan thought, but then he saw the third person.

His little sister, Eleanor.

Kristoff was holding her wrist tight. She was crying.

B rendan felt rage burning deep in his guts. Of all the nasty, underhanded things for Kristoff to do, he had to go after Eleanor? Why couldn't he come after Brendan? What a coward!

I'd show him too, Brendan thought. *Let Scott Calurio and his friends watch me take on Kristoff. We took care of him once; we'll do it again. He's nothing but a punk.* Brendan lunged forward, ready to go Three Musketeers with Will, swing down on a tapestry, and take care of Kristoff, but Will stopped him and pointed: *Listen.* Brendan tuned in to the conversation downstairs.

"So what exactly have I been paying you for?" Denver Kristoff asked the scared Angel. "You've been working with the Walkers for a month. You should be familiar with their daily routine by now!"

"Mr. Kristoff, I tried to explain—" said Angel.

"Just give me the information," demanded Kristoff. "Where would Cordelia go?"

"Usually she'd be volunteering after school," said Angel, "but yesterday she started acting very strange, because of this thing with her teeth—"

"You already told me about that. Good God, man, you're useless!" said Kristoff.

Brendan seethed as he realized: *Angel's been working for Kristoff! When we put up the partition in the limo for privacy, he probably had a microphone back there to record us!*

Kristoff continued. "Angel, all you needed to do today was pick up the Walkers and bring them to me. How could you fail in such a simple task?"

"Because Mr. Walker fired me! I couldn't help it! He said he needed to save money."

"The weak-minded fool," said Kristoff. "I never expected it to be so easy. All I had to do was sit down next to him at a bar and convince him to bet on *one basketball game*—now he's run through almost his entire fortune." Kristoff shook his head. "I shouldn't be surprised. His great-grandfather was the same way: simpering, soft, and weak. No core."

Brendan's hate grew as he heard Kristoff talk about Rutherford Walker, his great-great-grandfather, who had helped discover *The Book of Doom and Desire*. *It's not enough for him to ruin my present-day family, he has to talk trash about my ancestors too?*

Eleanor, meanwhile, took advantage of Kristoff's yammering and broke away from him, running for the door.

"Don't waste your time," Kristoff called after her. "The doors are all locked. You can't get out."

Eleanor beat on one of the big wooden doors that encircled the room, shrieking, *"Somebody! Help!! Get me out of here!"*

Brendan wanted desperately to help—but inside the Bohemian Club, Denver Kristoff wouldn't have to worry about people seeing his disfigured face or calling the cops. He could go full Storm King and blast them all to bits.

Will shifted as Kristoff went to Eleanor and picked her up, kicking and screaming. He felt something jab against his thigh, inside Dr. Walker's pants pocket. He pulled out a tiny green pencil and a score card from the Presidio Golf Club. He wrote something on the card and showed it to Brendan: *What do we do?*

Brendan took the card and wrote: *U were right. We just listen.*

Kristoff was trying to talk to Eleanor as he carried her. "I'm going to ask you one more time: Where is your sister? We need to find Cordelia. If we find her, we find my daughter, and then everyone's happy. And we can all go on with what's left of our lives."

"*Help me! Someone!!*" Eleanor yelled. It was all Brendan could do not to charge down the stairs and pull her away from Kristoff and hug her. Even if he got killed immediately afterward, it would be worth it to comfort his little sister. Eleanor didn't deserve this.

But before Brendan could react, Eleanor kicked Kristoff between his legs.

"Urp!" he managed, dropping her.

"I hope that's as broken as your *face!*" Eleanor yelled, running back to one of the doors. "*Help me! Someone!!*"

Eleanor's kick had done some damage. Kristoff was doubled over in pain, making squeaking noises. Brendan smiled. "*No core.*" *Yeah, right. We have a core.*

Angel stifled a laugh. Kristoff glared at him, still bent over. "You—find this—humorous?"

"No sir," said a terrified Angel. "Not at all—"

Kristoff reached up with a look of rage, chanting, starting to generate a blue lightning bolt over his palm.

"No! Mr. Kristoff! Please!" cried Angel, trying to hide under the table.

Kristoff gritted his teeth as the bolt grew larger, eyeing Angel with intent to fry, when one of the doors opened.

T he man who entered the room wore a black velvet robe and a tall, powdered wig, but he was so old and crooked that the wig didn't stand properly on his head—it pointed forward like the prow of a ship. He hobbled up with a cane, tapping, until he got to Kristoff, who promptly dropped to one knee.

"Aldrich," Kristoff said, kissing the old man's hand.

Brendan wrote: *Aldrich* Hayes!

Will mouthed, *Who?*

Aldrich Hayes turned his head (and wig) up so that he could look at Kristoff. This movement revealed his face, which, despite the very serious situation, almost made Brendan laugh. The old man looked like a mad Ringling

Brothers clown, with bright white powder caked from his chin to his forehead. His cheeks even had a rosy glow brought out by two bright red spots.

After Brendan stifled his laugh, he thought, *If that's really Aldrich Hayes, leader of the Lorekeepers, he should technically be a corpse! He looks great for his age!*

"Denver," Hayes said. His voice was throaty and strong; it easily filled the room. "How often must I remind you? When you are inside the Bohemian Club, you are required to wear our wigs and makeup."

"With all due respect," said Kristoff, gesturing to himself, "I think that would be like putting lipstick on a pig."

Hayes regarded the putrid flaps and scars of Denver Kristoff's face. "You do have a point," he said. "There probably isn't enough makeup in this entire city to hide your grotesque complexion! Now what sort of trouble have you gotten into? Who is she?"

Eleanor spoke up. "He kidnapped me from my riding lesson—"

"You *kidnapped a child?*" said Hayes.

"I had no other options—"

"And who is this man hiding under the table?"

"That's Angel, a driver, he works for me—"

"Denver!" Hayes bellowed. "When you arrived, I never expected you to bring all this trouble. 'Weaving Spiders Come Not Here,' am I right?"

Brendan was writing: *That's Aldrich Hayes. Leader of the Lorekeepers. The dude was old in 1906! He must be magically preserved.*

"Hey! Ancient guy!" Eleanor said. "If you get me out of here, my dad can recommend a really good surgeon for your hip or whatever—"

"Quiet," snapped Hayes.

Kristoff said, "I apologize if I've caused trouble. I'm forever in your debt. But I will remind you that over a century ago, I made a great sacrifice for this club."

"And what was that?"

"I discovered the hidden powers of *The Book of Doom and Desire*," said Kristoff. "And did I keep them to myself? No. I hid the book away in my own work to keep it from threatening the world."

"Which is why I welcomed you back," Hayes said. "But my generosity only goes so far—"

"*I need to find Cordelia Walker*," Kristoff said, cutting him off. "I cannot waste time. I'm certain that Cordelia knows where my daughter is."

"Your daughter is *dead*," said Hayes. "The Walkers got rid of her."

"I thought she was gone too," said Kristoff, "but not anymore."

"And why not?"

"Because I've been keeping tabs on the Walkers."

"What?"

"Following them to school, getting reports from Angel—"

"You've been going out in public? Are you insane?"

"Listen to me," said Kristoff. "I've learned that the Walkers didn't precisely *kill* Dahlia. This child *banished* her."

"To where, exactly?" asked Hayes, turning to Eleanor.

"I dunno," said Eleanor. "I just said 'the worst place ever.' I didn't exactly have time to think clearly on account of trying not to get killed an' all!"

"So we really have no idea where your daughter is," said Hayes.

"No," said Kristoff. "But I think the answer may start with Cordelia Walker. I couldn't find her, so I took Eleanor instead. These children are like wild dogs: They operate in packs. It's only a matter of time before Cordelia shows up. And when she does, I believe she will lead me to Dahlia."

"That all sounds very logical, except for one thing," said Hayes.

"What's that?"

"Why would you even want to find your daughter? The last time she saw you, she tried to *kill you*!"

"Ah, but you don't understand daughters," said Kristoff. "One moment they despise you, the next they love you."

That's actually true, Brendan wrote to Will.

"This has gone on long enough," Hayes said. He stepped

closer to Kristoff, slinking under him and looking up like a snake. "Do you understand the enormous historical significance of this organization? The Bohemian Club has *shaped the world*! We have *chosen presidents*! We have influenced world politics! And we thrive on one thing . . . secrecy. But you have broken the rules by *kidnapping a child and bringing her here!!*"

Hayes cracked his cane on Kristoff's foot.

"I'm sorry. I just want to see Dahlia. . . . I just want to get my daughter back," said Kristoff. His voice hitched.

Brendan felt something unspool in his chest. He couldn't believe it, but he suddenly understood the man. Kristoff was trying to do the same thing his mom was: keep a family together.

Eleanor had no such sympathies: "Hey, waffle face, if you want a family so much, join a zombie dating service! I want to go home!"

"You will, little girl, soon enough," Hayes said, turning to Angel. "You!"

Angel looked up from under the table.

"Leave this place and never tell anyone about what you saw."

"But what am I supposed to do?" complained Angel, climbing out. "I quit my old job to work for Mr. Kristoff. How am I supposed to get a new one?"

"Start over," said Hayes.

"I'm too old to start over," said Angel.

Hayes answered by unscrewing the top of his cane. Brendan was sure he was going to draw out a sword and skewer Angel with it, but instead he pulled out a tightly rolled piece of paper. *A spell scroll*, Brendan thought. Hayes declared, "*Famulus famuli mei, transfigura!*"

An explosion of smoke obscured Angel's body. For a moment Brendan thought Hayes had made him disappear. But when the smoke cleared, and the driver stepped out . . .

He was seventeen years old!

Angel looked like a million bucks. He was tall and muscular, without any of the padding he'd picked up driving limos.

"You're a senior in high school again. You have a second chance to make something of yourself. Study, find a nice girl, and play some baseball," Hayes said, unlocking one of the doors.

Angel wasted no time hustling out, grinning as he took a selfie with his phone.

"You should have killed him," said Kristoff.

"That's where you and I differ," said Hayes. "You'd resort to violence to keep Angel quiet. I give him hope, a new life, and he'll still keep quiet."

"My methods are more secure," said Kristoff.

"Your methods are more emotional," Hayes said, "and clearly you won't listen to reason." He began to pace in a circle. "So perhaps you'll listen to proof."

"Excuse me?"

"What if I could contact your daughter's spirit?" Hayes looked up. Brendan followed his eyes to the portraits that hung over the room, featuring the old Bohemian Club members. "What if I used the help of our brothers to summon her soul, and communicate with it? *Then* would you believe she was well and truly gone?"

Kristoff stammered . . . as Hayes started lighting candles.

"I don't want you to do a séance, please," Eleanor begged. She was getting very frightened as the crouched, makeup-caked Aldrich Hayes placed a wooden board on the long table in the Bohemian Club's great hall. The table was lit up with candles like a birthday cake. Eleanor was holding still, her shoulder in the grip of Denver Kristoff's big hand, but now she was getting way too scared to be here. If Hayes were really going to do a séance, that meant ghosts and spirits, and Eleanor wasn't sticking around for that. Luckily, by not moving for so long, she had made Denver Kristoff relax his grip, and with Hayes tending to the table, she broke free!

Eleanor ran toward the doorway that Angel had just

walked out of. Kristoff called angrily after her, but she didn't turn around—and then she heard Hayes's voice, calm: "Wait, little one. You'll be needing some money."

Eleanor stopped, turned back. *Did I hear that right?*

Apparently she did. Because Hayes was holding out a hundred-dollar bill.

"I want you to get a taxi, go back to your parents, and never tell anyone about being here. And keep the change. Understand?"

"You're letting me go?"

"Mr. Kristoff was wrong to bring you here."

Eleanor glanced at Kristoff, who stood behind Hayes. He was clearly angry but also powerless. The old man really was his boss. Eleanor hesitantly took the hundred-dollar bill and strode toward the door. Behind her, she heard Kristoff whisper to Hayes: "You're making a mistake. We should get rid of her. Permanently. I know a place under the Bay Bridge where we can dispose of the body—"

"Enough. Make yourself useful and bring me more candles—"

"I'm not your servant—"

"You are in *my* home and you will follow *my* rules."

Eleanor paused as she approached the door, catching sight of something above. She turned slowly, so Hayes and Kristoff wouldn't notice—

And saw Brendan staring down at her.

He was upstairs, on the balcony, next to Will!

Have they been up there the whole time?

Eleanor had to get to them.

Two sets of doors stood in front of her: one that led out of the great hall and one that led to the street. She went through the first set and opened the second, so it would sound like she was leaving . . . but then she dashed left, climbing the stairs to the balcony. She squeezed her eyes shut as she passed a pedestal holding a glass-encased stuffed falcon with huge, sharp claws. She had to get past all the scary stuff in this place. She had to get to Brendan and Will. And there they were! So close . . .

Control yourself, stay steady, no sudden movements, she thought, but it was all she could do not to cry out as she fell into them.

Their three-way hug was as strong as it was silent. It had only been a few hours since Eleanor had finished her riding lesson with Crow, but she thought she was never going to see her family again, and knowing that Bren and Will had come reminded her: *Sometimes your siblings annoy you, but sometimes they save your life.*

Then, all of a sudden, the lights in the Bohemian Club went out.

22

Eleanor, Brendan, and Will turned to the great room below, where there was a faint glow.

The white candles on the long table were arranged in a figure eight stretching from one end to the other. Hayes and Kristoff stood at the center of the table. Beside them was an ancient record player, equipped with a rusted windup crank and a large metal horn. Next to it was the wooden board that Hayes had brought to the table before. Brendan and Eleanor didn't recognize it, but Will knew it was a planchette, a board used for "automatic writing." A pencil was stuck through its middle, and the idea was that if a spirit contacted you during a séance, you placed your hand on the board and allowed the spirit to guide you, spelling out the words it wanted to say automatically on paper below. Planchettes were forerunners to the Ouija board, which Will knew since the whole idea of speaking with spirits was very popular in his time.

Hayes put a black vinyl record on the record player, dropped the needle, and turned the crank. A squeaky, wince-inducing sound filled the room. Brendan, Eleanor, and Will held their breaths.

The record player let out a loud crack, and then staccato pops, signaling that music could start at any moment.

But the sound that followed wasn't music.

It was a heartbeat—but very, *very* slow, as if a human heart had been slowed by a factor of fifty. It sounded like a cross between interstellar static and a giant's footsteps. *Fat Jagger's footsteps!* Eleanor thought, suddenly missing the brave and simpleminded colossus the Walkers had met in their last adventure. *If only Fat Jagger were here, he would get us out of this. He was my friend.*

As the slowed-down heartbeat played, a mist came out of nowhere—*like the water on our car in the morning,* thought Eleanor. It filled the room, from the air around Eleanor's fingers to the space between the portraits of the old Bohemian Club members. And as it drifted around the room, the heartbeat began to get faster, just a tiny bit. Hayes and Kristoff started chanting.

"*Diablo tan-tun-ka.*" "*Diablo tan-tun-ka.*"

They reached for each other across the table. Their fingertips were just able to touch. They moved their arms back and forth in a fluid ellipse, almost as if they were dancing.

"*Diablo tan-tun-ka.*" "*Diablo tan-tun-ka.*"

The heartbeat got faster, like the heart of someone who had just run a marathon. And it wasn't stopping. It galloped ahead, quicker and quicker, as the light from the candles began to change.

"*Diablo tan-TUN-ka!*" "*Diablo tan-TUN-ka!*"

The candles were bloodred. The mist became red too, looking as if it had soaked up the spray of a battlefield. Eleanor heard a scratching sound and turned—that stuffed falcon she had noticed? It was alive! Scraping its talons against the glass that trapped it, twitching its eyes—

Eleanor screamed, but Brendan covered her mouth. Will elbowed Brendan and Eleanor, pointing to the wall behind them. Two swords mounted there were twisting back and forth, like scissors. Drops of blood beaded up on the metal to plop fatly on the floor.

"*Spirits of our brothers!*" called Hayes. "*We summon you!*"

"*Diablo tan-TUN-ka!*" Kristoff said. "*Diablo tan-TUN-ka!*"

"*We wish to speak to one departed! We seek . . . Dahlia Kristoff!*"

A great groan came from the ceiling, and when Brendan, Eleanor, and Will looked up, they couldn't believe what they were seeing.

The Bohemian Club portraits were coming alive. Teddy Roosevelt, Richard Nixon, and several other stern-looking men were *moving*, moaning and rolling their jaws, as if to test that their mouths still worked.

"Brothers, help us!" Hayes implored from the table below. The red candles flickered around him. The cloud of mist above obscured the portraits—until Richard Nixon leaned out of his frame, puffed out his cheeks, and blew down a gust of air.

The mist drifted to the sides of the room. Hayes and Kristoff looked up at portraits that now twitched and harrumphed in their frames. Along with Roosevelt and Nixon, with their names engraved in gold in each frame, were nineteenth-century satirist Ambrose Bierce; *National Review* founder William F. Buckley Jr.; President Dwight D. Eisenhower; Joseph Coors of the Coors Brewing Company; Mark Twain; *Call of the Wild* author Jack London; "most trusted man in America" Walter Cronkite; and President Herbert Hoover.

"How da-aaare you dist-urrrb us?" Richard Nixon asked, his jowls shaking as he drew out the question. He climbed out of his portrait and sat on the edge of the frame, his legs dangling, revealing bright yellow socks. He glared down at Hayes. "We're all perfectly happy being dead! It's relaxing! Why would you wake us? It had better be important!"

"I know you seek peace, brothers, and I truly do hate disturbing you," Hayes said. "But perhaps you can answer a question?"

"What question?"

"Where is Dahlia Kristoff?"

"Who?" President Eisenhower asked. "Who is he talking about?"

"Dahlia Kristoff," Hayes repeated. "Of San Francisco. Daughter of our esteemed club member Denver Kristoff. It is vital that we find out if her spirit is among the dead."

"Vital to whom?" Nixon said. "I could care less about a missing girl. She's probably gone off to some debauched hippie commune—"

"Shut your mouth!" Denver Kristoff interrupted, leaping onto the table. "Do you know whom you're talking to? Aldrich Hayes built this place. None of you would have achieved wealth and fame if it weren't for the Bohemian Club and the Lorekeepers."

The faces in the portraits glanced at one another.

"That's right! Nixon, how do you think an unattractive dolt like you with a lousy personality, foul breath, and yellow socks could ever be elected president? Because of the Lorekeepers!"

Nixon reached down and pulled at the bottom of his cuffed trousers, trying to hide his yellow socks.

"And Eisenhower?" shouted Kristoff. "Who do you think is really responsible for all of your military victories?"

"The Lorekeepers," muttered an embarrassed Eisenhower.

"And Teddy Roosevelt?" barked Kristoff. "Do you think it's just a coincidence that a mean-spirited lush like you won the Nobel Prize? Now, as a fellow Lorekeeper, I implore you . . . help me find my daughter. Help me find out if she's alive or dead."

"Never," said Herbert Hoover. "Not after the way you spoke to us."

"Usually, when we're disturbed," said Teddy Roosevelt, "it's an extremely serious situation. An event that threatens the Bohemian Club itself."

"And I don't know about you fellas, but I don't appreciate these insults," said Nixon. "If I wanted to be treated like this, I'd move back into the White House. I'm going back to being dead." Nixon began to return to his frame.

"No!" Kristoff grabbed Hayes's hand and cranked up the record player. He began pulling Hayes in a circle, repeating their earlier movements, chanting *"Diablo tan-TUN-ka!"*

"Will you stop that?" Teddy Roosevelt said.

Kristoff ignored them all and bellowed, *"Spirits of San Francisco! Come do what the Lorekeepers cannot! Show yourselves in our time of need!"*

Up on the balcony, a *plink* hit Eleanor's back. It was as if a thumbtack had fallen on her. She turned to look up—but Brendan held her still, trying to keep her quiet. She looked to her side and saw a human tooth on the ground! Eleanor couldn't believe it, but before she could grab it—

Kerrrrrash!—the skylight above the portraits shattered into a million tiny pieces!

Hayes and Kristoff were dusted with falling glass. As they shook themselves off, there was an otherworldly *whoosh* . . .

And a horde of ghosts entered the Bohemian Club.

24

Eleanor had never seen ghosts before, but she knew what she was looking at. Their bodies were long and made of mist. They had howling faces with mouths that stretched into distorted ovals. They flew around like a tornado, streaking past Kristoff and Hayes and swirling on the balcony. They seemed to fly *through* Eleanor, Brendan, and Will, who clutched one another in terror.

The room was overrun with spirits.

"*I'm looking for Dahlia Kristoff!*" Denver yelled to the ghosts. "Dahlia, if you are among the spirits . . . reveal yourself to me!"

Now Eleanor could see the ghosts more closely. Their colorless hair floated behind them as if they were underwater.

Some wore bonnets and dresses from the nineteenth century; others had snazzy three-piece suits with wide lapels from the eighties.

What are they going to do to us?

The tooth was still sitting next to Eleanor, but as she watched, a hippie ghost in a flower-print dress kicked it away. *I didn't know ghosts could kick things.* The spirits peered in nooks and crannies, making faint moans; the Bohemian Club almost sounded as if it were hosting a party. After a few minutes it became clear that the ghosts weren't going to kill anyone.

"Did anyone see that tooth?" Eleanor whispered to Brendan and Will.

"What tooth?" Brendan responded. "I'm looking at *that guy!*"

Everyone turned to see the ghost of Jerry Garcia, in tan shorts, flip-flops, and a tie-dyed shirt, strumming an acoustic guitar. His spectral beard buzzed and snapped as if it were made of baby eels. His eyes were spinning green neon spirals.

"'What's all this 'bout a missing girl? Ain't nobody missing in this world . . . ,'" Jerry sang.

"Who is *that?*" Aldrich Hayes asked.

"It's Jerry Garcia, even I know that," Kristoff told him.

"The guy from the Ben and Jerry's flavor?" Eleanor whispered.

"'I'm just lookin' for peace, ya hear, for finding some girl who I know is near . . .'"

Jerry Garcia looked up. Eleanor looked with him, directly above her, and saw where the tooth had come from.

Clinging to a wooden beam of the Bohemian Club's ceiling was someone who was *not* a ghost. It was a teenage girl, scared and shivering, who looked like the traumatized survivor of a war.

It was Cordelia Walker.

"There's your girl," Jerry Garcia said, pointing. "Dahlia Kristoff."

"No!" Eleanor yelled.

Cordelia unhooked her limbs from the beam and jumped down.

"There!" yelled Denver Kristoff from below, grinning. "I knew if I captured one Walker, the others would appear. And look, they've brought a friend!" He pointed to Will.

"You idiot," said Hayes, "you've compromised our club even further. And how is this going to get you your daughter?"

"Look closely," said Kristoff. "That's not Cordelia Walker up there, not by a long shot."

It appeared that Kristoff was correct, because the skinny girl who had jumped down from the ceiling in front of Brendan, Eleanor, and Will hardly resembled Cordelia. She was crouched on her hindquarters, snarling like a wild animal who had just emerged from an underground cave.

"Deal?" asked Brendan. "What's wrong with you?"

He reached out his hand to her. Cordelia swiped at it, scratching her brother's wrist. Eyes wide and murderous, she madly glanced back and forth from her siblings to Will, growling.

"Brendan," asked Eleanor, "why is she acting like this?"

"She's certainly not herself," said Will, trying to make a joke that no one found funny.

"You were right, Hayes," said Kristoff from below. "These ghosts have given me an answer, but not the one you expected. Dahlia's spirit *is* here—in the body of Cordelia Walker."

"What? How do you know?" asked Hayes.

"Because the little one claimed she banished my daughter to 'the worst place ever.' You tell me: Is there any place worse, any place more isolated and treacherous . . . than the heart of a teenager?"

Kristoff didn't give Hayes a chance to answer. With a victorious laugh, he grabbed the vinyl off the record player and blew out one of the bloodred candles. "*Ite, omnes!*" he yelled to the spirits. "You are no longer needed!"

With one candle blown out, all the others extinguished in an elegant wave. The spell was broken. The ghosts rushed backward toward the skylight, caterwauling and reaching for the animated portraits, who were busy climbing back inside their picture frames. Then the portraits went still and lifeless as the ghosts spiraled out of the Bohemian Club in a wispy jet over San Francisco.

"Now join me in my moment of triumph!" Kristoff told Hayes, hoisting the older man onto his back.

Meanwhile, on the balcony, Brendan, Eleanor, and Will circled the thing that looked like Cordelia Walker. It was a broken thing, on all fours, darting its head back and forth, running forward on its hands and feet, then dashing back. It looked at Brendan, and for a moment he could see the sharp eyes of his real sister, and the thing said, "*Brr . . . ?*"

But then it shuddered and slapped at the ground.

"Cordelia, it's *us*!" Will yelled, sounding desperate.

Cordelia lunged forward. Brendan pulled Will back. Cordelia snapped her teeth—even though most of them were gone, the canines were still intact, giving her the mouth of a bat.

"*All of you stand back!*" Denver Kristoff bellowed.

He was at the top of the stairs, holding Hayes on his back, with Hayes's wig sticking up behind his head. Kristoff put Hayes down gently.

"Brendan, you horrid little brat," he said. "You will pay dearly for sneaking in here. And you!" he told Eleanor. "You had the chance to leave safely. Unfortunately for you—"

But now even Kristoff had to stop midsentence.

Because Cordelia Walker was screaming at the ceiling

in a painful, high-pitched wail.

"Leave her alone!" Kristoff yelled. "Don't touch her! That's not your sister! That's my daughter, Dahlia, who has been *inside her body* these last six weeks! You thought you could get rid of her with your childish wish, but she was stronger than you! The Kristoffs have *always* been stronger than the Walkers!"

Brendan shuddered. He couldn't take his eyes off Cordelia, and he couldn't shake the growing horror in his heart. Cordelia was still screaming like a wild beast—but now something worse was happening—something that reminded Brendan of a thing he'd seen on TV. It was from a show called *Deep Deadly Creatures*, on the Discovery Channel.

She was doing what the sea slugs did.

Brendan had seen sea slugs on this show—and even though they were already gross looking, the grossest thing about them was that they would *push their stomachs out of their mouths to eat*. Literally, they would turn inside out, and now . . . Brendan couldn't believe it . . . Cordelia was doing the same thing, *pushing something out of her mouth*, but it wasn't her stomach—

It was another person.

As it moved from inside her, Cordelia's own mouth hinged back, like a snake dislocating its jaw to consume an egg. There was a tremendous *crack*.

"Stop!" Brendan cried. He surged forward—and heard a sizzling, zapping sound, followed by a burning sensation that shot through his chest. He looked down and saw that his T-shirt was blackened and smoking. Kristoff had blasted him with a bit of blue lightning to keep him away from Cordelia.

"*Can't you see she's dying?*" Brendan yelled, tears streaming down his face. "*Please, let me help her!*"

"You can't help her," Kristoff said coldly. He was looking at Cordelia as if she were a fascinating experiment.

Now Cordelia's mouth was stretched unimaginably wide, nearly the size of a basketball hoop. She was facing the ceiling, her screams muffled by the size of the person coming out of her.

Kristoff recognized his daughter immediately. Brendan didn't take much longer. The first thing he saw was an old, crooked mouth with thin lips and gnarled, yellow teeth. A pinched nose, grayish skin, a mottled bald head . . .

The Wind Witch.

"*No!*" Eleanor yelled.

But there was no stopping her

now. The Wind Witch pushed through Cordelia. There was no blood, only the sound of bones cracking. The Wind Witch slid out of Cordelia's body as if she were wiggling out of a worn dress. Cordelia's arms and legs lost all of their rigidity, becoming a sad, discarded pile of skin on the floor. The Cordelia Walker that Brendan loved was now something like an exoskeleton, with dead eyes.

"*Ahhhhhh,*" said the Wind Witch as she stretched out luxuriously, unfurling her wings. She wrapped them around her body and cracked her neck. She smiled as she stepped away from Cordelia's husk.

"Did you miss me?"

26

"Dahlia!"

Denver Kristoff smiled. Even the side of his mouth that curved down seemed to temporarily twist upward. It was a smile Brendan knew from his own father, when Bren would correctly spell a word or solve a math problem and Dr. Walker would say, "Your daddy's proud of you." Unfortunately, it had been a long time since Brendan's father had given Brendan much praise. Or much attention at all.

"My darling daughter, I thought you were gone forever," Kristoff said, holding his arms out to the Wind Witch. "How did you manage it?"

"I've inhabited several bodies in my time, but hers was

the most difficult," said the Wind Witch. "What a nightmare! Her palms were always wet. Her face was constantly breaking out in patches of acne. So many petty thoughts about student elections and what to wear!"

"How did you manage to get out?" asked Kristoff.

"Every day, I took gradual control of Cordelia's body. Bit by bit, piece by piece. And I started to grow more powerful. Until finally—*ahhhhh*"—the Wind Witched stretched her back—"I could break free."

Eleanor wasn't listening. As she had seen Cordelia transform into the Wind Witch, she had become numb. It simply wasn't something she could handle. Cordelia was the person she looked up to, almost more than her mother. Cordelia was who she wanted to be when she grew up. And now Cordelia was gone—except . . .

The husk on the floor was moving.

Will didn't see. He had closed his eyes. His heart was in a million pieces. But now he felt a hand tugging on his sleeve.

"Look!" Eleanor whispered.

Cordelia's body was beginning to regain its shape.

It started with the tips of her feet, which still were attached to her shoes. The feet puffed outward to fill the shoes, sticking out straight, like the feet of a doll propped against a wall.

"Bloody hell—" Will said.

"Are we seeing things?" Eleanor asked.

"Deal!" Brendan yelled.

Now Cordelia's waist and body were taking shape. It was as if someone had attached a blow-dryer to her deflated shell and were pumping it full of air—and of life. Cordelia's fingers popped back up, one through ten, *pop-pop-pop-pop-pop*. Her arms inflated back to their normal size. Her neck returned. And then, like Dracula waking up from his casket, Cordelia's face rose, her cheeks expanded, her nose snapped outward. Cordelia's eyes rolled down from their sockets; her thin lips became full; her mouth returned to its normal size; and her teeth . . . her teeth grew back completely intact. Whiter than usual, in fact.

"*Wuh . . . ?*" she asked.

"Deal!" Eleanor yelled, bursting into tears as she rushed up to her sister. "You're alive!"

Will was right behind Eleanor, hugging both sisters at once, whooping with glee. He didn't care how it happened; he was just happy to have Cordelia back, happier than he could remember being in his entire life. Brendan was there too, squeezed in the middle.

The Wind Witch turned to her father. "What is this?" she asked, betrayed. "Is this one of your tricks?"

"Of course not," Denver Kristoff said, as Aldrich Hayes craned his neck to look at the incredible sight of Cordelia, palming her clothes to make sure she was still alive, surrounded by her tearful siblings and Will. "I don't know how that happened."

"She was dead as a doornail! *You* brought her back to life!"

"Of course I didn't, Dahlia! Why would I do that? I hate the Walkers as much as you!"

"*Liar!*"

The Wind Witch rose above the floor, flapping her wings, hovering over Kristoff and Hayes.

"You two are always up to your little tricks. You think I'm not aware what you're capable of? *You* brought her back to life!"

"Dahlia, please," said Denver Kristoff. "Just come down. We can talk about this—"

"My magic never fails me," said the Wind Witch. "When I kill someone, they stay dead. Maybe I should test that out . . . on you!"

The Wind Witch swooped toward Kristoff. Brendan grabbed his sisters and Will, animated by opportunity. If Dahlia and Denver were going to have a father-daughter moment, it was time to escape. Brendan inched backward—

"*Where do you think you're going?!*" the Wind Witch said, her body spinning toward the Walkers. "Stay put!"

The kids all froze.

"Excuse me," Cordelia said. She had finally managed to gather her bearings. Now she knew it had been the Wind

Witch—the Wind Witch all along, transforming her from the inside out. Cordelia wasn't even sure which parts of her over the last few weeks had been *her*.

"I thought you actually liked me," she told the Wind Witch. "I thought you respected my intelligence, Dahlia. Isn't that why you helped me on Sangray's ship? Why would you turn on me now?"

"Yeah, in other words: What's your problem?" asked Brendan.

"The four of you prevented me from getting the book," Dahlia Kristoff said. Her one good arm had been lost in the Walkers' last adventure, and her jeweled prosthetics had apparently not made the journey out of Cordelia's body, so she had two ragged stumps where her wrists should be. "I'll deal with you . . . just as soon as I deal with my lying father."

Two columns of air spiraled out of the Wind Witch's stumps and knocked Denver Kristoff off his feet. He hit the ground with a thud.

"I won't fight you!" Kristoff said. He raised his hand, trying to shield himself from the intense wind being blasted at him.

"Kristoff, she means to kill you!" Aldrich Hayes said. He threw down his cane and raised his arms, chanting. Fire appeared between his fingertips—

But he was too slow. The Wind Witch shot a blast of wind at his face and threw him down the stairs.

"C'mon," Brendan said, pulling the others. There was a large tapestry on the far wall of the balcony. It extended from the second floor to the main room. If they could reach it, they'd be able to climb down.

"What have you done?" Kristoff yelled, rushing to Hayes, who had landed on his back and was rolling over, trying to cast a healing spell on his broken ankle.

The Wind Witch screeched, flying out over the main room, under the busted skylight. She seemed to relish having her body back; she dipped and twirled like a dolphin at play before she took up a position next to Richard Nixon's portrait. She raised her arms as her wings flapped. Tiny updrafts lifted countless bits of the shattered skylight glass from the floor. The glass began to swirl around the Wind Witch, gaining speed, forming a very sharp and deadly ring.

Hayes was moaning. Kristoff saw that he was trying to heal his ankle, but his wrist was bent back the wrong way, and he couldn't cast a spell with a broken wrist. He tried to reach for his cane, but his hand could barely function.

"*Agh!*" Hayes said. "Kristoff! Get . . . a spell scroll. It will destroy her. She's better off . . . dead."

"Please don't say that," Kristoff said. "She's my daughter—"

"No," said Hayes. "She's something horrible, something evil—"

"I still love her—"

"*Love!*" the Wind Witch cackled in a mocking tone. "Father . . . do you remember why we fought last time?"

"Because you were mad," Denver Kristoff said. "Crazy for *The Book of Doom and Desire.*"

"And you stopped me from getting it. Which makes you just as bad as the Walker brats!"

"No," Denver Kristoff said. He stepped away from Hayes and spoke calmly, in a way that was somehow more powerful than Dahlia's screeching. "I'm not like them. I'm your father. Now, please. Come down. We can leave this place. Together. Make a fresh start. Be a normal family."

"Are you delusional? Look at yourself! You don't even have a *face!*"

"I can start writing again," pleaded Kristoff. "You can meet a nice fellow—"

"*A nice fellow?!*" said the Wind Witch. "Have you looked at *me?* The only thing that could make me attractive . . . is *power!* So tell me where the book is!"

"I have no idea," said Kristoff.

"And you're telling the truth?"

"With all my heart."

"Then you're no longer of use to me."

The spinning glass that had been circling Dahlia Kristoff's body formed a bullet-shaped cloud. It hovered in front of Dahlia for a moment, and then, with the speed of a subway train, shot toward her father.

Kristoff raised his arms. Blue lightning crackled in an arc over him—but the shower of glass slammed into him.

It hit Hayes as well. The shards entered the skin of the two men with such force that they were instantly turned into something resembling Swarovski porcupines. Kristoff tried to blink, but pieces of glass were lodged in the tops and bottoms of his eyelids, forcing them open.

Brendan was horrified. He knew the Wind Witch was capable of great evil, but he never knew she could be so cruel to her own father. Brendan would never forget the look of shock on Kristoff's face, a look that said it wasn't just his eyes, but his heart that had been broken. Brendan grabbed a section of the tapestry with Cordelia, Eleanor, and Will. "Hurry up," he said, starting to climb down. The others followed. The Wind Witch turned.

"Trying to escape?!" she asked, lifting more glass from the floor and shooting it at the tapestry. The glass tore through the fabric like a million tiny razor blades. The tapestry ripped in half and fluttered to the ground with the kids still holding on to it. Fortunately the ancient decoration was thick; they landed on it safely, tangled in fabric.

The Wind Witch turned to Kristoff and Hayes, who were screaming in terrible pain. She raised one of her stumps and blew open the Bohemian Club's double doors.

Brendan saw the streets of San Francisco outside. It was late at night, but the world was out there: a real world with red lights and supermarkets and cell phones, nothing like this insane nightmare he had been plunged into.

The Wind Witch pointed her stumps at the open doors and flung Kristoff and Hayes out of the building.

The wind carried the men out of the doors and into the street—where they were hit by a passing Muni bus. They sailed off the front of the bus and through the window of a closed Chinese restaurant, smashing into tables and chairs before going still on the floor.

The Wind Witch inhaled deeply. The doors to the Bohemian Club slammed shut. She turned to the pile of kids in the fallen tapestry. "Now I can deal with you."

27

The Wind Witch eased down slowly. When she landed, she beckoned with her stump, and the half of the tapestry that she had cut loose slid away from the Walkers and Will. Like a devoted pet, it crawled across the floor to her. She turned her stumps in small spirals, and the fabric wound around her until she was wearing it as a sleeveless dress.

"How do I look?"

"Like an old bag wearing an old bag," said Brendan.

Cordelia knew that Dahlia Kristoff was vain; a little compliment might go a long way. She said, "Brendan's a boy. He doesn't know anything. You look great."

The Wind Witch moved toward the kids like an animal

approaching dead meat. Her eyes seared into Cordelia's. "Don't mock me. You don't want to end up like my late father."

"You're more twisted than we even thought," Brendan said. "What kind of screwed-up person kills their dad?"

Eleanor glared at her brother: *Don't you know anything?* If he kept mouthing off they wouldn't stand a chance.

The Wind Witch patted Eleanor's head. "Don't worry. Follow me."

Eleanor was shocked, but she had no choice but to follow the Wind Witch as the gaunt figure strode through the great hall, which was now filled with overturned, broken chairs. Eleanor beckoned *c'mon!* to Brendan, Cordelia, and Will. Outside, they could hear ambulance sirens arriving. Someone must have reported Denver Kristoff and Aldrich Hayes flying through the restaurant window.

"Cordelia," the Wind Witch said, "you mentioned how I complimented your intelligence once." She was leading them all up to the balcony. "I *do* respect you. And I have to admit: All of you Walker children are more resilient than I ever imagined. Cordelia, I am still trying to figure out how you came back to life."

They stood over the place where Cordelia's lifeless husk had lain on the floor. The only sign that it had been there were the drops of spittle that had come out of Cordelia's mouth when she released the Wind Witch.

"Maybe I'm a witch," Cordelia said. "Like you."

"Possibly. But it would take a very experienced witch to reanimate themselves, someone much older and wiser than you. I still suspect it was a trick of my father's. But no matter. Now that he's gone, we can have a civilized conversation. And I'd like to make it clear to all of you . . . that I never meant to hurt you."

"No," said Brendan, "you just used Cordelia's body like an incubation tank. And then there was that time when you threatened to cut off Eleanor's fingers, fry them, and eat them."

"I was only trying to get the book," said the Wind Witch. "It wasn't personal. In many ways, you *all* remind me of myself."

"Yeah, right! On what planet?" asked Brendan.

"You have a father who says he loves you but truly doesn't."

"No," said Eleanor. "No matter what, our dad still loves us."

"Really?" asked the Wind Witch. "Is that why he continues to gamble away your fortune?"

"He's trying to change."

"He won't change. Fathers never do. My father was power-mad when I was a little girl, and he stayed that way for the rest of his life."

"But he was asking you to love him," Eleanor said. "He

just wanted you guys to be a family again."

"That's what he wanted you to think," said the Wind Witch. "That could never be possible as long as he kept *The Book of Doom and Desire* hidden from me."

She raised her stumps in front of the children.

"Now, my father said he didn't know where the book was. And you three were the last ones to possess it. And because of the curse he put on the book, you're the only ones who can open it. So can you please just tell me where it is? And I won't have to hurt you."

"*Are you serious?!*" shouted Brendan. "You just said you never meant to hurt us! Now, like thirty seconds later, you're threatening us! Lady, you need to seriously think about getting some therapy!"

The Wind Witch smiled. "Have you finished?"

"No, I *haven't!* I—"

"*I* think you have," the Wind Witch said. Brendan suddenly shrank back; he had momentarily forgotten who he was screaming at. "I think you've run your mouth enough for an entire lifetime."

The Wind Witch stood over Brendan now, sneering, focused. She began to move the stumps of her arms. Behind her, Cordelia edged toward a stuffed armadillo on a pedestal.

"You're nothing but an ignorant little boy," said the Wind Witch. "You've never used the book. You don't understand its power. You never will, until you open it yourself.

I'll let you, you know, if you help me. Then you'll under-stand what *true* power is. It's not the power to be popular or rich. It's the power of a *leader*. The power to look at the faces of those under you, thousands of them . . . staring up at you, quaking in fear—like you're doing right now—that's when you know what it's like to be a king. Or a queen."

The Wind Witch shot out her arms at Brendan. Unfor-tunately for her, she did it at the same time that Cordelia whacked her in the back with the armadillo.

It threw off the Wind Witch's aim. The torrent of air that spilled from her stumps hit the floor instead of Brendan. Wood flew up in big splinters as if it had been sandblasted, leaving a hole—and then, with a creak and snap, a whole section of the balcony fell away! Brendan dropped with it, but Will grabbed his wrists. Wooden beams crashed below; it looked like Jaws had taken a bite out of the balcony. The Wind Witch rose with her wings flapping.

"Come!" Will said. The Wind Witch swung her arms and another jet of air rushed toward Brendan. He ducked it, picked up Eleanor, and rushed downstairs with Cordelia and Will.

"This way," Eleanor said, heading for the double doors at the front of the Bohemian Club—

"Stop!" Brendan yelled. "There are gonna be cops and ambulances! This way!"

Brendan doubled back as the Wind Witch blew a sword off the wall. It did a midair flip and flew straight at him. He dove to the ground face-first; Eleanor jumped off him; the sword passed between them. They managed to get up and follow Will, who was going to the basement stairs, before the Wind Witch mounted another attack.

They followed Will into the basement. Their footsteps echoed against the concrete walls. Will flung open the door to the laundry room.

"What are we doing here?" Eleanor asked, breathless.

"Up!" Will said, pointing to the air duct. He interlocked his hands to make a foothold. Cordelia put her foot in there and sprang up like a jack-in-the-box. They all followed suit. Once they were in the duct, they crawled single file; the metal shuddered and clanged under their weight. In five minutes they were in the alley next to the Bohemian Club, dusting themselves off, and then they headed to the street.

There were seven police cars at the scene of the accident. They had cordoned off the area with yellow tape; surrounding it were news vans and ambulances and gawkers from a local sports bar who had put their bottles on the ground to take pictures. The bus that had hit Denver Kristoff and Aldrich Hayes was stopped in the street; the passengers were on the sidewalk talking to EMTs. Brendan saw one guy rub his neck and say, "Who do I sue? Muni? Or the idiots who jumped the bus?"

"The idiots are dead," said the EMT. "The only judge they'll be facing has a long white beard and a courtroom in the clouds."

Brendan couldn't believe it, but Denver Kristoff *was* dead. Hayes too.

He peered at the Chinese restaurant—their bodies were covered in sheets. A hard-looking detective in a trench coat spotted him.

"Hey!" the detective shouted. Brendan turned, and the Walkers and Will were off, pounding pavement, hailing a cab.

"What's wrong, you kids okay?" the cab driver asked as they piled in.

"One twenty-eight Sea Cliff Avenue," Brendan said. "Our grandfather was in that accident and we have to tell our parents."

The driver turned onto Mason Street. Brendan swiveled to look: The detective came into view, huffing and puffing, as the cab pulled away.

They rode in silent worry, except for the driver's Metallica music. Brendan was sure the detective had seen the number on the cab and they were all going to get arrested, but the only drama happened at the end of the ride, when the cab pulled up to their house and the driver asked, "Who's payin'?"

"Uh . . . ," Brendan said, digging in his pockets. "I'm

sorry. I don't—Deal?"

She gave him a look: *You do realize I was* dead *less than an hour ago?* "I don't have anything on me, Bren."

"Nell?"

Nell whipped out the hundred-dollar bill Hayes had given to her. She handed it to the cab driver.

"Keep the change," she gallantly told him as they stepped out of the cab.

Brendan hurried up the path to Kristoff House. His family and Will walked more slowly behind him. It felt good to be home. He was trying to convince himself that the worst was over: *Everything's going to be fine. Mom and Dad will be inside and everything will be normal.* But when he entered the house and left the door open for the others, the Wind Witch was standing in the hallway.

"Welcome home, darling."

28

"Something's wrong," Cordelia said, seeing Brendan suddenly disappear from the front door as if he'd been grabbed. She rushed to Kristoff House with the others—

The Wind Witch had Brendan suspended in midair.

She was in the front hall with one arm raised, using tiny gusts of wind to keep him floating near the ceiling. The anger and hatred on her face made her look almost foreshortened, like a snake.

"*For the power of the great book!*" she yelled.

The Wind Witch raised her other arm, creating a strong blast of wind that gripped Will and the girls in its invisible clutch. They were lifted off their feet and shunted into the living room. Brendan floated with them, and Cordelia saw that he was limp, lolling his head back and forth.

"You killed him!" she said in shock. "Brendan! *What did you do?*"

"He's only unconscious," said the Wind Witch. "I couldn't bear to listen to any more of his inane wisecracks."

Once she had them all floating above the Chester chair and grand piano that made the Walkers' living room so luxurious, she unfolded her wings and flew up herself.

"What are you doing?" Cordelia said—and then two quick bursts of air shut her mouth so tight, all she could do was scream into her own lips.

The Wind Witch tightened her brow. She was concentrating with inhuman precision. She waved her stumps to keep her victims suspended in place as she began to flap around them.

Whoosh—she passed Cordelia's terrified face. *Whoosh*—she flew by again. She was circling faster and faster, but always bending her neck to stare at Cordelia and the others, never losing focus.

"*Nnnnn*—!" Cordelia screeched through her forcefully closed mouth. It was like being on an amusement park ride gone terribly wrong.

The Wind Witch swished by again and again, creating a nauseating strobe effect, blurring—until her parched, patchy face seemed to become the center of a hall of mirrors. She was surrounding Cordelia from every angle at once. Screaming.

"That you will find what you so carelessly lost! That I shall have what I deserve!"

Cordelia tried to close her eyes, but the rushing air kept them open, making tears fly out and spiral behind her.

Then she began to experience a horrible *shrinking*.

It happened to all the kids. Their bones tightened. Their skin clenched around them. Their organs pressed painfully against one another. Their eyes grew smaller—and the Wind Witch's omnipresent face, and the room, grew larger.

Everything was spinning now. The house itself howled as it moved with the Wind Witch: The Chester chair had become a brown blur, the fireplace was disappearing and reappearing like a smear of brick—and the shrinking continued. Cordelia and the others were diminishing in size, becoming the size of Chihuahuas, of mice, of peas.

Cordelia looked below her. Three books floated there. She couldn't read the titles because they were distorted, too gigantic, getting bigger every second. They were like ridges on textured terrain, the way book titles might appear to a fly, or an ant, or . . .

How small are we getting? Cordelia asked herself. *And why is it different this time? We're being sucked into those books like a milkshake being sucked through a straw.*

It angered Cordelia that she couldn't read any of the books' titles as she hit one—and then all was dark and silent.

29

Cordelia woke up on the floor in the living room. Next to her were Will, Eleanor, and Brendan, also coming to. She blinked and got up on one elbow as she became conscious of a noise. It sounded like the cheers of a football game.

"Brendan?" she asked. "You okay?"

"The Wind Whacko knocked me out as soon as I walked in the front door," he said, looking around. "Oh, no, no . . . did she do it again?"

"That's an affirmative," said Will.

"She banished us?" asked Eleanor.

Brendan nodded. "Just like last time."

"But last time the whole house got destroyed," Eleanor

pointed out. "This time she kept the furniture and everything else pretty much in place."

"I can't believe she did this on a weekend," complained Brendan. "I'm not even getting to miss school."

"I'd like to know what world we've been sent to," said Will.

"Three of Kristoff's books again," said Cordelia. "I saw them right before I blacked out."

"Did you see the titles?"

"Couldn't make them out."

"Maybe we got sent to the same place as last time," Brendan said, "and now we have a serious advantage. We know how to deal with Slayne; we know how to handle the pirates—"

"But if it's like last time, doesn't that mean Will is going to fly in on a plane and save us?" Eleanor said. "That would make two Wills!"

"Two of me," Will said, intrigued by the idea. "Hmmm, that could be fortuitous."

"How's that?"

"Two strong, handsome leaders are better than one."

"One egomaniac is plenty," said Cordelia. "Besides, I think we've been sent somewhere new. Because what's that noise?"

"Yeah," Eleanor said. They could still hear a crowd. Outside the house. "Are we in the middle of a football game?"

They all paused for a moment and listened. The sound of the crowd surrounded the entire house. But all the windows and shutters were closed. The Walkers and Will seemed trapped like mice in an experiment.

Cordelia headed for the nearest window. "Do we have a weapon?"

Will looked around, made fists. Eleanor did the same.

"*Fists?*" said Brendan. "Really? It sounds like there's a thousand people out there, and what are we going to do, punch them?"

"Have you got a better idea?" asked Will.

Brendan paused, looked around, and picked up a small Japanese table lamp, holding it like a mini baseball bat.

"Of course," said a sarcastic Will. "Lamps happen to be quite effective at stopping angry mobs."

"Shut up, Will."

"All right, let's do this," Cordelia ordered. She was about to open the window when she noticed Will staring at her. "What?"

"You're taking charge. It suits you."

"It's cute?"

"No. *It suits you.* But it *is* cute."

"Will, listen," Cordelia said, stepping away from the window. "I know I haven't been myself so maybe you forgot who you're dealing with. But I'm not interested in being trapped in mystical worlds for the rest of my life. I need to get back home, to go to school. So we're going to see what's out there, secure the house, get *The Book of Doom and Desire* as soon as possible, and get out. *No adventures.*"

"Yes, ma'am," Will said, saluting.

"I'm not an old lady, don't call me that."

"But wait, Deal," Eleanor said. "If we get the book, won't we be doing exactly what the Wind Witch wants us to do?"

"If it gets us home, Nell? I don't care."

Brendan was tired of everybody talking. He ran off and yanked open the window Cordelia was at, which usually had a gorgeous view of the Golden Gate Bridge. Then he completely stopped, frozen, at the incredible sight he was looking at.

At the same time, someone grabbed Cordelia's leg.

Eleanor pointed at the entrance to the living room. "L . . . Li . . ."

Brendan stared out the window. "Guys? I think we're in a . . ."

But he didn't need to say it. Cordelia suddenly understood what the crowd noise was.

Facing her at the front of the living room, with its shoulders up and knotted, sniffing, was a full-grown lion.

"Oh my—" Cordelia started.

"How did that get in here?!" Will yelled, flabbergasted.

"Hide!" said Eleanor.

Cordelia grabbed her sister and ran for the couch. But

Brendan had no idea about the lion; he couldn't even hear his sisters and Will yelling. He was completely engrossed by the incredible view outside.

He was looking at the Roman Colosseum.

From smack-dab in the center of the arena.

The Colosseum was gorgeous, splendid, majestic. Giant outcroppings of stone held seats containing tens of thousands of people. It was like the Giants' baseball stadium in San Francisco, but so much older and more beautiful—in fact, it made that stadium look cheap. And Brendan was right where the pitcher's mound would be! This was the real deal: No one had gotten a chance to see the Colosseum this way for thousands of years, and here Brendan was, right in the middle of it.

He'd always wanted to see the Colosseum. There wasn't a cooler building in world history. When you were talking about ancient Rome, you were talking about plumbing, voting, and death by countless stab wounds. . . . The Romans were the definition of "ahead of their time." And this building was the *one* place people always talked about when they talked about Rome. It was like the Super Bowl and the Olympic Village rolled into one!

Brendan saw men in white togas in the stands, with some of the togas so white that they seemed to be bleached and hurt his eyes, and others with red stripes. There were a few purple togas, decorated with gold, but only the men who sat close to the arena wore them. There weren't any women, except in the nosebleed seats at the very top, where Brendan saw a few dressed in flowing robes that resembled what the Statue of Liberty wore.

Everyone was cheering at the top of their lungs, on their feet, pointing at Kristoff House. *And why wouldn't they? We just showed up in the middle of an event!*

Two deer were cornered with spears at one side of the arena, but the warriors holding the spears weren't paying attention to the deer anymore. The animals leaped away. The warriors stared at Brendan with open mouths. *They're looking at the house!* Another group in tunics with bows and arrows were putting their weapons down, calling and pointing. Clearly some kind of mock hunt had been going on—but it was on hold for now.

Brendan's eye flicked to a man seated in what Brendan would call one of the Colosseum's end zones, high up in a sealed-off box. *That has to be the emperor,* Brendan decided.

The man wore a garish purple toga with a dash of white and a golden crown lined with sparkling jewels. He was extremely short, under five feet tall, and nearly that wide. Soft and delicate, with eyes set too far apart and completely without hair, he stood and waved one hand at the crowd as if he were shooing away an insect.

The crowd went silent.

Man, Brendan thought, *that is one powerful dude.*

The man began to speak, but of course no one could hear him. He was one small (tiny, really) figure in a huge arena. So a manservant next to him stepped up to a giant bronze cone mounted on a tripod. The cone acted as a primitive megaphone, amplifying the manservant's voice throughout the Colosseum.

"Speaks Emperor Occipus the First!" the manservant declared. "'Do not be frightened by this odd structure! It is the work of enemy sorcerers, a hell house conjured from Hades! But I, your emperor, will protect you. If there are monsters in the house, I will exterminate them! Send in another beast!'"

Emperor Occipus, Brendan thought. *I've heard that name before. . . .*

A metal gate below Emperor Occipus's box winched open. From the dark inside, two guards with helmets and whips emerged, leading out a lion.

"Uh-oh," Brendan said. "Uh, incoming, twelve o-clock . . ."

That was when he realized: He hadn't heard from his sisters or Will in a long time.

Brendan whirled around. What had he been doing? He'd just been geeking out about ancient Rome, completely forgetting that he was trapped here, in deep doo-doo—

He saw the lion in the living room. It was as big as the one outside, nosing at the cushions on the couch. Cordelia, Eleanor, and Will were hiding behind that couch, completely still, trying not to breathe. But the lion had caught their scent; it jumped on the couch, sniffing for them.

Bren! Cordelia mouthed. Her face looked utterly terrified. Brendan hated to see her in such a panic. She had already been through so much. Couldn't somebody give them all a break? It wasn't fair to send a bunch of kids through these horrible problems. They would turn out disturbed, changed.

Do something! Cordelia mouthed.

Brendan had no idea what to do, but then he noticed two things: First, the lion didn't look like the healthiest specimen in Rome. It was thin, with ribs visible through its chest, and its mane was mangy and buzzing with flies. *It should probably be reported to the ASPCA,* Brendan thought.

The second thing he noticed was that he was still holding the Japanese lamp.

"Hey! You! Get outta here!" Brendan yelled.

He ran toward the lion, brandishing the lamp. He knew from the Discovery Channel that if people behave aggressively, a lot of wild animals get scared—people are big and they're hard to kill.

The lion, however, did not seem to understand this fact. *"RRRRRRAAAAGH!"*

It jumped off the couch at Brendan, sharp claws extended, mouth wide open. Brendan froze, preparing for the excruciating pain of having his entire face bitten off— but at the last moment, Will leaped up from behind the couch and pulled him aside.

The lion landed by the Chester chair. Will dragged a stunned Brendan out of the room with Cordelia and Eleanor as the lion tore the chair's cushion to bits, sending balls of white cotton flying through the air, like an indoor snowstorm.

"Why's he so obsessed with that chair?" whispered Will.

"Uh . . . I hide pepperoni in that chair," said Brendan.

Everyone looked at him.

"What? I hate pepperoni! You know that, Deal. I always ask you to order plain cheese, but *nooooo*! You have to get pepperoni!"

"How can you be so lazy? You know there's this thing called compost—" said Cordelia.

"You're not supposed to put meat in the compost, only vegetables—" said Eleanor.

"Guys, stop!" said Will. "We need to go before—"

"*Hnuff.*"

Will got quiet. The second lion, from outside, had entered the front door of the house and was walking toward them.

"Follow me!" Eleanor hissed, heading for the kitchen.

It was the only option. The first lion, swallowing a mouthful of moldy blue pepperoni, met the second lion in the hall and turned toward the kids. The Walkers and Will managed to close the door to the kitchen—but it was a swinging door; it wouldn't lock! The lions charged down the hall and burst into the kitchen as the kids dashed up the spiral stairs at the back of the room. The lions followed. The Walkers and Will were only a hair's breadth ahead of them—but the lions had difficulty navigating the curving steps. One slammed its head against the wall and shook its mane out, growling, as the other tried to leap over it and fell backward, clawing at the steps like a cat trying to climb out of a bathtub.

The Walkers and Will reached the second floor and pulled the rope for the attic stairs. Then they went into Brendan's not-quite-a-man cave (Eleanor couldn't help scrunching her nose; it had that older-brother smell), turned back, and tried to yank up the stairs—but the lions were already climbing them!

The kids backed toward the far wall of the attic.

"We only have one option," Cordelia said, ripping a sheet off Brendan's San Francisco Giants desk calendar and grabbing a pen. "We have to summon the book."

"What?" Brendan asked. "*The* book? Isn't that the problem in the first place?"

"The Wind Witch was smart," said Cordelia, and Brendan noticed that she didn't look scared now. She looked determined, driven, like a person who would do anything to save herself—no matter the cost. "She sent us to a place where we would immediately be in danger. And the only way to get out is to summon *The Book of Doom and Desire* and make a wish."

"At which point she'll swoop in and make us use it for *her*," Brendan said.

"What other choice do we have?"

"We can't let her near that book, Deal!"

"We'll worry about that when it happens. Okay, you guys know how this works. . . . To make the book appear, we have to think selfish thoughts. So, everybody! Go! Think the most selfish thoughts you can!"

31

The lions covered both sides of the attic, moving forward with their heads down. Drool from their mouths hit Brendan's dirty laundry. The last thing they probably expected was for their prey to go quiet and still, eyes closed, but the Walkers and Will began to concentrate.

Brendan: *I want to be Occipus. The emperor! I would just be chilling all day if I had that kind of power. I'd never have to worry about anything. And I'd have all these people hanging on my every word. I wouldn't even have to speak that much. I could make things happen just by my movements. The way Occipus raised his hand and everybody in the Colosseum got quiet? How cool would that be? That's what I call power!*

Cordelia: *Now that the Wind Witch is out of my body, I can* feel what thoughts are mine, and what were hers. And the tutoring program I set up, and me thinking about running for class president . . . that wasn't her. That was me. I did a good job. I really helped people. And if I can help people at a competitive place like Bay Academy Prep, maybe I can help people on a bigger level. Why not dream really big? Harvard. Yale Law. And then politics, elections, and then . . . president! Why not? I wouldn't even be doing it for myself, I'd be doing it for all the girls who would look up to me, and for all the women who came before, who wanted to be president when they didn't have a chance. The history books would write about me: President Cordelia Walker!

Eleanor: I want to win that horse competition with Crow. I want to get the ribbons for us and lead Crow around in a circle with everybody cheering. And I want Ruby and Zoe there watching me—and Crow can just lift his tail and drop a big old pile of poo right in front of them. And then we can leave Bay Academy Prep, go back to our old school, and forget that any of this craziness ever happened.

Will: I want to be back in England. In my own time. Flying for my country. I want to be in a world where I belong. And I want to find my mum. I want to have tea with her, ask her all sorts of questions. I'd like to find out if I have any other family. Maybe an auntie or a grandfather. What good is a person with no roots? And I want Cordelia with me.

With a quiet, gentle rush of displaced air, *The Book of Doom and Desire* appeared and fell to the floor.

Cordelia froze. It was a simple leather book, with no title, just an eye on the cover, and a stylized eye at that. It had a dot with a semicircle over it and a semicircle under it, carved into the leather. *The most powerful book in the world.*

Cordelia didn't expect to feel so connected to it, but she remembered how it had been when she first opened it, how it showed her a whole new world, how it was filled with swirling half letters like nothing she'd ever seen. It had made her feel that she was learning truths she had always been denied. She had an overwhelming urge to open it right then and just lose herself in its pages, lions or no lions.

She felt something pull on her leg. Eleanor.

"Deal, stay with us! Don't get lost again."

Cordelia realized she was halfway toward the book, walking to it like a zombie. Then she saw Brendan. He had snatched up a pen and paper and written something. The lions were sniffing and batting at the book with their paws as if to check that it was real, but when Brendan got close they roared at him.

Brendan gulped, dove forward, and opened the book.

One of the lions swung a paw at his shoulder. Brendan felt hot pain explode down his arm. Four curved claws in his flesh! The lions bore down on him with their jaws wide as he slipped the paper in the book and closed it—

And suddenly . . . the lions made gulping, curious noises, as if something were happening to them that they couldn't believe. It sounded like "Mrrrrp?"

The Walkers and Will stared in disbelief.

The lions were getting fat.

It started in their midsections. The sharp ribs that Brendan had seen when they entered the house were suddenly hidden by expanding fur. The creatures' legs, which had been thin enough for the sinuous tendons to be visible, ballooned up in seconds to the size of elephant feet. And the lions' faces comically doubled in width, pushing their manes out and making them look like cartoons.

"Raarrr!" one of them said to the other, in clear shock.

"What's going on?" Will asked.

"I wrote, 'The lions get really fat!'" Brendan explained. "I figured that'd slow 'em down and we could escape—plus the poor guys looked like they were starving."

With howls of confusion, the lions turned and ran toward the attic exit—but they couldn't run very well. They bounced into each other and had to squeeze down the steps, their bodies still expanding.

Cordelia ran to the window and looked outside. The lions shoved their way out the front door, moving slowly, wobbling, and breathing heavily. Roman guards smiled—the crowd cheered.

"They think we've been eaten!" Cordelia said. Then she started yelling and waving: "Hey! Look! We're still here! Alive! *Hello!*"

When the thousands in the Colosseum saw her, they went quiet—and then started speaking excitedly among themselves, trying to figure out what was going on. If those lions didn't have a bellyful of humans, why *were* they so fat?

Just then the amplified voice of Occipus's manservant rang out across the arena.

"Emperor Occipus speaks: 'Two African lions, turned into overweight mice by means of powerful sorcery! What sort of child witch lives inside the Hades house?'"

"Oh great," Cordelia said. "Now I'm a witch. *And* a child."

"Why are they speaking English?" Eleanor asked.

"It must be because they're all characters in a Kristoff book, and Kristoff spoke English," said Cordelia.

"Uh-oh," said Eleanor. "Look!"

A dozen armed Roman guards were marching toward Kristoff House, past the lions, who had finally stopped growing and were sitting and panting, looking like giant beanbag Buddhas. Eleanor's eyes went wide as she saw their pointy spears and armor. She was terribly scared.

Brendan sat up in pain, clutching his clawed shoulder, and saw what was happening. He tried to reassure his sister. "Don't worry, Nell. Those guards aren't going to hurt us. Emperor Occipus isn't totally mean; he's quite a character."

"How do you know?" asked Eleanor.

"I've read about him," Brendan said. "In Kristoff's book *Gladius Rex*. I read the beginning of it on our last adventure. It must be one of the books we're trapped in. And it's not so bad. There are a lot of cool feasts in that book, and battles, and chariots. . . . I'd almost like to meet the emperor. He seems really cool for a short, hairless guy."

"Bren, we need to get you home," said Cordelia. "You're hurt. You might be getting delirious. You're not in a position to meet a fictional Roman emperor or anyone else."

"But Deal . . . don't you think it's weird that here inside Kristoff's books we do such amazing things? We're so strong, we're like superheroes. But then back in the real world, where everything counts, we can't even stand up to the normal stuff that happens to everybody all the time. Why?"

"I don't know, Bren. Maybe for the same reason that Denver Kristoff wrote these books to begin with."

"Why's that?" Will asked, bringing one of Brendan's T-shirts to him to try to help his wound.

"Because the real world isn't always all that great," Cordelia said. "It's boring and tedious, especially if you don't have any power. So you escape to a place where you do have power."

Brendan said, "I want to keep escaping."

"You can't. We don't belong here."

"Why not? At least here we don't have to go to school."

"You *do* have to go to school. Only the school here is worse."

Eleanor looked away as Will pulled Brendan's shirt off and started wrapping the claw wound with the T-shirt he had brought. She couldn't stand the sight of blood, and she was still worried about those Roman guards with spears outside the house. But they had stopped; they were just standing there, making sure that no one went in or out, as the crowd continued murmuring among themselves. Eleanor thought, nervous: *All those people are talking about us, wondering who's inside this house. What are they going to do when they find out it's just three kids and a recently homeless British guy? We have to get home. And fast!*

And then Eleanor looked at *The Book of Doom and Desire*. *There's our way home. Right there! All I have to do is write a wish and slip it inside. Then this can all be over. No more hungry lions, no more bleeding Brendan . . .*

She grabbed another sheet off Brendan's desk calendar and a pen. She walked toward the book—and as she got closer to it, it seemed to get bigger, almost as if it were expanding in her mind. Eleanor didn't want to admit it, but the book had the same effect on her that it did on Cordelia. It called to her, told her that it had power inside, tempted her. *Fine, let it try to get me, because I'm going to use it, for good,* she thought—but just as she was about to reach it, a strong blast of air knocked her to the ground.

Eleanor tensed up. It wasn't fear that filled her anymore, but anger. She knew who had done that. She didn't even have to turn around. But she did.

The Wind Witch was in the attic with a big smile on her face.

"Well done, children," she said. "You summoned the book. And now, little Eleanor, I have a wish for you to place in it."

The Wind Witch held up a piece of paper.

It said: *Dahlia Kristoff shall rule the world.*

33

"Well, at least you're consistent," said Brendan, reading the note. "That's the same psycho thing you always wish for—"

"Silence!" the Wind Witch said. "I'm speaking to your sister."

Eleanor was in a panic. Sweat poured out of her forehead. The Wind Witch was even scarier than before, because she had fastened two new chrome hands onto her stubs: One hand was positioned with the finger and thumb pinched together, holding the note; the other was shaped like a fist. Eleanor stayed right where she was, on the floor, staring, and her thoughts started running in a loop: *What do I do what do I do how do we get out of this what do I do?*

"Do you actually expect us to help you?" Brendan said. He didn't seem to be scared, but Eleanor knew it was an act. Just as her response to the Wind Witch was to become extremely tense and speechless, Brendan's was to run off his mouth. "The curse that keeps you from getting close to that book is the best idea your father ever had. Maybe his *only* good idea. And you want us to put that lame wish, 'Dahlia Kristoff shall rule the world,' inside the book for you? Do you think we're idiots?! If we do that, it's kind of like we mess up the entire earth. No thanks."

"Maybe I can change your mind," said the Wind Witch, staring at Brendan's bandage. "Pain can be *so* persuasive."

The Wind Witch extended a chrome hand. A gust of air swirled out and blew off the T-shirt that was bandaging Brendan's shoulder. Brendan felt the sharp pain of the skin around his wound separating, letting cold air touch the inside of his flesh. . . . It was like being pierced by hundreds of sharp needles. He couldn't help but scream. Eleanor wanted to scream too, but she bit her tongue. Her heart was thudding inside her, shaking her whole body . . . but she had to be brave. Maybe she could do something. Maybe she could turn her fear into something useful. She started to think of a plan as her sister yelled, "Stop!"

Cordelia faced the Wind Witch. "Stop, please! Don't hurt my brother. We've been through enough. We'll do what you want."

"What?" Brendan said.

"I'm tired of fighting, Bren. I want to go back. I want to see Mom and Dad again. Don't you?"

"You can't negotiate with the Wind Witch, Deal! She's like a terrorist. Only worse."

"I *am* negotiating with her," said Cordelia, turning back. "Dahlia, is it really necessary that you rule the *entire world*? Couldn't you just wish for maybe being president of the United States? I mean, I might be running for class president next year—"

"I'm well aware of that," said an annoyed Wind Witch.

"Then you know how important that is to me," said Cordelia. "But being president of the United States . . . that would be a whole lot of power . . . leader of the free world and all . . . and you'd be the first woman president—"

"You're a bright girl, Cordelia," said the Wind Witch. "But you think small. I want to rule the entire world!"

"Okay," said Cordelia. "So let's say you do get your wish . . . what happens to us?"

"A world ruled by me will have a very special place for you three," the Wind Witch said. She was smiling wider than Cordelia had ever seen. "I'll never forget that you did a favor for me. You'll always be with your parents, always be happy, always be rich. You won't have a care in the world."

"And what about Will?" Cordelia continued. "You'd need to give him what he wants."

Cordelia took Will's hand, which she thought Will might really like. But Will shook his hand away.

"Don't touch me. You're colluding with the enemy. You should be ashamed of yourself."

Cordelia gave Will a quick look that said: *Trust me.* Eleanor saw it too. And then Cordelia glanced at Eleanor, as if to say, *Your move!* Eleanor realized then that her big sister didn't mean to work with the Wind Witch at all. She had only been buying time for Eleanor, who was closest to *The Book of Doom and Desire.* Which was good, because Eleanor had a plan.

Eleanor had written on the calendar paper she tore off, being as quiet as she could, worrying that the sound of the pen itself would alert the Wind Witch. She couldn't misspell any words either. She crept toward the book.

Cordelia stepped forward and took the Wind Witch's note. "It would be my honor to make your wish come true," she said. Dahlia Kristoff bowed her head to Cordelia, a solemn look on her face. Cordelia returned a grateful smile, even though she had no intention of doing what the Wind Witch desired. She was a better politician than perhaps any of them realized.

Eleanor reached the book, put her note in, and slammed it shut.

"No!" the Wind Witch yelled, frantically trying to open the book with wind.

But it was too late.

The book was held closed by an unseen force.

And then it vanished.

The Book of Doom and Desire was completely gone, as if it had just winked out of existence.

"Eleanor?" Cordelia asked. "What did you just do?"

Before Eleanor could answer, a disturbance appeared around Brendan's shoulder. A small cyclone hovered in place there, looping inside his claw wound to send soothing coolness into him. This wasn't the Wind Witch's doing. She stared at the magic along with everyone else. Within seconds it proved to be a healing spell for Brendan's wound. The claw marks closed up, the blood faded, and Brendan's skin became smooth and clear. There was no evidence of the tiniest scratch.

"Wow, thanks!" said Brendan. "Nell, did you do that?"

Eleanor nodded.

"*Where did you send the book?*" screeched the Wind Witch.

"It's gone," said Eleanor. She wasn't afraid of Dahlia

Kristoff anymore. Not after doing what she just did. Something so brave and smart.

"What do you mean, 'gone'? Why did it disappear?!"

"I asked it to," said Eleanor.

"You what?"

"I wrote on the paper, 'Brendan's shoulder gets healed . . . the book goes away and can never return.'"

The Wind Witch's face turned bright red. Veins popped out of her temples.

"So," said Eleanor, narrowing her eyes at the Wind Witch, trying to look tough, "now what are you gonna do?"

"You . . . ," Dahlia said, and for once she couldn't find any words. She extended her prosthetic hands and sent a blast of air toward Brendan's bed, blowing the covers off. Then she went to the bed and started looking for the book, getting on her hands and knees as if it had slipped underneath. "You can't have gotten rid of the book. You can't! Why would you do that? The book is power . . . it's everything. . . ."

"It's gone," Eleanor said.

Cordelia hugged Eleanor as the Wind Witch continued to tear the sheets from the bed like a crazy person.

"Let me get this straight," Cordelia whispered. "You used *The Book of Doom and Desire* to get rid of itself?"

"Yes."

"That was very brave, Nell—but how are we supposed to get home?"

"I don't . . ." Eleanor's face fell. "I wasn't thinking about that! I was just thinking: Now she won't be able to bother us anymore!"

"I thought you were going to make the *Wind Witch* disappear, not the *book*!"

"I tried to make her disappear before and it didn't work!"

"*No!*" the Wind Witch suddenly said. She had frantically searched every nook and corner of the room. "You brat! You really did it! *It's completely gone!*"

"That's right," Eleanor said. "You'd better get used to life without it."

"*Die!*" the Wind Witch screamed.

A tremendous blast of wind pinned Eleanor against the opposite wall, knocking Cordelia away.

Brendan and Will rushed the Wind Witch, but she kicked them to the floor. She was hovering, flapping her wings, shooting hurricane-force winds at Eleanor's face. Cordelia hit her head against the attic wall. Eleanor was facing a blast that seemed to come from the world's most powerful wind tunnel. *How dumb was I to try and take her on? How could I really think I was smarter?*

"*I'm going to blow the flesh clean off your bones!*"

Eleanor couldn't close her eyes. The wind was keeping them open. It rushed into her ears and nose. It trapped her against the wall, tore her shirt sleeves off, and rippled her whole body. She saw the skin of her arms starting to move toward her shoulders, as if someone were kneading it; she knew that when the wind got stronger she was going to tear and peel open. The Wind Witch screamed—but Eleanor heard something in her scream she didn't expect.

Frustration.

The Wind Witch's plan was not working.

Will and Brendan and Cordelia stood back, equally impressed and amazed with what they were seeing.

Eleanor was held in stasis. She looked at her pants, her shoes. Her pants were tearing away in tiny strips. Her shoelaces went straight back, as if they had magnets on the ends.

But her skin was holding together.

"Why can't you just . . . die! Die! Die!!!" the Wind Witch gasped, gritting her teeth, turning her face into a horrible mask of frustration and anger.

And then she lowered her arms.

She had been defeated.

Eleanor fell forward, no longer pinned to the wall. She was exhausted and terrified, but she had survived. Even when it was impossible to do so.

The Wind Witch dropped to her knees.

"You should be dead!" she snarled at Eleanor, then turned to Brendan, Cordelia, and Will. "My powers have never failed. Not once! But I'll get to the bottom of this. You'll see! And then I'll return to kill all of you!"

She clasped her hands together over her head and started

to spin like a top. A purple glow surrounded the Wind Witch as the air around her swirled faster and faster—and then she was gone.

"What was *that*?" Brendan called, running to Eleanor, hugging her. He held her tighter than he ever had before, and within seconds Cordelia joined him, and then Will. "Are you all right?"

"I think so," Eleanor said. "But I felt her trying to kill me with everything she had, because I made the book go away."

"She couldn't," Will said. "You were too strong."

"I don't . . . I don't feel strong," Eleanor said. It was all she could do to catch her breath. She wanted to lie down and rest for about two hundred years. She wanted a bath and to watch some TV. But then she heard the crowd outside. *All this craziness and we're still stuck here! With no Mom or Dad!*

"There's something else going on here," Cordelia said. "What the Wind Witch just did . . . that was a full-fledged attack. It would have killed any of us. But Eleanor lived."

"Maybe it has to do with the book being gone," Brendan said. "Maybe the Wind Witch's power comes from the book."

"Whatever happened," Cordelia said, "without that book, I don't know how we get home."

Eleanor nodded. She had temporarily forgotten about her huge mistake. Now, having it pointed out, she felt like the dumbest person in the world.

"I'm sorry . . . I wasn't thinking about that. . . ."

"It's okay," Brendan said. "We'll figure something out. The most important thing is that you're okay."

"Maybe there's another book," Eleanor said. "Or another . . . something. Somewhere in this house. We know that Denver Kristoff used to travel into his books. And didn't he write over a hundred books? So maybe he used one of them to get in and out of the others."

They all looked at her. At that moment, they didn't see their little sister. They saw a brave warrior who would one day grow into a confident, powerful person. Brendan thought, *Someday I might be asking her for a job.*

"That's exactly right," resolved Cordelia. "We'll start looking for another way home. But first we're going to have to hug you a little bit longer, because you were so brave."

"Uh, Deal?" Eleanor said. "I don't think you can."

"Why not?"

"Because we have visitors."

Eleanor pointed to the attic door.

35

In person, Emperor Occipus looked like a big thumb. But his posse made up for it. His manservant/announcer was beside him, along with three tall guards who carried spears and stood at attention with shimmering chest muscles and massive biceps. Behind them was a beautiful woman with jet-black hair that had bright silver threads woven into it. They all stood in the attic. The guards had carried Occipus up as if he were a toddler.

"Well?" Occipus said. Without an announcer translating his words, he possessed a flat, froggy voice.

The announcer, who had long, curly blond hair that hung to his shoulders, reminded Brendan of Roger Daltrey, the vain lead singer of his dad's favorite band, the Who. He whipped back his long mane and said, "Emperor Occipus says, 'Well?'"

Brendan dropped into a deep bow. The others followed. Occipus was confused; bowing was not a Roman custom.

"Raise your heads and tell me where you hail from!" Occipus said; it was hard not to laugh at his blatting tone. "And which one of you turned my lions into clumsy, portly creatures?"

Brendan gulped. "Ummm . . . I guess . . . I did, sir. Your highness. Emperor-ness."

"You will address my master as 'Supreme Emperor,'" the announcer said.

"Now, Rodicus, no need to frighten the boy," said Occipus. "Boy? What is your name?"

"Brendan, Supreme Emperor."

"And who are your retinue?"

"Reti-what?" whispered Eleanor.

"Retinue, as in people who follow Brendan around," Cordelia said. "The Supreme Emperor thinks we're his servants."

"Well?" Occipus insisted.

"These are my sisters,

Cordelia and Eleanor, and my friend Will," said Brendan.

"What odd names. Where are you from?"

"Brittania," said Will, "and New Brittania, for these youngsters. A land you have yet to conquer." Occipus stared at him expectantly. "Supreme Emperor."

"A land I haven't conquered?" Occipus shared a smile with the dark-haired woman. "How unexpected! You will have to tell me all about it. Now, can you hear the voices outside?"

They did. The people in the Colosseum were cheering, chanting.

"The crowd is cheering for Brendan here, who performed magic on the lions. I was certain those lions would drag out anyone they found alive."

"You mean they wouldn't have bitten my face off?"

"Oh, they would have definitely bitten your face off," said Occipus. "Then they would have moved on to the more fleshy bits, finishing off with your scrumptious internal bits."

"Ohhhh," said Brendan, the color leaving his face.

"But they'll only do it in front of spectators," said Occipus. "They're trained to kill in the presence of a crowd, so everyone can get their money's worth. Are you the same way, Brendan of New Brittania? Trained to kill?"

"I'm not really a killer, Supreme Emperor," said Brendan.

"But you defeated those beasts. I say it's time to meet your public."

"My what?" asked Brendan, but then he realized what was happening. All that cheering and chanting . . . it was for him.

A slow, satisfied smile grew across Brendan's face. Cordelia, Eleanor, and Will looked at one another, thinking, *This is not good.*

A few minutes later they were all outside, standing in front of Kristoff House surrounded by fifty thousand screaming men and women under a scorching blue sky. The Colosseum smelled of food and sweat and char and dirt and blood. It was as if they had journeyed into a deeper part of humanity, a part that later generations had paved over.

Occipus spoke and Rodicus amplified his words through his primitive megaphone, which had been wheeled into the arena. As the speech went on, Cordelia saw the black-haired woman rubbing Occipus's doughy shoulder.

"The emperor has discovered a shocking secret that will be the talk of Rome for days! Our lions were magically defeated by a *band of wild children from afar*, led by Brendan of New Brittania!"

Rodicus ushered the other kids aside so the crowd could get a good look at Brendan.

"*Lion tamer! Lion tamer!*" the crowd roared.

Brendan waved. He had a feeling in his chest that he

hadn't felt for a long time. Back before he started at Bay Academy Prep, at his old school, he had been on the lacrosse team, and this was the feeling he would get when he scored a goal in front of the home-team crowd. It was the warmth that came from admiration, from being a star. He hadn't realized until just now how absent it had been from his life. At Bay Academy he was never the star; he was always the joke, always out of place. But the glow in his chest now, set off by this crowd, made him feel that the last place he expected was the place he belonged: ancient Rome.

"*Lion tamer!*"

He had done that. He had stopped a lion—no, two. He could imagine people saying, "Did you hear about the boy who beat two lions?" Within a few days he would be one of the most famous people in Rome.

Brendan wasn't sure how long this feeling would last, so he kept waving, basking in the crowd's admiration. Then he turned back to Eleanor and said, "Maybe it's not such a bad thing that you got rid of the book. I think this might be a great place for us."

"You mean for *you*," said Eleanor.

"Watch it," said Brendan with a smile, "you're talking to the lion tamer!"

Eleanor could tell he meant it as a joke, but there was some truth behind it. Brendan was starting to think of himself as someone different. This wasn't going to end well.

36

The Walkers and Will spent the rest of the day in Emperor Occipus's royal stadium box. Despite being desperate to get home, and worried about their parents, they had to admit it was pretty luxurious.

First, they were escorted across the Colosseum as the crowd chanted and Brendan stopped every few steps to wave. It took a good ten minutes of him preening and prancing around like a rock star before they finally made it to the gate under the box. Then they went up a secret, guarded passageway and emerged on the platform, which was like the observation deck of a skyscraper. It put them right over the arena, able to see the crowd and battlefield. Occipus's black-haired female companion snapped her fingers, and the area's many servants disappeared and came back with food: olives, fresh-baked bread, rich cheese and wine, and a roast suckling pig, which Cordelia thought was disgusting. (Will had no problem snatching the apple from the pig's mouth and taking a bite, proclaiming, "Lovely.")

"Can you believe how many servants work for this dude?" Brendan said. He was lounging on a gold-plated divan, trying not to stare at the blushing girls who served him food but kept their distance.

"They're not servants," Will said. "The word for them in Latin may be *servus*, but they aren't getting paid. They're slaves." Will turned to Cordelia. "Did you forget that I took Latin in school?"

"Very impressive," Cordelia said, rolling her eyes.

"Do you think I'm allowed to talk to the slave girls?" Brendan asked. "They're looking at me! And smiling! And that red-haired one . . . she winked at me!"

"Brendan, they're not here for your amusement," Will warned. "They're trapped here, just as we are."

For that, Cordelia gave Will's hand a squeeze. "Did you do women's studies in school as well?"

Will gave her a blank look. "What's that?"

"Hold on a minute," Brendan said. "I thought these girls liked me! I thought they liked my jokes."

"Has anyone ever liked your jokes?" Cordelia asked.

"Well . . . no."

"Don't worry, Bren," said Eleanor, patting his hand. "Someday you'll find a real girl who thinks you're funny."

Brendan flashed on Celene, the girl he had seen all too briefly the last time he was in one of Kristoff's worlds. Celene would probably declare right away that the emperor was oppressing the people and needed to be removed. Which is what Cordelia would say—but Celene was so much prettier than Cordelia! It didn't matter. She was in some other book. Brendan bit into a pork chop.

"Guys," said Cordelia, "I think we should eat and run. We need to get back to our house, which luckily is still in the middle of the arena. I don't know how long the Romans are going to let it stay there."

"Why do you want to go back to Kristoff House?" asked Brendan, juice dripping down his chin.

"Because we need to find a way home. We should look around in the library to see if there's another book like *The Book of Doom and Desire* that can bring us back to Mom and Dad."

"I want to see them too," Brendan said, "but do we have to start *right now*? I mean, it's pretty sweet up here! They're treating us like royalty."

"No, Bren, they're treating *you* like royalty," said Cordelia, nodding to his pork chop.

"So? You guys are along for the ride. What's so bad about being my retinue?"

"I'm going to do you a favor and forget you said that."

"I just don't get it. You'd rather go into a house where we almost got killed by lions than hang out up here, eating olives and drinking wine."

"Brendan! You're not supposed to drink the wine!"

"I'm just tasting it."

Brendan grabbed the silver goblet in front of him and took a hefty sip of wine, sloshing it around in his mouth. His face turned green and he spat the wine out onto the floor. Everyone in the balcony turned, including Emperor Occipus.

"Ughhh, that stuff tastes like vomit mixed with cat litter!"

Occipus laughed—and all his slaves laughed too. "Our child warrior has never tasted wine! Bring him some goat's milk and honey so he can enjoy himself."

A slave hustled off and returned with a soft skin like a canteen, full of goat's milk. Brendan took a sip and found it just as gross as the wine. He stuck with water.

Meanwhile, below the emperor's viewing area, a half-dozen gladiators entered the arena and positioned themselves in a circle. One at a time, they began demonstrating their weapons, showing off swords, axes, and daggers in solo feats of spinning skill. Brendan was entranced. It was so cool the way the warriors moved, the way they had complete control over their weapons. Brendan found himself standing up and imitating them, pretending to hold a sword, which Occipus and his entourage found very amusing. When Occipus laughed, it sounded like a burp—and then he often did burp at the same time, which made him laugh more. It was all very hilarious to him and Brendan, less so to Cordelia, Eleanor, and Will.

Kristoff House was still in the center of the arena, looking like a misplaced toy. Cordelia was trying to figure out how to get down there as Occipus received a tray of meats that appeared to weigh as much as he did. He ate by throwing his food in the air and catching it with his wide, puffy-lipped mouth. The pieces that hit the floor he allowed to be consumed by the slave girls. When Occipus's belly was full, the slave girls, along with the help of some burly male workers, picked up the emperor and carried him to a sofa. They laid Occipus down there and girls fed him grapes dipped in honey.

Only when Occipus seemed about to burst, burping constantly, surrounded by the odors of his own flatulence, did he beckon the Walkers and Will over, avoiding eye contact as he spoke.

"You see how happy the crowd is, yes?"

"Yes, Supreme Emperor," Brendan said. Everyone else nodded. (Eleanor held her nose.)

"A happy crowd means a happy public," said Occipus. "A man can live on one slice of bread and a thimble of water, as long as he's entertained. So you see what a stroke of luck this is, all of you appearing in my Colosseum. Everyone is talking about your Hades house, fascinated by it, actually."

He pointed to Kristoff House, in the center of the arena. Chariots were racing around it now.

"They think it's a trick. 'An illusion,' they say. 'The Emperor spent a mighty bit of coin on that one.' But I know better. I know that house *just appeared out of thin air.*"

The emperor stared at them all in turn, his eyes set back in fleshy lids.

"Which one of you can tell me how this house got here?"

"I can," said Cordelia, "on one condition."

"Which is?"

"Let us return to the house. All of our belongings are inside. Things that we need."

"Do you think I'm an idiot? *Bwark*—" Occipus burped, then sloshed his mouth around and swallowed, as if something had come up. "If I let you back inside that house, I may never see you again."

"Would that be so bad?" Cordelia asked. "Look at us! We don't belong here. Think about it . . . have you ever seen anyone like us? With our clothes?"

"I must admit, I have been admiring the little one's shoes," said Occipus, pointing to Eleanor's pink Converse high-tops.

"That's what I mean," said Cordelia. "We're from the future."

"The future?"

"And we just want to get back."

"You speak of sorcery."

"Yes . . . I suppose. But it wasn't *our* sorcery—"

"I knew it!" said Emperor Occipus. "That's how you managed to transform my lions! So tell me . . . what is your secret? What else can you do?" He grabbed Cordelia's collar. "Can you control the weather? Do you breathe fire? *Tell me!* With your power I will not only be supreme emperor of Rome . . . but the entire world!"

"Why is it that almost everybody we meet in these books wants to rule the world so bad?" muttered Eleanor.

"Because armies will fear me," screamed Occipus. "Foreign leaders will cower in my presence. I will be respected wherever I go! Now tell me . . . *how do you perform your magic?*"

Cordelia froze. Occipus's hands were horribly fat and clammy against her skin. Rodicus leaned over his shoulder: "Maybe she needs a little convincing, master. We can hang her up by her fingernails and cover her body with leeches. That usually makes them talk."

"Hold on, there, Supreme Emperor," said Will, stepping forward. "There's no need for that. Allow me to show you one of our secrets."

"What?" asked the emperor.

Will pulled a gray cigarette lighter out of his pocket—

"Wait, what is *that?*" Eleanor interrupted. "Will . . . you *smoke?!*"

"Of course not," said Will. "I . . . I keep this nearby for emergency situations."

"What kind of emergency situations?"

"You know," said Will. "If I'm ever in a plane . . . and I'm shot down . . . I could be stranded in the cold . . . I'd need to light a fire."

Will showed Cordelia and Eleanor the lighter. It wasn't a modern lighter—it was an old-school World War I lighter made of tin. Occipus grabbed it.

"Explain this to me."

"Supreme Emperor chap, you just place your thumb on that wheel . . . and look!"

Occipus lit the lighter. A small flame danced out. Occipus sloshed back and fell off the sofa. Everyone—his mistress, Rodicus, the slaves—gathered around to pick him up as Will picked the lighter up.

"It's sorcery!" "A flame from that little box!"

"Give it to me," Occipus ordered, standing up. Will handed him back the lighter.

"I will keep this," said Occipus. "For it is written that any item inside the Colosseum becomes the property of the Supreme Emperor! Including your home!"

The Walkers and Will exchanged a worried look.

Occipus snapped his fingers. "Rodicus."

Rodicus dashed away.

"No!" said Cordelia, but it was too late. Below them, in the arena, an army of a hundred slaves or more streamed toward Kristoff House. They were carrying long ropes, fashioned with hooks. They attached them to the house and started dragging it away.

37

"Where are you taking our home?" Cordelia said.

"You mean *my* home," said the emperor. "I'm moving it to an area where it can be easily searched."

"Searched for what?"

"First of all, jewelry!" Emperor Occipus said. He held up his arms. They were clanging with jeweled bracelets. "I love precious jewels, foreign jewels most of all, and I'll add to my collection. Secondly, I will confiscate any magical devices we find. Perhaps another fire machine . . . or a machine that can generate water . . . wouldn't that be grand?" Occipus tested the lighter again; it gave him such pleasure. Cordelia was about to cry out—*What are we going to do without Kristoff House? How are we ever going to get back to Mom and*

Dad?—but as she opened her mouth, Rodicus grabbed her.

"Hold your tongue. The Supreme Emperor hates being distracted when his favorite gladiator is in the arena."

Rodicus pointed. Down below, with the house gone, it was easy to see the gladiators being quiet and still as a young man stepped into view. He was tall and muscular, not like those creepy bodybuilders who win contests with bulgy veins and skintight briefs, but lean and rock-solid, like an Olympian athlete.

He raised his sword and began a display of mastery. He cut the blade through the air, diving into somersaults, jabbing and slashing at imaginary enemies. The crowd cheered him on. He executed an upward thrust and stabbed down into the dirt. He called out a battle cry as his sword vibrated back and forth with a *bwanggg*.

The gladiator took off his helmet. He was young, with close-cropped hair, piercing brown eyes, a cleft chin, and a killer smile.

"Who's he?" Cordelia asked.

"Felix the Greek," Rodicus said, applauding loudly.

The emperor applauded as well. Everyone did. Brendan felt a twinge of jealousy.

Felix, in the arena below, looked up at the emperor's sitting area. Cordelia felt as if he were staring right at her. She gave a slight smile. She could have sworn he returned it.

"Who is that?" Will asked, standing next to Cordelia.

"Some gladiator named Felix."

"And why are you smiling at him?"

"Um . . . did you see what he did? It was really cool . . . like a solo ballet with a sword."

"A rather girlish display, in my opinion," Will said, and he didn't have to say any more.

Is Will jealous? Cordelia thought.

"Bravo, Felix!" the emperor called. "Let the battles begin!"

Rodicus grabbed the giant bronze tripod cone: "Your Supreme Emperor is ready for entertainment!"

"Entertainment? So what was the rest of that stuff?" Brendan asked.

Felix put his helmet on. The black gate rose underneath where the Walkers were sitting. This time, instead of lions, some animals came out that made Brendan's jaw drop.

The color was what startled him at first. The creatures were white. Brendan thought they were Siberian tigers, or giant snow leopards, because it didn't make sense for polar bears to be in the Colosseum . . .

But they were polar bears.

Shuffling, angry, *hot* polar bears.

Guards whipped at the bears as they lumbered forward. There were two; they moved toward Felix, who raised his sword. The gladiators formed a ring around the bears and their fellow fighter.

"Oh man, I should have read more of *Gladius Rex*," Brendan said. "I guess Kristoff went a little nuts with the exotic animals."

"What are they going to do with the bears?" Eleanor exclaimed. "That guy's not going to fight *bears*, is he? They're innocent!"

"They're hungry," Brendan said.

"Wait!" Eleanor ran up to the emperor and pulled on his robe. "You can't do this! It's cruelty to animals!"

A shocked Rodicus grabbed her, but the emperor responded: "Cruelty? How ridiculous." He pulled a string of meat from one of his back teeth. "What you call 'cruelty' is a natural part of the world. Have you ever seen a cat bounce a live mouse between its paws until the mouse dies? That's not cruelty. That's pure joy."

"And you're pure gross!" Eleanor said. "A horrible, bloated—"

Brendan put his hand over Eleanor's mouth and gave the emperor a big, fake grin. "Your Supremeness, I got this." He took Nell into a corner and whispered, "You ever hear that expression 'when in Rome'? You've got to play along—"

"Play along? Those two beautiful polar bears are about to be slaughtered! You used to care about stuff like that! What's happened to you? You're becoming as disturbed as Blob-ipus!"

"I'm trying to keep us *alive* and I've done a good job so far. And if you want to stay safe I suggest you turn away from this battle. Then you won't have to see what happens to the bears, or to that guy who's fighting them. You know, the bears may win."

"I hope they do. I'll be *glad-they-ate-him!*"

Cordelia watched the bears approach Felix the Greek. The first one took a swipe at him. The crowd all gasped at once, as if the Colosseum were one big mouth. Felix ducked and slashed at the bear's paw, but the animal drew away as the second bear charged him from behind. Felix jumped and the two bears tumbled into each other! They rolled and battled on the ground. The spectators laughed.

Eleanor yelled to the crowd, "That's not funny! That's mean! You're all a bunch of—"

Brendan's hand strategically covered her mouth.

The bears advanced on Felix. He tossed his sword from one hand to the other. Felix was in trouble—he had more than enough of his body exposed for polar bear teeth to chomp through. The bear on the left roared and charged—

And Felix flipped his sword backward and knocked it in the chin with the hilt!

The bear stumbled back as if punched. Felix whirled and took a swipe at the other animal, cutting off some fur underneath its chin.

"See, he's not so bad!" Brendan told Eleanor. "He could've cut that bear to ribbons but he didn't."

The crowd cheered louder than they had for Brendan: "*Felix! Felix!*" The bears got ready for another attack.

Cordelia was riveted. The gladiator—a kid, really—had such a great smile. But if he weren't as talented as his confidence indicated, he would end up Hamburger Helper. It would be such a shame. She understood suddenly why people went to bullfights. She found herself chanting: "*Felix! Felix!*"

The bears ran at the warrior full-on. He readied his sword. But this time the animals were smarter; when they got within striking distance, one of them leaped over Felix, slashing down with its claws, as the other barreled into him. Felix's attention was split—he tried to attack up and down at the same time—and one bear took out his legs while the other knocked him forward. He hit the ground . . . *and now the two bears were on top of him*, their mouths heaving, long runners of spit hanging from their teeth, about to chow down.

"*Stop!*" Cordelia yelled. "Supreme Emperor, please make it stop!"

Occipus raised his eyebrows. Something in Cordelia was making a major impression on him. And he suddenly had a truly spectacular idea, one that would absolutely dazzle the crowd. Occipus whispered something to Rodicus, who smiled, then shouted into the ancient megaphone, "*Stop the battle!*"

The guards who had formed a perimeter around Felix whipped at the bears, forcing them back. The crowd *booed*. Occipus grabbed Cordelia's wrist and started to lead her away from his viewing area.

"Where are we going?"

"Into the arena," said Occipus.

"Hey, wait!" Brendan said, shocked. Will and Eleanor backed him up. "Don't take my sister away!"

Occipus laughed: a deep, burbling sound that resembled bubbling muck. Then he snapped his fingers and the guards grabbed Brendan, Eleanor, and Will.

"This is my Colosseum!" Occipus declared. "I can do whatever I want. And I want to bring Cordelia into the arena, to meet the man she admires!"

"Wait! No, stop—" Cordelia said, but Occipus was done talking. He dragged her down the dark staircase that led into the arena. His small hands were very strong, and his determined, stubby legs moved quickly. In seconds, he pulled Cordelia onto the dusty field, where the polar bears were being led back inside the black gate. Felix stood at attention. As they got close to him, Rodicus narrated their progress from the balcony.

"The emperor is bringing Cordelia from New Brittania to meet Felix the Greek. She has just begged the emperor for Felix's life! It can only mean one thing, esteemed citizens! Yes, that's right . . . now the Supreme Emperor is clasping their hands together! The vows will begin shortly."

"What do you mean, 'vows'?" said Brendan.

"Wedding vows," said Rodicus. "Our laws dictate that if a young maiden saves the life of a gladiator, she must marry him."

"*What?*" asked a stunned Will.

"In a few moments," said Rodicus, "the Supreme Emperor will perform the ceremony. Then Felix and Cordelia will be man and wife."

38

In the center of the arena, Cordelia was overwhelmed with noise and attention. The entire crowd was on its feet, wildly cheering for Felix—*And for me, I guess?* she asked herself. She hadn't heard Rodicus say the word *vows* over the cheers; she didn't realize what was going on. She just knew that Occipus's clammy hand was holding hers and Felix's together.

Felix, however, understood how to use the attention of the crowd. He took off his helmet and waved. Everyone cheered. He spoke to Cordelia without looking at her: "Thank you for saving me."

"You're welcome," said Cordelia. The crowd was so loud that they could speak freely. "I need to get back to my house. You know the one that just appeared in the arena? It's my family's. But the guards took it away with hooks and ropes—"

"I'll help you get it back," Felix said. He had a slow, even voice. "I'll help any way I can. But the emperor will get angry if we leave before—"

"And now," called Rodicus from the balcony, "the Supreme Emperor will begin the wedding ceremony!"

"Wedding ceremony?" asked Cordelia. "What wedding ceremony?"

"Uh . . . ours?" said Felix.

"*Ours?* Are you kidding me? Why would I marry you? We just met!"

"Roman law," said Felix. "When a woman saves a gladiator from death, she is required to marry him. Didn't you know that?"

"There's no such law. That's not historically accurate! It's totally made up!"

"It was created by Occipus."

Cordelia paused. *Of course. We're in one of Kristoff's books. It's all fiction. Kristoff made up this stupid rule just to make the plot of his book more exciting! And now I'm the victim of some writer's whimsy!*

"Felix the Greek," said Occipus, still holding their hands, "do you take the lovely Cordelia of New Brittania to be your bride?"

Felix smiled into Cordelia's terrified face. His eyes seemed to say: *Don't worry, I'll take care of you.* But it didn't make Cordelia feel any better. She wasn't going to be stuck in some arranged marriage, even if it was in a magical world and would never be technically recognized by the state of California—

"Wait a minute!" Cordelia said. "I'm only fifteen years old!"

"So?" Occipus said.

"I'm still a minor. It's illegal for me to marry anyone! Isn't that a law here?"

"Hmmm . . . ," Occipus said. "Did you say you were fifteen?"

"Yes!"

"Well, Felix is seventeen. So no problem there."

"What?" Cordelia turned to Felix. "How can you be a gladiator at seventeen?"

"I was sold to Rome when I was a toddler."

"Besides," Occipus said, "the legal age for marriage under my rule is thirteen."

"Thirteen?!" shouted Cordelia. "You are one sick—"

"I suggest you hold your tongue, young lady," said Occipus, "or I will have it removed, and Felix will have the distinction of being married to a wife who cannot speak!"

Cordelia stayed silent, terrified. *What can I do? Nothing for now. I have to play along. This is all about survival. All about getting from moment to moment, until I can find a way to sneak us all back into our home. Once we're there, we know all the secret passages. The Roman guards will be at a disadvantage. And we'll find a way back to Mom and Dad. Just play along, Cordelia, and survive.*

"Now," said Occipus. "The next two words out of your mouth should be *I do.*"

"I do," Felix said.

Cordelia swung her gaze around the arena, where everyone was on their feet, eagerly watching the ceremony. Emperor Occipus gave one thumb up to Rodicus.

"It looks like the groom has accepted the marriage proposal. But what about our bride?"

"Cordelia," said Occipus, "do you take Felix the Greek as your husband?"

Cordelia felt as if she were about to faint, throw up, and wet her pants all at the same time. She had been through some pretty scary life-and-death situations, but nothing quite as gut-wrenching as marrying someone she just met.

Occipus raised an eyebrow. "Your answer, please?"

"*No, no, no, no, no!*" interrupted Brendan, shouting as he ran across the arena. "Her answer's *no!!*"

"How dare you interrupt my ceremony?" said Occipus. "How did you escape?" But then he saw his dark-haired mistress following and realized she had let them come down from their seats. Eleanor and Will were being held back by guards in the upstairs viewing area.

Occipus smiled. Of course, this could all be part of the grand spectacle. Brendan's appearance created more drama, more conflict for the crowd. And they loved it! The Colosseum sounded like it was full of excited hyenas.

Occipus dropped Cordelia's and Felix's hands. He stepped toward Brendan, making grandiose gestures as if he were in a play.

"You think you can speak to me as if I were a commoner? Why don't you give me one good reason not to have you *executed, 'lion tamer'*?"

The emperor drew his finger across his throat. Seeing this, Rodicus announced to the crowd: "It looks as though Brendan has offended our great emperor! We may have a wedding *and* a crucifixion in the Colosseum today!"

The crowd screamed and whooped. Brendan dropped to his knees.

"Okay, fine, sorry!" he said. "It won't happen again!"

"That's more appropriate," said Occipus, and he helped Brendan up, waving to the crowd as if to say, *I'll let this one live.*

Rodicus announced: "The emperor's empathy knows no bounds!"

The crowd cheered. And Brendan realized that Occipus had the Roman people completely under his thumb. As long as he kept up bizarre stunts like marrying Cordelia off and threatening Brendan, they would be entertained—and he would hold on to power. It was brilliant, really.

"Back to our lovely couple," said Occipus. "Miss Cordelia, do you take Felix the Greek to be your husband?"

Cordelia had a plan. She looked at the emperor and said, "I'm starting to understand how wise you are. A marriage to a gladiator I favor would be wonderful. But where will we live?"

"Live? You'll live in the slaves' quarters."

Cordelia had to fight to hold down her disgust. Her feelings about this stubby, selfish emperor were exactly the opposite of Brendan's. Where Brendan saw a skilled manipulator, she saw someone who had squandered an opportunity to lead. If she ever got home, ever got to grow up and become a leader, she would use her power wisely, to help people, not gorge herself on food and stage wasteful stunts.

"Supreme Emperor, as you know," she said in her most delicate voice, "my family and I are not from here. We traveled here through the magic of our house. And we need to stay in that house."

"Why?"

"To make sure that you and your people aren't hurt by the house's magic."

"Are you threatening me?" asked Occipus.

"I'm protecting you."

Occipus jutted out his lip, pondering Cordelia's words. Then he nodded at one of the guards, who ran off the field toward the black gates where the lions and polar bears had emerged.

The gates raised. In a few minutes, a line of slaves stepped out of the darkness within. The slaves were all hunched forward, with ropes slung over their shoulders, heaving as hard as they could. Line after line came out, each pulling a heavy rope.

Inch by inch, Kristoff House came into the arena.

"You've got your wish, young lady," Occipus said. "Are you ready to complete the ceremony?"

Cordelia stared at the house. The barrels underneath it were still intact; the slaves were using them to roll the house forward. (Kristoff House had been on stilts back in San Francisco, with barrels attached to its underside, to help it float in case it ever fell off the cliff where it was perched.) Even in this strange place, it was her home, and it nearly brought a tear to her eye.

Cordelia took a deep breath. *The marriage won't count anywhere but here. And in a few hours we'll be back inside Kristoff House, and then we'll find some way to get back to San Francisco, and then anybody who says he's my husband will go to jail.*

She glanced at Felix—he was giving her the same kind, reassuring look he had before. She looked up to the emperor's balcony, at Will, held captive by guards with swords; he didn't have his gun; he shook his head ominously. She looked to Eleanor, next to Will; she shrugged.

Cordelia decided that no matter what happened, she could take care of herself. She was a Walker. Surely she could handle a phony marriage.

"I do."

Occipus clasped her hand to Felix's and raised them both. "I pronounce you man and wife!"

The crowd roared. Occipus stepped away satisfied. Cordelia realized that Felix's face was very close to hers. *Oh no, I'm supposed to kiss him!*

Oh well, Cordelia thought. *Keep your mouth closed tight, grit your teeth, and give one lightning-fast kiss the way you used to with Granny, who had pointy black moles and a prickly mustache. It'll be over in no time!*

But as Felix leaned toward her lips, Cordelia saw something inside Kristoff House that stunned her. She opened her mouth wide, but not to give Felix a kiss. To scream.

39

"What did you do to Kristoff House?"

Cordelia could see through one of the living-room windows—and inside, the house was totally trashed! It looked like burglars had gone through it and dumped everything on the floor—plus a bunch of furniture was missing. She broke away from Felix and ran to the house, as Felix protested and Occipus laughed wetly.

"What did you do?" Cordelia yelled to the emperor. "Why would you mess up our house like that?"

"For this," said Occipus, as a slave approached him with Cordelia's mother's silver tray that she used for fancy dinners. On top of the tray was all of the jewelry in Kristoff House: Mrs. Walker's necklaces, rings, bracelets, earrings . . . even

Dr. Walker's Keith Richards skull ring that somebody gave him as a joke. Emperor Occipus stuck his hand into the pile and started putting things on.

"Hey! That stuff belongs to my mom!" said Cordelia.

"Not anymore," said the emperor. "I've also made sure that the slaves removed any bedding and furniture that I thought would be appropriate for my personal quarters. Plus any books that may fit well in my library. But I'm sure there are a few things left in the house for you to enjoy, since you insist on living there."

Occipus turned to the crowd and shrugged with his hands full of Walker family heirlooms.

"I declare these games to be over!" Occipus said, making a signal to Rodicus, who repeated the announcement at high volume.

The people cheered for minutes as Occipus waved. It sounded as if they had just witnessed the Super Bowl, and Cordelia could picture them all going home, talking to one another, recapping the day's events and ignoring the fact that they each had a life expectancy of about forty-five. She hated Rome.

"My wife," Felix said, "are you coming?"

Cordelia flashed red, then looked up to see Will, Brendan, Eleanor, and Felix headed toward Kristoff House's front door, being led by the emperor. Felix held his hand out to her. She reluctantly approached, refusing to take it, and heard Occipus speak:

"There will be guards posted outside all night, to prevent you from escaping."

"Why would we want to escape?" asked Felix. "I've got a beautiful new bride!"

Cordelia almost threw up on her shoes.

"I can't take any chances," said Occipus. "You see, everyone who was here will be telling their friends and families how incredible today's performance was. Tomorrow, they will be lining up to get in. To see all of you young witches and warlocks in your Hades house. And I can't take a chance that you won't be here!"

The Walkers exchanged a worried look with Will.

"How long will you keep us?" asked Eleanor.

"For the rest of your lives," said the emperor casually.

"What—?" "Hold on a minute—" "Listen—"

"You can never leave. What would the public say?"

Once again, Cordelia was about to throw up on her shoes. But she suppressed the urge, took in a few deep breaths, and was able to keep it down.

"Very well. I'll leave you in peace. And if you do manage to get past the guards, Felix here knows where his allegiances lie. Isn't that right, my boy?"

"Yes, Supreme Emperor," said Felix. Will and Cordelia looked at him with disgust.

"Very well! *Vale!*"

Occipus joined his raven-haired mistress and they walked arm in arm into the bowels of the Colosseum. Felix, the Walkers, and Will entered Kristoff House. It was chaotic and desolate inside, with papers and clothes thrown everywhere. The Romans had apparently not been interested in any modern American food, because they had thrown cereal all over the place and tossed soda cans in a big pile in the living room. Felix turned to Cordelia.

"So, my dear, this is where we'll be living?"

This time, Cordelia did throw up on her shoes.

40

Everything felt horrible for Cordelia now, inside and out. She was trapped. Trapped in every way she could be.

Felix knelt, took a tossed-aside washcloth, and wiped Cordelia's shoes clean. He really was very nice, and Cordelia did sort of like him . . . *but.*

"You know our marriage isn't real, right, Felix?" asked Cordelia.

"It's not? But the emperor just—"

"I know," said Cordelia. "But like I told you. Things are different where we come from. Maybe we should explain. . . ."

The Walkers and Will started filling Felix in on their

unbelievable story, and the sun had set by the time they finished. They were surprised at how well he took it.

"None of this bothers you?" Brendan asked.

"My parents fear the wrath of Poseidon and try to please him with fat oxen," said Felix. "This all makes sense."

"Good," said Cordelia. They were sitting on the floor in the kitchen, because there were no longer any stools, and eating the yogurt and cookies that the Romans had left behind.

"Here's the thing, though," Cordelia said to Felix. "We *didn't* grow up hearing stories about Poseidon. We grew up with order, logic. We have real, normal lives somewhere else, with a mom and dad who love us and need us, and we need to get back to them."

"How do you intend to do that?"

"We thought we'd find a clue inside one of the books in this house. But your people have taken the books."

It was true. Kristoff's novels in the library were gone. Cordelia had hoped that *Gladius Rex* would still be here, so they could at least learn about how to navigate their way through ancient Rome.

Will took notice of how closely Cordelia was speaking with Felix. He didn't like this, so he interrupted: "I've got an idea for how we can get everything back."

"Excuse me," said Felix. "My wife and I are having a conversation."

"Ugh, can you please stop calling her that?" asked Eleanor. Eleanor didn't like Felix at all, from the moment she saw him fighting polar bears. "'*My wife*' this, '*my wife*' that. It grosses me out!"

"Not me," said Brendan, raising his eyebrows. "I think it's fun to watch Cordelia squirm."

Cordelia punched his arm. Hard.

"Will you just listen to me?" Will said. "Actually, on second thought, maybe Felix the Greek should go to another room."

"Why?" asked Felix.

"You're a spy," said Will.

"I am nothing of the sort," Felix said. "I'm a gladiator."

"Well, you're clearly the favorite of Emperor Blobipus—"

"Emperor Occipus—"

"I'll call him what I like," said Will, smiling at Eleanor. Eleanor beamed, glad someone was on her side. "And I suspect that once we've all gone to sleep, you're going to report back to him *exactly* what I called him, along with everything we've discussed!"

"You question my word?" Felix asked, standing to face Will.

"I do," said Will, moving closer to Felix. "You're just another one of Denver Kristoff's characters. Just like me. Only I was written as an honorable, handsome, brave hero."

"So was I!" said Felix.

"I doubt that. Once we get our hands on *Gladius Rex*, we'll find out your true personality!"

"And what would that be?"

"A conniving, sneaky, venomous serpent!"

Felix had his gladiator sword strapped to his belt. Will instinctively reached for the Webley Mark VI pistol that he had lost long ago in San Francisco.

"Looking for a weapon?" Felix asked.

"Don't need one," Will said, putting up his fists. "Let's settle this with our dukes!"

"Nothing I'd like better," said Felix.

"*Both of you STOP!*" Cordelia yelled.

Will dropped his fists. He didn't want to, but something in Cordelia's tone made him.

"Just as I thought," Felix said. "You're not so brave. And if you are such a hero . . . tell me, what exactly have you done to help out Cordelia, Brendan, and Eleanor since you arrived here?"

"I . . . well . . . I got Occipus's attention. Yes, I did," said Will. "I gave him the lighter."

"A whole lotta good that did us," mumbled Brendan. "Now he thinks we're magicians and he wants to keep us here forever."

Will gave Brendan a startled look: *Now you're turning on me?*

"Just sayin'," said Brendan sheepishly.

Will glanced down. He never would have admitted it, but he was deeply ashamed at how the last few hours had gone. Ever since he had met the Walkers, he had helped and protected them. But what Felix said was true: In this world, what use was he to anybody? He didn't have his gun—or his plane. He didn't belong here just like he didn't belong in twenty-first-century San Francisco. *Maybe I don't belong anywhere,* he thought, *except back in the book where I came from.*

Then, just as he was about to burst into tears, something he hadn't done since he was an infant—*But was I ever an infant? Did Kristoff even* write *me* as an infant?—Will remembered what he had been going to tell Cordelia a few minutes before he got distracted by Felix. His whole demeanor changed in an instant.

"You want to see how useful I can be?" he said. "Follow me."

41

Will remembered exactly where to go. In the hallway between the front door and the kitchen was the spot where he and Brendan had busted into the hollow walls of Kristoff House on their last adventure. He stood there with Brendan, Cordelia, Eleanor, and Felix.

"There's a passageway behind this wall," said Will.

Cordelia slapped Felix's hand away from hers. He was trying to hold her hand whenever they walked anywhere, telling her, "It's a husband's right."

"Would you stop calling yourself that?" Cordelia said.

"Maybe if you don't want me to hold your hand, my shoulder can just touch your shoulder," Felix said. "See?" He tapped against her. His shoulder was about twice as big as hers. "Is that so bad?"

"Yes!"

"Ahem," Will said. "Are you two finished?"

Cordelia and Felix nodded. Will stared at the wall: "One place I bet these grotty Roman blighters never got to was inside here. And last time, we discovered all sorts of things in these walls."

"Like what?" Brendan asked. "Wine? Those creeped-out books? They didn't really help."

Will didn't appreciate his attitude. "Have you forgotten Penelope Hope?"

The Walkers glanced at one another. Penelope Hope wasn't a good memory. She had been another character from Kristoff's books, but they hadn't been able to keep her safe. Now she was gone.

"Penelope told us that the inside of this house goes on and on," Will reminded them. "That there are endless mysteries inside its walls. There's no telling what we might find in there. Maybe another *Book of Doom and Desire* that can get us all home."

"But how do we get through the wall?" Eleanor asked.

"That's what we need to figure out," said Will. "You can't expect me to come up with everything."

"Maybe I can help," Felix said.

"And exactly how do you plan on doing that? With your sword? Perhaps you can chop your way through the wall, the way you beat those polar bears? Oh, wait . . . hold on . . . that's right . . . you almost got *eaten* by those polar bears!"

Cordelia laughed. She couldn't help it. When Will started dishing it out, not even Brendan could match him.

"I don't need my sword," the gladiator responded. Then he wet his thumbs and ran them through his close-cropped hair.

"What are you doing?" Cordelia asked.

"When I started gladiator training," Felix said, "they put me through many difficult and painful trials. Tell me, Will . . . are you able to tow a chariot with your teeth?"

"Can't say I've tried," said Will.

"Well, I can. First you strap a harness to a gigantic ox and put a rope on it. Then you take a gladiator-in-training like myself and put the rope in his mouth. The ox drags the gladiator-in-training through the field for eight hours while he holds on by his teeth. You do that for sixty days and you'll be able to pull *anything* with your teeth."

"That's torture," Brendan said.

"No. Torture is when they hurt you for secrets. Training is when they hurt you to make you strong."

"What else did you learn?" Eleanor asked. She was starting to hate Felix less, impressed by how straightforward he was. Will was always making a wisecrack or bragging about his talents and exploits, but with Felix, what you saw was what you got.

"This," Felix said.

He took a deep breath . . . and puffed out his cheeks, making them nearly the size of water balloons!

He looked like a frog, or like the great trumpeter Dizzy Gillespie. His cheeks were puffed out so far that they were making his ears stick forward from his head. His eyes bulged too.

"That's disgusting," Brendan said as Felix turned in a circle, making them laugh—even Will.

Felix exhaled and his face went back to normal. "It's a defense. If your enemy is close by, puff out. This will make him jump, and then—"

Felix drew his sword.

"Very nice," Will said. "You're quite the human curiosity box. When your gladiator days are over you should get yourself a job in a traveling circus."

"Sounds like fun," said Felix. "I'll perform feats of strength and you can be the clown. Seeing as that's all you're good for."

"That's it," shouted Will, pulling back his fists, ready to punch Felix. Eleanor got between them.

"Guys, guys, the wall, please?"

Will sighed, stepping back. "Very well, but pulling chariots with your teeth and puffing out your cheeks won't break through this surface!"

"This will," said Felix, rapping on his skull.

"What?"

"That's right. Another thing we did as soon-to-be gladiators was 'inverted noggin training.'"

"Inverted noggin training? How does *that* work?" asked Eleanor.

"They made us stand on our hands and heads, on a large flat rock. We would do this for an hour at a time. Then, after a month, we would remove our hands and *just* stand on our heads, with our trainers holding our ankles. After another month of that, we could stand on our heads indefinitely!"

"No way," Brendan said. "You'd pass out."

"Not if you continuously move your feet to keep the blood flowing. It's all been medically proven by physicians."

"Who cares how long you can stand on your head?" Will asked, but then Felix charged the wall.

Everybody jumped back. Felix ran forward with his head down, hitting the wall—

Crack!

He busted through! The wall was no match for his stone-callused noggin. His head was gone from view and his chest, legs, and arms were sticking into the hallway.

"*I'm okay,*" Felix's muffled voice yelled, "*but what's this gammadion doing here?*"

The Walkers and Will looked at one another. *Huh?*

"The gladiator's been using his numb skull too many times," Will said.

But Eleanor was more concerned: "What do you mean, Felix? What's a gum-aid-eon?"

"Pull me out and I'll show you!"

They grabbed Felix's feet and tugged him out of the wall; he landed in the hallway with a dusty thump.

"We've got to clear away the rest of that wall," he declared. "There's a piece of fabric on the floor, adorned with this symbol known as a gammadion. It represents the four corners of the world; I remember back in Greece seeing it etched on the coins."

"So?" Cordelia asked.

"So maybe there's some Greek living in the walls of this house. Could be one of my relatives. . . ."

Will rolled his eyes and they all exchanged looks, but Eleanor mouthed, *Don't be mean.* Felix reminded Eleanor of Fat Jagger, her colossus friend, only a lot smaller and much more vocal. He seemed to really want to help. Eleanor didn't think he was a spy. As long as he stopped saying gross things about her sister being his wife, he might actually be a lot of help. And a lot of fun.

The Walkers and Will started grabbing chunks of the wall near the hole, pulling away pieces. Plaster hit the floor. In a few minutes they had cleared a human-sized opening in the wall. They all stepped into the hidden passageway on the other side and looked around.

"Where's the gamma-thingy?" Eleanor asked.

Felix pointed. In a pool of light that came through the wall was a loop of red fabric with a sewn-on black-on-white symbol. Eleanor squinted at it—and gasped.

"Nazis!"

42

"W hat?" Brendan asked. "What do you mean, Nazis?"

Eleanor knelt and picked up the fabric, pinching it with two fingers as if it were a dead rodent. Brendan saw it and shouted, "A Nazi armband!"

"The gammadion," Felix said. He pointed to the fabric, on which was sewn a very clear swastika. "It reminds me of home!"

"Home?" Cordelia cried. "That symbol is the personification of pure evil!"

"What do you mean?"

"It's part of a Nazi uniform," Brendan said.

"What's a Nazi?"

"A bad guy," Eleanor interrupted. "Like really, really bad. The ultimate bad guys."

"The Nazis started World War Two," Brendan explained, "and they killed six million Jewish people in the Holocaust."

"Six *million?*" Felix asked, his expression turning to shock. "That's just horrible. Why have I never heard about this?"

"Because it happens in the future," Cordelia said. "The twentieth century."

"Which century is that again? Is that the one you're from?"

"Never mind," Eleanor said. "You just need to trust us: Anything you see with that symbol on it, it's not a gamma-whatever, it's a . . . uh . . . a swa-sticker."

"A swastika," Brendan corrected.

"Yeah, and it stands for a dangerous, screwed-up bunch of people who we don't want anything to do with. So give it to me." Eleanor took the armband, tore the swastika off it, threw it to the ground, and stomped on it. And then for good measure, she did something she rarely did. She spat on it.

"Question is, how did it get here?" said Brendan. "It must be from another one of the books we're trapped in!"

"Except this *can't* be from one of Kristoff's novels," said Cordelia.

"Why not?"

"Because he was writing before Nazis existed. He published his last book in 1928. Then he disappeared."

"And became the Storm King," said Eleanor.

Will walked to the torches on the wall, fully intending to light one with his lighter, and then remembered.

"Bloody emperor took my light. Any matches in the house?"

"Romans took them," said Cordelia. "What's your plan anyway?"

"We head this way," said Will, nodding down the hall. "As I recall, it leads to the wine cellar."

"The wine cellar?" Cordelia asked. "Is that your big plan, to hit the wine cellar? We need to go somewhere we haven't been, to look for clues we don't know exist. Which means we go *that* way, not toward the wine cellar."

"How are we going to see?" Eleanor asked.

"We're not," said Cordelia. "We'll just have to move slowly, hold each other's hands, and make our way as best we can."

"Finally I get to hold my wife's hand," said Felix.

"Call me that one more time and I'll smack you!" said Cordelia.

The Walkers, Will, and Felix started down the hallway, leaving behind the spat-on Nazi armband. Soon the light from their makeshift entryway had faded. They were in total darkness. Felix held one of Cordelia's hands and Will held the other. The group stayed in a line with Brendan at the front, touching the walls with their fingers. There were many trips and a few "oofs" as they went around pitch-black corners. They suddenly stopped at a place where they could feel the passage fork in two.

"Which way?" asked Brendan.

"Right," Eleanor said. "We should always go right. Then it'll be easier to remember how to get back when we turn around."

"Good point," Will said.

"Leave it to the dyslexic to figure out stuff like that," said Brendan, actually meaning it as a compliment.

They went right, again and again. *Feels like we should've come full circle by now*, Brendan thought. And then he stopped.

"Guys? The wall's not made of wood anymore."

They all started pressing it with their palms. There was a clear seam where the wood stopped and turned into wet, jagged stone.

"How is this possible?" Will asked. "There's a rock wall *inside the house?*"

"We heard about this!" said Eleanor. "Remember how Penelope Hope told us about that cave? The one where Denver Kristoff snuck off to use the book, to create his evil wishes?" She shuddered. "Maybe we should go back—"

"You can't act out of fear, Nell," said Cordelia. "We need

to move forward. No matter what we find."

The group kept going, slowly and cautiously. Water droplets plinked in the stone tunnel. Suddenly, Brendan spotted a faint light, shining out of the floor up ahead.

"Guys! Check it out!" shouted Brendan.

The light was about as bright as the glow of a computer screen leaking from a bedroom, but it looked like the sun to Brendan. He broke free and ran toward it.

"Bren, what are you doing?"

Brendan stared at the light as he got closer. At first it just seemed like a reflection of something in the ceiling, but there was nothing up there, only blackness. Then it looked like a sheet of ice on the floor, or maybe a pile of blue-white gems, and only when Brendan got very close did he realize what it was—

A pool.

A still, glowing pool of water, right in the middle of the ground.

It looked as if a full moon were floating inside the pool, shining up. The water illuminated the surrounding walls, which were no longer close to Brendan. He was in a real cave, not huge—but big enough to pitch a tent in. The shimmering light made it quite beautiful.

"What is it?" Eleanor asked, rushing up. They all looked into the glowing pool. The water was blue—gemstone blue, as if it were a sparkling mineral that had been liquefied—and resting below the surface was something familiar.

A bookshelf.

It looked like the driftwood bookshelf they had seen on their last adventure. It was completely submerged in the pool. And on its shelves, perfectly visible in the water, were

dozens of manuscripts.

"Books," Brendan muttered. "More books."

The top row of manuscripts lay just below the surface of the water. *But they don't even look wet,* thought Cordelia. *That's weird: If Kristoff left them down here all those years ago, they should have disintegrated into pulpy mush. . . .*

Cordelia reached out to touch a manuscript—but Brendan grabbed her wrist.

"What are you doing?"

"Trying to get a book."

"I think before you touch anything, you should ask me."

"Excuse me?" Cordelia drew back. "You want me to ask *you* for permission?"

"I'm just trying to keep you safe."

"That doesn't mean you can order me around—"

"It does if I'm protecting you."

As Cordelia and Brendan argued, Eleanor reached into the pool and pulled out a manuscript before anyone could stop her. She plopped it on the ground; it was a stack of papers held together with a leather strap. Eleanor started undoing the strap. The liquid that came off the manuscript didn't seem to be water. It felt thicker and softer, like oil. Eleanor put a drop on her fingertip. It sat there, glowing from within.

Cordelia and Brendan whirled around—but neither of them could get mad at Eleanor.

"What's the book covered in? Some phosphorescent preservative?" Cordelia asked.

"Just be careful, Nell," warned Brendan.

Eleanor looked at the first page of the manuscript. Whatever the liquid was, it *had* protected the pages, because they looked as pristine as if they had just come out of a printer.

"Red...D...Dalmatian?" she asked.

Felix looked over her shoulder, pretending to concentrate on the title Eleanor was trying to read. The young gladiator didn't know how to read at all.

"Red Dominion," corrected Cordelia.

"By Denver Kristoff," continued Eleanor.

Felix nodded as if that made perfect sense.

"Jeez, how many books did this guy write?" asked Brendan.

"Enough to need a magical underwater bookcase," said Eleanor.

But Cordelia said over her shoulder: "This is very weird." She read aloud: "'Red Dominion. Chapter One. It was 1959, and the Iron Curtain was about to erupt into a wall of fire.' Brendan, when did the Iron Curtain begin?"

"That's the Cold War, so probably 1945—"

"Cold War?" Eleanor asked. "What's that?"

"Arms-building race between the Americans and Russians," Brendan said. "Almost went nuclear."

"Is this more information from the future that I need to know?" asked Felix.

"It's definitely interesting," said Brendan. "The U.S. called the barriers Russia created between themselves and Europe the 'Iron Curtain.'"

"These are books Kristoff wrote after he became the

Storm King," Cordelia said. "Check the others."

Brendan reached into the blue pool and pulled out a manuscript called *Fields of Vietnam*. Then another: *Flying Saucer Apocalypse*.

"Look at this," he said. "It's like, 'Kristoff, the Secret Works.'"

"This is terrible," said Cordelia. "Now there are twice as many books we could be trapped in. What if Japanese kamikaze planes show up? Or Iraq War drones? We have to get out of here!"

"You're saying that like we have a choice," Brendan said, "but there *is* no way to get out of here."

"If we keep going past this cave, maybe we'll find one—"

"Hold on," Brendan said. "We're not going any farther tonight. We need to go back and get some sleep. You heard the emperor. He wants us to be in tomorrow's games."

"So?" Cordelia asked.

"So? We're his biggest stars ever. We've got to be ready. Aren't you guys excited to be in the games? A little?"

They all looked at one another. No one answered.

"Of course you are! Will? Felix? Felix, I know you're excited."

"I don't really like the games," Felix said. "I'm good at them, but I don't enjoy them." He turned to Cordelia. "I'd rather explore more of these books with you. Books are things I don't know much about. Maybe I could learn—"

"You guys are out of your minds!" Brendan said. "Tomorrow there's going to be *more* feasts, *more* entertainment, *more* of those little grapes with the honey—and you want to hang out in a cave all night *reading?*"

"Brendan . . . ," Will said. "You're getting a little too enthusiastic about the Roman lifestyle. You do realize it's not going to last. . . ."

"Why not?" Brendan asked. "I mean . . . at this point we don't have a way to get home. And why would we even want to go back? Guys, I know Occipus is a pain in the butt, but this is so much more fun than going to school, where I have to deal with that stupid bully, Scott, and then coming home and listening to Mom and Dad argue all night! We should take advantage of this. Start having fun. You know what I think? I think you're all just jealous because I'm the emperor's favorite!"

"His favorite? He almost had you executed," said Eleanor.

"We understand each other," said Brendan, and then he stormed away from the glowing pool, back toward the corridor. "I'm going back," he called without looking. "See you guys later! Maybe I can get the emperor to give me my old bed back in his personal quarters. . . ." He kept muttering, but his voice faded.

"What do we do?" asked Eleanor.

"Stay put," said Will. "We need to study these carefully.

There may be a clue inside to find a way home."

"And leave Brendan all by himself?"

"Definitely," said Will. "He needs to grow up. If he does talk to that slimy emperor, I predict that by tomorrow, he'll be thrown into the middle of the arena, all alone, fighting polar bears and lions, crying his eyes out, screaming for us to come and save him."

"But what if something happens to him before we get there?" asked a frightened Eleanor.

"At least," said Will, "he will have learned a valuable lesson."

As Brendan ran away from Kristoff House in the dark night (the Roman guards let him pass once he explained he was going to Occipus for special training for tomorrow's games), he started to have doubts. *I've never been on my own before, never really been away from my family. But I've got to stay tough. Maybe being a Roman is what I've always been destined for. I always thought I was meant to be a lacrosse star or a player for the Giants, but I'm not really that great at those things. But here . . . maybe I can be great. I'm already close to the emperor. He seems to like me. And I think he respects me. But what if I never see Deal or Nell or Mom and Dad again? . . . No, you can't think like that. You have to keep going, keep going, keep going—*

"STOP!!"

Brendan froze in his tracks, and slowly turned. It was the Wind Witch.

She floated a few feet above the ground, on a gentle gust of air. She wore her new chrome false hands, which glowed, and a long cape that flowed behind her. The curve of her smile and the curve of her bald head reminded Brendan of the eye symbol on *The Book of Doom and Desire*.

"What do you want?" Brendan asked.

"One final test," said the Wind Witch.

"Test?"

The Wind Witch stuck one of her false hands under her armpit and pulled it off. Beneath it was another metallic item attached to her stub: a long, razor-sharp, curved knife.

The Wind Witch lowered herself to the ground and started to walk toward Brendan. As she got close, she extended the knife.

The Colosseum was empty. Kristoff House was too far away—if Brendan called for help, no one would be able to reach him until it was too late. He stalled.

"What are you doing?" asked Brendan, his voice shaking.

"I tried to kill your sister Cordelia," said the Wind Witch. "And I failed. I tried to kill Eleanor. And I failed again. As you can imagine, it's all very confusing and disturbing to me. I don't know why my power has weakened. And in my search for an answer, I realized one very important thing: *I haven't tried to kill you."*

"Look, lady," said Brendan, trying to stop his voice from trembling. "I just want to get back to the emperor. . . . I'm not trying to hurt you. . . . Do you really need to do a test on me? I mean—"

Before Brendan could say another word, the Wind Witch's arm shot forward, plunging the knife deep into his chest.

Deep into his heart.

Brendan gasped. It hurt. It took his breath away. He felt his heartbeat starting to slow. He couldn't speak. He looked down. Blood poured from the wound, down his chest. The Wind Witch pulled out the knife and smiled. Brendan fell to his knees and felt himself losing consciousness.

"It worked," said the Wind Witch. "My power has returned."

Brendan's heart stopped beating. Everything around him spun. But before he collapsed on the ground . . .

The wound in his chest began to close back up. He could feel his heart muscles rethreading. And he felt a thump of life inside him. He was confused, overjoyed, terrified. It was like nothing he had ever experienced. Within seconds, he was able to breathe again. The color returned to his face.

"Nooo!" screamed the Wind Witch.

Brendan stumbled back to his feet and placed his hand on his restored chest, feeling his heartbeat. He smiled at the

Wind Witch. It felt like he had just won a huge gladiator fight, like he had beaten her in front of a packed crowd.

"Guess your mojo's gone, Baldy!"

Hearing that, the Wind Witch shot up in the air like a rocket, screaming *"It can't be!!"* before disappearing into the night sky.

Brendan turned away and, with a renewed sense of confidence, raced toward the entrance to the emperor's palace.

This is a sign, he thought. *I'm not just supposed to be a Roman. I'm invincible! I'm supposed to be a gladiator! Maybe . . . the greatest gladiator of all time!*

45

Cordelia, Eleanor, Will, and Felix spent the night in the Kristoff House living room, with as many manuscripts as they could carry from the underwater bookshelf. They used them as pillows, and even blankets, since there was no bedding, lying down in piles of books.

The next morning, Eleanor awoke to see Felix kneeling over some of the manuscripts. He had placed them in neat rows, faceup, with the title pages displayed.

"What are you doing?" Eleanor asked. Will and Cordelia were still asleep. Gray light stretched across the living room; the sun hadn't risen but there was a hint of heat in the air. It was going to be a scorcher in the Colosseum.

"Nothing," Felix said, quickly turning away from the

manuscripts. "Just . . . guarding these."

"Guarding them? You're trying to *read* them." Eleanor approached. "*Can* you read them?"

Felix hung his head, too embarrassed to say no. But Eleanor understood.

"That's all right," she said. "I'll teach you."

"Really?"

"Yeah. At least while Deal's asleep. When she wakes up she'll be like, 'Step aside, Nell. You're the last person who should be teaching people to read.'"

"Why's that?" Felix asked.

"Because I'm . . ." Eleanor was going to explain, but then she thought, *What's the point? Felix doesn't know!* "Never mind. Where do we start? Do you know your alphabet?"

"Like all the letters?" Felix shook his head. "All I know is how to write my name. But the others . . . ?"

"Oh boy, we're starting right from the beginning," Eleanor said.

"Is that a bad thing?"

"No, it's great. The beginning is what I know best."

Eleanor started with the letter *A* and all the different sounds it could make. As she spoke, she realized how difficult English was. A lot of the letters could make more than one sound depending on what other letters were near them. O could make about four different sounds, and she had a feeling there were more. If you wanted to design a language to be difficult, it couldn't get much tougher than English. Really, it was amazing anybody could read it.

"Why do C and K sound alike?" Felix said. "Shouldn't they just get rid of one?"

"They *should*," said Eleanor, "but you'd have to email the dictionary people about that."

Felix nodded as if that made total sense before he started sounding out the title of one of the books. Then Will woke up and tapped Cordelia.

"Look at this," Will said. "Your sister's teaching the Greek to read."

"You could help," said Cordelia. "Be the bigger man after almost getting in a fistfight with him."

"Good point," said Will, thinking to himself, *"Be the bigger man." I like the sound of that!* He walked over to Eleanor and Felix.

"Would you two fancy some assistance from an educated Englishman?"

Felix was wary at first, but then allowed Will to join them. Soon the pilot was helping the gladiator sound out letters, and when Cordelia joined in, Felix felt a bolt of pride as he accurately sounded out an entire title.

"At . . . *Atlantis Brigade!*"

Everyone applauded.

"Excellent," said Eleanor. "If you keep practicing, you'll be able to read the whole book."

Felix's voice shook as he spoke: "Eleanor—all of you—I was raised to be a gladiator. My strength training involved the most difficult and deadly exercises. But never once in my life did I have the strength, or more importantly, the courage . . . to attempt to read. And now . . . I've actually done it. Because of you. It's a miracle!"

"Wish Bren were here to see," said Eleanor wistfully.

They all took a moment to think about Brendan and what kind of trouble he could be getting into, and then Cordelia took charge and started organizing a reading of the books. Eleanor and Felix kept looking at *Atlantis Brigade*. Cordelia and Will began skimming manuscript titles—*The Mine Field Under the Sea*; *The Lunar Odyssey*—in an attempt to find what other books they might be trapped in. It was sobering; Cordelia's head began to fill with all the horrible and deadly scenarios that were inside each manuscript. They had a tough enough time with gladiators; what if they were attacked by a spaceship or prehistoric creatures?

In the middle of this investigation, Brendan returned to the house. He wore a purple toga, like the men who sat close to the action in the Colosseum, and a golden, vine-shaped crown. His body glistened, covered with oil; he walked with his chest held high as if he had something long and straight sticking up his backside.

"Good morning," he said. Roman guards stood behind him.

"Brendan!" Cordelia gushed, despite still being angry at how he had left them. "Where have you been?"

"With Occipus," Brendan answered. He seemed cagey; he looked at his feet, which were adorned with brand-new leather sandals. "I've been in his palace. We feasted until I don't know when last night; I just woke up. Check out my cool outfit!"

"Bren, don't leave us again," Eleanor said. "We had a horrible night. There were no blankets or anything, and believe it or not, we actually missed all of your dumb jokes and complaining."

"Yeah, well . . . ," Brendan said. He kept staring at his toes. "The people in Occipus's palace were really nice. I mean, nicer to me than anybody back home . . ."

"Brendan—" started Eleanor, but her brother took a deep breath and interrupted.

"You have to let me finish, Nell. Ever since we came back from our last adventure, I haven't been happy. I mean, our family has all this money, but we're not happy, and now we're at a school with kids who have more money anyway. And the harder I try to fit in—like getting that backpack—the more people make fun of me. And I don't really feel like I belong, you know?"

"That's called being a teenager, Bren," Cordelia said. "We all feel it, even Nell, and she's only nine."

"A very *mature* nine," said Eleanor.

"But *here*," Brendan continued, "I do feel like I belong. I'm special here, and no one will ever take that away from me. I'll be a guest of honor as long as Occipus is in power."

"And then, when he's kicked off the throne or hanged . . . you'll take over, right?" Cordelia asked in a mocking tone.

"I don't want to take over," Brendan said. "I just want to stay."

"You're not serious, are you?" Eleanor asked.

"I'm more serious than I've ever been," Brendan said. "I know you guys are all used to me making jokes. But this isn't a joke. I don't want to go home. I want to stay in ancient Rome for good."

Everyone looked around, waiting to see who would speak first. Cordelia stepped forward.

"Bren, you really need to think about what you just said," she exclaimed, suddenly panicked. "We can't break up this family. We work together, and it's the only way we've managed to survive. We're going to need your help to find a way back to Mom and Dad. I think the Wind Witch—"

"I don't care about the Wind Witch," Brendan said. "I don't want to have to worry about her ever again. Especially after last night—"

"What happened last night?"

"After I left," said Brendan, "she showed up. Said she had to try to kill me to see if she really lost her power. . . ."

"And?"

"Well, I'm here, aren't I?"

"So she can't kill any of us," pondered Cordelia. "Why do you think that is?"

"I don't care," said Brendan. "I just want to hang out at the Colosseum, eat some cured meat, rock in the hammock, watch the gladiator games—"

"What kind of horrible person have you turned into?" Eleanor burst out. "What would Mom and Dad think? I mean . . . don't you even miss them?"

"Of course I miss them," Brendan said. "But sometimes kids leave their parents early on. Not everybody has to stay home until they're thirty or whatever. It used to be that you went off and made your fortune as soon as you could. And that's what I'm trying to do—"

"You won't make any fortune here," Cordelia said. "In a few weeks you'll be lying in a ditch. Maybe the Wind Witch can't kill you, but there are plenty of other things that can. This is a really dangerous place. Your notoriety won't last forever—"

Brendan dismissively waved his hand at them, the way he had seen Occipus do. Everyone just rolled their eyes. He really was turning into an annoying, pompous egomaniac.

"This isn't only something I'm doing for myself," he said. "All of you are invited to join me. Cordelia, do you really want to go back to school after having one of your teeth fall out? The kids are going to tear you apart! Eleanor— would you rather go to horseback lessons twice a week, or have your own elephant imported from Africa? Will—you hate San Francisco, why not try something different? And Felix—you belong here anyway!" Brendan sighed. "You know I love you guys, but this is my chance for an extra-ordinary life. Shouldn't I take it?"

Eleanor grabbed Brendan. "No! Don't go! Stay with us!"

The Roman guards who had been standing behind

Brendan stepped forward. One of them said, "Keep away from the general."

"The general?" Cordelia asked.

"It's Occipus's name for me," said Brendan. "Isn't it awesome?" And then the guards put their big hands on Eleanor and pulled her off her brother.

"Hey!" Brendan said. "You don't need to do that—"

"Emperor's orders," said one of the guards. "No one is to touch General Brendan."

"But she's my sister," Brendan said.

"Very well, then we won't hurt her," said a guard. "Have you finished saying your good-byes?"

"Your good-byes?" asked Eleanor. "Is this the last time we're going to see you?" She started to cry. "Bren, you don't mean this! You're just confused. You want to stay with us, not that fat emperor with the ugly frog voice!"

"Watch it," said one of the guards.

Brendan stared at the floor. He hadn't thought this would be so hard. But then he closed his eyes and pictured the emperor's quarters, and the great food, and the awesome weapons, and the beautiful girls bringing him whatever he wanted.... Brendan felt like someone different when he was with the emperor, someone better than a kid who got beat up by Scott Calurio. He had seen an escape hatch through which he wouldn't have to deal with homework, or designer backpacks, or girls he was supposed to talk to, or college, or getting a job, ever again! He didn't want all that stuff. He knew from the adults in his life that that stuff wasn't fun. No. It was better to stay in Rome.

"I have to go," Brendan said. "I'm sorry." He turned and rushed out of the house. He didn't want anyone to see that he was crying.

The guards let go of Eleanor and followed him.

"*Bren!*" Cordelia screamed. "*Come back! You don't want this!*"

But Brendan wouldn't turn around. He walked into the arena with his head held high, ignoring his sister's pleas.

"Should I try to get him back?" Felix asked, pulling his sword out halfway.

"That won't work," said Cordelia. "He made his decision."

"Maybe if we just talk to him a little longer," said Will.

"I don't think so," said Eleanor. "Bren's stubborn. Like me." She held on to Cordelia's arm and sobbed. Losing her brother was like losing herself. She felt hollow inside. The three of them belonged together. Couldn't Bren see that?

"I think the only thing we can do is hope and pray that he comes around," said Cordelia. "And in the meantime we need to explore more of the house, see if we can find clues to get home—"

"But I don't *want* to go home without Bren!" Eleanor insisted. Cordelia wiped her tear-streaked hair away from her face. *How the heck are we going to get through this?*

All of a sudden they heard a huge *crack* outside.

Will flinched. He knew that sound.

"What was that?" Felix asked.

"Artillery," said Will, not believing the word even as it came out of his mouth.

Everyone looked out the window. The Roman guards who had left with Brendan were running across the arena. Brendan was running himself, his purple toga looking like a smear of jam because he was moving so fast.

Another huge crack sounded, followed by a massive crushing and crumbling, like an avalanche.

"Is it Fat Jagger?" Eleanor asked, hopeful to see her old friend.

"Who's Fat Jagger?" asked Felix.

"He was a friend of mine, a really good friend of mine."

"No, it's not him!" said Will. "That sounded like an armor-piercing shell. And—"

Cordelia and Eleanor yelled, *"Tank!"*

They saw it through the front door.

46

A dark green tank had burst through the walls of the Colosseum.

Luckily it was still early morning and there weren't any people in the stands. But a large portion of the curved building, where yesterday thousands of spectators had sat, was now a pile of chunky rubble on the ground. And the tank, looking like an impenetrable, determined robot, rolled right through this rubble, heading toward Kristoff House.

Eleanor pointed and shouted, "*Nazis!*"

Painted on the front of the tank was a giant swastika.

"Bloody hell," Will said. "Krauts."

"They've got to be from another Kristoff book!" Cordelia yelled. "We should've known when we found that

armband. Two of the worlds are coming together!" She rushed to the pile of manuscripts to find one about World War II. Eleanor grabbed her.

"There's no time, Deal. It's happening now!"

The tank, a *Wehrmacht* Tiger I with two hatches on top and a huge 88-millimeter tank gun mounted to its turret, rolled to a stop a few feet from Kristoff House. Behind it, through the hole in the Colosseum, Cordelia saw terrified Roman citizens running for their lives. To them the tank must have looked like a monster of legend.

"What sort of creature is this?" Felix asked.

"It's a machine," Will said, "and it looks like they made some major improvements over the ones in the Great War."

Suddenly one of the tank hatches popped open and a Nazi soldier stuck his head out. The soldier was tall and muscular, with bright blond hair. He wore a gray-green uniform and a swastika armband matching the one the Walkers had found in the hallway.

"There's the house!" he yelled, pointing at Kristoff House. "Just as our spies informed us! Get the towline!"

The blond soldier disappeared and another Nazi, in a scooped *Stahlhelm* helmet, climbed out. This one hit the ground running and grabbed a long metal towline that anchored to a winch on the tank. The line unwound as the soldier ran around Kristoff House.

"What is—*hey!*" Cordelia yelled out the front door.

Will pulled her back. "*Shhh.* Quiet. He could shoot you."

"But look what he's doing—"

Now the soldier was running back to the tank, having encircled Kristoff House. He clipped the towline to the winch. The winch started and tightened the line as the tank began to back out of the Colosseum. The giant vehicle groaned at the task of pulling the full weight of the house . . . but the Walkers, Will, and Felix felt the ground shift beneath their feet.

The house was moving, dragged by the Nazi tank.

"Oh, this really isn't good," Eleanor said. She saw

Brendan standing outside the house, in the exact same place where, the day before, he had victoriously danced around after defeating the lions. Now he was just staring at the house with a mixture of shock, dismay, and regret on his face. Kristoff House was going. And his family was going with it.

The house crunched and squealed over rocks as it went through the blown-out Colosseum wall. Now the Walkers, Will, and Felix were moving through the streets of Rome, toward an intersection, where a group of Nazi soldiers stood in four open-bed trucks.

Cordelia saw several Roman citizens fleeing the streets in terror: Some hid in alleyways; others bolted the doors of their homes. "These poor people have no idea what hit them," she said.

Just then, an angry young Roman, dressed in a dirty toga, charged out of his home, brandishing a knife. In a window behind him, a woman who must have been his wife screamed, clutching a baby, telling him to come back. But the man raised his knife and slashed at the tank—when machine-gun fire cut him down.

The gunfire came from the trucks that the Walkers had now reached. Cordelia turned away. She covered Eleanor's eyes. Will turned away as well. But Felix couldn't help but watch; he was fascinated and horrified.

"What just happened to that man?"

"He was shot," Will said with a sigh.

"Is he . . . dead?" asked Felix.

Will nodded.

"How?"

"They're called guns. They shoot tiny, sharp pieces of metal, strong enough to pierce the flesh. It's how we do things in the future."

Felix's heart sank. "I've seen ugly, awful things in the arena," he said, "but where is the honor in these guns?"

"There isn't any. Only efficiency," said Cordelia.

The Nazi trucks started their engines and surrounded the tank, forming a convoy. The tank, house, and trucks began to move through the streets; no one else tried to play hero.

Cordelia went to the pile of manuscripts in the living room and tore through them—then found what she was looking for. *Assault of the Nazi C—*. The title was incomplete; the lower half of the cover and first few pages were ripped off. "*Nazi Commander*," Cordelia assumed. The book opened with a description of the blitzkrieg—the "lightning war" that sent Nazis into Poland with such speed that there could be no resistance. *They could've won*, Cordelia realized with a chill.

"What are you reading?" Felix asked. "Shouldn't we be trying to escape?"

"If we try to escape, we'll be shot," Cordelia said. "I'm

just getting to a description of the soldiers who captured us. They're methodical and cold. They lack emotion, have no compassion."

"Are we mentioned in that book?" asked Felix. "Is this house written about? Is it being pulled through Roman streets?"

"No, so far it's just about the Nazi campaign on the western front. Last time, when we were sent into Kristoff's novels, we were stuck in a mash-up of three. Now it appears we've been sent into *Gladius Rex*—which the Romans stole from the library—and this one, *Assault of the Nazi* . . . whatever. The wild card is the third book."

"We should find it," said Felix.

That gave Cordelia an idea. "Can you stay with Will and Eleanor, Felix? Guard them?"

"Of course. Will seems to think he doesn't need my help, but—"

"Give him a chance. He likes you, really. He's just a little sensitive."

Cordelia grabbed Felix's hand and gave it a squeeze.

From across the room, Will saw that, and frowned—he certainly *was* sensitive when it came to Cordelia touching Felix. Felix shrugged, trying not to start trouble, as Cordelia took off down a corridor of Kristoff House.

47

*C*ordelia climbed into the secret passage that Felix had opened up with his powerful noggin. She moved quickly through the darkness. It wasn't as scary as before, but she didn't have much time—there was no telling when the house would stop moving and the Nazis would start checking out who was inside.

She knew that logically, the stone-walled chamber they had discovered should be long gone. If Kristoff House connected to a cave system, that cave system shouldn't travel from San Francisco. But magic had its own logic.

Cordelia's eyes detected the glow of the pool. The walls pulled away as she entered. She approached the underwater bookshelf; the top of it had been cleaned out by the kids, but there were more manuscripts below.

Cordelia got ready to fish them out, about to climb into the water. She paused. This wasn't quite water but some sort of liquid that gave the pool its glow. *That stuff might give me some horrible disease that I'll carry around for the rest of my life.* But she had no choice. She was doing this for the safety of her family. Cordelia took a deep breath and placed her feet in the water. It clung to her like oil, shining from inside.

She slipped into the pool with her clothes on. It was terribly thick and sticky. She felt like she was entering a hardening Jell-O mold. She had to push with her arms and legs to get down to the second level of the shelf, all the time terrified that the liquid would force its way into her lungs—even her brain, where it would swell her head to the size of an alien's and explode.

She grabbed seven manuscripts and brought them out of the pool, heaving them onto the stone floor. She couldn't read the titles with the thick liquid dripping off her eyelashes. Along with the manuscripts, she found one book that looked different from the others. It was smaller and hardbound—almost like a diary.

Cordelia wiped her eyes and tried to open the smaller book, but it was locked. It had a tiny metal keyhole on the front; it *was* a diary. Written on its cover in precise cursive script was:

Property of Eliza May Kristoff

Denver Kristoff's wife? Cordelia thought. *This is an incredible discovery! Who knows what secrets are in here?*

She stuck the book in the back of her pants as she returned through the corridor. All she had to do now was find the key.

48

Cordelia didn't tell Eleanor, Will, or Felix about the diary. *I need to open it first. It might be a hoax.* And (a deeper impulse, one she was ashamed of): *I'm the one who found it. I should open it.*

She placed the seven Kristoff manuscripts she had recovered on the floor and began to sort through them: *Under the Mummy, The Monks' Sacrifice, The Space-Time Disaster.* None of the books seemed to describe a third world that the Walkers were trapped in, but maybe they were about to enter that world, because they had finally left Rome.

The last city dwellings were behind them now. Kristoff House was being dragged through open country. Green fields stretched out; a river sparkled in the distance. It was a beautiful vista at complete odds with the situation.

"They're taking us into the middle of nowhere," said Will. "Based on personal experience, that's where you take your enemies to have them shot."

"Don't say that . . . ," said Eleanor.

"Don't worry, Eleanor," Felix said. "I'll protect you."

"Felix, old chap, you may be extraordinarily courageous . . . but guns beat swords. Those Nazis will shoot you where you stand."

"What if I'm faster?"

"Excuse me?"

"What if I slash the guns out of their hands?"

"That's—"

Will was about to say that was ridiculous, but Cordelia cut him off: "That's very brave, and we're lucky to have such a brave warrior on our side." She didn't want Felix to get demoralized. No matter how bad the situation got, they all needed to have hope.

Suddenly the tank, the house, and the trucks stopped. For a moment no one dared to breathe. They heard crickets chirping.

"I wish Brendan were here," Eleanor said.

"Because he'd have a plan?" Cordelia asked.

"Because he's my brother and I miss him," Eleanor said.

The hatches on the tank popped open. Out climbed a Nazi soldier dressed differently from the rest. There were red stripes on his helmet and gold-threaded swastikas in his shoulder pads. He was over six feet tall, with broad, muscular shoulders and a huge cleft chin. His hair was bright blond and tightly cropped. His eyes were steely blue. When he opened his mouth, his teeth were blindingly white. Everything about him was perfect.

"I speak now to the inhabitants of this house!" the Nazi called in a German accent. "My name is Heinrich Volnheim, *Generalleutnant* of the Fifteenth Panzergrenadier Division! We know you are there; we have seen you in the windows! Come out with your hands up!"

"What are we gonna do?" asked Eleanor.

"We can't go out there," said Cordelia. "It's certain death."

"We'll fight," Felix whispered, drawing his weapon—

"Felix!" Will scolded. "Guns . . . ?"

"There's always a way to turn a battle to your side."

"You have thirty seconds to show yourselves!" shouted Volnheim.

Cordelia gulped. Felix was brandishing his sword, ready to fight, no matter what the odds. Cordelia noticed, and grew strength.

"All right. If we're gonna do this, we need weapons. Follow me!"

Cordelia led everyone into the kitchen, where they grabbed things to defend themselves with against the Nazis. Will picked up the Wusthof knife block, tucked it under his arm, and pulled out a long serrated blade. Eleanor found a battery-operated metal cake mixer. She held it out like a gun and hit the On button. The metal whisks spun quickly.

"Really, Nell?!" said Cordelia. "You're gonna bake them a cake?"

"No," said Eleanor. "These mixers can really mess you up. I got my finger caught in 'em once . . . remember?"

"Oh, right," said Cordelia. "Fourteen stitches." Cordelia picked up a five-gallon water-cooler jug, about halfway full, and hoisted it over her shoulder.

"What are you going to do with that?" asked Will.

"If one of them gets too close, I'll drop it on his head," said Cordelia.

"Heinz, Franz," came Volnheim's voice from outside. He was strangely calm, as if he were waiting for some food to finish in the microwave. "The children have not shown themselves and it has been thirty seconds. Go in and retrieve them. And don't shoot. I want them alive."

"All right!" Will said. "We might get the jump on these guys. Cordelia, go upstairs. Felix and I will try to fight them off." He handed Felix a knife.

"No," said Cordelia. "Stop ordering us around—"

Just then, the front door burst open, and Heinz and Franz stepped in. They had arrived at the front door much faster than was humanly possible—faster than anyone could run. And they looked exactly like Volnheim. Both over six feet tall, with square jaws and blue, soulless eyes. They both held Luger pistols.

"*Get out of this house!*" Felix yelled, rushing down the hall.

He slashed at Heinz's arm. There was a loud clang. Heinz dropped his gun to the floor and Felix dropped his sword—but quickly retrieved it.

The Nazi glanced to where Felix had struck him. Heinz's uniform sleeve was torn and his skin was sliced open, but there was no blood.

Only a shimmer of bright silver beneath the skin.

That's odd, thought Felix—and then he swung at Heinz's face. The blade cut across the Nazi's cheek and chin, but Heinz only smiled, as if he were being tickled by a feather.

Felix stared in shock. "What . . . ?"

Heinz grabbed Felix's sword and snapped the blade in two with his bare hands. Franz, who had been standing behind Heinz, punched Felix in the jaw. *Dong!*

The gladiator had never been hit so hard in his life. Franz's fist felt like a can of paint. Felix fell backward and hit the floor. Out cold.

Will, back in the kitchen, viewed all of this with increasing panic. But he couldn't abandon Cordelia and Eleanor, and the Nazis had orders to take them alive, so maybe they wouldn't shoot him. He charged with the Wusthof block under his arm like a football, whipping out a knife—

When it hit Franz, the blade snapped in two.

Will lifted the cutlery block over Franz's head and brought it down. The heavy wooden block just bounced off.

"*What?*" said Will.

Franz pulled back his arm, hitting Will square in the jaw with his elbow. There was a sound of metal connecting with flesh, and Will hit the floor like a sack of potatoes.

Cordelia and Eleanor were confused and horrified.

"What's up with these Nazis?" asked Eleanor, clutching her cake mixer. "They're like Superman, only meaner!"

"I think I have an idea—" started Cordelia, but she had no time to explain, because Heinz and Franz were aiming their guns.

"Come with us," said Heinz, "and no one will get hurt." Eleanor and Cordelia ran up the spiral stairs, with Cordelia struggling mightily to bring along the five-gallon water jug she had brought as a weapon.

The Nazis followed, their boots hitting the floor with mechanical precision as they went through the kitchen and up the stairs. Cordelia raised the water jug over her head. As soon as the Nazis came into view, she threw it. The water bottle hit the stairs directly in front of Heinz and Franz and burst open, drenching them in two-and-a-half gallons of water. It dripped off their faces as they stopped and shook their hands to get it off.

"Deal, you missed! That's just gonna make them mad—"

"Watch."

There was a sizzling sound. It got louder and louder, echoing from inside the Nazis' bodies. Smoke began to seep from their ears, mouths, and nostrils. Loud, crackling pops and grinding whirs came from their chests. "What the . . . ?" Eleanor said.

Showers of bright sparks suddenly shot out of the Nazis' bodies, spewing up the stairs. The kids ducked away as Franz and Heinz fell backward and tumbled head over heels, hitting the wall as the staircase curved down to the kitchen. When they reached the bottom, they remained still, lying on their backs, their bodies smoking and crackling. Cordelia and Eleanor went halfway down the steps to look at them. Every now and then, stray sparks would shoot from their open mouths and ears. But the Nazis stayed motionless. Silent.

"What just happened?" asked Eleanor.

"We found their weakness," said Cordelia.

The sound of metal—whirring, grinding, clicking—continued to come from the Nazis' bodies. And then, without warning, the front of Heinz's face literally popped off and bounced across the floor.

It came to a stop in the corner of the room. The metal face wasn't a face at all, but a faceplate. It resembled a sophisticated Halloween mask, no more than a quarter-inch thick. Cordelia and Eleanor looked down at the wide opening that was now Heinz's head. Inside, there were no visible muscles or blood vessels.

Only a mass of wires, gears, and black oil.

Will and Felix were getting back on their feet, rubbing their heads in pain. They joined Eleanor and Cordelia over the bodies of the fallen Nazis. They stared in horror at the complex mechanical workings of Heinz's head.

"Poor chap's got a rather nasty complexion," said Will.

"He's a cyborg," said Cordelia.

"A cy-*what*?"

"That's the title of Kristoff's book. *Assault of the Nazi Cyborgs!*"

"What are cyborgs?" asked Felix.

"Robots."

"What are robots?"

"Oh boy," said Eleanor, doing a facepalm. "This is gonna take a while to explain."

"Never mind that—what do we do now?" asked Will.

Outside the house, Volnheim spoke—now the kids recognized his voice as not just calm, but robotic —"Beckler. Dingler. Heinz and Franz have not returned from their mission. Go and see what is taking so long."

Two identical Nazis stepped forward—and then they warp-walked to the house, their feet moving so fast that they were a blur, appearing at the front door in an instant. This time all the kids saw it.

"That's messed up," Eleanor said.

"I'm on it," said Cordelia. She was kneeling, holding the faceplate of Heinz, searching for something. There it was: the serial number.

Cordelia ran into the living room.

"*Deal?!*" shouted Eleanor. "Where are you going?!"

"You will come with us," said Beckler, pointing his gun from down the hall.

"One moment," said Will, who quickly dove to the floor and grabbed Heinz's gun. Will rolled onto his stomach, propped himself on his elbows, and took aim. He fired several shots at the two Nazis.

The bullets just bounced off.

The two Nazis grinned.

Will got to his feet and tossed the gun on the floor.

"German engineering," he muttered.

Beckler and Dingler moved toward Eleanor, when suddenly they stopped in their tracks, held still for a moment . . . and began to walk *backward*.

They moved in a herky-jerky motion, like characters being rewound on a DVD. They started to speak. It sounded like gibberish, like someone was playing a recording in reverse. When they reached the door, they stopped again. Frozen.

Will, Felix, and Eleanor exchanged a stunned look—and then Cordelia stepped out of the living room. She was pointing a high-tech universal remote at the Nazi cyborgs.

"Deal!" shouted Eleanor. "What are you doing?"

"I programmed the cyborg's serial number into the remote," said Cordelia. "I figured it might be able to control them somehow . . . and it worked!!"

Cordelia hit Reverse four times on the remote.

The Nazis moved backward at four times their normal speed. They resembled an old Charlie Chaplin movie as they skittered out the front door, backing away from Kristoff House and speaking to each other in reverse chipmunk voices.

Outside, Volnheim and his Nazi brigade watched in disbelief.

"Beckler! Dingler! Have you lost your minds? Get back inside!"

But the two Nazis kept walking backward, oblivious to their leader. They reverse marched all the way through the assembled troops and across a field, disappearing into a forest hundreds of yards away.

"What just happened?" asked Volnheim, looking at his equally perplexed troops. "Anyone?"

The Walkers, Felix, and Will stepped out of the house. Everywhere they looked, there were Nazis. Standing in the four trucks, on top of the tank, lined up in formation . . . nearly one hundred of them. And they all looked exactly like Volnheim.

"Stop right there," shouted the *Generalleutnant*. "What did you do to my men? You played with their minds. It's witchcraft—"

Cordelia hit Pause.

Volnheim shut up immediately, and the entire Nazi cyborg army froze in place.

"That's awesome, Deal!" said Eleanor.

"Dad spent a really long time researching this remote," said Cordelia. "He got the best one."

"But why does it work against those Nazi cy-bros?" asked Felix.

"*Cyborgs*," corrected Eleanor.

"I put in the Nazi's serial number, and he came up as being a brand Loewe AG television," said Cordelia. "I don't know how much time we have. Let's grab as many of their weapons as we can and go back inside to figure out our next move."

"Good idea," said Felix.

The four of them began walking through the army of statue-like Nazi cyborgs and taking all their Luger pistols. Also their grenades and daggers. It was a difficult task to remove the weapons from the mechanically clenched metal hands of the soldiers. As Eleanor tried to pry a gun from one Nazi's fingers, it fired!

Eleanor stared at the hole in the ground, inches from her foot.

She was frozen in fear. "I'm sorry!" she said, starting to cry.

"Don't worry," said Cordelia. "Hopefully we won't have to use the guns. Let's head back to the house."

The four of them were a few feet from the front porch when a hand reached out and grabbed Eleanor's shoulder.

49

Eleanor whirled around. One of the Nazis had come back to life. He was gripping her shoulder with one hand, holding a knife to her throat with the other.

"Deal!" cried Eleanor.

Cordelia saw motion out of the corner of her eye—*all the soldiers were coming back to life.* She dropped what she was doing and pulled out the universal remote.

She hit Pause.

It didn't work this time. The Nazis were moving, looking for their missing guns and daggers.

Cordelia hit Pause again. And again.

But it was useless.

The Nazis were very much alive.

And that's when she noticed the flashing Battery Low light.

"No way!"

The Nazis who still had their guns surrounded the kids.

"Drop the weapons," said Volnheim, pushing through the group with a Luger pointed forward. Cordelia, Eleanor, Will, and Felix complied. The Nazis slowly took every single one of their weapons back from the children. Then Volnheim stood in front of Cordelia.

"Hand over the device."

Cordelia gave him the universal remote. Volnheim took it, turned it over, and carefully examined it from all sides.

"What is this magic? Clever. Very clever."

Volnheim tossed the remote high in the air, raised his gun, and fired, blowing it into several pieces. He turned back to Cordelia. "Are you the owners of this house?"

"Well, technically, my parents, but yeah."

"It's quite beautiful," said Volnheim. "Our spies spotted it yesterday, just after the Great Time Disturbance."

"Great Time Disturbance?" Cordelia asked.

"Yes. The Great Time Disturbance that caused Germany to suddenly be connected to ancient Rome." Volnheim's eyes narrowed. "Are you responsible for that as well?"

"No . . . ," said Cordelia, but Volnheim didn't buy it.

"You're lying. It's your house and you know all its secrets, which is why I'm keeping you alive. I want you to show me everything about this residence. Lead the way."

The group exchanged worried glances as they led Volnheim, and only Volnheim, into the house. There he proceeded to pace and examine.

"Who ransacked this house? The Romans?"

Cordelia nodded.

"Typical Italians," said Volnheim. "No elegance, no artistic sensibility. You do know that the entire Renaissance was a hoax?"

"No," said Cordelia. "I wasn't aware of that—"

"Yes," said Volnheim. "The Sistine Chapel was actually painted by a German."

"Interesting," said Cordelia, who had decided it was a good idea to agree with anything said by the Nazi cyborg.

"Is there an attic?" asked Volnheim.

"Yeah . . . ," Eleanor said.

"Wonderful!" Volnheim clapped his hands, making a metallic ringing noise. "*Der Führer* loves attics!"

"Uh . . . *Der Führer*?" Cordelia asked. "You don't mean . . ."

"Of course," said Volnheim. "My master and creator. *Der Führer* is the only one worthy of living in this house. Which is why he sent me to appraise it. You see, he has purchased a lakeside lot. Several acres. This will work quite well as his summer home."

Felix whispered to Cordelia: "I don't understand, who is this *Führer?*"

"Only the most reprehensible and evil dictator in world history," said Cordelia. "Certainly one of the top five."

"Silence!" shouted Volnheim. "How dare you speak that way about *mein Führer!*"

Volnheim suddenly stopped in the kitchen, looking down at Heinz and Franz. He frowned, brow tightening.

"I assume you are responsible for this?" he asked.

No one said a word. Volnheim clenched his jaw. Then he led Felix, Will, and the Walkers back outside, addressing his army.

"I have found the home to be satisfactory. We will bring it to the *Führer's* lakeside property. And these four—"

He looked at Cordelia, Eleanor, Will, and Felix.

"We shoot."

The Nazi cyborgs let out a hearty cheer, which sounded a little robotic, like someone yelling through a fan. Eleanor screamed. Will and Felix tried to shield the Walker sisters. Cordelia squeezed her eyes shut. The Nazis drew their guns. But before they could fire off a shot, a loud laugh stopped everyone in their tracks.

50

In the past, Cordelia had felt a range of emotions when she heard the Wind Witch—terror, anger, resignation—but now, for the first time, she felt excitement. There was only one person who laughed that way, high and cackling.

She flew down from the sky with her wings flapping and her bald head glistening in the sun.

"*Leave them alone!*" she commanded. "*The Walkers belong to me!*"

Commander Volnheim was taken aback by the sight of her, but he wasn't too surprised. He was a cyborg, after all.

"Stay out of this," he ordered.

In response, the Wind Witch pointed one of her false

hands at a Nazi truck and let fly a blast of concentrated air. The truck flew upward, flipping end over end, sending Nazis flying everywhere.

Volnheim screamed to his men: *"Kill her!"*

Nazis opened fire on the Wind Witch, using rifles and pistols and machine guns from the trucks. Volnheim ducked into the Tiger I tank; within moments, the turret began rotating, the cannon pointing upward.

The Wind Witch took off, climbing up, up, up, far away from where the bullets could reach her. She was lost in the clouds within seconds, able to see the entire panoramic view of Kristoff House and the trucks below. But she saw something else. Something fast, coming toward her with a flurry of deafening propeller noise.

And it had a star painted on its side.

Meanwhile, the Walkers, Will, and Felix ran back inside Kristoff House, racing for their lives as Nazi cyborgs streamed in. Cordelia led them into the attic. Eleanor was confused.

"I thought the Wind Witch was bad, so why is she helping us now?"

"I don't know," Cordelia said. "I need to learn more." She thought of Eliza May Kristoff's diary, which she had taken from the cave in the wall. It was still stuffed in her jeans. Maybe the answers were within, but now was not the time to check.

Back in the sky, the Wind Witch had met the other primary characters from Kristoff's *Assault of the Nazi Cyborgs*: the Americans.

She was flying alongside an airplane, and behind it were two dozen others: an entire squadron of U.S. P-51 Mustangs with silver wings, crosshatched red tails, and big propellers spinning on their noses. The pilot of the lead plane stared at the Wind Witch through his cockpit window. She blew him a kiss, waved her arms, and started to move bits and pieces of the clouds, forming a white, puffy swastika shape. She pointed behind the pilot and down, emphatically. The pilot nodded and gave a thumbs-up, then rolled into a big U-turn and led the other planes back the way they had come, toward the Nazis. Once she was sure she had made her point, the Wind Witch flew that way herself, streaking toward the ground like a bird about to grab its prey. She plummeted faster, faster, and she couldn't resist—she opened her mouth to let out a gleeful scream.

Cordelia heard it from the attic. *"Look!"*

The Wind Witch dove straight for the Tiger I tank, extending her arms, gathering a cyclone of wind that surely would have turned everyone inside the vehicle into sparking spare parts—

But the tank fired.

It was the same intense blast that had busted a hole in the Colosseum wall: a twenty-two-pound, armor-piercing ballistic shell. The Wind Witch was no match for it. At the last moment she redirected the air that was circling her to form a protective shield. This cushioned the blow, but only slightly. She was knocked backward in a tremendous explosion, flying away from the tank like a baseball cracked over the left-field wall. Screaming in pain, she disappeared behind a hill, where she presumably hit the ground more than a mile away.

"They got her!" Cordelia yelled. "She was our last hope!"

A cluster of Nazi cyborgs climbed into the attic and drew their pistols, pointing them at the Walkers, Felix, and Will. Volnheim was in the lead.

"Turn around and face the wall."

Terrified, realizing that this was the end, they faced the back wall of the attic. Cordelia took Eleanor's trembling hand. Will and Felix fumbled for Cordelia's other hand—and they both ended up holding it.

They all closed their eyes, waiting for the blazing round of gunfire—but they heard a tremendous *KABOOOOM* outside that didn't sound like a gun.

It sounded like a bomb.

Eleanor was hit from behind with a blast of splintered wood and a Nazi *Shahlhelm*, which *bong*ed off her head. She turned, dazed, and saw that the front of the attic had been blown off.

Nazi cyborgs were crawling on the ground, some blown to pieces, one headless, wires bursting from the hole in his neck, blindly searching for his missing head. The place where the front wall had been was a gaping hole; outside and below, a crater smoldered. The buzzing in Eleanor's ears became a different kind of buzzing: a plane overhead.

"Americans!" she yelled.

Everyone looked. The Mustang P-51s, which were so classic in their design that they seemed like toys, soared away from Kristoff House—and then turned around in long, beautiful arcs that made the stars on their sides glint and wink.

"*Verdammt*," Volnheim said. "They're coming back. To the trucks."

The fritzed-out cyborgs began to rush out of the attic and jump to the ground, pulling their damaged bodies back to the truck convoy, but it was too late. The planes released two more bombs.

The oblong shapes fell slowly. It was almost as if time stopped while they were in the air. One of the Nazis yelled "*Take cover!*" as cyborgs scurried this way and that, but they didn't have anywhere to go before the bombs reached the ground, and then—

The army of Nazi cyborgs got turned into a big pile of spare parts.

Up in the attic, the kids had been huddling scared, but now, in the sudden quiet, they crept forward and surveyed the scene.

The field in front of Kristoff House was a junkyard of

burning robotic heads. The bombs had largely disassembled the Nazi cyborgs, leaving arms and feet twitching and torsos spattered in black oil.

"We did it!" Felix yelled. "We're safe!"

"Well, *we* didn't do much of anything," said Will. "The American planes did."

"And the Wind Witch," reminded Eleanor.

"Yes, that is strange," said Cordelia.

"Where's the tank headed?" Will asked. The Tiger I was crawling down the road, making a hasty retreat.

"Volnheim!" Felix said. "He's leaving his men. Or his cyborgs. Coward. Even if the men are made of metal, that still makes him a coward."

Cordelia and the group went downstairs and outside as six American planes touched down: five near the house, one far down the road to block the tank. Pilots stepped out of the planes and started to deactivate any Nazi cyborgs that were still moving, unscrewing power panels in their lower backs and pulling out their batteries. Then one of the pilots noticed the kids. The American pilot was Sergeant Jerrold "Jerry" Hargrove: square-jawed, with a three-day growth of beard, a shearling-lined flight cap, a brown bomber jacket, and killer aviator shades.

"Who the heck are you?" he asked.

Cordelia stared to answer him: "We—"

"Allow me to explain," Will interrupted, stepping

forward. He couldn't let his friends botch this up. He was absolutely stunned at the quality of the American planes. He thought maybe if he showed his leadership and courage, he'd get a chance to fly one.

"I'm Wing Commander Will Draper, sir," he said with a salute. "Royal Flying Corps, Squadron Seventy."

"Hold on," Hargrove said. "The RFC hasn't been around for years."

"Right, bear with me, sir, it's going to take some time to explain." Will took a deep breath and laid it out—who the Walkers were, the fact that they were all trapped in novels by Denver Kristoff, the fact that those novels were coming together, and the manner by which Felix had joined the group. When Will finished, Hargrove scrunched his brow, turned, and called, "Lieutenant Laramer, sir? You gotta hear this."

Lieutenant Laramer was a tall, rangy type. His shiny brass buttons meant he outranked Hargrove by quite a bit. He came over holding what looked like a water gun pointed at the back of Volnheim.

"Look who I found! The lead unit. You can tell from his Nazi stripes." Lieutenant Laramer shook his head and chuckled. "Trying to outrun a plane in a tank. He ain't the brightest 'borg in the bunch." Laramer had the same cool-looking aviator shades as Hargrove. *If Brendan were here, he'd be trying to get his hands on those*, thought Will. *I miss him.*

Hargrove explained the implausible story to Laramer. Volnheim listened in; as crazy as the explanation was, it made sense to him: The Great Time Disturbance had, in fact, been two fictional worlds coming together. And the *real* world was the world these children were from. Volnheim's robot mind began to spin with possibility.

Lieutenant Laramer shook his head: "You know, Draper . . . a guy tells me a story like that, usually I'd figure him for a crackpot . . . but do you know why I decided to strike against this Nazi force?"

"No, sir."

"We were running recon," said Lieutenant Laramer, "and a flying bald woman appeared in the air. Now I've seen plenty of nutty stuff in this war—after all, we're fighting a bunch of robots designed by Hitler—but a flying bald woman? Anyway . . . she waved at me and made a signal in the clouds, pointing to the exact location of the Nazi cyborgs. This woman sounds a lot like your 'Wind Witch.'"

"It *was* the Wind Witch!" said Eleanor.

"Plus," continued the lieutenant, "I find it pretty odd that yesterday we were fighting in Salerno and now we're almost three hundred kilometers northwest. I don't have a single memory of us flying that distance or receiving orders to fly it. Do you, Hargrove?"

"No, sir."

"I think these kids are tellin' the truth," said the

lieutenant. "They're real American heroes! Jerry, I want you to transport them wherever they want to go—"

"Rome," said everyone at once.

"Rome, why?"

"To find our brother," said Cordelia.

"Not just her brother, one of my best friends," said Will. "Brendan Walker."

"You got it," said Laramer. "Hargrove, take them to Rome."

"How?" said Jerry. "They won't all fit in the plane, sir."

"Take the Tiger."

"I—excuse me, sir? You want me to take the *tank?*"

"That's right. If you encounter any German 'bots, they'll think twice before attacking their own tank. Heck, they're practically tanks themselves."

"But I don't know how to drive a tank, sir!" said Hargrove.

"Jerry . . . how many times have we had to sit in some trattoria, after a couple jugs of vino, listening to you brag about being the best pilot in the squadron?" Laramer changed the tone of his voice, doing a very good impression of Jerry. "*I can guide any vehicle made by man!*"

"Well, yes, sir, but that was a figure of speech—"

"Airmen in my squadron don't make figures of speech, Jerry. They make commitments!"

"But sir, the dials and controls are in German!"

"Then take Volnheim with you."

And that was how Cordelia and Eleanor found themselves walking toward the Tiger I, getting ready to take a trip back to Rome. Volnheim, handcuffed and clanking his wrists against his cuffs, approached the two girls.

"I have a proposition for you two," he said with a perfect smile.

"Leave us alone, you creep," said Cordelia.

"I could," said Volnheim, "or I could tell you about the treasure map."

51

"What?" asked Eleanor. "What treasure map?"

"One of the spoils of our battle victories," said Volnheim, "is the great treasures—paintings, jewels, gold—that we have taken over the years. This map will lead you to the place that stores all of these great treasures."

"No, thanks," said Eleanor. "We don't want your Nazi gold. That's a disgusting, awful—"

"*Great* idea," interrupted Cordelia. She looked around to make sure that Will, Felix, and Jerry were out of earshot. They were standing by the tank. She leaned close to Volnheim and whispered: "Where's the map?"

"What?" cried Eleanor. "You're gonna actually talk to him?!"

Cordelia gave her a look: *Gimme a sec, I'm working on something.* Eleanor backed off, although she didn't trust her sister. Volnheim whispered, "The map is hidden in the walls of the tank. But if I show you where it is, you must promise me one thing."

"What's that?"

"You will take me to your world—to the *real world*—when this is over."

"It's a deal," said Cordelia.

"Have you totally lost it?" Eleanor hissed as Jerry came over, grabbed Volnheim, and led him to the tank.

"Calm down, Nell," Cordelia said. "You know it's really true that there's a lot of treasure never recovered from the Nazis? If that guy has a real treasure map and we can bring some treasure home, there will be a huge reward for returning it to the rightful owners."

"That's horrible, Deal. That's really kinda greedy."

"No," argued Cordelia, "it's about helping our family survive—and protecting our good name. What if we do manage to save Brendan and get home? What kind of home are we going back to? Dad's gambling away all our money. I don't want to go back just so we can get kicked out of Kristoff House!"

"I do. I want things to go back to how they were before."

"You mean when Dad got fired and we had nowhere to live?"

"Okay, maybe things weren't so great. But here's another issue.... *You just promised a Nazi you'd take him back to our home!!*"

"That's *all* I promised him," said Cordelia. "What I didn't promise him is that he'd be free. As soon as we get home I plan on turning him over to the authorities for perpetrating hate crimes. Or maybe I'll give him to a museum and they'll unplug him and put him on display. Not many people have seen a Nazi cyborg."

Will called from the tank: "Cordelia, Eleanor! Come on, then."

The girls climbed inside the Tiger I. Will was sitting in the driver's seat under the turret. It wasn't like the driver's seat of a car; there was no windshield. The only way to see was through the telescopic range finder in front of Will. *Once again*, he thought, *Brendan would love this.*

The tank was a lot like a submarine, a tight maze of protruding metal, endlessly complex and requiring careful movement to navigate. Volnheim took the gunner's seat. Jerry took the commander's seat behind him, so he could keep tabs on the Nazi. Felix got in the mortar seat below. Cordelia and Eleanor scrunched together uncomfortably in the radio operator's position.

"Let's go!" Jerry said, closing the hatch. Will hit a button and the tank came to life with a deep thrumming. It sounded like the inside of a factory, and after a few minutes they were moving down the road, past the field where the

Nazis had suffered their losses.

"Farewell, Kristoff House," Will said.

"Can I see?" asked Eleanor, climbing up to Will and trying to peek through the range finder.

"Sorry, dear, it's a tank, not a tour bus."

They rolled through the Italian countryside, with Volnheim instructing Will on how to maneuver the tank.

Soon the sun began to set. Everyone started feeling hungry.

"Is there anything to eat in here?" asked Will.

"In that compartment," said Volnheim. Will opened a small door to find several cans of motor oil.

"Motor oil?!" asked Will. "You call that food?"

"That's the only food we need," said Volnheim.

"Bloody cyborgs," said Will as he slammed the compartment door shut. "And by the way, it's getting too dark to see."

"Just continue to follow the instrument panel, and you should be fine," said Volnheim.

"But what if there's a person in the way . . . or a harmless farm animal?" asked Eleanor.

"We will feel a slight bump," said Volnheim with a mean-spirited chuckle. He was the only one who found this amusing.

As the tank continued on, it got much colder inside. Eleanor and Cordelia were glad that they were sitting with each other, because they could keep warm. Felix could suddenly see his breath.

"What's going on?" Will asked. "My temperature reads zero."

"Zero?" Eleanor said. "We're gonna freeze to death!"

Cordelia explained, "It's Celsius, not Fahrenheit, so it's only thirty-two—"

"That's still pretty cold!"

"This shouldn't be happening . . . ," Volnheim said. He looked at the instruments in the gunner's chair. Particularly the compass. The arrow indicating which way they were going pointed southeast. But it was turning, creeping toward north.

"Are you turning the wheel?" Volnheim asked.

"No!" Will said. "I'm going completely straight!"

But the compass was moving, inching up . . . and then it began to spin as if someone had hit a spring inside. The arrow circled past west, south, east, north—

"What is this? What's going on?" Volnheim screamed.

"You tell us!" shouted Jerry. "Is this some sorta Nazi trick?"

"No! Stop the tank—"

"I've already stopped it! I'm not touching anything," said Will. "And look at the altimeter!"

"What?" asked Cordelia.

Will explained, "It measures the altitude of the vehicle in meters—"

"How did this happen?" Jerry screamed. "Where are we?!"

"We must have hit a seam in Kristoff's books," Cordelia said, "and crossed into another one of his worlds."

"What does that mean? *How do we get off this mountain?*" Jerry looked down to Cordelia, taking his eyes off Volnheim for a moment. The Nazi knocked Jerry's water pistol out of his hand and scrambled through the hatch.

"Hey, get back here!" Jerry climbed out after Volnheim. On top of the tank, he grabbed Volnheim's ankle. The Nazi kicked at him. The two began fighting, grappling, rolling away from the hatch on top of the tank.

"Uh-oh," Will said. Snow blew down on him. "We have

to go, people. And bundle up . . . it's freezing up there!"

Felix grabbed wool blankets for everyone, and they climbed out of the hatch and stared in shock at the swirling snow.

The tank was completely surrounded by mountains. Jerry and Volnheim were rolling toward the front of it, punching and kicking—all while the tank was about to fall off the cliff!

Cordelia was immediately cored out by the cold, as if the Wind Witch had returned to possess her body.

"Come on!" Eleanor yelled. "Let's get off this thing!"

"We can't leave Jerry!" said Felix.

"That's right!" said Will. "We'd be cowards—"

Creeeaak—the tank yawned over the chasm where it was perched. Jerry and Volnheim now clung to the barrel of the 88-millimeter gun, holding on for dear life, only able to kick at each other. Jerry's hands were becoming ineffective in the merciless cold. But Volnheim had no problem. Jerry called to the kids.

"Get outta here! Forget about us—"

Volnheim slammed his boot into Jerry's stomach, nearly knocking him into thin air. The Nazi cyborg then swung his legs up, wrapping them around the gun barrel. Now he was hanging upside down.

Volnheim cracked a smile as he shuffled rapidly forward with his legs along the barrel of the gun, toward the front, causing the tank to tip farther over the cliff's edge.

"What are you doing?" shouted Will to the Nazi.

"What I should have done earlier. Kill all of you!"

Volnheim hoisted himself onto the end of the barrel and started wrenching it up and down, like a monkey trying to shake coconuts off a tree, moving faster and faster, as if Cordelia had the remote and were fast-forwarding. The vibrations of his heavy metallic body tilted the tank forward, bringing it closer to the chasm.

Will saw his chance.

He ducked back into the tank and sat in the gunner's position. He knew that the tank was armed; he knew that firing it was a one-man job. He reached his finger toward the button that read: *Feuer*.

And Will shot the cannon.

Up on the tank, Felix, Cordelia, and Eleanor were blown back and nearly deafened. But that didn't compare to what happened to Volnheim. Since he was holding on to the end of the barrel, he got hit point-blank; he was blasted off the tank into black space and gyrating snow. Jerry, also hanging on the barrel, saw Volnheim get blown into countless pieces of metal, wiring, and gears, as well as a splash of motor oil— and then the shell detonated against a mountain nearby.

It was like a spectacular NASCAR crash in the middle of the Swiss Alps: For a moment, the mountainside was bright as the sun, and Jerry could see all the tiny pieces of

Volnheim fluttering down to the snowbanks far below.

The mountains echoed: *kabooom*.

Cordelia, Eleanor, and Felix landed in snow. But Jerry couldn't get off the gun barrel. And the tank, which had been knocked back by the recoil of the cannon, was now being drawn into the abyss. Will climbed out and crawled toward the barrel, extending his hand to Jerry.

"Get closer! I'll pull you up!"

Jerry reached up—but his fingers were frozen. Jerry looked at his hands, betrayed, as he slipped off the Tiger I.

Will screamed.

Now the tank was going over too, groaning as it slid off the cliff. Will stumbled, trying to leap off—

But it was too late.

"*Will!*" Cordelia and Eleanor yelled.

There was no way he was going to survive. Except . . . Felix was diving toward the edge of the cliff, landing in snow and whipping his German wool blanket forward, holding it with one hand.

The tank fell away, sending out a shower of sparks as it went down and screaked against the rocky cliff face, finally detonating in a muffled explosion below.

But Cordelia saw: *Felix's blanket was tense, like a rope.*

She ran toward Felix. She started pulling his legs. Eleanor followed and pulled *her* waist. They all worked together, grunting and groaning, trying to keep from being drawn off the cliff, and hauled Will onto the white and desolate mountain.

Then they huddled under German blankets next to a snowbank.

"Where are we . . . ?" Eleanor said weakly over the wind.

"The third Kristoff book," said Cordelia. "Whatever that is."

"It looks like a ski resort," said Eleanor. "Remember when everything was good at home and Dad would take us on ski trips to Lake Tahoe? Hey, maybe we're back home. . . . Tahoe's only a few hours from San Francisco. . . ."

"This doesn't look anything like Tahoe," said Cordelia. "It looks like hell after it freezes over."

"Is it just me?" asked Felix. "Or is it getting even colder?"

"It's not just you," said Cordelia. "Look at Will's lips."

They all turned to Will. His lips were blue. His skin was turning white. His eyebrows were flecked with frozen snow.

"We need to g-g-g-get out of here," said Will. "We'll d-d-d-die of hypothermia."

"What's h-hypothermia?" asked Felix, starting to shiver as well.

"Starts with a t-t-t-tingling sensation," said Will. "Followed by b-b-b-blisters, b-blackened skin. You start to get confused, become very sleepy, d-d-d-drift off, and d-d-d-d-d . . ."

"That sounds aw-awful," said Felix.

"I've heard it's actually rather p-pleasant once the f-frost-bite sets in. You p-p-perish rather quickly. And best of all, you leave a perfectly preserved c-c-c-corpse—"

"*Guys,*" shouted Eleanor. "Will you stop talking about c-corpses?"

They sat in silence for several minutes. Sadly, besides corpses, they didn't have much to talk about.

"We should huddle c-c-c-close," said Will. "Use our h-h-heat . . ."

"What's the p-p-p-point?" asked a deflated Cordelia. "I mean . . . there's no way off this mountain. There's no one around to help us. Why p-prolong the inevitable? I hate to say it—"

"Then don't," interrupted Eleanor. "We've come too far to g-give up now. We have to get B-B-Brendan. We have to get back home. And after t-t-t-today, I'll have to start therapy!"

Nobody laughed.

"That was a j-j-j-joke," said Eleanor. "Remember how Bren used to handle stuff like this?"

They all got closer together. Soon, they all began to feel very, very tired. One by one, they lost consciousness in the cold. Felix was first, followed by Will and Cordelia. Eleanor held on longest.

And that's when she saw the shadowy figure, a silhouette

really, approaching in the snow. It looked like a man, a very small man. As he got closer, Eleanor could see that he was wearing a giant fur coat with a thick hood. When the man arrived in front of Eleanor, he knelt down and moved his face close to hers. She couldn't see his features, hidden by the shadows of his hood. She wanted to shout to the others, tell them to wake up . . . but she was too weak to speak.

The man opened his mouth and exhaled.

A thick, red puff of smoke flew out of his mouth. The smoke encircled Eleanor's face. It smelled like cinnamon. And suddenly, Eleanor was no longer cold. Every inch of her body was filled with a burst of wonderful heat, surging through her limbs, reviving her.

And then she passed out.

53

The first thing Cordelia noticed was the smell: vanilla, cloves, and butter. It woke her up from the deep slumber that she, Eleanor, Will, and Felix had been in. When she looked down, she saw that it was coming from a cup of tea. The cup had no handle, but it was covered in soft brown fur, so even though Cordelia's hands were wrapped around it, she wasn't burning her palms. *That's nice*, she thought.

The steam from the tea was so strong and delicious that it made her lightheaded. The beverage seemed too hot to drink. She let it warm her for a moment before she looked around to see where she was. A room with red stone walls. A huge fireplace with a roaring fire. Animal pelts and antlers on the wall, and on the floor, a rug that might have once belonged to a buffalo. She was sitting on it, wrapped in a thick wool blanket, surrounded by Eleanor and Will and Felix, who likewise held cups of tea in their hands.

Cordelia suddenly had a flash of worry and checked her back pocket. Yes, there it was, damaged by the snow: Eliza May Kristoff's diary. She had to get it open as soon as she could.

"Ahem," said a voice above her.

Standing over Cordelia was a stooped man with craggy, tan features. He wore a woolly tunic, and underneath, pants adorned with red feathers. He was completely bald, and his cheeks were sprinkled with chunky moles. White, whisker-like hairs, over two inches long, stuck out of the moles.

"Ahhhh . . . ," he said. "The tea does the trick. Every time!"

"Who are you?" Will asked.

"My name is Wangchuk."

"Where are we?" asked Cordelia.

"I will explain everything in time," Wangchuk said, "but first, honored guests, I urge you to relax and drink. I know the journey has been weary."

They all looked at one another. Cordelia and Eleanor were nervous about eating and drinking. Back on the pirate ship in their last adventure, magical steak and fries they'd eaten had caused a bunch of skeletons to come to life. But

Will was already drinking the tea.

"*Mmmmmm,*" he said, and then noticed them looking at him. "What?"

They all took sips. The drink warmed them to the tips of their toes. It was unlike any tea they had ever tasted: laced with cream and honey, rich and thick, as if some world-class chef had invented milkshake tea.

"What's in here?" Eleanor asked.

Wangchuk stood over them proudly: "Yak belly."

"Excuse me?"

"We scrape the fat from a yak's stomach—"

Pffffft—Eleanor spat her tea back into the cup.

"What's the matter?" Wangchuk said.

"*Yak belly?*" said Eleanor. "That's totally gross! And what if the *yak* was eating something gross too?!"

"Yak-belly tea is served to only our most distinguished and honored guests," said Wangchuk. "I've even added two special ingredients to make it more delicious."

"What's that?"

"Monkey sweat—"

Now Cordelia spat her tea back into its cup.

"And donkey spit."

Will dropped his cup to the floor. Only Felix was left happily gulping the tea.

"Oh, I see," said Wangchuk. "None of you are accustomed to our . . . rather exotic food. But we only want to please you. We've been waiting so long for you. That's why my brothers and I braved death to get you off the mountain."

"What brothers?" asked Felix.

"Why, the monks of Batan Chekrat," Wangchuk said. "Who else?"

"You'll have to pardon us," Cordelia said. "We're not that familiar with this book—I mean, this part of the world."

"And why have you been waiting for us?" asked Eleanor. "How did you even *know* about us?"

"Because of the prophecy."

"What prophecy?" Will said.

"Legend has it," said Wangchuk, "that a band of warriors will one day arrive and help us defeat the frost beasts."

"*Frost beasts?*" Cordelia asked.

Wangchuk clapped his hands, five times in a specific rhythm, and barked: "*Brothers!*"

A door at the back of the room opened. A dozen monks—who were dressed like Wangchuk, their pants adorned with white feathers instead of red ones—quickly filed in and sat down by the fire. What was curious about them was that they didn't look very similar to Wangchuk. Some looked European, some Asian, some African; they looked like they had come from all over the world, or had been handpicked by a reality television show to represent all possible nationalities. They were also different ages, young and old. But they had two noticeable things in common: shaved heads and a musty, lived-in smell, like a pair of jeans worn three days in a row.

"Please direct your attention to the opposite wall," Wangchuk said.

Cordelia and the others turned. The leaping firelight cast shadows on the wall. The monks extended their arms in front of the flames, bringing their hands into very precise positions . . . and suddenly, shadows took shape, forming the perfect silhouette of a tall mountain, with a castle perched on top.

"Wow," Eleanor said.

"This is the monastery of Batan Chekrat," Wangchuk said. The monks fluttered their hands and the castle-shadow vibrated. It was really quite spectacular. "The highest monastery in the world. Built three thousand years ago by the Gautama Buddha."

The shadows of the monks' arms shifted shape to become the familiar fat silhouette of the Buddha, then slipped back into the monastery image.

"Gautama Buddha founded no other monasteries during his long life. This is a sacred and singular place. But soon after it was built, the frost beasts attacked."

The arms of several monks contorted. The shadow of the monastery transformed into three nasty shadows. Each one looked like the offspring of the abominable snowman and a werewolf, with oversize arms, stubby legs, and mounds of muscles, covered in hair. Cordelia looked at the monks casting the shadows. They were creating these hairy silhouettes using the hair on their own arms and hands. It was one of the few things Cordelia could think of that was a good use for hairy hands.

"The frost beasts come at night," Wangchuk explained. "They're over ten feet tall and ferocious, with blood that runs cold as ice. If they so desired, they could scale the walls of the monastery and kill us. But by letting us live, they ensure a more steady food source."

Two of the monks twisted their hands into the shapes of yaks, which looked like big, shaggy cows. They moved the shadow yaks outside the shadow monastery, where the frost-beast silhouettes snatched them up. Then they made caterwauling yak noises to establish their point.

"You feed them *yaks?*" Eleanor asked. "That's terrible! Poor yaks!"

"Unfortunately, it isn't enough," Wangchuk said. "Every month we are also forced to give them two members of our order. As a sacrifice."

"Oh no!" said Eleanor. The monks now created the shadows of monks themselves, who were tossed out of the monastery and caught in midair by the frost beasts.

"Yes," said Wangchuk in a quiet voice. "The frost beasts love human flesh most of all. But they are a primitive species, lacking in certain skills . . . for instance, they have no idea how to create fire. So they bring their human meals to their cave"—now the monastery became an overarching cave made of interlocking arms—"where they eat them slowly. And raw. One limb at a time."

The monks moved closer to the fire, which made the shadow beasts appear much larger. The wall became an abstract combination of silhouettes, hungry mouths, and razor-sharp teeth. The monks made chewing and crunching noises, followed by slurping sounds, like a person trying to get every last bit of meat out of a chicken bone.

"These monks have a bit too much time on their hands," whispered Will.

"This is the most horrible thing I've ever heard," Cordelia said to Wangchuk. "You just stand back and let these monsters eat you every month? How can you live with yourselves?"

"We have no choice," said Wangchuk.

"You could fight back," said Felix.

"No. Fighting is against our code of conduct. We are peaceful men."

"You are cowardly men," said Felix.

"I would not expect you to understand," said Wangchuk. "But you must accept that is the way of our order. To accept what we cannot control, and to persevere."

"But there have to be some people around here who *can* fight," Eleanor said. "Like warriors or soldiers, living outside the monastery . . ."

"We are all alone on this mountain," said Wangchuk. "There is no way to get here, except through the Door of Ways."

"Door of Ways? What's that?" Eleanor asked.

"It's deep inside the frost beasts' cave," said Wangchuk. "Deep in the mountain: a magical portal to the outside world."

"A way out?" asked an intrigued Cordelia.

"A way in," said Wangchuk. "Every year, monk initiates who want to join our order come through it from faraway lands. But very few make it through the frost beasts' cave and to the front gates without getting eaten."

"Why would anybody ever want to be a monk here?" asked Cordelia.

"Because we have enlightenment here," Wangchuk said. "True peace, through meditation. And besides: *Now you are here.* Our traveling warriors. *You* shall rid us of the frost beasts."

Cordelia, Eleanor, Will, and Felix glanced at one another. They weren't sure who was going to speak first. Then Felix said, "Very well. Where are these beasts? I'll show you cowards how to fight!"

"Wait a minute, hold on," Cordelia said. "We hate to tell you this, Mr. Wangchuk . . . but we're not the warriors you're waiting for."

"Yeah," Eleanor said, "we're just kids trying to get home."

"That can't be true," said Wangchuk. "First of all, you came here without using the Door of Ways, which no one has ever done. Secondly, you came with a war machine. I saw it with my own eyes. It's at the bottom of the chasm."

"That's called a tank, and it isn't ours," Cordelia said. "It belonged to the Nazis. And we don't ever want to see them again." *Although . . . ,* she thought.

"But without a war machine, how will you fulfill the

prophecy?" Wangchuk asked.

"Please, mate," Will said. "Stop babbling nonsense. They're telling you the truth."

Wangchuk paused, as if pondering this, and sighed.

"Then I'm afraid we have only one choice," he said.

"What's that?"

"To feed you, shelter you, and provide you with a warm bed."

"Sounds like a spectacular idea," said Will, grinning in relief. "As you said, we're rather exhausted."

"However," said Wangchuk, "it is written that only *warriors* who protect our monastery may be given shelter. All others must join the order of the monks."

"Fine," said Will. "What do we need to do? Say some prayers? Drink tea made of goat vomit?"

"Shave your heads," said Wangchuk, before turning and shouting: "*Brothers!*"

All the monks stood up in a flash, pulling out rusty scissors and sharp razor blades. They grabbed Cordelia, Eleanor, Will, and Felix to chop off huge chunks of their hair. Everyone squirmed and protested. One of the monks dipped a straight razor into a porcelain bowl of yak shaving cream and brought it up to Cordelia's head—

"*Wait!! Stop!!*" she yelled.

The monks paused, looking at the kids.

"Okay, okay," Cordelia said. "Maybe you *are* right.

Maybe we *were* sent here to help you. Let's just put a hold on this head-shaving stuff, and we'll start working on a way to beat the frost beasts!"

Wangchuk held up his hand; the monks backed off. As they were putting away their scissors and razor blades, Eleanor whispered to Cordelia, "Do you really think it's worth risking our lives against some horrible monsters just to save our hair?"

"I don't know about you," said Cordelia, "but I've had enough embarrassing episodes at school with my tooth falling out. I'm not going back all bald and Joan of Arc–like. Can you imagine walking down the halls? Nope." She dropped her voice to a whisper: "And maybe, while we're fighting these frost-beast things, we can get into that Nazi tank."

"You want to *go back inside* the tank?" said Eleanor. "What for?"

"To find the treasure map."

54

A world away—literally—Brendan Walker was having the time of his life. Since watching the tank tow
Kristoff House out of the Colosseum, he had done everything he could to not think about what was happening to
his sisters, and Will, and Felix—and he had succeeded. *If
you go to enough feasts and dances,* he now realized, *you don't
have to think about anything.*

First, in the aftermath of the tank attack, Brendan
had dashed back desperately to the emperor. When he
reached Occipus and his mistress (along with that annoying announcer, Rodicus), he told them that the Nazis were
part of a powerful sorcery and had sprung from a magical
book.

"Are they coming back, General Brendan?" Occipus asked.

"Luckily, Supreme Emperor," Brendan said, "I've read the book. And now that they have passed through Rome, these Nazis will never return."

Of course Brendan hadn't read any book; he didn't even know *Assault of the Nazi Cyborgs* existed. But he was getting good at lying. *If somebody asked me now how good of a liar I am,* he thought, *I'd say, "Seven out of ten." But really I'd be lying. I'm a ten out of ten.*

"I wouldn't trust this one," Rodicus whispered to the emperor. "We have reports that these 'Nazis' are right outside the city, perhaps gathering reinforcements. The people are certain that they're coming back with their crack-sticks"—this had become the Roman word for *gun*—"to kill us all!"

"Well then," Occipus said, picking lint out of his belly button, "we will see soon if General Brendan speaks truth."

Rodicus frowned, clearly annoyed.

The day went on and no Nazis returned to Rome. Occipus was overjoyed—and quite impressed with Brendan's predictive abilities, even though Brendan had only been guessing. To honor him, Occipus arranged to throw a feast. Brendan was led into the emperor's Jovian Banquet Hall, beside the Colosseum, and seated at the head of a table that was over one hundred feet long.

The room was arched like a cathedral, with columns depicting ancient Greek legends. The table was made of silver-flecked white marble; when Brendan sat down, it was already filled with roasted pork, figs, veal, cheesecake, goose, rabbit, and boats of gravy. Brendan couldn't identify many of the dishes, but he wasn't going to be rude—he took huge helpings and ate as much as he could stomach.

Suddenly, after all dishes, glasses, and silverware had been cleared, the table began to descend shakily into the ground.

"What's happening?" Brendan asked. "Is it a sinkhole?"

The Roman dignitaries laughed. They were all very familiar with this trick. Brendan felt ashamed for not understanding what was going on, but Occipus patted his shoulder. "Relax, General. Just watch."

The table's top was well below the floor when Brendan heard a gurgling sound. Water began to flood the hollow space, and after a minute, what had been the table was now a long, clear pool. Crawfish, lobster, and trout were released by tiny metal gates, swarming into the water. Slaves appeared with spears and nets and caught the fresh seafood, carrying it away before the pool drained off and the table rose back into the room. Water sheeted off it.

"How did you do that?" Brendan asked the emperor.

"A complex system of hydraulics and pulleys," the emperor said. "And now we're ready for the second course."

"Wait? All that stuff I ate . . . that was all just one *course*? How many courses are there?"

"Twelve."

"What? Are you kidding me?" Brendan was genuinely worried about being able to eat that much, plus he felt a little guilty. He didn't deserve this—and where were his sisters? And Will? Did the Nazis get to them? . . . No, he couldn't think about that. Hopefully Felix had defended them. He seemed tough enough.

By the time the fourth course was delivered, Brendan was having a difficult time swallowing. His waist had expanded several inches. He was feeling sick. The luxuries of the Roman feast were starting to look disgusting to him. *I gotta get out of here*, he thought. *I have to find my sisters. I never should have left them.*

Brendan stood up to leave—but Occipus gently sat him down. "Where are you going? Don't you want to see the juggler?"

A juggler carrying several lit torches appeared. Behind him, the slaves brought in course number five—stuffed doves—and as the juggler started juggling the torches, Brendan noticed the huge armed guards who stood at each door. *Like those guards would ever let me leave. I'm trapped!*

But a strange thing happened as the meal went on. Brendan began to enjoy himself again. All he had to do was force himself not to think about his family. It wasn't easy, but as he spoke to the other people at the table, and they seemed genuinely excited to meet him, and looked at him with sparkling eyes because he was so interesting, he found it easier. The reactions he got from the Romans were the exact opposite of those he got from people like Scott Calurio. People respected him here. And wasn't that why he had stayed? Hadn't he argued to his sisters that this was the better life for him? He couldn't go back on his word.

At the end of the feast, the conversation turned to music. Several guests were asked to perform a song for the emperor. The performances were out of tune, warbly, and operatic. When it was Brendan's turn to sing, he knew he could outdo everyone. He stood up and began a sing-along of his dad's favorite song, Bruce Springsteen's "Glory Days." He felt a bit melancholy at first, singing something that reminded him so much of his father; Brendan and Dr. Walker had sung "Glory Days" together when it was just the two of them in the car, nobody to judge. But then Brendan remembered: *That was a long time ago, in a different time and place. Why should I be missing Dad now? He only thinks about himself these days. I'll bet he's still back in San Francisco gambling our money away. Meanwhile, I'm the hottest thing in Rome.*

The Romans loved Brendan's performance. They applauded wildly, asking him to sing the song again and again. After the fifth performance, which lasted for fifteen minutes, Occipus declared "Glory Days" to be Rome's new national anthem.

"You'll go down in history!" he told Brendan. "A great singer *and* a great warrior!"

Then things started getting weird.

55

The feast ended. The guests stumbled out. Brendan tried to exit with Occipus, but a freakishly muscular slave with intricate, gory tattoos grabbed him. The slave pulled Brendan aside.

"What are you doing?" Brendan asked. "Get your hands off me!"

"No, no, it's all right, General," said Emperor Occipus. "This is Ungil. He's to escort you to your room."

"I thought I'd be staying in the Royal Bedrooms. . . ."

"Brendan, Brendan," said the emperor, "you're to be a great warrior—and great warriors don't sleep in the Royal Bedrooms."

"Why not?"

"Because great warriors *don't sleep.*"

"Huh?!"

Ungil grabbed Brendan's elbow and pulled him out of the Jovian Banquet Hall. The last thing Brendan saw was the emperor waving good-bye. Ungil led him to a winding stone staircase that smelled like burned, rotten eggs. Then he pulled off Brendan's Roman sandals and threw them away.

"Hey! Stop! Where are you taking me?" Brendan demanded, but Ungil didn't answer—and then two more ridiculously muscle-bound slaves approached, holding knives to Brendan's throat.

"Keep yer mouth shut, boy," one of them said.

Brendan descended the smelly steps. He noticed water seeping out of the walls, dribbling over the sharp stones; the water stank. He must be near some underground sulfur spring. And he was only going deeper.

The staircase brought Brendan to a hallway from which different bedchambers branched off. But these looked nothing like the Royal Bedrooms that Brendan stayed in the night before. They were small, barred spaces with no beds to speak of, containing large jars for human waste.

"This is a dungeon!" Brendan protested. Ungil and the slaves laughed as they moved him along.

The barred rooms seemed empty at first, but as Brendan went past, people called out: *"Fresh meat!"* "Where'd *they find you, at the baths?"* One of the cell occupants, a sinewy man with long, shaggy hair and a black beard, ran up to the bars and taunted Brendan: *"Is this what they call a gladiator these days? A skinny, soft little baby? Go back to yer mother's milk, sonny!"* Some of the others stayed back, restrained by metal cuffs or strapped to wooden beams. Brendan gasped at one man who was hanging upside down, whimpering.

"Here you go," Ungil said as he opened the last cell in the corridor. "This'll make you a gladiator in no time."

Brendan squirmed, trying to release himself from Ungil's grip, which was impossible. "I changed my mind! I'm not a warrior! Let me out! I don't belong with these people! I'm not like Felix—"

Ungil slapped him. Brendan jumped back.

"Felix the Greek was trained by me. And now Occipus wants me to train you. And the emperor's wish is . . ."

Ungil let the actions of his fellow slaves finish the sentence. They pulled Brendan inside the cell and turned him upside down, clamping his ankles into manacles that hung from the ceiling.

"No, no!" Brendan said. "What is this? Is this 'inverted noggin training'?! You can't put me through that. I'll black out!"

"You'll die, in fact," said Ungil, "but we'll come in and rotate you periodically so the blood doesn't flood your brain. And you won't black out. The pain will keep you from doing that."

"What pain?" asked a terrified Brendan.

Ungil reached into a miniature barrel stored in a corner of the cell. He pulled out a handful of stinky soft cheese.

"What are you—*ugggh!*" Brendan said.

Ungil smeared the cheese on Brendan's face. Huge soft chunks entered his mouth. The cheese tasted like the bottom of an old compost bin.

But Ungil wasn't finished. He and his fellow slaves dug their hands into the barrel and coated Brendan's entire body with the pungent, repugnant cheese.

The smell was unbearable; Brendan felt as if he were going to upchuck all twelve courses of his recent meal. But Ungil still wasn't finished. He tied a blindfold around Brendan's cheesy, upside-down head; one of the other slaves handed Brendan a short sword.

"What's this?" Brendan asked—but he quickly figured it out and started swinging wildly, trying to get the slaves, who laughed. They were out of range.

"Bring him down!" ordered Ungil.

A slave pulled a lever on the wall. Brendan was lowered until his hair (which was covered in cheese like the rest of him) just touched the floor. He continued swinging the sword, but hearing the slaves' laughter, he gave up. He wasn't there to entertain them.

"Release the vermin," Ungil said. One of the slaves hit another lever on the wall.

Brendan knew what had happened even though he couldn't see. He remembered Occipus explaining about a "complex system of hydraulics and pulleys"; now he could hear a similar system at work all around him. Panels in the walls slid away. Ungil and his slaves stepped out. The cell door locked. And Brendan heard the chittering of rats.

An army of them.

"Why are you doing this?" yelled Brendan.

"Gladiators need to rely on their speed and accuracy," said Ungil through the bars. "This is the first part of that training. Cut the rats ... and not your-self."

"But that's impossible—"

"Not for a great gladiator," said Ungil. "Oh, it doesn't happen overnight. Training like this usually goes on for several weeks—"

"Several *weeks?*"

"Until you can kill the rats without leaving any scratches on your body," said Ungil, as he and the other slaves exited. "See you in the morning! Good luck."

The first rat came up to Brendan's hair. Brendan swung his sword and missed, hitting the ground, sending up sparks. Other rats seemed to laugh at him: *Chee chee chee.* An intrepid one climbed up his hair, scaled his face, and went up his chest before it began to eat the cheese nestled around Brendan's belly button. This made matters worse because Brendan was extremely ticklish; as the rat nibbled, he found himself laughing while slashing wildly. He managed to cut the rat in two, but also nicked the skin above his pelvis. As a giant rat started to eat cheese off his eyebrow, he screamed.

56

Meanwhile, a long, long way away, Cordelia, Eleanor, Felix, and Will got a tour of the monastery. They had had a good night's rest on straw mattresses—or at least, better than they had had the night before, when they slept on a bunch of manuscripts.

Batan Chekrat was a grand fortress made of rust-colored rock held in place with frozen mud. In the summer, Wangchuk explained, the snow melted, and for two weeks the land was a paradise of grass and butterflies. But even then the frost beasts did not let up. They still demanded their sacrifices, and their appearance was even more horrible in the summer. They molted, losing great patches of hair all over their bodies, like giant mangy dogs.

Wangchuk showed the kids the monastery kitchen. There they learned that there were 432 monks in the monastery, among them a head chef and two sous chefs. There were seventy-five yaks on the premises as well, kept outside in a walled-off pen that the frost beasts couldn't reach.

"Are *all* these yaks going to be sacrificed to the frost beasts?" Eleanor asked worriedly as they toured the pen, wearing bulky coats that the monks had lent them.

"We eat them too," Wangchuk said, petting a giant, shaggy yak with big wet eyes. "But right now they're our pets."

Eleanor felt sick. She had learned in school that you needed to respect other people's cultures, but it was really hard to understand the monks' customs and eating habits. And although Cordelia and Will and Felix thought yak meat was pretty tasty after breakfast—and were looking forward to more at lunch—Eleanor didn't. *I can't eat yak sausage and yak meatballs when I think of all those poor yaks staring at me with their big, sad yak eyes! I need to get out of here,* she thought, *but first I need to learn more about this Door of Ways.*

After lunch, Wangchuk brought them to the monastery's atrium, which doubled as a library. It was a domed room with rows and rows of ancient books and glass drawers filled with scrolls.

"Do you have any books about the Door of Ways?" Eleanor asked.

"Why, of course," Wangchuk said. "On the top shelf. Over there. But those are sacred documents. Only meant for the eyes of our brotherhood."

Eleanor stared, obsessed with learning more. But Wangchuk was ushering everyone out of the library, telling the "traveling warriors" that it was time to see the meditation room.

This was a large space where monks sat in lotus position every day for hours in complete stillness. The room had a grass floor and warm steam floating through bamboo pipes. It was completely quiet. Inside it, the buzzing of a fly was a momentous event. Cordelia, Eleanor, Will, and Felix joined the meditation. Wangchuk led, instructing everyone to imagine the pain of life as a large red balloon, floating directly above them. With each passing minute, the balloon would float farther and farther upward . . . until it disappeared among the clouds.

During meditation, one of the monks paced around the room with a bamboo stick, ready to whack anyone on their skulls if they fell asleep. This would have scared Eleanor, except she wasn't close to falling asleep—she actually loved meditating!

She found it hard at first; it didn't make any sense to sit and think about a red balloon. But as Wangchuk instructed her to make her breathing very regular, and to *think* about each breath, she slowly entered a clear place where she could see the balloon, and could imagine that it really did hold all her crazy thoughts and pain. "Our mind is the sword that cannot cut itself," Wangchuk said. "I ask you to remove the barrier between your mind and what you are aware of. Banish all thoughts of the past and future. Immerse yourself in the present, in the *here and now*. Only then will you conquer your pain. Only then will you find enlightenment."

Eleanor didn't understand everything the monk said, but she did realize that she spent a lot of time thinking about her past and future, instead of the present moment. It was only when her breathing was slow and regular, and she was thinking, *Breathe*, that she suddenly saw how, right here and now, she was *perfect*—she wasn't hungry (she had found some non-yak tofu paste at lunch); she wasn't cold; she wasn't tired; she wasn't in pain. She missed her parents—but getting them back was something she would do in the future; she wasn't allowed to think about that now. She was only a body breathing in a room, and she was alive, and that was something to celebrate. The red balloon floated into the sky.

Cordelia, Will, and Felix had no such luck with their meditations. They immediately fell asleep, and the monk with the bamboo stick came up behind them—

"Stop," whispered Wangchuk. "They need their rest if they're going to face the frost beasts."

"But master," said the monk, "do you really believe that these four have the ability to kill such creatures?"

"Of course I do."

"But every other time you've told visitors the traveling-warrior story, the frost beasts have killed them—"

"Hush! They'll hear you!"

"They're sleeping!"

"Not that one," said Wangchuk, pointing at Eleanor.

The monk with the stick pushed Eleanor's back. She fell forward, pretending to be asleep.

"See? She's out too."

"Well, don't hit them," Wangchuk said. "These four may truly be the chosen ones."

On the floor, Eleanor was no longer picturing a red balloon. She was thinking, *Wangchuk's a liar, and we're being set up!*

At dinner that night Eleanor had a hard time keeping her mouth shut. She wanted desperately to get a moment alone with her friends and explain to them that Wangchuk wasn't telling them the whole truth, but she couldn't get away from the monks. They were constantly shadowing the kids. While they ate, they asked a bunch of overly nice questions about what it must be like to be traveling warriors. Then Wangchuk stood up:

"Esteemed guests, it is time to see what you will be facing!"

The monks rose from their seats and started leaving the dining hall, which was filled with soft-splintered benches lined up around huge tables. The kids couldn't do anything but follow. They climbed a long stone staircase out into the freezing, whipping cold. They were on top of the monastery walls. And they heard a bloodcurdling roar below.

The noise was almost human, like the sound a person would make if trapped under a pile of collapsed rubble. But it was deeper, and incredibly long—whatever made this noise had huge lungs.

"Oh my God, guys, look," said Cordelia. "Down there—"

Standing directly below them were two frost beasts. The first thing Eleanor noticed were the creatures' huge hands, which were bunched into shaggy fists, pounding on the walls. The frost beasts were covered in an almost psychedelic color combination of blue, white, brown, black, and gray fur; the only place they didn't have hair was at the tops of their heads. Their naked scalps steamed where snow melted off them. Presumably they were burning a lot of calories doing what they were doing, which was beating at the walls, scratching, and roaring. Eleanor looked into their mouths, which were bloody-looking Os, filled with giant, pearl-white teeth.

"They obviously floss," said Cordelia.

"With human innards," said Will.

The beasts continued to roar and pound against the monastery walls.

"Look at the tops of their heads," Cordelia said in fascination. "That spot where they don't have hair? It almost looks like they have fontanels."

"Fontanels?" Eleanor asked. "What's that?"

"They're the soft spots on babies' heads," said Cordelia. "When you were a baby, Mom would always freak out if I got close to your head. Because she said if I accidentally pressed on your fontanel, it could really hurt you—*oh!*"

Cordelia fell forward as one of the frost beasts hit the monastery wall so hard, the whole building shook. Will caught her and pulled her back before she could tumble over the side. She immediately checked her pockets and breathed a sigh of relief. She still had the diary.

"It's not safe for us to be here!" Cordelia told Wangchuk.

"Keep watching," said the head monk.

"Why? You're not . . ." Eleanor looked at the gathered monks. "You're not going to feed them, are you?"

"Perhaps," Wangchuk said.

"Are you going to feed them one of your brothers?"

"No."

"Are you going to throw them one of *us?*"

"Of course not!" Wangchuk said. A few of the monks turned away and went over to a hand-drawn elevator that connected to the kitchens below. After heaving on a rope for several minutes, they pulled out a stretcher made of crisscrossed wood that held something huge and moving, covered in a sheet.

"It's a yak!" Eleanor said.

"Of course," said Wangchuk.

"But . . . he's still alive!"

"Of course. His name is Savir."

"He's got a name? Awwww! That makes it even worse."

It took ten monks working in unison to push the struggling and stubborn Savir up and over the wall.

The two frost beasts caught him in midair.

Eleanor looked away, hearing a squelch as Savir was torn in two.

Then the frost beasts walked off together, each carrying a half-a-yak meal.

"Are they gone?" Eleanor asked.

"Yes," said Wangchuk.

"Are more coming?"

"Not today. But tomorrow, yes. And they'll be demanding a human sacrifice then."

"How many of these fiends are there?" asked Felix.

"Fifty."

"*Fifty?!* And how exactly are we supposed to kill them?"

"We are men of peace," said Wangchuk. "You are the warriors."

Eleanor struggled to hold her tongue: *No we're not! You just made that up!*

"What happens if we refuse your challenge?" asked Will.

"As we said earlier," said Wangchuk, "you will be forced to join the order of the monks. And then, following the ceremony . . . we will prepare you for tomorrow's sacrifice."

"What?" Cordelia exclaimed.

"You—" started Will.

Eleanor cut them off. "So it's finally out in the open, Wangchuk," she said, stepping forward. "You *are* going to sacrifice us."

"Only if you refuse to help," said the monk.

"You're a monster!" Eleanor yelled. "You'd throw all four of us to those things?!"

Wangchuk nodded.

"But I was under the impression you only sacrificed two monks at a time," said Will.

"I'm hopeful that if we give the frost beasts four, they will give us an extra month of peace."

The monks all nodded in agreement. Cordelia, Will, and Felix exchanged shocked glances. But Eleanor took a deep breath. Her plan was taking shape. "Hold on, every-one! I know what we can do," she said.

"What's that?" Felix asked.

"Leave."

"What?" asked Wangchuk. "You can't leave. You'll die out there!"

"Better than dying here," said Eleanor. "We're not fight-ing the frost beasts—and we're not getting sacrificed. We'll take our chances on the mountain. We've survived worse things."

"Wait, Nell," said Cordelia. "Remember how close we all were to dying of hypothermia?"

"What's wrong with you?" Felix piped up. "Listen to this brave one. We'll go out on our own terms instead of being pushed around by these monks. Eleanor has the heart of a great warrior!"

Cordelia looked at Eleanor as if to say, *What are you up to?*

Eleanor winked: *You'll see.*

"If you insist on leaving, I'll let you stay one more night, just to sleep on it," said Wangchuk. "But then, once you step out the doors, I can't help you."

"Perfect," said Eleanor, ready to put her plan in motion.

B ack in Rome the next day, Brendan stirred....
  "Wakey-wakey! Sleep well?" Ungil asked.

Brendan raised his head (upside down) and managed
to mumble a curse. He had spent the night alternating
between fitful sleep, the painful slicing of his own body,
and the slaves coming in and flipping him around so he
wouldn't die. He stank of cheese and was surrounded by
dead rodents. He held the hilt of his sword like a life pre-
server.

"You killed a few!" Ungil said. "I must say, I'm surprised." He entered the dungeon with his two slave helpers
and unshackled Brendan, who collapsed in a heap on the
floor.

"Ah, look at him," said one of the slaves. "He's still a child, boss. All wiry and scrawny? Is he strong enough for this?"

"Of course," said Ungil. "I've trained 'em younger. Pick him up!"

Brendan was carried through the dungeons and back up the stone stairs. Every muscle in his body throbbed with pain. He was plopped down on a bench and given a fork. He looked at the rotten wooden table in front of him and was scared out of his wits: It was crowded with smelly, shirtless gladiators-in-training.

The boys were Brendan's age, but they had hulking, powerful bodies. They reminded Brendan of the people at school he called "scary jocks," like Scott—the wrestling kids who looked forward to staying after school to pummel one another. There was one big difference, though—nobody ever died in school wrestling.

Ungil and the slaves stepped back. Brendan reached timidly for a piece of bread, took a bite—and immediately realized how hungry he was. His fear vanished in the presence of his desire to eat. The table might not have held last night's feast, but it was piled high with roasted turkey, chicken, and beef, and Brendan dug in with the enthusiasm of a death-row prisoner, even though it wasn't breakfast food. The other gladiators-in-training did the same, stuffing themselves with meat. None of them paid much attention to Brendan, and Brendan realized maybe he didn't have to be scared of them. Maybe if he just minded his own business, they would mind theirs. . . . *And if I ever get back home, that policy might work with Scott too.*

Brendan laughed inside his head: *Or maybe no one is messing with me because I smell like cheese.*

Then he got sad—he wished his sisters were there to hear that joke.

When breakfast was over, Ungil took Brendan to the baths, a collection of large underground pools. He stepped into the ice-cold water and scrubbed the cheese from his skin and hair. The water actually felt good, temporarily cooling the sting from the countless scratches and cuts on his body. Following his bath, Brendan was led with the others to a thin hallway with wide slits carved in the ceiling. Light poured in, and Brendan realized he was beneath the Colosseum, in the network of corridors that allowed gladiators to pop out of the floor in unexpected places and keep the games interesting. He wondered if there were any games today, and if he were going to be thrown to the lions. But there was no applause. *That's good,* Brendan thought. *I bet we've been brought here to practice.*

Ungil nudged Brendan up some stairs and handed him a sword. Brendan stepped into the blinding light of day. Squinting, he saw that the stands were empty. The arena had been organized into a half-dozen fighting rings.

Two gladiators were practicing in each ring, sparring with swords and spears.

"Emperor Occipus is pleased to see General Brendan!" called a voice from above.

Brendan looked up and saw Rodicus. Next to him was Emperor Occipus, yawning. Brendan glared at him. Only yesterday he felt that Occipus was a powerful and enviable figure; now, lounging shirtless with a bunch of grapes on his belly and a slave girl fanning his hairless, sweaty body, he looked more like a giant wet slug.

"*Occipus!*" Brendan yelled. "*Why are you doing this to me?*"

"The gladiator dares to speak?" announced Rodicus. He turned and listened to Occipus, then continued: "'The emperor wishes to remind General Brendan that he has been given the highest honor in Rome: the opportunity to fight in the Colosseum!'"

"It's not such an honor now," Brendan responded, pointing to the giant hole in the structure where the Nazi tank had busted through.

"*No one is to look at the hole!*" announced Rodicus. "Now begin!"

Occipus clapped like an excited child as Brendan began his first sparring match.

This actually doesn't look so bad, Brendan thought. His sparring partner was an extremely skinny, weak-looking kid who resembled a sickly King Tut. He carried no weapon and just stared at Brendan with hollow, expressionless eyes. Brendan suddenly felt bad for him. He didn't want to fight this kid, who looked like a refugee from Egypt. He wanted to give him a cheeseburger.

A guard beside them hit a small bell. Brendan took a few halting steps toward his adversary, but then realized there was a big problem here: He had a sword, but his opponent had no weapon at all.

"What am I supposed to do?" Brendan asked the guard. "Just start attacking him? I mean . . . I'm really gonna hurt him if I slash him. This is supposed to be sparring, right? We're not supposed to actually—"

"Fight as you would for the crowd," the guard intoned, and before Brendan could figure out what that meant, his face became an explosion of buzzy pain.

Brendan dropped his sword, held on to the side of his face, and looked at his opponent. The Egyptian kid was smiling. And that's when Brendan realized . . .

The kid had spin-kicked him.

Brendan couldn't believe it. His sparring partner stood in a boxer's stance, bouncing his fists and waiting for Brendan to get close.

"Nice trick," Brendan said, bending to retrieve his sword—

And the kid spin-kicked him again.

It was lightning fast: The skinny boy planted himself

on his left foot and whirled around, bringing his right heel down like an ax on Brendan's temple. Brendan hit the ground, almost knocked unconscious.

"What's up with that?" he asked. "You can at least let me get—"

"'Fight as you would for the crowd,'" the skinny boy repeated, whirling quickly, sending a swift kick into Brendan's ribs while he was down. Brendan thought he heard a rib snap. He held up his hands and screamed, "I give up! Just leave me alone!"

"*The emperor wishes to know what is wrong with General Brendan!*" Rodicus called from the balcony. "*Why will he not use his magic?*"

Brendan saw that Occipus wasn't lying down anymore; he was standing, his expression quite furious. Brendan struggled to get to his feet. A hush rippled through the gladiators as Occipus left his seating area and emerged into the arena to speak to Brendan.

"What is going on?" the emperor whispered. "How is it possible that this ninety-five-pound child from Thebes defeated you so swiftly? I thought you would become the greatest gladiator this arena had ever seen!"

The other gladiators all stared at Brendan, amazed that he was being granted a personal audience with the emperor. One large and hormonally imbalanced fighter, Gaius, cracked his knuckles.

"Emperor, I have to admit something," Brendan said. "The power that I had . . . the magic . . . it came from a book. And the book . . . is gone."

Occipus slapped him across the face.

"*Ow!*" Brendan grabbed his cheek. The other fighters laughed.

"Don't make excuses," Occipus hissed. "And do not embarrass me. I have given you special treatment, believed in you . . . and now you stand here like a quivering little child, telling me *you can't do it?* You performed your special magic two days ago and you *will* do it again today!"

"I understand," Brendan said, deciding to rely on the one thing that had worked for him in Rome: lying. "I misspoke, Emperor. What I meant to say is that I need to save my magic for the games. If I use it now, I won't be able to entertain your crowds later."

"Well," Occipus said, "of course that's reasonable—"

Slap!!

"*Owww!* What was that for?"

"Lying!" screamed the emperor. "Do you take me for a fool? Enough of your excuses. You'll fight now!"

He turned to the assembled fighters: "Who is my strongest warrior-in-training?"

"That would be me, Emperor," said Gaius, stepping forward.

"Lovely," said Occipus. "Then let's begin, the two of you."

A tremendous clang sounded as Gaius swung his sword down at Brendan's head. Only the reflex action of Brendan's sword, blocking, ensured that he still *had* a head. The fighters and guards formed a circle around Brendan and Gaius, to watch.

Brendan gritted his teeth and began to stalk around Gaius, who he remembered reading about in *Gladius Rex*. The brute had a huge scar over his left eye, causing a thick flap of skin to cover a section of his eyeball, giving him an obstructed view. Brendan knew that if he triangulated his left-hand side, he'd be able to sneak in a blow. But Brendan found it difficult to concentrate. *How did I get here?* he thought suddenly. *I should have stayed with Deal and Nell—are they even thinking about me? Do they even miss me? Probably not, because I've been such a horrible brother—*

Gaius lunged forward, nearly slicing Brendan's stomach open. *If that were an inch closer, my guts would be spilling out,* Brendan thought—and then he had a sudden, certain realization.

This isn't like the other night with the Wind Witch. This time I won't be coming back to life. This time it's really over.

The thought came to him from a numb, flat place. A dull blur seemed to hover in front of him.

"I'm sorry," Brendan said to no one—or to everyone. He was speaking to his sisters, to Will, to Felix—to his mom and dad. His simple words didn't do justice to his thoughts, which looped: *I'm sorry, Mom, I'm sorry, Deal, I turned into an awful person. I started to think about only myself. And I left you, I left you guys and I miss you—*

"*Brendan! Fight back!*" Occipus yelled, but there was no fight in Brendan. Gaius was stronger, bigger, and faster.

Brendan fell to his knees and dropped his sword. He closed his eyes, about to pass out. Gaius stepped over him—

And pressed his sword against Brendan's neck.

58

Back in the monastery of Batan Chekrat, Eleanor arose from her straw bed in the middle of the night. She had told her sister, Will, and Felix, who had all gone to sleep nearby, that she didn't *really* intend for them to walk out on the monks the next day. But if they were going to fight the frost beasts, she needed to confirm something that she suspected. And she was going to do that now. She started to tiptoe out of the room when she heard "*Psst! What are you doing?*"

Cordelia was also awake, sitting up, with a book on her lap.

"I'm . . . well . . . ," Eleanor started. "What is *that*?"

Cordelia hesitated—but then showed Eleanor the diary

of Eliza May Kristoff. "I'm trying to get it open."

Eleanor took a closer look. "It's by the Wind Witch's *mom*? You *have* to get it open!"

"I know, but the key must be back in Kristoff House—"

"Why didn't you tell us about this? Deal! This is like a huge clue!"

"I know, but it may be a fake. I didn't want to say anything until I actually get it open and read it. I'm trying to use this." Cordelia held up a crooked bobby pin. "But apparently I'm not a safecracker. But more importantly . . . what are you doing? What's your big, secret plan?"

"The library," said Eleanor. "I'm going to see if I can get some information about this Door of Ways."

"You're going to sneak around in the middle of the night to check out a book?" Cordelia said. "You *are* my sister!"

Eleanor smiled. But Cordelia's expression turned serious. "I'm going with you."

"No, Deal," said Eleanor.

"But what if you get caught?"

"There's more of a chance that two of us will get caught than one. Besides, I'm smaller. I'm better at hiding."

"Okay," sighed Cordelia. "Just, please . . . be careful."

Eleanor gave her a fist bump. "I will."

Once she was out of the room, Eleanor snuck through the winding corridors and large, open spaces of the monastery. She thought about how mice move, always staying close to the wall, and tried to imitate that. She thought if she were out in the open, it would be easy to get caught by one of the monks—and to be tossed to the frost beasts prematurely.

She nearly shrieked as a monk with a *huge* forehead approached—then realized it was the shadow of a statue in the moonlight. She arrived at a hallway that split in two directions and tried to remember which way the library was located. After a few moments of deliberation, she decided to make a left turn. She passed two giant doors behind which she assumed there was some kind of indoor yak pen, because she smelled an earthy odor—but then she heard, "*Aaarf! Rrraf! Rraaf!*"

It was dogs. Louder and more vicious than Eleanor had ever heard. And she heard a *thump* as something big threw itself against the doors.

Eleanor ran away. *That was larger than any dog! Maybe it was a yak. Maybe yaks can bark. But no, I could almost hear the spit in the jaws, just like you see on a pit bull. It was dogs! Giant attack dogs! Oh, stop being a baby and stop worrying!! Just keep moving!*

Finally Eleanor came to the monks' atrium and entered. She looked for the shelf that Wangchuk had pointed out—the one that featured books about the Door of Ways—but she couldn't find it in the dark. So she just began examining all the books, checking out the titles: *Martial Arts for Monks*, *Monk Folk Dancing*, *30-Minute Meals for Monks* . . . nothing about the Door of Ways. Then she froze.

There was someone else there, standing by one of the shelves.

"Eleanor?"

Wangchuk. Eleanor was terrified—but she couldn't show it. She had come too far to back down now.

"Yes," she said. "Yes, it's me." She stepped forward.

"What are you doing here?" asked Wangchuk. "You know it is forbidden for anyone to be here after hours."

"I came to learn about the Door of Ways," she said.

"I'm sorry," said Wangchuk. "But that is a sacred subject. The words are not meant for your ears."

"Oh really?" asked Eleanor. "Just like the words I heard today?"

"What words?"

"What your 'brother' said. The one with the bamboo stick. I know this traveling-warriors thing is a made-up story. You've been lying."

"That isn't true," said Wangchuk. "There is truly a prophecy that someday, someone who arrives here will be able to defeat the beasts—"

"And they always end up dead," said Eleanor.

"Well, yes. That has been somewhat of an issue. But it only proves one thing . . . that those who came were not strong enough. But I believe you may be."

"You are so full of it. . . ."

Suddenly Wangchuk held up his hand and shut his fingers and thumb tightly.

Eleanor's voice died in her throat.

She suddenly couldn't talk!

What are you doing to me? she tried to say.

"The brothers of Batan Chekrat possess more than insight," Wangchuk said. "I did not want to use my magic on you, but I also do not appreciate being insulted. Now wait here."

Wangchuk turned and walked to a far corner of the library. He climbed a ladder and removed a book from the top shelf: a large, yak-fur-bound book. He opened it, holding it out in front of him.

"Our sacred text of ancient prophecies," he said. "In it are the words that predict the coming of the traveling warriors."

And as he spoke, letters began to magically lift off the pages. They formed sentences in midair in front of Eleanor.

"Go on, Eleanor," said Wangchuk. "Read. Maybe this will make you believe that I am telling the truth."

All this time, Wangchuk had been holding his fingers and thumb together, and now he opened them.

Eleanor could speak again.

Amazed, she placed her finger on the floating letters in front of her face.

"'There will be *traveling warriors*,'" read Eleanor aloud, slowly, making sure she didn't mix up the words. "'And they shall display remarkable courage.'"

As Eleanor read each word, the letters floated back down and returned to the pages of the book, soon replaced by more sentences. Eleanor looked at Wangchuk, her expression curious.

"Continue," said Wangchuk.

"'These warriors,'" read Eleanor, "'will be greatly rewarded.'"

"That is correct," said Wangchuk. "And the greatest reward is the Door of Ways. I admit I *have* withheld information from you. The Door is not only where aspiring monks arrive. Entering it is the highest achievement for any warrior. And if you defeat the frost beasts, you and your friends will be able to do so."

"But how will the Door help us?"

"It will take you home."

"Are you sure?" Eleanor asked.

"It is very dangerous to be sure of anything," Wangchuk said. "The Door of Ways does not grant its secrets lightly.

There will be a final challenge for each of you. A test."

"What kind of test?"

"Unfortunately, I know nothing about that," said Wangchuk, closing the book. "Now go back to your room and get sleep. You'll need much energy for battle. Unless, of course, you are still planning to leave?"

"No," said Eleanor. "We're going to stay, and we're going to fight. I was wrong about you, Wangchuk. I think you're a good person, even if you're harsh, and kinda weird."

"What do you expect?" Wangchuk said. "I'm a monk!"

"There is one more thing: If we beat the frost beasts, after we go, all of you monks need to become vegetarians. I feel so bad for the poor yaks. I thought monks were vegetarians anyway!"

"We'll consider it," Wangchuk said.

"Oh, and there's one *more* thing," said Eleanor. "We're not fighting the frost beasts alone. You're going to help us beat them."

"Me? That is not possible," said Wangchuk. "I don't fight. *You* are the traveling warriors."

"Enough of that!" said Eleanor. "And we're not only going to need you. Your brothers need to help as well."

"But—"

"Don't argue," said Eleanor, her voice surprisingly strong and commanding. "You have powerful magic. First, you did that cinnamony thing on the mountain, where you revived us when we were practically dead. Then you just made me shut my mouth and not be able to speak—which *nobody* can do. We aren't going to be able to beat the frost beasts without your magic."

"But ancient legend says that the traveling warriors will—"

"I don't care what ancient legend says!" Eleanor said. "We're making our own legends now. And one of the things that warriors do is lead people. So we're going to help you, but only if you help us. Is that clear?"

Wangchuk hesitated, but then a big smile came over his face. "Very well."

"What's so funny? Why are you smiling?"

"The traveling-warrior legend says that there will be one who is greatest of all," said Wangchuk. "One who shall display remarkable courage. And now I know which one that is."

Eleanor beamed with pride.

"Hey, one more thing!" she said. "Do you have magic that can open a lock?"

59

Cordelia was awake when Eleanor came into the room with Wangchuk. She had been up worried about her sister and was overjoyed when Eleanor filled her in on what had happened. With the monks' magic on their side, Cordelia felt the same way as Eleanor: They might actually beat the beasts.

Cordelia gave Eliza May Kristoff's diary to Wangchuk. He examined the book's metal lock and spread his fingers across it. He muttered a few words, in a language that Cordelia and Eleanor could not understand, and the book's lock exploded in several pieces. The cover popped open.

"I think you're tele . . . telkin . . . ," Eleanor started.

"Telekinetic," said Cordelia.

Wangchuk bowed and departed.

"I'm going to check out the diary, just a little, and then we're going to get some sleep," Cordelia said. "I can't believe Will and Felix are still out."

"They're like animals," Eleanor said, nudging a snoring Felix.

Cordelia began paging through the diary.

Her eyes widened as she read. A look of shock and surprise covered her face. Eleanor was watching.

"What?" she asked. "Something important?"

"Nothing," said Cordelia. "Boring stuff. So far it's a real slog to get through." She squirmed inside. She hated lying to her sister, but she didn't know what else to do.

Eleanor knew Cordelia. If Eliza May Kristoff's diary were really boring, Cordelia wouldn't be reading it. Nor would she be staring at the pages in horror.

Eleanor was hurt. But if she had been able to peer into Cordelia's thoughts, she would know the real reason Cordelia wasn't talking.

It was because she was thinking: *No, no! This can't be true!*

As the oldest, Cordelia promised herself she would never tell anyone the horrible secret she was discovering. Her family had already been through enough. *This . . .* this was something they didn't need to know.

60

The next morning at breakfast (yak bacon), Will was having a hard time agreeing with Eleanor's decision to fight the frost beasts.

"It's madness," he said. "We'll be eaten before you can say 'Yorkshire pudding.'"

"If we survive, we'll get to the Door of Ways," said Eleanor, "which will get us home—so long as we pass its test."

"No," said Will. "There's no such thing as this door. It's a fairy story, a whole lot of rubbish. These people will say anything to get us to do their heavy lifting. I don't know why you trust them. There's something very strange about a group of men who live alone on top of a mountain—"

"They're characters in a book," Eleanor said, "just like

you. Give them a break!"

That stung Will. He spent a good part of each day forgetting that he wasn't a true flesh-and-blood person. Eleanor saw his face fall.

"I'm sorry—that was mean," she said. "You're much more than a character in a book to us. You're a real person. And we love you. But you should have some sympathy for these monks. They're trapped here. All they want is to be free."

"I understand," said Will.

"Me too," said Felix. "All I ever wanted was to be free."

"You're right," said Will. "I think one of the things we share . . . those of us who are from these books . . . is this sense that we're trapped. Whether we're fighting a war that never seems to end, or fighting in an arena for days and days . . . it always seems to go on and on, with no end in sight. It's a bit like a curse . . . we all long for something more than Kristoff wrote for us."

"Look, Will," said Eleanor. "You and Deal won't even have to fight the frost beasts."

"What are you talking about?" asked Cordelia.

"I've been thinking about this," said Eleanor. "I can fight the frost beasts. With Felix."

"What?" Felix asked. "Just us?"

"Someone has to go back to Rome to get Brendan," said Eleanor, "so we split up. Two and two. Felix will stay with me because he's used to fighting a lot of creatures at once—"

"Nell, you're out of your mind!" Cordelia said. "You and Felix can't fight these things on your own—"

"I'd like to point out," said Felix, "that I've never fought fifty large animals at once. I mean, I *can* do it. But it is going to be a challenge."

"No kidding," said Cordelia.

"It'll be fine. I'm fast," said Eleanor. "Superfast. And we'll have the monks to help us."

"Are you feeling all right, Nell?" asked Will. "All of a sudden you've become a mini Winston Churchill."

"For the first time in forever, I actually can see a way home!" Eleanor said. "I know we can do this!"

"But can you get your sister to agree?" asked Will.

"It's fine," said Cordelia, giving up. It was hard for her to focus. Her mind wouldn't stop reeling from what she had read in the diary the night before. Every time she thought she wasn't thinking about it—there it was.

After breakfast, on hearing Eleanor's plan, Wangchuk led the kids to the giant double doors that Eleanor had passed the night before. Eleanor got more and more scared as they approached and she heard the vicious barking.

"Don't be scared, brave warrior," said Wangchuk. "I'm about to help your sister get back to Rome."

Wangchuk lifted a wooden bar to open the doors. They all entered—and gasped. In front of them were eight incredibly large sled dogs, rising up from beds of hay. The dogs resembled Siberian huskies, but twice as big. Gigantic bowls filled with yak bones sat at their feet. Their mouths were big enough to consume each of the kids' faces with one quick chomp. The dogs snarled and bit as Wangchuk walked deeper into the barn. They were kept at bay by harnesses, attached to metal posts driven deep into the ground.

"Meet the Batan sled dogs," Wangchuk said.

"What's a sled dog?" Felix asked. "Actually . . . what's a sled?"

"It's kind of like a chariot that's got rails instead of wheels," Cordelia explained. "But a sled isn't as big as a chariot—"

"This one is," said Wangchuk, pulling a tarp off a giant machine.

The sled was almost as tall as the barn, constructed of polished red wood, covered with ancient symbols. Two large chairs, upholstered with dark leather cushions, were attached to the top of it. It resembled the vehicle that Cinderella rode in to the ball before it turned into a pumpkin, only without the pumpkin parts.

"The Great Sled of the Buddha," Wangchuk said. "It will take you where you need to go."

Eleanor hugged her sister while Felix held back. He was afraid to say good-bye to Cordelia and Will, unsure of how permanent this parting would be.

"Good luck, Deal," Eleanor said, holding her sister tight, squeezing her with not only her arms, but with each finger. "Bring Brendan back to us."

"I will," said Cordelia. "Love you."

"Love you more," said Eleanor.

Felix moved forward to hug Cordelia himself. To his surprise—and heart-stopping pleasure—Cordelia kissed him on the cheek.

"I thought you didn't like me that way," he said.

"Just because I don't want to be your wife, Felix, doesn't mean I can't give you a kiss good-bye."

Will rolled his eyes, but he gave Felix a hearty hug himself before he got into one of the sled's massive chairs. Cordelia sat next to him, and they fastened a thick rope (an ancient version of a seat belt) around their waists.

Wangchuk, who held his hands closed to keep the dogs from barking, attached them to the sled's chain with a rope as thick as his arm. Then all eight of the dogs rose to stand in two rows, widely spaced. Ahead, the monks had opened two huge doors that led out of the monastery. There was a straight path leading out of the dogs' giant kennel and into the mountains.

"Remember!" Wangchuk said. "If the terrain gets too treacherous, these dogs have special powers."

"What kind of powers?" Cordelia asked.

Wangchuk didn't answer. Instead, he tossed two

multicolored fur coats to Cordelia and Will. Cordelia caught hers and held it over the edge of the sled with two fingers.

"I don't wear fur," she said.

"It's from dead frost beasts!"

"I'm sorry," said Cordelia, "but I'm totally against it."

"If you don't wear it, you'll freeze to death! And this time, I won't be around to save you."

Cordelia put on the coat and Will smiled; he could see how warm it made her feel. He was standing majestically at the front of the sled.

"Mush!" Will said.

The dogs didn't move. One of them turned to look at Will: *"Rrrr?"*

"Why didn't my command work?" Will asked Wangchuk.

"You've got to tell them where you want to go!"

"Rome!" Will called.

The sled dogs tore off, knocking him back into his seat.

61

Will had never experienced anything like gliding over snowy mountains at high speed. The snow was blinding white, and he had to scrunch his face up; he thought, *I probably look like Wangchuk.* The air was so cold that it cut into his lungs, but it was also impossibly fresh. And the views were so spectacular—the blue mountains patchy with snow, the deep valleys with scrubby bushes like puffs of green paint—that it felt like he'd been lifted into heaven.

"Isn't this wonderful?" he asked Cordelia.

She smiled; Will didn't think she could hear him. The wind was too loud. She looked glorious in her multicolored coat with her hair flowing behind her. Will thought he'd never seen anyone so beautiful.

The Great Sled of Buddha rounded a curve, throwing Will and Cordelia into the sides of their seats. The sled skidded precariously close to a cliff's edge and, just as it felt they were going over, righted itself. The dogs displayed no dismay or deceleration. They were professionals.

The thudding, whooshing snow under the sled and the frantic pace of the dogs seemed to make time slow down, and the sun put Will and Cordelia in such a daze that neither could say for sure how far they had traveled or for how long.

Then it happened.

It started with Cordelia's hair. As the Great Sled took a sharp turn, a huge swath of it slapped Will's face and triggered a sneeze. He emitted a great *aaachoo* into the air (his hands were holding the reins of the dogs), and then something odd took place—

The sneeze didn't stop.

It bounced off the mountain in front of him: *aaachoo!*

The mountain behind him: *aaachooo!*

The one to the side of him: *aaaaa-choo!!*

It continued to echo all around the speeding sled, like some nightmare version of surround sound, an innocuous sneeze turning into something much more dangerous, much more terrible. . . .

Then he saw it, above and to the left.

A chunk of the mountain was moving. There was a tiny black gap in the whiteness. A monumental slab of snow was rumbling toward the sled.

Will yelled: "*Ava—*"

Cordelia finished: "*—lanche!*"

It was moving down the mountain like a cloud, only this cloud had weight that could kill. It was tough to comprehend, because it was just snow; it defied perspective—somehow seeming slow and fast at once. It was the most terrifying thing Will had ever seen.

Will tugged the reins, trying to get the dogs to move faster than the avalanche. Maybe, just maybe, they could outrun this thing. But the snow was getting closer. In a few minutes, they would be engulfed. The sled dogs turned—now they were heading away from the avalanche . . .

Toward the edge of a cliff.

"*Other way!*" Cordelia screamed.

"*I'm trying!*" screamed Will. "*But the dogs . . . they're taking control!*"

The two of them took the reins together, pulling with all their strength, but the animals were determined to go over the edge. The thousand-foot wall of snow was inches from crushing them. . . .

And the Great Sled of Buddha flew off the mountain.

Will would later remember it only in glimpses: Cordelia closing her eyes and putting her arms around him; the snow cascading over the side of the mountain; the sun shining down with uncaring clarity.

But of course what he would remember most were the Batan sled dogs.

They changed.

It was a beautiful transformation, unlike the Wind Witch's bone-cracking affairs. It was as if the dogs had been meant to do this all along. The fur that lined their enormous midsections folded out from under their shoulders—

And formed into glorious furry wings.

Then, in sequence, they all began to flap.

"No *way!*" Cordelia yelled.

Now Will understood the reason there was so much space between each dog at the front of the sled; it was so they could spread their wings and fly. The animals' legs kept moving, running on air, flapping and pawing as they flew over a crevasse far below.

As the avalanche finished crashing over the cliff behind them, they flew through the mountains like Santa Claus.

"Those *are* some special powers," remarked Will in awe, and it was quiet enough for Cordelia to hear him. She clasped his hand.

In a few hours, the scenery below had changed, from white peaks to brown mountainsides to green hills. Then Will spotted something, far beneath him on the ground.

"Is that . . . ?" he asked Cordelia.

"Yes," she said. "Maybe the avalanche represented the same kind of seam between two worlds that the tank went through when we flew up on the mountain."

"*Kristoff House*," said Will. "I'm glad to see you again."

B ack in Rome, somewhere in a dark room, Brendan
woke up and immediately asked, "Deal? Nell?" He
was certain that everything he had been through was only
a bad dream. "Will?" he continued . . . and then the world
flooded in on him and he remembered what had happened
in the arena.

"Sorry to disappoint you," said Emperor Occipus. "It's
only me."

Brendan heard a click and saw a flame above him. Will's
lighter! It was in Occipus's hand, pointing up at his face,
giving it an eerie glow.

"Where am I?" Brendan asked. "What happened?"

"Below the arena, in a sick bay," said Occipus. "Many

gladiators are brought here when they have been pierced or bludgeoned in battle. But you didn't suffer an honorable injury. You passed out when your opponent had you beaten. It was one of the most cowardly performances I have ever seen."

Emperor Occipus let the lighter go out. Brendan was back in darkness. He felt something drip on his forehead and realized it was Occipus's sweat. He tried to get up, but found that he was strapped to his bed, which wasn't really a bed at all, but a stone slab.

"How long have I been here?" Brendan asked.

"Not even a day," said Occipus, "but it has been quite a humiliating day. Word of your failure to fight has spread far and wide. You are no ordinary young man, after all; you are General Brendan, the lion tamer. You skyrocketed to fame. Your name was on everyone's lips until those Nazis showed up. Even afterward, there were many who said that you would be the one to conquer them."

Brendan started to say, "But the Nazis haven't come back, just like I told you, Supreme Emperor"—but then he thought, *No more lies.* Because whatever else had happened, he had been given another chance at life. He had a heartbeat; he could breathe. *There must be a reason I'm still here, still alive. And when there's life, there's hope. Who told me that? Wasn't it Will? . . . Yes,* Brendan decided. *And from now on I'm living my life differently. I'm going to get out of here and find Nell and*

Deal, and find a way home. And then I'm going to tell Mom and Dad I love them, no matter what.

Emperor Occipus lit his lighter and menaced Brendan. "So put yourself in my position. Which is something I know you like to do—I see the way you look at me. I have created a superstar gladiator who has proven himself to be nothing but a liar and a charlatan. My people are now whispering behind my back, doubting me, losing faith in me. They have started to ask questions. There is even talk they are looking for my replacement!"

"If I were in your position," Brendan said, "I would stop these games entirely."

"Why?"

"They're wrong. People are getting killed every day. Not to mention helpless animals."

"I can't stop the games. In fact, the games are the only way I can regain the trust and love of my people."

"How?"

"By making you today's star attraction!"

Brendan gulped: "Star attraction" didn't sound as great to him as it once had. He thought about that *Twilight Zone* episode he'd watched with Eleanor last year, titled "To Serve Man."

"This afternoon," said Occipus, "will be the first and only day in Roman history that I will allow all Romans free admission to the Colosseum. And not just the citizens: the slaves, too. They will all crowd into the stands. I will serve them free, unlimited food and drink. And when all of their stomachs are full, when they have all had enough wine to make them giddy with happiness, you will be led into the arena."

"And . . . ," Brendan said shakily.

"I will make a speech," said Occipus, "as I am wont to do. A very humble speech where I will beg for forgiveness. I will admit that I made a big mistake, that I misjudged your character. In my left hand, I will be clutching a sliced onion. And when I raise my hand to my face, this onion will bring tears to my eyes. Crying always manages to create sympathy. Then I will conclude the speech by making my usual empty promises that can never be fulfilled. But I will be so passionate and engaging, my people will believe every word. And they will trust me again. And then, to wipe away any doubts that may still be lingering about me, I will do something that will restore all of Rome's belief in my power, 'General' Brendan."

"What's that?"

"Feed you to the lions."

63

Will had a plan. He came up with it moments after spotting Kristoff House in the Italian countryside. It was comforting to see the house, to know that they were on the right course flying back to Rome. But something beside the house was more important: an American P-51 Mustang.

"We need to get that plane," Will told Cordelia.

"No, we need to get to Rome and save Brendan."

"I agree," said Will, "but we have no idea what the Romans are going to fight us with. Personally, I'd feel better arriving in a plane with artillery, rather than on a sled with flying dogs."

One of the Batan sled dogs snapped its teeth at Will.

He whispered to Cordelia: "I forgot they could under-stand us. Anyway, I'd feel safer in a plane."

"You have a point," said Cordelia, "but apologize to the dogs."

"I'm terribly sorry. I promise—" said Will to the dogs. He suddenly stopped midsentence, feeling very silly. "*Oh, bloody hell*, this is absolutely ridiculous! Talking to a bunch of mutts!"

All the dogs turned and snapped their teeth at Will. And growled ferociously.

"All right, all right, don't worry . . . ," said Will. "I truly am sorry. Won't happen again."

The dogs ended up landing on green grass behind a hill a few hundred feet from Kristoff House. Their wings folded beneath them and they curled up for some much-needed rest. Will helped Cordelia out of the sled, and the two of them reached the top of the hill and looked down. Below was Kristoff House. Next to it was a bored-looking pilot leaning against the P-51 Mustang.

"Americans keeping guard," Will said. "They know there's something unusual about this house."

"Well, we're not letting them occupy it either!" Cordelia said.

"Relax," said Will. "I've got a plan."

"What's that?" asked Cordelia.

"We're gonna pull a fast one, kiddo."

Cordelia squinted. "Why are you doing an American accent?"

"You'll find out soon enough, sweetheart," said Will.

"It's not half bad," she said.

"Thanks. All of us Brits can do Yank. We learned from your Westerns and gangster pictures, partner."

"That was a little forced," said Cordelia. "That time you sounded too 'movie cowboy.'"

"Just what I had in mind, sister," said Will, now sounding more like a Roaring Twenties cinema gangster.

"You have to pick between gangster . . . and cowboy," said Cordelia.

"I'll stay somewhere in between," said Will. "Now, time to put your hair up, little lady."

Cordelia laughed as Will wrapped her hair up over her head. It wouldn't stay put until he found a twig and stuck it through. Then he took the hood of her multicolored fur coat and pulled it over her eyes.

"Hmmm," he said. "Almost."

He smudged his finger in some dirt and smeared it on her face.

"What the heck are you doing?" Cordelia asked.

"Isn't it obvious? I'm trying to make you look like a boy."

"By getting me *dirty*? For your information, girls get dirty too. We play sports, we—"

"Just bear with me," Will said. He pressed his hand

against her lips. "What is this? Are you wearing lipstick?"

"That's my normal lip color! Leave my lips alone!"

"Oh," Will said. "Oh. Wow. Really?" He looked at her face again. *Darn*, he thought. *She still looks completely beautiful!*

"Hey! You two!"

The air force pilot standing at the plane yelled up at them: "What're you doing?! This ain't lover's lane!"

Will put on his American accent: "Ya got me wrong, buddy! This isn't my main squeeze, it's my assistant."

The pilot aimed a pistol at Will. "Who are you?"

"The name's Marvelous Marcus, Master of the Mystic Arts," said Will. "And this is Jimmy Hobbs."

"Jimmy?" said the suspicious pilot. "He's no Jimmy. More like a Judy."

"Believe me, partner," said Will. "This here's a young man. He's been my assistant for five years."

"Look, buddy," said the pilot, "I don't got time for nonsense. This whole area is US-seized property, and you have point-five seconds to explain what you're doing, before I blow you and your 'assistant' away."

"I'm a world-famous magician," said Will. "I've been sent here by the good ole U.S. of A. to entertain the troops with incredible feats of magic and illusion!"

"Oh yeah?" said the pilot. "Well, I've been stationed here for the last two years, and I ain't seen any entertainment. Betty Grable was supposed to show up and never came.

Neither did Bob Hope. And I sure as hell never heard of any Marvelous Marcus. So get down on the ground with your hands on your heads. Both of you—"

"Let us show you something!" said Will. "Something *so magical, so fantastic* . . . that you'll have to believe us."

The pilot paused, intrigued. Back home, he used to love going to magic shows with his father.

"You're going to enjoy this," said Will. "I promise."

"You got thirty seconds," said the pilot.

Will turned back and shouted: "*Batan sled dogs! Fly!*"

A moment passed. Cordelia looked at Will. *Uh-oh. Is this going to work? Maybe the dogs are asleep, or maybe they're still ticked off at Will for insulting them.*

Then suddenly they appeared, flying over the top of the hill. Wings spread wide. Soaring high in the air. Like Rudolph and his reindeer friends, but a lot cooler.

The pilot's jaw dropped. His eyes nearly popped out of his skull. Will turned to him. "Convinced?"

The pilot could manage only a small, shocked nod.

"Would you like to see more?" asked Will.

The pilot smiled, like a young child witnessing his first circus. Will turned back to the dogs: "Do a few more tricks for the chap!"

"Hold on," said the pilot, "why are you suddenly talkin' like a Brit?"

Will exchanged a startled look with Cordelia. Without

missing a beat, she spoke up in a perfect British accent of her own: "It's all part of the show, mate. When we're onstage, we pretend we're British."

The pilot was about to ask Will why Jimmy Hobbs sounded like a girl. But Will interrupted: "*Fly, boys!*"

The dogs soared even higher into the air. The pilot

watched, amazed, as they began to perform a stunning aerial show. They flipped, doing loop-the-loops, and then dove at an incredibly fast rate. Just moments before impact, they swooped back up into the sky, and the pilot actually dropped his gun and applauded.

Will nudged Cordelia. They sneaked away from the pilot and climbed into the cockpit of the P-51 Mustang. Will started the engines, causing the pilot to turn.

"Hey! What do you think you're doin'—?"

But Will hit the gas and the plane sped off, toward the pilot. He leaped out of the way as the plane went airborne. The duped pilot picked up his gun, got to his feet, and shot at the departing craft, but it was too late. The plane disappeared into the clouds, flying toward Rome, with the sled dogs following close behind.

64

Back in the Himalayas, Eleanor was having a tense moment with Wangchuk. "What do you mean, 'This is it'?" she asked.

The monk shrugged at her. The two of them, along with Felix, were standing in the Batan Chekrat dining hall, staring at a pile of butter knives and spoons.

Eleanor said, "You expect us to fight the frost beasts with *butter knives and spoons?*"

"They're not butter knives," Wangchuk said, "they're yak knives."

"I don't want to hear that word ever again!" Eleanor tapped her finger on the knives. "Look at these! They're not even sharp. We're supposed to be getting ready for a battle, not a cookout."

"I apologize," Wangchuk said. "But yak meat is extremely tender. We don't require anything sharper."

"We. Need. Weapons!"

Felix could see that Eleanor was getting worked up, nearing tantrum-level anger. Since Cordelia wasn't around to put a hand on her shoulder, Felix did it.

"We are men of peace," said Wangchuk.

"We've *heard*," grumbled Eleanor.

"You have already convinced us to join you in battle," said Wangchuk. "You have to be reasonable. It is *you*, the warriors, who are responsible for bringing the weapons."

"And where should we get them?" asked Eleanor, slightly less angry. Felix's hand was steady—and it helped her be, too.

"You came in a war machine," said Wangchuk. "Are there no weapons inside?"

Eleanor could have slapped her forehead, it was so obvious. She had completely forgotten! And weapons weren't the only thing that was in that tank. There was also the very special thing Volnheim had told them about. . . .

"You're right," she said. "Wangchuk, we *do* have weapons. Gather your brothers, some warm coats, some Uggs—"

"Uggs?"

"Snow boots?"

"We have snowshoes."

"Those will work," said Eleanor. "Follow me."

An hour later they were joined by a bunch of monks outside the monastery's great doors, all wearing shoes that looked like oversize tennis rackets strung together with dried yak guts. Eleanor, Felix, and Wangchuk had frost-beast coats, but there weren't enough for everyone, so the others wore yak-fur coats. Eleanor jumped as the doors closed with a thunderous clang. Anything could get her out here. *At least I'm not alone,* she thought, looking at Felix.

"I'm staying close to you," she told him.

"We'll stay close to each other," he said. "I'll watch your back. You watch mine."

"Lead the way, little warrior!" Wangchuk called.

Eleanor started off, then stopped. "Wait a minute—what if frost beasts come?"

"They only come out at night," Wangchuk. "All we have to worry about is the cold."

"Oh. Just that. No problem," said Eleanor. Wind screamed past her face, and she could hardly see with the dizzying reflections of snow all around her. Her nose was running, forming tiny mucus icicles over her top lip. The cold made her move slowly, almost dreamily, and more than once she wanted to lie down and make a snow angel; but any time she stumbled, Felix helped her up, and a monk gave her fortifying tea from a yak-belly flask.

"We're getting close," Eleanor said as they came to the

edge of a huge ravine. Below them was a path leading down, like the narrow donkey path that snaked along the side of the Grand Canyon, which she had seen with her family two years before.

"Look," Wangchuk said, pointing to a mountain beside the chasm, where a large, vaulted cave sat in the rock. "That's where they bring their victims."

A path beaten down by the frost beasts ran up to the cave. Eleanor turned away; she didn't want to think about the frost beasts yet. It was easier to contemplate the long journey to the bottom of the chasm, where she could see a faint discoloration.

The tank.

Or what was left of it.

It took half a day to get down. The Tiger I was epic in its annihilation. What had been a pinnacle of engineering was now a twisted hunk of metal that could be mistaken for a sculpture from a modern art museum. The tank was burned and blackened; the housing was sticking out in several different directions. Snow had piled on top of it, turning it into a striking combination of the artificial and the natural.

"Wow," Eleanor said. "It looks like Fat Jagger crumpled up the tank and put it in a wastepaper basket."

"I hear so much about this Fat Jagger person," said Felix. "When will I get to meet him?"

"Not much chance of that," Eleanor said. "He's in a different book. But I think you'd really like him."

Eleanor turned to the monks. "Okay! So this is the war machine. And what we're looking for are weapons. I'm thinking the Nazis probably stashed their knives, guns, and grenades. . . . We'll look for anything that could help against the frost beasts. Oh, this stuff counts as weapons too."

She dug a hunk of scrap metal out of the snow. It had been blown off when the tank hit the ground. It was torqued and sharp, like a spearhead.

"Pieces of the tank are supersharp. If we come back with a bag full of this stuff, we'll be able to mount it on sticks and make some pretty awesome weapons. So let's get to it! Felix and I will go in first—"

"Wait," shouted one of the monks to Wangchuk. "Isn't this against our code of conduct?"

Wangchuk took a deep breath. "The rules have changed," he said. "We're living by our own code now."

"And we're making our own legends," said Eleanor. She walked up to the entrance of the tank, which was not really an entrance at all, just a blown-open hole, and stepped in.

The inside of the tank was like an alien world, with arcs of metal and coils of wire and stenciled German letters peeking out of mounds of snow. It was graveyard-quiet; the only sound Eleanor heard was the soft pat of her snowshoes. She saw the steering column that Will had used to guide the tank and the massive cannon that shot Volnheim, which was now sticking vertically into the ground. She even saw what appeared to be *one of the cyborg's eyes*—a mechanical orb with gears behind it and a wire leading off. It was connected to a charred battery pack. Eleanor saw a tiny stencil above the eye. It was the same golden swastika she had seen on Volnheim's uniform. *Is this Volnheim's eye?*

"Weird . . ." She picked it up. The iris seemed to be made of mother-of-pearl, the pupil a clear gemstone. Watch-sized gears were placed behind the eye parts. The eye *moved in her hand*, glancing to the right. Eleanor dropped it.

"Oh my gosh!"

"What?" Felix said. He was on the other side of the tank, searching through a bunch of wet dossiers for the Nazi treasure map, which Eleanor had told him to look for.

"This eye of Volnheim's—it's still alive!"

"Throw it away," Felix said. "I'd crush it under my snow-shoe if I were you."

But Eleanor was noticing something. If she held the eye to the left, it kept looking right. If she held it up, it kept looking right. No matter where she positioned it, it trained its gaze on something.

Eleanor followed its sight line. It led to a lockbox in the snow.

The box was black with no writing or decoration. It almost looked like a lunch box from prison. It was secured with a padlock, so Eleanor brought it out to Wangchuk and asked him to use his magic to open it. When he turned aside and spoke a few words, the lock snapped open. Eleanor opened the box and reached inside.

There was only one thing there: a worn, yellowed, folded map of Europe, with a very clear X-marks-the-spot.

"We got it!" Eleanor told Felix. Then she handed him the eye. "*Now* you can crush this."

"What are you going to do with the map?" asked Felix.

"My sister wants to keep it, to try and find the treasure to get reward money and help our family . . . ," Eleanor said. "But I don't want our family to be rich anymore. And if I leave it out here, she might find it. So after the battle . . . I'm taking it back to the monastery."

"To do what?"

"I'm gonna burn it."

65

Will was back in the cockpit of an airplane; he'd never felt better. He soared and dipped, showing off the P-51 Mustang for Cordelia, pulling every maneuver short of a barrel roll to get her to laugh and scream. The sled dogs behind copied his moves.

"Do you realize how lucky I am?" he asked as they flew over an aqueduct with flabbergasted farmers standing beside it.

"No, why?" Cordelia said.

"Because I know what I love!"

Cordelia found it hard to appreciate Will's enthusiasm. Her mind was being weighed on by the big secret she had learned in Eliza May Kristoff's diary. She wanted to tell

Will about it—but she had promised herself to never tell anyone. At least not until the right moment. And she had no idea when that might be.

Will dove the plane and pulled up, buzzing the tops of some oaks.

"Careful—"

"Flying is what I was meant to do! I may never land!"

"Will," said Cordelia. "We can't forget Brendan—"

"Of course I haven't forgotten him! One last maneuver!"

Will turned—and kissed Cordelia. He managed to hold his face by Cordelia's lips for a full second before she pushed him away.

"Will! What are you doing?"

"Cordelia, I need to tell you something," Will said. "We're going to reach Rome soon, and I don't know if I'll have the chance to tell you again. So here goes. I know it's crazy—"

"Will . . ."

"I love you."

"Oh, Will," Cordelia said. "Should you really be doing this now?"

"Why not? Life is fleeting! Surely we've seen too many examples of that lately. I know I love you, and I know how we can be together. We can stay here, in Kristoff's worlds. We don't have to go back to San Francisco. Your modern world is an awful place anyway."

"What are you talking about?" Cordelia said, suddenly feeling like she had to defend her entire way of life. "San Francisco is wonderful."

"Really? With people always staring intently at their phones, fingers tapping? I see them through coffee-shop windows . . . poking away as if they have a disease."

"You're being way too harsh—"

"And what about these places you call fitness centers? All of those people attached to *machines*, running in place like hamsters? What's the point?"

"To stay in shape."

"So why not gather up some friends for a round of football? The point is that people of your world would rather be alone than with another person. But here"—Will dipped the plane and brought it up again, making Cordelia scream—"here we have adventure!"

"Will, stop!" Cordelia said.

"And one more thing!" Will said, completely misunderstanding the terrifying effect he was having on Cordelia. "I've begun to have little flashbacks of my mum. I think Kristoff may have written about her. Somewhere in one of these books. And I'd like to find her, with you—"

"*All right, stop!*" Cordelia screamed. Will gripped the controls tightly and went silent.

"I'm not ready to be with anybody," Cordelia said gently. "I'm not interested in being anybody's girlfriend. I have an incredible amount on my mind and I'm still trying to find out who I am, what I want to do with my life. And I don't know what it is, but it's not *spending the rest of my life living in a fantasy world.*" She sighed. "Not even with you."

"Oh," Will said. His heart felt like it had been freeze-dried and dropped into his shoes. "I see."

"I like you as a friend," Cordelia said. "But I'm not ready for more, and I'm certainly not ready to stay here with you. Is that okay?"

"Looks like I don't have much of a choice," Will said. He was looking for something to help pick his heart back up and put it in the right place. "I guess we can work as friends."

"It's a very contemporary concept," Cordelia said. "A guy and girl, great friends, who love each other."

Will let out a sigh. "I can do that."

Cordelia wrapped her arms around him and hugged him as Rome appeared on the horizon.

66

Brendan's ankles were clamped together with big black manacles and he was being pulled forward by a heavy chain. Ungil—the slave with a face even a mother couldn't love—was in front of him, in the corridor under the Colosseum. Shafts of light edged down from the slits in the ceiling. It reminded Brendan of the gladiator practice he had been through the day before—only now the Colosseum was filled with a deafening roar. This was no practice. These were the real games. And with Occipus's open-admission policy, they might be the biggest games Rome ever saw.

"Please," Brendan said. "Please stop. I have to see Occipus."

"Oh, you'll see him," said Ungil. "You'll be in the arena, and he'll be in the stands. You'll see each other just fine."

"Seriously, maybe we can work something out, if we talk—"

"The time for talking is over!" Ungil said. "Now it's time for entertainment."

Brendan stayed quiet, but as Ungil continued to pull him along, his brain worked a mile a minute. There had to be a way to escape. They reached an iron staircase that led to a trapdoor. Ungil unshackled Brendan's feet. Brendan rubbed his ankles. Ungil pulled out a leather club and slapped it in his palm: *Slap. Slap.*

"Climb the stairs! The crowd's waiting."

"But what about my gladiator training? You said it took *years* to train gladiators. Don't I have to fight some more rats or hang upside down some more?"

"No. *Gladiators* I train for years. People who get thrown to the lions I don't have to train at all."

Stall, Brendan told himself.

"Ungil, I know you're a smart guy. And like you said, it's time for entertainment. But I gotta ask: Where's the entertainment value in me getting taken down by a lion? I mean . . . that'll probably take ten, fifteen seconds at the most. Nobody pays good money for a fight that lasts under a minute."

"Not with you, boy. You betrayed their trust. They want

to see your limbs"—Ungil moved his arms apart—"in two different places."

There. Brendan saw his chance. He rushed Ungil—

And Ungil smacked him down with the club.

"Owww!"

"No tricks, boy! Get up there!"

Brendan rubbed the back of his head, trying to see something other than stars. "Please . . . just give me a weapon . . . a garden hoe, your club, anything. . . . It'll make this event exciting!"

"I have my orders."

"Then what about some clothes?"

"You're wearing clothes."

"This?" Brendan pinched the garment that was tied around his waist. It was a piece of burlap the size of a handkerchief. The only other thing on his body was a dazzling gold wreath stuck down over his head that felt like it weighed twenty pounds. "This is like the tiniest loincloth ever! You can see my—"

"It doesn't matter what we can see," Ungil said, "as long as the crowd will be able to see every bit of you that gets eaten."

"But—"

Ungil leaned in. "I know you've probably spent all your life using words to get out of bad situations. But that's because you've been using words on educated people. I am not an educated person."

With no weapon, in a skimpy loincloth that looked like something worn by a dancer in a hip-hop video, Brendan ascended the steps and entered the arena. His head was down; he was out of options.

He saw the crowd; they cheered. He heard a grunt and saw two lions—but not just any lions. These were the creatures he had made fat before . . . and now they were ripped! They had obviously been to lion boot camp, or maybe Brendan's wish had a cruel twist embedded in it. Their stomachs, which had before been ballooned to gargantuan proportions, were now lean and muscled. Their legs were thick and powerful. And they had a glint in their eyes that wasn't just hunger. *They recognize me! They want revenge!*

The lions were penned inside a metal cage with Brendan, in the center of the arena. One lion was sitting with its paws folded under its chest; the other paced. A metal fence separated Brendan from the lions. Two guards stood outside the cage, ready to pull the fence aside, so that there would be no barrier between predator and prey.

It was pretty obvious who would come out alive.

Brendan saw Occipus, with his mistress and Rodicus, lounging eagerly in the stands. On their faces were the same looks that his friends had when they were passing around their phones, watching some cool new YouTube video. Brendan had never thought about what it would be like to *be* the video.

He sat down.

The crowd booed.

Rodicus called, "Let us welcome Brendan the Brave! Or should we call him Brendan the Betrayer? The boy who—"

Suddenly there was a commotion in the emperor's seating area. Emperor Occipus pushed Rodicus out of the way and stood at the ancient megaphone himself. The crowd gasped. The emperor rarely spoke directly to the people.

"My fellow Romans!" Occipus bellowed. His naturally crabby and froggy voice achieved unexpected heft when he spoke loud enough. He reminded Brendan of Richard Nixon speaking in the Bohemian Club. "It gives me nothing but pain and grief to see this poor boy harmed, for he is only a child! And yet"—here the emperor turned aside, as if to cough, but Brendan saw him rub his eyes with the flat half of a sliced onion and turn back to the megaphone with big tears running down his cheeks—"he has b-betrayed my trust! He has made me into a f-f-fool! What will this do to the enemies of Rome?" Occipus's tears turned to anger: "They will take it as a sign of weakness! They will try to invade! And they will take advantage of dissenters among you who have been questioning my authority. All because of this meddling boy! And so, as much as it hurts me to say it"—Occipus hit the onion again—"the boy must die!"

Occipus stepped away from the announcer's cone as

riotous applause rippled through the Colosseum. But when Rodicus whispered something in the emperor's ear, he returned: "And remember to stick around for *ludi* games afterward. We will be entertained by the famous Cretan mimes!"

The crowd cheered. *Gotta give the dude credit,* Brendan thought. *That was a pretty great performance.* Brendan wasn't moving; he was just picking at the dirt around him.

The guards opened the metal fence.

The seated lion started grunting. It was low at first, but then each grunt got louder and louder, like an engine warming up, until the lion let out a roar that drove the arena wild. The two lions approached Brendan.

Brendan didn't move.

"Fight!" the crowd yelled, and when that didn't get a reaction, they appealed to Brendan's vanity.

"Fight, General Brendan!" "Brendan the Brave!" "You can stop the lions!"

Brendan shrugged: *Sorry, folks!* He wasn't going to give the crowd the satisfaction of watching him fight. It was the only power play he had left.

The crowd hissed and jeered. The lions were as confused by Brendan as the audience was. The animals circled, sniffing Brendan's hair and body. They seemed to assume he was sick, not worth their time. But the crowd egged on the animals, throwing food and sandals.

"Kill him!" "Eat him!"

One of the lions bent down and opened its warm, smelly mouth.

Brendan looked up, wanting to look into the eyes of the animal that would take his life.

And then a strange thing happened.

As Brendan raised his head, his golden head wreath reflected the hot Roman sun directly into the lion's eyes. The lion blinked, distracted, got spooked, and backed off. But as soon as Brendan changed position, the sun's reflection disappeared. The lion roared, moving back toward Brendan.

Brendan suddenly saw how he could save himself. He jumped to his feet, tore the gold wreath off his head, and held it in front of him, moving his hand into the perfect position to catch the sun's rays and shoot them back into the eyes of the lion. Momentarily blinded, the animal retreated again—but the second lion charged Brendan. Brendan spun around and flashed the beam of light into its eyes. The second lion squinted, backing off.

"That's right!" Brendan said to himself. "I'm not done yet, baby!"

The crowd cheered as Brendan continued to keep the lions at bay. He swiveled back and forth between the two beasts, arm extended, holding the wreath like a pistol, blinding one lion for a few seconds, then the other. *Awesome,* thought Brendan. *I can keep this up all day and as long as the sun stays up, the lions won't get anywhere near me!*

But suddenly, Brendan heard a *whzzzz*—something was coming at him. He turned and saw an arrow spiraling in his direction. It was moving too fast for Brendan to get out of the way. But the arrow wasn't coming for his body. It was aimed at the wreath in his hand. The arrow hit the wreath and sent it flying to the side of the cage. Before Brendan could grab it, a slave unlocked a door to the cage and snatched the wreath away. Brendan turned to see who had fired the arrow. Ungil held up a bow.

"Now *that's* what I call entertainment!" said Ungil, grinning.

For once, Brendan had no comeback. Ungil turned to the audience and waved. People stood on their feet and cheered wildly. With the wreath gone, there was nothing to keep the beasts from attacking.

The lions bent their heads, growled, and moved toward Brendan.

Brendan had one last idea. He had seen plenty of National

Geographic shows about Africa and its wildlife ... and one thing he remembered was that lions were afraid of loud noises and clapping. And he thought he had a way to make them hear louder noises and more clapping than they had ever heard in their lives. So, with the beasts only a few feet from him, Brendan leaped up, put his hands together, and started clapping and singing at the top of his lungs. ...

"I had a friend was big baseball player, back in high school," sang Brendan.

It was Springsteen's "Glory Days."

The official theme song of the Roman Empire.

The entire crowd tried to join in. The Romans had heard about Brendan's musical skill and wanted to sing along—but unfortunately they didn't know the words or melody, so what came out was truly hideous noise. Inside the cage, the lions looked around, skittish and frightened by the cacophony. They backed away, cowering in the corner. Brendan took the opportunity to take center stage and start dancing and singing. He had gone to see Springsteen at least five times with his dad, so he knew the Boss's moves, and he knew how to get the crowd whipped into a frenzy.

"I'm just a prisoner of rock and roll!" Brendan shouted, in a perfect rock-star voice. Unfortunately no one could hear him because he had no microphone. The crowd, however, began chanting and demanding to hear what he was singing. Occipus, knowing that he had to keep the crowd

happy, nudged Rodicus, who stepped up to the primitive megaphone and began bellowing out some version of the words to "Glory Days" as he had heard it at Brendan's feast. Rodicus actually had a better voice than Brendan, and that got the audience even more worked up and excited. Eventually, furious as he was, Occipus himself had to get to his feet, shaking his booty and raising his fists. But as Brendan tired, he realized that this could not go on forever. Soon he would have to finish, and then . . .

Death by lion.

He kept singing, repeating the chorus over and over. . . .

There was a loud roar, the loudest yet.

This wasn't a lion.

But it was loud enough to make the arena go silent.

Even before he saw it, Brendan had a hope in his heart who it would be—and then he looked up and saw the P-51 Mustang, and his heart swelled with a flood of joy.

His family. The only people who could save him now.

67

"There!" Will yelled to Cordelia. The sled dogs were still behind them. Brendan was on his last legs dancing in the arena, but he was infusing "Glory Days" with the energy that came from hope.

"*What's going on?*" Cordelia said. "Is he . . . is Brendan pretending to be a rock star?"

"Not for long," Will said, and pulled a trigger.

Acka-acka-acka-acka!

Bullets hit the arena floor, sending blasts of dirt everywhere. The Roman audience gasped as the World War II plane, followed by a team of flying dogs and a sled, dove into the Colosseum and circled Brendan. Everybody was in shock—it seemed that the gods themselves had come to put on a show.

Never one to miss an opportunity, Occipus nudged Rodicus.

"Ladies and gentlemen, behold the emperor's display of aerial wonderment!"

Will circled, steering the plane so close to the stands that the spectators' hair was blown back. He wanted to land in the middle of the arena, but that's exactly where Brendan was standing. So Will steered the plane toward the far end of the Colosseum.

It dipped lower, inches from the arena floor—and crashed.

First, the back landing gear snapped off. Then the entire underside of the plane started screeching against the dirt, spewing sparks as it careened forward. Then the propeller blades hit the ground, bent, and zinged off, spinning into the air, whizzing toward Brendan—and breaking open the door of his cage.

Brendan ran toward freedom.

The plane had stripped as it slowed, losing the wing with the beautiful star on the top before stopping. It was a smashed, smoking mess.

The cockpit door opened. Will and Cordelia tumbled out, coughing. They took off their flight helmets and looked at the utter chaos around them.

The Romans had figured out that this wasn't part of the show. Fearing for their safety, they were streaming out of the Colosseum through the hole the Nazi tank had made. Occipus, in his viewing area, was screaming to his guards, pointing at the plane. On the arena floor, the guards drew their weapons and moved toward it, but Will leaped back inside the cockpit, pulled the trigger. . . .

Acka-acka-acka-acka!! The bullets hit the ground in front of the guards. They scrambled, running for their lives.

"Stop!" screamed Occipus. "*You cowards! Go back! Fight!*"

But the guards followed the spectators out of the Colosseum.

Occipus looked around, seeing that even his mistress and Rodicus were running away. He grabbed a sword and eyed Brendan on the arena floor.

Brendan rushed toward the cockpit.

"Deal! Will!"

He ran into his sister and hugged her. He was more grateful than he had ever been in his life. Cordelia hugged him back—*My little brother.* But the blown-open cage door had created an escape hatch for the lions. They charged—

"Bren!" shouted Cordelia, turning him around. "What do we do?"

The lions were rushing right toward them when Will yelled, "*Batan sled dogs! Attack!!*"

The dogs and their sled were circling above. But as one

of the lions reached Brendan and eclipsed his face, its sharp teeth and rotten breath filling his world—

"Awoooooooooo!"

The lion suddenly wrenched back. The Batan sled dogs had arrived.

In the eternal battle of cats versus dogs, the Batan sled dogs put a win in the canine category that day. They were nearly as big as the lions and there were eight of them. They jumped on the lions and pulled them down. It was a brutal, bloodthirsty battle. In the midst of this—with dogs ripping the lions to shreds—Brendan put his head on Cordelia's shoulder and almost cried.

"You guys came back for me! Even though I behaved like a complete—"

"*Shh,*" Cordelia said. "It's okay. What happened to you?"

"They made me a gladiator-in-training . . . with *him!*" said Brendan, pointing to Ungil.

Ungil was shouting at his guards, frantically trying to gather them back together, but the guards would have none of it, running out with the crowd through the open Colosseum wall. Meanwhile, the dogs had completely dispatched the lions, and Will saw it was time to beat a hasty retreat.

"Come on!" he said. "To the sled!"

They headed for the Great Sled of Buddha, but not before Emperor Occipus appeared, running into the arena with his sword, staring up at the emptying stands, tears—this time real tears—pouring from his eyes.

"My people have abandoned me," cried Occipus. "They're all leaving! It's over for me! My empire is in ruins!"

He turned to Brendan. His face was bright red with anger, his mouth twisted into a cruel frown.

"You're responsible for this." Occipus raised his sword. *"You'll die for this!"*

Occipus ran toward Brendan. Will stepped between them and, with a quick punch to the emperor's nose and another to his gut, sent Occipus to the ground. Nearly unconscious and out of breath, groaning and whining, holding his Buddha belly, Occipus didn't look like much of an emperor anymore. He was just a sad, hurt, weak man.

"Serves you right," Cordelia said.

"Let's get out of here," said Brendan.

Will called the dogs into position and they arrived with the sled. Occipus was panting hard on the ground. Will and Cordelia got into the sled, and Brendan started climbing up—

When Occipus grabbed Brendan's ankle.

Brendan screamed; the sled dogs spooked; all of a sudden the Great Sled was taking off, and as it soared high into the air, Emperor Occipus clung to Brendan, trying to pull him to his death!

"Get offa me, you fat phony!" screamed Brendan, trying to kick the emperor down.

But Occipus hung on as the sled rose higher: "Never! I'm taking you with me!"

Hundreds of feet above the Colosseum, Occipus's added weight was too much. Brendan was using both of his arms to hold on to the sled—but he was starting to weaken, to feel that he might even be pulled apart.

Occipus gurgled and reached up, trying to clutch at Brendan's torso, and he wound up grabbing Brendan's loincloth—

Which suddenly slipped clean off!

Occipus found himself in a weird moment—an almost comic moment, if it hadn't been for the fact that he was no longer holding on to anything solid. He looked at the loincloth in his hand—

And screamed as he fell away from the sled.

Brendan climbed up into the sled. Completely spent. Safe. And naked.

"Take my jacket," Will ordered. Brendan was only too happy to have a cool vintage bomber jacket, even if he was wearing it as pants.

On the arena floor, Ungil frankly wasn't sure what to do. He was surrounded by chaos, screaming spectators, and fleeing guards. No one was listening to him. And then he heard a whooshing sound, followed by the growing scream of Emperor Occipus. He looked up—

And saw the emperor much too late.

Before he could move out of the way, Ungil was crushed with a squelch.

Cordelia gave Brendan a hug. "We missed you so much! Don't ever leave us again. Please."

"I won't," Brendan said, finally letting all of the fear and panic of the last few days out, crying without the aid of any onion. "I won't I won't I won't. I love you guys so much . . . hey . . . where's Nell? And Felix?"

"They're fine," Cordelia said. "We're going to them now."

Before they left the arena, Brendan looked down. It was the last look he would have of the Colosseum—*Unless I go and visit, which I can't imagine ever wanting to do.*

Emperor Occipus was dead in the middle of the arena. The head of Ungil peered up from behind Occipus's shoulder; the rest of him could not be seen. Ungil's eyes were wide open; even though Brendan was high in the sky, he could see that they were big and white, as if they had literally bulged out under Occipus's weight—and they were moving. Ungil was still alive.

Brendan shouted to him: *"Now that's what I call entertainment!"*

68

"Who's going first?" Wangchuk asked.

"I'll do it," said Eleanor, stepping forward.

"No," said Felix, pushing her aside. "It should be me."

Even though Felix stood with his chest puffed out, proud and strong, inside he was feeling uncertain about taking the lead. He did not want to be here, in the Himalayas with Eleanor and the monks in a bulky frost-beast coat. He was accustomed to fighting under the blazing Roman sun. The cold made his muscles feel dense and slow. Nevertheless, they were about to enter the cave of the frost beasts. And he wasn't going to let little Eleanor be the leader this time.

"We can't go anyway," said Eleanor. "Someone has to give a speech. The monks are terrified."

Eleanor, Felix, and Wangchuk faced the crowd. The monks were far fewer than the 432 who lived in the monastery. After different monks had claimed they were too old or had injuries that prevented them from fighting or had a phobia of frost beasts, fewer than forty monks had actually shown up. And they had refused to bring any of the guns, knives, or grenades that they found in the tank! They just stood there with bits of tank shrapnel crudely attached to wooden sticks.

"Who will give the speech?" he asked.

"You do it," said Eleanor.

Felix opened his mouth to speak . . . but he couldn't. He turned to Eleanor and whispered: "I'm not sure this is a good idea."

"It's *not* a good idea, but it's the *only* idea." Eleanor was scared too—but she couldn't show it. "Just get them fired up. You can do that, right?"

"I've never given a speech," said Felix. "I'm not really good with . . . with words. . . ."

"You need to do this," said Eleanor, putting her hand on his arm. "Our lives depend on it."

Felix paused and took a deep breath.

"Look at all you fearsome warriors! If I were a frost beast right now, I'd be turning the snow yellow!"

The monks laughed. Eleanor thought it was a gross opening, but it worked. Felix continued.

"You may not be the most experienced fighters I've ever seen. But you have something that no one can take away from you: anger. It may not be obvious on the surface, but I know it's there, deep down inside you. For years you have been oppressed by these creatures. You have sacrificed your brothers to them! You have watched your closest friends die!" Felix paused a moment, wondering why these words seemed so familiar to him. Then he realized: *I saw plenty of my own brothers die in the arena, all under the thumb of that horrible slave . . . Ungil. And I never had the opportunity to do anything about it.*

"When you channel your anger into energy, there's nothing you can't accomplish! You must attack these beasts as if, with each thrust of your blades, you were taking back a fallen brother!"

The monks cheered in unison, raising their makeshift

weapons high in the air.

"Do this for the memory and the glory and the spirit of your brothers!" shouted Felix.

The monks shouted again, this time louder, more ferociously, and with great passion.

Eleanor pulled on Felix's sleeve and whispered in his ear. "One more thing: They have to use their magic!"

"Oh yes," Felix said. "You must remember . . . we cannot win this battle with strength alone! You must tap into the mystic arts that you have learned. Otherwise we will have no hope!"

One of the monks raised his hand.

"Yes?"

"We have never learned how to use our magic to help us fight. We only use it in meditation and healing."

All the monks nodded and agreed. But Wangchuk spoke up: "Trust in yourselves, brothers. When the time is right, the magic will come."

"I certainly hope so," mumbled Eleanor.

Felix went on with his speech. Eleanor looked at the cave behind him. The wide, tall entrance was big enough for Kristoff House to fit in. It looked too perfect to be a cave. *Maybe the frost beasts made it wider. Maybe they dug little pieces out bit by bit over the years to turn it into their home. Maybe they're smart,* Eleanor thought. *And if they're smart . . .*

Felix was still talking. "Hold on to your weapons. They

will be your greatest allies in this battle. Never give up. And most importantly, never back down. Remember: You are no longer the monks of Batan Chekrat. You are the *warriors of Batan Chekrat!*"

The monks raised their shrapnel sticks high over their heads and cheered louder than ever. Felix flushed with pride; the only way he'd ever known to please a crowd was through fighting, but here he'd done it with words. He smiled at Eleanor, who had helped show him what words could do.

The two shared a heartfelt look—

And the frost beasts attacked.

They didn't come out of the cave as anyone expected. With bloodcurdling roars, three of them jumped down from *above* the entrance. *They* are *smart!* Eleanor thought. *They were hiding!*

The first was the leader, six feet taller and wider than the other two. The beast continued its strangled-human cry as it hit the ground in front of the monks. Then it beat its fists against its chest, before snapping its face upward. The beast's mouth opened wide, baring all its sharp white teeth.

"*Braaaaaoaar!*"

It was a threat display, and it worked. Eleanor huddled behind Felix, her heart pounding. If he hadn't been there she would have run away, possibly tumbling down the mountain, never to return. Ten of the monks *did* run away, bolting back toward the monastery as fast as they could on the path the frost beasts had made in the snow.

The other two beasts, standing beside the leader (who Eleanor thought of as "Broar" because of the sound he had made), copied him by beating their chests and roaring. As Eleanor was forcing herself to be brave, remembering that this was her idea, she noticed what Cordelia had pointed out before: the tops of the frost beasts' heads, where there was no hair. It really *did* look like they had baby soft-spot fontanels, very pink and thin. She thought, *I wonder what would happen if I got one of the frost beasts right in the fontanel?*

"Attack!" Felix called.

But Broar attacked first, slamming his paw into a monk, sending him flying backward, tumbling down the mountain. The beast behind him turned to Felix, who whirled around and swung his knife, slicing the creature's paw. The third beast slashed at Felix's side; Felix swirled and jabbed like a small whirlwind as the monsters surrounded him.

"Save him!" Eleanor called, raising her weapon, and the monks charged.

Wangchuk was the one who surprised Eleanor most. He had more courage inside him than his wrinkled skin would let on. Now his mouth was frozen in a battle cry as he rushed forward with a dozen monks behind him. They all plunged into the two lesser frost beasts, burying their makeshift weapons in the animals' backs. Eleanor, who had kept a knife from the tank, jumped onto one of the frost beasts' legs and started to climb upward.

The beasts turned from Felix and attacked the monks. They used their enormous arms the way a human might sweep ants off a table, sending their assailants stumbling, rolling several of them down the mountain, jabbing others—

But Eleanor didn't give up.

She continued to climb up the frost beast's back, determined to get to its shoulders. She grunted and hissed and gritted her teeth. The creature roared and grabbed for her—but like a pesky itch, Eleanor stayed in the center of its back, where the beast couldn't reach her.

"Eleanor!" Felix yelled. He was having his own problems ducking and weaving, trying to avoid Broar's swinging arms. "What are you doing?"

"Their heads are the weak spots!" Eleanor yelled. "Aim for the fontanels!"

Eleanor's beast reached up and grabbed her, squeezing her torso. But Eleanor held up her knife even as the creature began to squeeze its hands around her, crushing her insides. . . .

She plunged her blade down.

The beast's eyes rolled back. Its legs went out from under it. It loosened its grip on Eleanor and fell forward.

Eleanor rode its shoulders the entire way down—

and when the beast hit the ground with a loud *KER-THUNNKKK!*, she flew off and rolled into a snowdrift.

Eleanor sat up, momentarily dazed. Directly in front of her, the frost beast lay sprawled on the ground.

Completely still.

Completely dead.

Felix turned back and continued to battle Broar.

"*Rrragh!*" the giant frost beast bellowed, diving at Felix like a major-league shortstop. Felix jumped, aimed his knife down—

And pierced the beast's head.

Broar gave a raspy breath, tried to reach up and wrench the knife out—but it was too late.

He went limp and collapsed beside the body of his subordinate.

Eleanor and Felix looked at the two fallen frost beasts in front of them. Each creature's fur shimmered and rippled, looking momentarily like an oil slick floating on water, and then went still. The third frost beast turned on his big ape feet and ran into the cave.

"Are you okay?" Felix asked Eleanor. "Are you hurt?"

It took a moment for Eleanor to catch her breath.

"No. I'm not okay. It's horrible to have to do this . . . I don't ever want to hurt a living thing again. My heart won't stop beating—I—I . . ."

"Maybe they're scared of us now," Felix said, hugging

her. "You saw that one run away from us. . . . Maybe the battle is over. Your plan worked! And you were so brave."

"*Is* it over?" asked Wangchuk. "I pray that's true. We lost ten brothers."

"There are always losses in battle," Felix said solemnly. "We just have to be ready for what's next."

"I am trying . . . ," Wangchuk said, but then his voice trailed off as he saw something behind the gladiator.

"What?"

"I'm not sure we *can* be ready for what's next."

"Why?"

"Because it's that."

Wangchuk pointed.

A dozen frost beasts had stepped out of the cave.

They were groggy, yawning, until they saw the humans in front of them. Then their faces changed into masks of animal predation. They huffed in the freezing air. Mist came out of their nostrils. They were a terrifying sight, but Wangchuk refused to back away.

"Come, brothers!" he said. "We must fight for our home!"

They all charged.

Twenty monks and a dozen frost beasts met in front of the cave. It was like gasoline meeting fire. The monks battled the beasts, slashing at the creatures' ankles and knees with their spears, trying to get them to fall so they had access to their sensitive fontanels.

But the frost beasts were bigger, stronger, faster . . . and had their ferocious claws and teeth always moving, jabbing, spinning. They cut several monks down, while picking up others and devouring them in a few nasty bites.

Eleanor took a deep breath, thinking: *I can do it! For Mom, for Dad, for Cordelia and Brendan!*

She climbed onto the back of a creature, avoiding its slashing claws, but as she reached the top of its head, she was knocked to the ground by another beast. Lying in the snow, her mind spinning, she managed to roll away from the stomping feet of the creatures. When she looked up, she saw the big picture of what was happening.

The frost beasts were winning.

The bodies of several monks lay on the ground. Others were being shoveled into the frost beasts' mouths. Felix was holding his own, keeping them away from him, but Wangchuk was surrounded, slashing blindly. There was an enormous cut on his forehead and blood streaming into his eyes. *He's spent most of his life meditating, performing shadow plays, and drinking tea,* Eleanor thought. *What were we thinking, forcing monks to fight? Fighting is supposed to be a last resort!*

Suddenly, Wangchuk fell to his knees and dropped his weapon.

"Wangchuk! No! Use your magic!" Eleanor called.

But the frost beast was too fast. The creature lifted

Wangchuk, bit off the top half of his body, and swallowed him whole.

"*Noooooo!*" Eleanor screamed.

The angry frost beast threw the lower half of Wangchuk's body into the snow.

At this rate, all the monks would be dead within minutes.

But then something very strange happened.

Eleanor watched as the frost beast stopped moving. The creature grimaced, growled, and clutched its stomach in tremendous pain. Swirling red smoke began to seep from its ears, nostrils, and particularly large belly button. The smoke had a familiar smell to it. Cinnamon and vanilla.

"Wuh . . . ?" Eleanor managed—but now she could hardly hear herself. The frost beast was screaming in agony, its body beginning to expand. Its arms, legs, and belly swelled up as if it were being inflated by a gas-station air pump. And then there was a loud—

Bannnggg!!!

The frost beast exploded into a million pieces. Chunks flew everywhere. And all that was left behind, propped up in the snow, was . . .

The upper torso of Wangchuk.

Very much alive.

And smiling.

Smoke spiraled out of Wangchuk's mouth, moving

toward the ground, to the lower part of his body. Eleanor watched the red smoke swirl around Wangchuk's detached legs and feet. Within seconds, the monk's lower torso and legs stood up. Then Wangchuk's upper body rose from the snow and floated, descending toward his lower half—

And *reattached itself.*

Soon, the smoke dissipated and Wangchuk was whole again. No trace of being bitten in half.

"Wangchuk!" Eleanor screamed. "You're . . . all together again!"

"Thanks to you!" said Wangchuk. "In the heat of the battle, I found the magic!"

That's when Eleanor heard another *bannngg!*

She turned and saw the last bits of an exploding beast. Inside, floating in midair, were a few sections of an eaten monk. Within seconds, red smoke began to swirl around the monk pieces and his body parts re-formed.

Banngg! Banngg! Banngg! Frost beasts were exploding all around them, and the monks were coming back to life! Even the monks who were dead on the ground gathered up their missing parts in a cinnamon haze, stood up, and joined their reanimated brethren. Only the ones who had been tossed down the mountain seemed lost for good.

Two of the beasts that Felix had been fighting blew up in front of him, bringing two more monks back to life. This left Felix with only one beast to deal with. Felix threw

69

It was the least he could do. Having selfishly abandoned his family in search of fame and glory, Brendan was filled with a deep guilt. He needed to prove himself to them again. So he stepped toward the cave and stood there for a few moments, peering into the darkness. As the monks stood guard in the event that the frost beasts returned, Cordelia and Eleanor stepped away to talk privately.

"Did you get the treasure map?" Cordelia asked.

Eleanor reached into her pocket, felt the map, and looked up at Cordelia. "No."

"You're lying, Nell."

"No, I'm not."

"Yes, you are," said Cordelia. "You just closed your eyes

and you always close your eyes when you tell a lie."

Eleanor sighed and pulled the map out. "Fine. Take it. I went down into the tank like you said and found the map, but I wanted to burn it."

"Why?"

"So our family would never be rich again," said Eleanor. "But I don't care anymore. . . . I just want to get *home*."

"We're going to get home," Cordelia said. "You don't think *I* want to get home? . . . It's gotten way too intense here. . . . I mean . . . Will tried to kiss me!"

"Oh my God," said Eleanor. "But you like him, right?"

"No way," said Cordelia. "My first boyfriend is going to be someone who exists in the real world. Someone who respects me for what I do as a normal person, not a fictional fighter pilot."

"So I guess Felix is out of the question."

"Completely!"

Eleanor smiled. "So why do you want to keep the map?"

"Insurance," Cordelia said. "Survival, if we lose everything. To protect Mom, Dad, Bren, and you."

"What do you mean?"

But Cordelia wouldn't say more. She took the map and put it in her pocket. Eleanor saw something else in that pocket: Eliza May Kristoff's diary.

"What about the diary?" asked Eleanor. "Are you going to tell me what you read in it?"

Cordelia shook her head. "I hope no one has to know."

"What's going on?" Brendan asked. "Are we going into this cave or what?"

"Let's do it," Cordelia said.

But before they could walk into the cave, they had to face Wangchuk and a line of all the monks.

Wangchuk spoke. "We are beyond grateful to you. You will always be remembered as the one and only . . . *traveling warriors*! The ones who helped us realize our true magic."

The monks bowed to the Walkers, Will, and Felix. But instead of raising their heads in unison, they raised them quizzically, at different times, because they heard the sound of whirling propellers overhead.

Brendan looked up.

It was an American P-51 Mustang.

"What do *they* want?" Brendan asked. The plane passed by and left someone behind, parachuting down, drifting back and forth. The monks all stared in astonishment as the parachutist landed on the ground. He detached himself from his parachute and took off his flight helmet.

It was Lieutenant Laramer, U.S. Army Air Force.

"Lieutenant!" said Will, snapping into a salute. "Greetings, sir!"

"What in the hell happened to *you*?" Laramer barked. "I had a homing beacon on that tank. After heading toward

Rome, it went AWOL; I ended up in some kinda freak windstorm that brought me to these mountains . . . and *what are these giant, dead ape-things?*"

Eleanor started to speak up, but Will knew how to handle military debriefings.

"Lieutenant, sir! The tank experienced the same phenomenon you did, sir! We crash-landed here! Then Volnheim attacked Jerry—"

"Hargrove?" asked Laramer. "Where *is* Hargrove?"

Now Felix stepped up. He saw the crisp and concise way that Will had spoken to Laramer, and he took note.

"Jerry was killed, sir," Felix said.

Lieutenant Laramer didn't show any emotion. He just gave a quick nod. "He was a good soldier."

"He died protecting us from Volnheim. He was the best, sir," continued Felix.

"Thank you both," Laramer said. "We'll give Jerry the proper honors."

Lieutenant Laramer began gathering up his parachute.

"Where are you going now, sir?" Will asked.

"Ten kilometers away, to the landing strip my copilot identified. He'll pick me up. Then it's back to fight the war. Just the way we have been. Every day."

Will looked at the Walkers, then at Laramer. The things he had said to Cordelia were absolutely true; he hated modern-day San Francisco. He knew this was going to be difficult, but he spoke to Laramer: "Do you need another soldier, sir?"

"What, Draper?"

"I'd like to volunteer, sir."

Cordelia's mouth hung open. "What? Will? You're not coming with us?"

Will turned to her. "I can't. This place—strange as it is—is closer to my home than your world. No cell phones or fitness hamster-machines. And you and I, if we're really friends, should be able to visit from time to time."

Cordelia looked away guiltily. Maybe if she hadn't been so harsh . . . maybe if she had let him down a little more gently . . . he would be returning to San Francisco with them.

"But Will," said Eleanor, "you have to come back with us! We'll miss you!"

"I'll miss you all," said Will, his eyes starting to tear up. "But my place is in the military. In the skies."

"Hold on, hold on," Lieutenant Laramer said. "I never said yes! A John Bull pilot in the USAAF? Whose flying experience comes from planes that haven't been used for twenty-five years? I appreciate your bravery, Draper, but you're not cut out."

"I can fly your planes, sir."

"Really? And how would you know that?"

"Because we stole one," Cordelia said, stepping in. She wanted Will to get his wish to fly again. Even if it would mean losing him.

"Excuse me?"

"Back by Kristoff House, Will and I stole a plane, and he flew it all the way to Rome—"

"You stole a plane? I ought to lead both of you out of here in handcuffs!"

"He landed it in the Colosseum to save my brother," said Cordelia.

"It's true," Brendan said.

"You can't land a P-51 in an arena!" Laramer exclaimed. "*Crashing* you can do. Maybe you *crashed* the plane, Draper."

"Point is, I'm still here, sir," Will said, putting his hand on his heart, "and I want to join your cause. Let's see: 'I pledge allegiance to the flag of the United States of America—'"

"Enough, that's not necessary!" Laramer said. "If you really did crash one of my planes, then you coming to fly for me is an appropriate punishment. Because I won't treat you with kid gloves, Draper. I'll work you hard, every single hour of every single day. You'll be eating K-rations and swabbing down planes even if the rest of my men are eating filet mignon in Chartres. Understand?"

"Yes, sir!"

"Then I'll take you on."

Will turned to the Walkers. "I'm sorry . . . ," he started to say, but before he could finish they all hugged him. They had been through so much with Will. He had saved their lives and they had saved his so many times, it was difficult to keep track. That's the way it is with family.

"I'm gonna miss you," Brendan said. "You were like the big brother I never had."

"And you were like the brave little brother who was never written for me."

They shared a warm smile.

Eleanor hugged Will one last time and spoke into his chest: "You be careful."

Cordelia was the last of the three to look Will in the eyes, and she wondered if she had made a terrible mistake by pushing him away in the plane. He was so much braver and more mature than any of the guys in her school.

"I hope you find everything you're looking for," said Cordelia, her eyes filling with tears.

"I know I won't find a better friend than you, my sweet Cordelia."

Then Cordelia kissed Will's cheek so hard he was worried that she would put a hole in it. Will sniffled, wiped his eyes, and abruptly turned. He sprinted off to catch Laramer, who was already moving through the snow. But there was another person with Laramer, a big strong figure walking beside him.

"Felix?" Eleanor called. "You're going *too*?"

Felix turned back.

"I have to," he said. "I'm a fighter, a simple person, not cut out for the life you three lead."

"You're more than a fighter!" Eleanor insisted, running up to Felix. He had become one of her best friends. "You're smart. You learn so fast. You can do anything you want to. You could end up being a great leader, much better than that awful Emperor Occipus."

"Then shouldn't I do it with the army?" Felix asked. "I can learn from the Americans, and then return to my people." He leaned in. "I know that the things we do in Rome will someday be part of your history. And I would rather be part of that history than study it."

"Not to be rude," Will said, standing with Laramer, "but what exactly will you do in the air force, Felix? You obviously can't fly a plane."

"No, but you know I learn fast. Can't you teach me?"

"He has a point," Lieutenant Laramer said. "I've always been a bit of a history buff . . . and one thing I learned is that there's never been stronger warriors than Roman gladiators. A gladiator pilot would be just the thing to toast those Nazi cyborgs. How about it, Draper? If you're such a hotshot, can't you teach him to fly?"

Will said, "Yes, sir."

Now the Walkers had to do another round of hugs and

good-byes. Eleanor cried into Felix's shoulder. It wasn't easy for anyone to let go of the gentle gladiator—or for him to let go of them. When he came to Cordelia, he kissed her, technically on the cheek but close enough to the lips to make her jump back, her cheeks burning red.

"Felix!"

"Consider it a parting gift from your not-quite-husband."

Then Felix was off with Lieutenant Laramer and Will. The Walkers waited for any of them to turn back as they departed, becoming specks in the snow, but only Will did, giving a wave and grin that was dashing, even though it was distant.

"Well," said Wangchuk, "it is getting dark now, almost bedtime for us monks. We cannot travel into the cave with you. But we wish you luck on your journey to find the Door of Ways, and to pass the test that it poses, to return safely home. We will never forget you, traveling warriors. Or should we say, traveling Walkers?"

"We sound like a band from the eighties," said Brendan.

Wangchuk bowed, and the rest of his monks bowed with him. The Walkers returned the gesture, and then as the sun began to edge behind a distant mountain, feeling very lonely as a trio, they held hands and entered the cave of the frost beasts.

70

The Walkers didn't know what to expect, so they expected the worst. That had proven effective in the past. The cave was huge and echoing; when they stepped in, they smelled sweet-spicy rot.

"Oh no, this is where the frost beasts had their meals," Eleanor said. "It's all going to be filled with yak bones and people's rotten old left-behind remains! Uggghhh . . . I feel like I'm gonna be sick."

"Don't think about it, Nell," said Brendan. "Just close your eyes. And keep holding hands."

Eleanor followed the instructions, allowing Brendan and Cordelia to lead her through the first huge chamber inside the cave, to a small passageway at the far side. Inside the passageway Eleanor began to notice a crispy clinking sound every time her feet touched the ground.

"Oh no," said Eleanor.

"What?"

"Bones," she said.

Brendan said, "Try to think of them as . . ."

"Rice Chex," suggested Cordelia.

"They don't sound like Rice Chex!"

"Then think of them as Lego blocks."

"But they're bones!"

Eleanor opened her eyes—and saw the bones all around her, reaching up the sides of the passageway, as if it were a clogged artery. This was clearly a space that had been used by the frost beasts to toss away centuries of inedible food parts. The bones were in layers like sedimentary rock, with the ones on top still attached to raggedy bits of flesh. . . .

Eleanor shut her eyes again.

"We're almost through," Brendan said. "Just stay strong."

But now Brendan was noticing something horrible about the bones. They weren't just lying there. They were moving slightly, because there were colonies of bugs living among them. Big black beetles that crawled and crept all over the bones. He realized he was stepping on them, crunching them under his feet, and he got ready to scream—when Cordelia put a hand over his eyes and mouth.

"Both of you need to get ahold of yourselves," she said. "They're just a bunch of bones and bugs. They're not going to hurt us. *Keep moving!*"

They came through the passageway into a second huge cavern. Cordelia was the only one with her eyes open at this point, and moving into the room answered a big question that had been bothering her since she entered the cave: *How is it that we're able to see?*

After all, the cave looked pitch-black from the outside. But walking through, everything was lit with a silver glow that seemed to come from nowhere, as if there were a very dim light set within the rocks themselves. Now Cordelia saw where that light was coming from, and she told her brother and sister to open their eyes.

The cavern they were in was over sixty feet high, and twice as wide.

And one entire wall was covered with a waterfall of light.

Cordelia didn't know how else to describe it. It was as if a cascade were coming from a wide opening in the top of the cave, but instead of water pouring out, light came down, shimmering and dancing as if it were alive, but holding a shape that had crisp edges and corners. The magical light illuminated the entire cavern and bled through the other parts of the cave.

Cordelia was completely mesmerized.

"The Door of Ways," said Eleanor, staring.

"It's a door?" asked Brendan.

"It's two doors, see?"

Brendan noticed that there was a small seam of blackness in the center of the cascade of light. And to either side of this seam, halfway down from the cave ceiling, were two dark circles, like doorknobs.

"It's beautiful . . . ," said Eleanor.

"And there's no bones in here," Brendan said.

"I'll bet this was some sort of sacred place to the frost beasts," suggested Cordelia. "They probably wouldn't bring any food or drinks inside."

"Like their church?" said Brendan.

"Maybe."

"So what do we do now?" Brendan asked.

"We go through the door," said Eleanor, "and face the test."

"You want me to walk through *that*?" asked Brendan.

Cordelia and Eleanor nodded.

"It's like you guys never watched any Star Trek movies!" shouted Brendan. "I mean . . . the first thing about a bright light like that . . . is that it's probably some kind of laser ray thing. . . . If we step through that, we're gonna get fried."

"Not according to the monks," said Eleanor. "According to Wangchuk, if we step through the Door of Ways . . . it will challenge us with a test, and then hopefully . . . it will bring us home."

"What kind of test are we talking about?"

"That I don't know, but I bet it won't be easy."

"Have we ever been through anything *easy* in these books?" asked Brendan. "Are you guys really sure about this?"

"Do we have another choice?" asked Cordelia. "We either go through the door or stay here for the rest of our lives."

Brendan sighed.

"Okay," he said. "Let's do it."

The Walkers went forward on smooth stones. The light seemed to separate and conjoin in tiny, infinite patterns as they approached. It gave off a pleasant hum. The light had some electrical aspect, because as the kids got nearer to it, their hair began to rise from their heads and point straight ahead.

"You look funny," Eleanor told Brendan. Brendan's hair was like a flattop on a cartoon character, making a beeline for the light.

"So do you," said Brendan. Eleanor's hair looked like Cousin Itt from the Addams family, shooting out horizontally instead of falling over her shoulders.

"I feel very calm . . . ," Cordelia said, staring through her own hair. "Is anyone else feeling that?"

"Yeah," said Eleanor. "I feel warm and safe all over, like all my worries are going away."

"Except for her," Brendan said.

Standing in front of the Door of Ways, twenty feet ahead, was the Wind Witch.

Backlit by the churning glow, she wore a robe that stretched out behind her and crackled where it kissed the light.

"My babies," she said.

"Not *you*!" Eleanor said. "Don't you know when enough is enough? Can't you just leave us alone? And don't call us 'my babies'! It's creepy enough when you call me 'little one'!"

The Wind Witch shook her head and smiled. She had a calm demeanor, as if she knew a secret that no one could take away from her.

"She knows what I'm talking about," the Wind Witch said, pointing to Cordelia. "Ask her."

Eleanor and Brendan turned to their sister, their profiles becoming bleached white.

"What's she talking about, Deal?" asked Brendan.

"The diary," said Eleanor.

Cordelia nodded, then shook her head. "Guys. The Wind Witch is . . ." But she stopped. She couldn't bring herself to say it.

"Oh, Cordelia," said the Wind Witch. "I thought you were so much stronger than that. If you don't have the courage to tell them, I will."

"Tell us what?" shouted Brendan.

The Wind Witch smiled, looked into the eyes of the three Walker children, and said:

"I'm your great-great-grandmother."

71

"That's impossible!" Brendan said, his guts twisting at the thought of being related to this monster. "There's not even a family resemblance! You're lying!"

"I'm not," said the Wind Witch. She began to pace in front of the Door of Ways, which made her look like the silhouette of a phantom in front of a burning star. "I always wondered why I could remember nearly everything about my life... except one year. My eighteenth year. It has always been a complete blank. It was only when I came out of Cordelia's body that I began to suspect the truth."

"And what's that?" said Brendan. "That you're crazy delusional?"

The Wind Witch ignored him. "Aldrich Hayes and the

Lorekeepers taught my father his magic. And one of the most important principles of Lorekeeper magic is that *no one can use it to kill their own child.* You can *hurt* your children with Lorekeeper magic—break their bones, crush their eyes—but they will never die; they will always come back."

"The way I did," said Cordelia, with dawning realization.

"That's right. When I came out of your body, I didn't know how you came back to life. You weren't my child. But could it be possible that the rule protected all descendants on the bloodline? I began to test my theory. I tried to kill you, Eleanor—and failed. I tried to kill you, Brendan—"

"And you totally failed."

The Wind Witch growled. "Horrible as it was to imagine, I realized that we *must* be related. And so I followed you three, protected you from the Nazis. I couldn't let them kill you. I needed more information. But their tank took a terrible toll on my body."

The Wind Witch raised her arms. She had a huge blackened hole in her stomach. It was being circled by purple lines of force—a healing spell repairing the damage. But it was still a deep pit that went all the way to her pelvis.

"When the tank's shell hit me, I was nearly destroyed. I was able to use my magic to slowly restore most of my body, but it's only now that I am able to walk and speak again. . . ."

"So exactly how do you figure that we're related?" asked Brendan.

"She had a child with Rutherford Walker," Cordelia said.

"What?" Brendan asked. "Ew! Someone had a relationship with the Wind Witch? That's like kissing a lizard."

Cordelia sighed and held up the diary. "It's all in here."

"That's right," said Dahlia. "You three know me as a bald old crone, but I didn't look like this when I was younger. I was quite attractive. And I hated my father, hated him with a passion that's only extinguished now because I've extinguished *him*. So when he banished *The Book of Doom and Desire* into his work, where I could never use it, I did the thing I knew would hurt him most."

"You had a child with his former best friend," Cordelia said.

"That's not a very nice thing for a lady to do," said Eleanor.

"Not if the lady is a tramp," said Brendan.

"Really?" said Cordelia, raising an eyebrow to Brendan.

"Couldn't resist," said Brendan, grinning. "Did ya miss me?"

"Anyway, I paid dearly," said the Wind Witch. "The baby was taken from me, passed off by Rutherford Walker and his wife as their own. My father did a spell that erased my memories of the entire year so I would never know about the child. But my mother, Eliza May . . . she knew. And she wrote about it."

"How did you find all this out without the diary?" Cordelia asked.

"Because you and I will always be connected, my dear. Now that I have been inside you, I get glimpses of your mind. I know your thoughts and feelings. I saw you reading that diary clear as day. The words leaped off the page and gave me the answers I sought. And now that the truth has been revealed . . . all of us can grow closer."

"What are you talking about?"

"Join me," said the Wind Witch. She spread her wings, creating a giant angel shadow in front of the Door of Ways.

"We can subjugate all of earth together! Along with the worlds my father created. You can be *kings and queens* with me. We don't need the book. I can teach you everything I know. We can be conquerors—together, we will take over city after city, country after country, making people *worship* us, ruling humanity the way humanity rules earth!"

"Ya know, Grandma," said Brendan. "I'm starting to think we *are* related to you. I mean, you're on one huge power trip. And I can relate. I mean . . . a couple days ago, I was the same way. And you know what?! I almost ended up dead because of it! But I got my family back. And there's no way I'm ever gonna turn my back on them again. So you can forget about the four of us going on the road together. I'm staying with my sisters. And I hope they feel the same way."

"I do," said Cordelia evenly.

"Me too," said Eleanor, with her chin jutting out.

"Very well," said the Wind Witch, folding her wings. "You can walk into the Door of Ways. But this door does test you, and do you know how? It shows you *what sort of life you will lead once you get home.*"

"It shows us our future?" asked Cordelia.

The Wind Witch nodded.

"So take a look," she said. "And if you don't like what you see, perhaps you'll reconsider joining my side."

"No way!" Brendan said. "I'm going home right now!" He brushed past the Wind Witch, stepped into the cascading patina of light—and disappeared.

72

Brendan felt the brightness of the Door of Ways grow in his eyes, until all he could see was a white churn— and then he was in a college dorm room.

He heard dim electronic music. He saw two twin beds on either side of a floor that was covered with remnants of pretzels, soda cans, pens, and wires leading to a laptop computer on top of a desk. Tapping away at the computer was Brendan, working on a document. But this wasn't Brendan as he appeared now. This was College Brendan.

Although College Brendan was older than Real Brendan—maybe twenty—he looked almost exactly the same, with spiky hair and a sports T-shirt and sneakers. He didn't notice Real Brendan, who stepped in front of him to look at his face and saw that he was sweating. *Oh man, what's wrong with me?* Real Brendan thought. College Brendan had bags under his eyes that were lined and drooping, that made him look like a zombie. His skin was pale white, as if he'd spent a month in this room, and he didn't even have the muscle tone that Brendan had already, from lacrosse. He was eating from a jumbo-size bag of Cheetos and drinking what appeared to be his fifth can of Pepsi. He looked like . . .

"A loser!" Brendan yelled at himself. "I'm a total loser! What is this?" He screamed in the face of his older counterpart. "Stop eating this junk! Look at me! What's wrong with you?"

But College Brendan just kept tapping away at the laptop, working furiously, completely unaware of Real Brendan's presence. College Brendan hit the Print command, got up, and grabbed ten new pages from the tray of his laser printer.

"What's going on?" yelled Real Brendan. "Why can't you hear me?!"

But then College Brendan heard the bedroom door slam open. Someone had barged into the room.

It was Scott Calurio.

Scott looked different too. Better. He had grown in height but more noticeably in the shoulder area. He wore a polo shirt under a varsity jacket, with jeans that weren't too tight or too loose.

"Hey, roomie," Scott barked at College Brendan.

"Scott Calurio's my *college roommate?!*" Real Brendan said to himself, in total shock.

"Did you finish my bio paper?" said Scott.

"Yep," said College Brendan, handing the ten freshly printed pages to Scott, who shoved them into his pants pocket and grabbed College Brendan by the front of his shirt.

"This one better be good," said Scott.

"It is," said College Brendan. "You'll definitely get a good grade."

"Better be an A," said Scott, tightening his grip on Brendan's shirt. "Not like last time."

"Last time you got an A minus," said Brendan.

"*My parents want A's!!!*" screamed Scott. "They see a minus on my report card and they drop my allowance!! And you know what happens if they drop my allowance?!"

"No—"

"*I drop a fist in your face!*"

"Well, no worries," said Brendan, visibly shaking. "Y-y-you'll definitely get an A on this one!"

And then Scott shoved Brendan in the chest, knocking Brendan to the floor.

Real Brendan ran over to his college counterpart, stood over him, and shouted: "What is wrong with you?! Why are you being such a coward? Such a little wimp? Get up and fight back!"

But College Brendan didn't move. He just stayed on the floor, looking up at Scott in fear.

"Time for you to get lost, Walker," said Scott.

"W-What?" asked Brendan. "But it's past two a.m. . . . I've been working on your paper for the last six hours and I got an early class. I just want to go to sleep—"

"And I just want to party," said Scott. "I got a bunch of friends comin' over, and the last thing they wanna see is your sorry face!"

"Can't I just get into my bed, pull the covers over my head?" asked College Brendan. "I'll put on my head-phones . . . you guys won't even know I'm here—"

"Everybody's gonna know you're here because you smell like loser sweat and Cheeto breath," said Scott. "Okay. Fine. We coulda done this the easy way. But I guess you're gonna make me do this the hard way."

Scott turned, opened the door, and sprinted into the hallway. He came back a few seconds later, holding a large red fire extinguisher.

He pointed it at College Brendan.

"*Wait, Scott!*" protested Real Brendan. "*Don't—*"

Scott pulled the fire extinguisher trigger and fired a powerful stream of white foam at College Brendan. He started at Brendan's face, then continued to spray downward, soaking his shirt, jeans, and sneakers. College Brendan ran to the door, trying to escape. But Scott chased after him and kept firing.

College Brendan made it into the hallway, but the thick, dripping foam made the soles of his shoes slippery. He slipped and fell to the floor.

Giggling sadistically, Scott continued to spray College Brendan, who was in the middle of a growing puddle of foam.

"Scott, please, stop . . . *mmmmmppphhhh*," pleaded College Brendan, who was coughing, choking on the foam.

Students were now coming out of their rooms, pointing and laughing at College Brendan, who was writhing on the floor, covered in white foam. He looked like a living, melting snowman.

Real Brendan rushed up, trying to punch and kick Scott to make him stop, but he was just a ghost; he couldn't help his older self.

Suddenly, the scene froze. "Have you seen enough?" the Wind Witch asked, stepping into the room.

"*This* is what happens after I go home?! I go to the same college as *Scott*? And we're roommates? And he humiliates me in front of everybody in my dorm?"

"Yes," said the Wind Witch, "it's one possible future for you. Are you ready to see another?"

She turned, walked toward the closed Exit stairway door, and passed right through. Brendan, who wanted desperately to get out of here, didn't hesitate. He walked to the door, passed through himself—and stepped onto Emperor Occipus's viewing area at the Roman Colosseum.

"What . . . ?" Brendan asked.

The roar of the crowd surrounded him. It was midmorning; the sun made everything sparkle; the smell of dust and sweat and food tickled Brendan's nose and brought back his best memories of Rome. He was floored by the breathtaking view, which let him see not only the Colosseum arena, but all the people in their togas, talking and cheering and laughing.

The Wind Witch was standing beside him, pouring a drink for the emperor, who lay in a hammock watching the games. She winked at Brendan, who came around to see.

The emperor was *him*.

"Emperor Walker," the Wind Witch said to this older version of Brendan, "would you like any grapes dipped in honey?"

Emperor Brendan nodded as Real Brendan took a moment to marvel at his adult body. Draped in royal robes, he looked *fantastic*, toned and muscular, as if he worked out for hours every day and got plenty of sleep every night. Golden necklaces, full of bright gems, hung from his neck.

"I never really wanted to wear jewelry," Real Brendan told the Wind Witch, "but that stuff looks cool."

"You haven't seen anything yet," said the Wind Witch. "If you choose to rule with me, you will have power over *all worlds.* Which means you can do things like . . . ah. Here we go."

Horns blasted in the arena. The crowd cheered. Real Brendan heard the black gate rising below him. Then he saw two lions coming forward, roaring and shaking their manes.

"Are those . . . ? Hey, those are my lions!" Real Brendan said.

The lions were quickly joined by two polar bears, and all four beasts lumbered forward to their target in the middle of the arena.

Scott Calurio.

He looked up pitifully, dressed in rags. Tears ran down his cheeks. He was shaking with fear.

"Emperor Brendan," shouted Scott. "Please spare me! I will be your faithful servant . . . for the rest of my life . . . if you would only save me!"

Emperor Brendan, tight-lipped, raised his fist in a thumbs-down. The crowd went wild. Real Brendan could see, on his emperor counterpart's face, the immense satisfaction that was about to result from seeing Scott Calurio torn limb from limb. Real Brendan hated himself for it, but he understood the feeling, and the adulation that came from the crowd. It was like he was singing Bruce Springsteen all over again. He was loved. Infinitely loved.

The lions and polar bears rushed Scott—and Real Brendan turned away.

He was suddenly ashamed of the idea that he could enjoy seeing Scott Calurio hurt. What had he wished for in Rome? That this kind of stuff would stop. No matter what Scott did to him in high school or college, he didn't deserve to die for sport. Brendan turned and moved toward the back of the viewing area, where he suddenly saw a glowing door, as the Wind Witch yelled, *"No! Wait!!"*

73

Back at the Door of Ways, Eleanor couldn't bear to see her brother disappear. She rushed forward past the Wind Witch—who was curiously silent and still, as if her mind had been transported to another place—and entered the shimmering light with her eyes closed, yelling, "Bren! Come back—"

Eleanor found herself at a funeral.

She was in a cemetery, under maple trees. The grass was perfectly manicured. A tentlike structure with a white canvas top stood over a grave, where a coffin covered with bright flowers was ready to be lowered into the ground. Standing next to it was an elderly priest, who said, "And we know that Dr. Walker loved his family most of all. . . ."

"*No!*" Eleanor yelled. "*Dad!*"

She rushed forward and saw the people at the funeral sitting in fold-up metal chairs. There was a carpet of fake grass on top of the real grass. In the front row were Brendan, Cordelia, and herself, looking only a few months older than she did now, along with her sobbing mother.

"Oh no . . . no . . . ," Real Eleanor said. "This doesn't really happen!"

But Mrs. Walker looked as if it were happening. Her face was a blotchy red mess. Her children bunched into her, trying to give her some strength, but they were crying themselves.

Eleanor—Real Eleanor, not Funeral Eleanor—saw the Wind Witch float across the cemetery over an angel mausoleum. She got up and ran to her angrily, but the Wind Witch grabbed her and comforted her.

"Shh, my darling. This isn't how it has to be."

"You monster!" Eleanor screamed, wrestling herself out of the Wind Witch's arms. "You killed my father!"

"I didn't kill him. He did that to himself."

"What?"

"The gambling . . . it only gets worse. And within a few months, he gets in some trouble with some very bad people . . . and this is how it ends."

"No! Mom won't be able to handle it!"

The Wind Witch sighed. "That's true. Your mother

snaps and ends up in a psychiatric hospital. And you go and live with him."

The Wind Witch pointed at a man dressed differently from the other mourners. They wore black and sat with erect postures, but this man was slouching, almost as if he was bored, in a brown coat, with wild, curly hair, a Hawaiian shirt, and cowboy boots. He glanced back, making sure no one was looking at him. He reached into his back pocket, pulled out a bottle, and took a long drink.

"Uncle Pete? No! I can't live with Uncle Pete. He's the worst."

"With your father dead and your mother unable to care for you, he becomes your legal guardian."

"But he spends all day drinking and watching old game shows on TV! He lives in a trailer . . . in the *desert*! I can't live with him!"

"Then let me show you another way."

The Wind Witch waved her hand, causing the ground below her to crumble into itself. Within a few seconds it was a gaping hole, and both she and Eleanor fell through, below the brown earth, past muddy walls . . . into a blue sky.

They were free-falling.

Eleanor squinted. The blue was so bright that it seemed to cut her. She was somewhere with pure air and sunlight and a wonderful fresh smell, but she was dropping fast.

"What?—Are you?—What's happening—?"

Eleanor landed on something soft.

It was a beige platform with a ridged, bouncy floor. If Eleanor pressed her hand into it, her hand came back. *Almost like* . . . She looked down . . .

"Fat Jagger!"

The colossus, six hundred feet tall, sat on top of a hill surrounded by a beautiful medieval festival. He was holding up his palm, and Eleanor was in it with the Wind Witch. Below were streamers and horses and knights jousting and vendors selling sausages and a sparkling lake. Next to Eleanor inside Fat Jagger's palm was another version of herself.

Princess Eleanor.

Fat Jagger moved his massive finger toward Princess Eleanor and stroked her cheek. *"Walk-er."* He looked up with his humongous eyes. He clearly loved Princess Eleanor—and Real Eleanor didn't think she looked bad either.

Princess Eleanor wore a golden crown with three rows of gems: ruby, diamond, and sapphire. She held a silver scepter with

447

a crystal horse carved at the top of it. Real Eleanor couldn't talk to Princess Eleanor—just the way Brendan couldn't talk to College Brendan—but she could see her beauty and poise. Princess Eleanor was the young woman Eleanor had always wanted to be: graceful, smart, and kind. Plus she was sitting above everyone else, in the hand of Fat Jagger.

"This is what happens if you stay with me," said the Wind Witch. "And this is only a small part of what I can give you. You are my blood, little one. And I want you to be happy."

"How . . . how do I choose?" Eleanor asked. Although she knew the Wind Witch was evil, this was not an easy decision: Go back to the real world with all the tragedy there, or stay here with Fat Jagger? *Who in their right mind would choose the real world?*

"Just say yes," the Wind Witch said, "and I will give you all of this. And so much more. Or you can go back through that door . . . into pain."

Eleanor looked up and saw the portal she had fallen through.

It was a black square cut out of the sky, leading back to the funeral. Eleanor could just see the green of the trees up there. And she had an idea.

"Fat Jagger! I don't trust the Wind Witch. I trust you. Can you put me where I'm supposed to be?"

"What are you doing?" asked the Wind Witch. "That ugly brute can't hear you!"

"Jagger! Please!" Eleanor said. "If you sit here, I'll join the Wind Witch, but if I'm not supposed to, just use your hand like an elevator . . . and put me through the door!"

"You're wasting your time," said the Wind Witch. "He's a total fool!"

All of a sudden Fat Jagger turned, narrowed his eyes, and growled. The Wind Witch looked surprised: "How are you hearing me?"

The giant started getting to his feet.

"He heard *me*!" Eleanor called. "He's listening!"

"Impossible," said the Wind Witch.

Now Jagger was standing at full height. He raised his hand toward the hole in the sky. And Eleanor—the real one—was able to jump off and grab the lip of the hole, pulling herself back up through the dirt, grabbing roots and rocks to climb into the funeral. And Fat Jagger looked up at the hole himself, his expression a mixture of fascination . . . and extreme curiosity.

Cordelia was standing petrified in front of the Door of Ways, unsure of what to do after seeing her brother and sister disappear. The Wind Witch—who had been in some kind of catatonic state—came back to her senses and beckoned her forward.

"Don't you think it's time we were together?" she said. "I won't hurt you, Cordelia. You were always my favorite."

Cordelia walked forward, barely in control of her feet, and passed into swirling brightness.

She found herself in a kitchen.

She was standing by the table, which wasn't a very nice table. It was chipped and wobbly, with a folded newspaper propped underneath one leg. In fact, the entire kitchen, and the small apartment it was attached to, was tattered and dingy.

Cordelia saw herself standing by the stove.

The Cordelia she saw was fifteen or twenty years older, with a drawn, defeated look on her face. Real Cordelia didn't know what else to call this version of herself besides "Old Cordelia."

Old Cordelia opened the stove, releasing a hot chemical smell. Real Cordelia knew it was the scent of fish sticks. She had always hated fish sticks. She once told her mom, "No species of animal should be made into a stick."

But here in this dim, messy kitchen, Old Cordelia was dutifully picking the fish sticks up with tongs, trying to get the bits of fried batter that stuck to the pan, and putting them on a plate.

A man came into the kitchen.

It was Tim Bradley, from Bay Academy Prep.

He was different now, of course—a man, not a boy, still handsome but seedy, and chunky, with a few days of beard and an old Metallica concert T-shirt. But he was definitely the same guy.

He looked at Old Cordelia and said, "*Mmm*, nice. Fish sticks. My favorite."

"I *married* him?" Real Cordelia cried.

"You did," the Wind Witch said, materializing from the fridge like a mist. "This is your 'happily ever after.'"

"There's no way I marry the *first guy who asks me out*," Cordelia said. "Why would I do that?"

"You don't immediately marry him, silly. But you date him after you become class president. You have quite a wonderful high-school career."

"Did you get my Red Bulls?" Tim asked Old Cordelia.

"You get into a good college," said the Wind Witch. "But Tim doesn't. He drags you down. You think you love him, you make sacrifices for him, and your political career goes away. Now your only chance is to take law classes at night school."

"Hey, Cordelia," said Tim excitedly, "we got a big week ahead of us. Friday's bingo night. And Saturday we're going to a NASCAR race."

"*This is not my future*," Real Cordelia said. "This can't be."

"It doesn't have to be," said the Wind Witch. "Would you like to see another?"

The Wind Witch opened the fridge. Inside, Cordelia saw luscious green hills, arrows flying through the air, and handsome knights on horseback.

"What is that?" Cordelia asked, and in answer, the Wind Witch took her hand—Cordelia felt a bit of desperation in her touch—and pulled her through the fridge into a field of battle.

Two armies attacked each other under the burning sun. One was dressed in black, the other in blue, each yelling orders and firing arrows and slashing and charging and regrouping. It looked like the battle that had taken place at the Wind Witch's castle in Cordelia's last adventure, but with more pomp and circumstance. There were streamers and war drums and trumpeters.

"This is one of your great victories," the Wind Witch told Cordelia. The two of them stood directly in the center of the battle, but it raged around them without leaving a scratch. "Your forces are in blue. You fight for your kingdom—one of many you rule. In the worlds we create together, you are second only to me."

"I'm a general?" Cordelia asked.

"Think more . . . Joan of Arc," said the Wind Witch.

Warrior Cordelia appeared and charged into battle.

She looked nothing like the lost and trapped woman who had pulled fish sticks from the oven. She sat on top of a regal horse whose hair had been painted blue to match her armor. She looked like she belonged on a stamp! She wore her hair short, tightly cropped, with blue streaks. She galloped down a hill with a banner held high, screaming, "For glory!" Real Cordelia felt proud to see herself this way—but also a little scared.

Warrior Cordelia—or Cordelia of Arc—threw down her banner and pulled out a sword. Then, from atop her steed, she bore down on an enemy knight and chunked into his shoulder. The knight fell from his horse. This was

Warrior Cordelia's first kill of the day, but it would not be her last.

"I'm . . . I'm a terrible person," Cordelia said.

"What?" said the Wind Witch. "You don't want the power?"

"I don't want to *fight battles*," Cordelia said. "I don't want to kill people. I want to help people!"

"But in this world, you're like Genghis Khan! People will speak your name for centuries! And back on earth, too, you won't be ignored! I can make this happen everywhere."

"This is wrong," Cordelia said. "This is evil."

"It's your destiny," said the Wind Witch.

"No," said Cordelia. "Not this."

"Then what is your destiny?" asked the Wind Witch. "A dreary life of monotony? Bingo and NASCAR?"

"No," said Cordelia. "Night school. Where I'll learn to be a lawyer, and then to change the system, any way I have to."

"You don't know what you're saying! Cordelia, stop! Don't go!"

But Cordelia had already made her decision. And the door—the same one that Brendan and Eleanor had seen, the true Door of Ways—appeared before her in the battlefield. She opened it and walked through. And when the Wind Witch saw her disappear, she let out a piercing scream and fell to her knees. She had lost all three of the Walker children. Everywhere around her, the battle between the black and blue armies raged on. But the Wind Witch was oblivious to it. For the first time since she could remember, real tears fell from her eyes. She had been truly defeated. She had lost her entire family.

75

The Walkers never woke up at the same time. One of their favorite things to do was wake up early and go to one another's rooms, hitting each other with pillows, yelling, *"Wakey-wakey!"* But now, in the same instant on a misty San Francisco morning, they all woke up in their beds in Kristoff House as if they had just had crazy dreams.

They ran into the upstairs hall.

Cordelia smacked into Eleanor. Brendan came down the ladder from the attic so fast, he nearly broke his hip. They all looked at one another in astonishment and started speaking at once.

"Did you—?"

"I saw—"

"What did she show you?"

They were overjoyed. More than anything, they felt a sense of peace. The adventures they had been on were so draining, so emotional and intense, especially at the end, that they felt like it might be easier to just lie down and give up. But they weren't lying down. They were laughing and hugging and jumping, so much so that they were shaking the lights downstairs.

"So, Deal," Eleanor asked, "who will you miss more? Will or Felix?"

"I'm not answering that."

"The question is," Brendan said, "who's a better kisser?"

"Too soon, Bren!"

Mrs. Walker came upstairs. "What's going on, you three? Why are you so happy?"

The Walkers nearly decapitated her with huge bear hugs.

"We're . . . ," Brendan started. "We're just happy to see you, Mom!"

"We love you!" Cordelia said.

"Well, that's just great," Mrs. Walker said, "but will you come downstairs? I need your help with the packing."

"Packing?" Eleanor asked.

The siblings looked at one another—and that's when they realized that their mother wasn't smiling. She didn't seem anywhere near as happy to see them as they were to see her. What was wrong? They followed her downstairs and saw a startling sight.

Everything in the kitchen was packed in cardboard boxes.

"We're moving?" Brendan asked.

"Of course we're moving," Mrs. Walker said. She looked as if she hadn't slept in a few days. "You knew that."

"Why?" Cordelia asked.

"Why? What do you mean, 'why'? Do you have a memory problem?"

"We're just confused, Mom," Eleanor said. "*Why* are we moving?"

Mrs. Walker gave Eleanor a very curious look.

"Because it's gone," she said with slow obviousness.

"What?" Brendan asked.

"Where have you kids been? We've lost everything—all the money. We have to move."

"When?" Eleanor asked.

"The movers are taking our boxes and personal stuff today," said Mrs. Walker. "Tomorrow they come for our beds and furniture."

"Where are we going to live?!" Cordelia asked, shocked.

"A sublet on Fisherman's Wharf," said Mrs. Walker, trying to hold back her emotions. "Hopefully we'll sell quickly. And I'm going to have you back at your old school next week."

"That might not be such a bad thing," Eleanor told Brendan and Cordelia as Mrs. Walker turned away, continuing to pack the boxes. But then Eleanor realized something and grabbed her siblings. "Oh no," she whispered. "This is what the Wind Witch showed me. It's all coming true! Dad really is going to die . . . and Mom's going to go crazy . . . and we're all going to live with Uncle Pete!"

"That's not what I saw," said Cordelia. "I saw myself in a dead-end marriage with Tim Bradley."

"There's no way those things *have* to come true," said Brendan. "Those are *possibilities*. The Wind Witch was just playing tricks on us. Nothing's set in stone."

"What are you three babbling about? Come and help me with these plates!"

The doorbell rang. Brendan answered it. He was shocked to see a man in a Spartan Movers outfit—the same man who had talked his ear off when he'd moved into Kristoff House just a few weeks before.

"Hey!" the moving man said. "The lacrosse player! Sorry to see you're moving out, kid. Easy come, easy go, huh?"

Brendan nodded mutely, flabbergasted and gutted. He followed the moving man up the stairs as other men in Spartan uniforms came into the kitchen and hauled boxes out. *It's one thing to run and fight in a fantasy world*, Brendan thought hollowly. *It's another to deal with problems in the real world.*

As Brendan went up the stairs, Cordelia turned to

Eleanor. "We're losing Kristoff House," she said.

"I know."

"I mean, we're really losing it. Tomorrow morning, we're going to be looking back at it through the trees, waving good-bye." Cordelia squeezed her eyes shut, trapping the tear that was about to come out of one of them. "It's a good thing I have this."

"What?" Eleanor asked.

Cordelia reached into her back pocket and pulled out a piece of paper.

"The Nazi treasure map!" Eleanor said.

"Insurance," Cordelia corrected. "If this map really leads to Nazi treasure, we can find it and give it back to the world, and save our family."

"But how do we know that map leads to real treasure? Couldn't it lead to a fictional treasure that's only in Kristoff's books?"

"I'm starting to think the real world and his world are more connected than we think. And no matter what—this is proof. This is an artifact from our adventures that no one can deny. We'll find a way to use what we know to save our family."

She folded the map up and put it in her pocket. Eleanor held her hand.

"Saving our family," Eleanor said, "is one of the things we do best."

Epilogue

Brendan sat in his almost vacant room, with only one remaining dresser and a nightstand. He stared at the ceiling, at the empty space where his posters used to be. There were small patches of paint missing from where he had taped them up. *How did we get here?* thought Brendan. *Things were bad before we left, but not this bad. And it feels like they're only gonna get worse. . . .*

Brendan's attic door swung open.

Eleanor climbed into the attic, followed by Cordelia.

"Hey, Bren," said Eleanor.

"Since it's our last night, we thought it'd be nice if we all sat out on the roof," said Cordelia. "We're probably never gonna have a view like this again."

"No kidding," said Brendan, opening the window and climbing outside, onto the rooftop. Cordelia and Eleanor followed.

They sat at the edge of the roof, where not so long ago, in another adventure, they once hid from bloodthirsty

pirates. The view was just as magical: San Francisco Bay, illuminated by a full moon and the glorious Golden Gate Bridge. A thick layer of fog swirled all around the bridge. They sat together in silence for a long time, enjoying the breeze, listening to the sound of a heavy fog horn. Finally, Brendan said what they were all thinking.

"Maybe we should've gone along with the Wind Witch."

"Yeah," said Eleanor. "At least I'd be a princess."

"I'd be Cordelia of Arc."

"But we wouldn't be together," said Brendan. "We wouldn't be here. Now."

"Yeah, and the three of us together . . . ," said Eleanor. "There's nothing stronger than that. We've beaten pirates, frost beasts, Nazis . . ."

That's when Eleanor noticed the shadow.

At first, it looked like another one of the oil tankers or sailboats in the bay. But the shadow was *slowly rising out of the water*, getting bigger and bigger. . . .

Now it stood nearly as tall as the top tier of the bridge. And it was no shadow. Backlit by fog, it was—

"Fat Jagger!"

Cordelia and Brendan stared open mouthed. Sure enough, it was Fat Jagger, standing in the middle of San Francisco Bay.

"That can't be . . . possible . . . ," said Cordelia.

"He followed me," said Eleanor.

"Followed you?"

"When the Wind Witch showed me my future with her, Fat Jagger was there," said Eleanor. "He helped me get to the Door of Ways . . . he watched me go through . . ."

And then Fat Jagger lifted his head toward the sky and howled at the moon.

"Waalllllk-errrr!!! Wallllk-eerrrrr!!!"

And then, as brake lights lit up on the few cars on the bridge, Fat Jagger slunk down and disappeared into the water, leaving a surprisingly small ripple.

"Oh man," Eleanor said. "Do you think anyone saw him?"

"*I* definitely didn't see him," Brendan said. "And even if I thought I did see him, which I'm sure I didn't . . . I—*we* can't deal with this right now."

"We have to," said Eleanor. "*Fat Jagger's our friend!* And he's all alone out there in the middle of the water. He's lost and scared."

"Get your coat," said Cordelia, already climbing down off the roof. "We need to go to the bridge and get to Fat Jagger before somebody else does."

"And how exactly do you *help* a sixty-story giant who's stuck in the middle of San Francisco?" asked Brendan.

"We've had tougher missions," said Eleanor.

So the Walkers went back downstairs, sneaked outside, and headed to the steep cliff that led to the beach. As they climbed down carefully, moving toward the water, they all looked at one another—and were surprised to see smiles on their faces. Despite Brendan's reservations, they couldn't help themselves. This is where they were meant to be. This is what they were meant to do.

They were the Walkers.

And they lived for adventure.

END OF BOOK 2

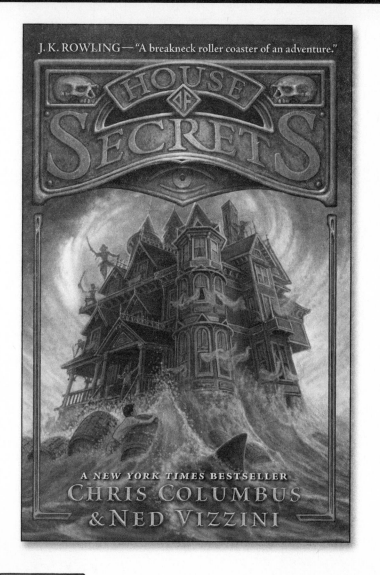